RAMAGE AND THE GUILLOTINE

LORD NICHOLAS RAMAGE, eldest son of the Tenth Earl of Blazey, Admiral of the White, was born in 1775 at Blazey Hall, St Kew, Cornwall. He entered the Royal Navy as a midshipman in 1788, at the age of thirteen. He has served with distinction in the Mediterranean, the Caribbean, and home waters during the war against France, participating in several major sea battles and numerous minor engagements. Despite political difficulties, his rise through the ranks has been rapid.

 In *Ramage and the Guillotine*, his sixth recorded adventure, Lieutenant Lord Ramage embarks on a spying mission to discover the strength of Napoleon's forces which are threatening British shores.

DUDLEY POPE, who comes from an old Cornish family and whose great-great-grandfather was a Plymouth shipowner in Nelson's time, is well known both as the creator of Lord Ramage and as a distinguished and entertaining naval historian, the author of nine scholarly works.

Actively encouraged by the late C. S. Forester, he has now written fourteen 'Ramage' novels about life at sea in Nelson's day. They are based on his own wartime experiences in the navy and peacetime exploits as a yachtsman as well as immense research into the naval history of the eighteenth century.

Available in Fontana by the same author

DUDLEY POPE

Ramage and
the Guillotine

FONTANA/Collins

First published in 1975 by
The Alison Press/Martin Secker & Warburg Ltd
First issued in Fontana Paperbacks 1977
Second impression November 1978
Third impression November 1981
Fourth impression November 1984

Made and printed in Great Britain by
William Collins Sons & Co. Ltd, Glasgow

For Peter J-S with thanks

CHAPTER ONE

Ramage reached across the breakfast table for the silver bell, shook it and waited. After more than a year at sea in one of the King's ships (when meals were usually dreaded as unimaginative variations on a theme of salt beef or salt pork, and bread was a polite name for hard biscuit that an honest baker would disown and a potter would proclaim a credit to his oven) his stomach still rebelled at the rich fare that old Mrs Hanson insisted on providing for every meal, including breakfast.

She had been the family cook and housekeeper at the London house for as long as Ramage could remember, and her short-sighted husband was the butler, a timid and wispy-haired man whose life seemed to be a sheepish hunt for his mislaid spectacles.

Mrs Hanson firmly believed that all sailors, be they admirals or seamen, lowly lieutenants like Ramage or portly masters, were deliberately underfed by a scheming Admiralty which calculated the scale of rations on the principle that fighting cocks were starved for hours before being put into the cockpit to battle for their lives. It seemed to Ramage that whenever he came up to London on leave she was determined to cram enough food into him to last another year at sea.

'You rang, my Lord?'

Ramage glanced up to find Hanson waiting expectantly, his spectacles slowly sliding down his stub of a nose. 'Ah – please thank Mrs Hanson for an excellent breakfast.'

'But you've hardly touched the cold tongue, sir,' Hanson protested plaintively. 'And the oysters – you haven't eaten a single one!'

'Hanson,' Ramage said sternly, knowing that to the butler he was still a small boy, to be humoured, but made to eat every scrap of food on his plate, 'you should remember I've always hated oysters; the mere thought of them makes me queasy.'

The butler shook his head sadly. 'Mrs Hanson will be upset; sets great store by oysters, she does; reckons they build you up. A score for breakfast, she says, and you'll never come to no 'arm for the rest of the day.'

'Just look at me,' Ramage said patiently. 'Do you think I'm fading away?'

'Bit on the lean side, my Lord,' Hanson said warily, remembering how sun-tanned his Lordship had been when he first arrived back from the West Indies. 'Your face is paler, too. My wife commented on it yesterday.'

'Remind Mrs Hanson that suntan doesn't last for ever.'

'Well, it's been raining hard,' Hanson said lamely as he began to clear away the plates, 'an' it'll rain again before the day's out.'

'I'm sure it will,' Ramage said soothingly. 'Is anyone else in the family up and about yet?'

'Your father and mother, sir, and hot water has been sent up for the Marchesa, so she'll be down presently.'

Ramage sniffed doubtfully. 'Very well – please fetch me a newspaper.'

'The *Morning Post* or *The Times*, sir?'

'I'll have plenty of time to read both before the Marchesa is ready.'

Hanson smiled happily, nodding his head at some private thought as he went to the door. 'A lovely lady,' he murmured to himself, 'and her a foreigner, too . . .'

Ramage grinned self-consciously and then felt foolish; praise for Gianna was not flattery for him! Still, Hanson's innocent remark emphasized that now was not the best of times to be a foreigner in England – in Great Britain and Ireland, he corrected himself. The Act of Union had become law while he was commanding the *Tritona* brig in the West Indies, and recently he had been trying to break himself of the habit – which infuriated the Scots and Welsh – of saying England when he meant Britain. The trouble was that foreigners always refer to 'you English,' not 'you British.'

He took the newspapers from the silver tray Hanson was holding and shook his head at the discreet, 'Would you prefer to sit in the drawing-room, sir . . .?'

His eye caught a name in the first item on the front page of the *Morning Post*:

'The public will learn with great satisfaction that LORD NELSON, the hero of Copenhagen and the Nile, will soon leave Town on a SECRET mission which will rid the country of the Corsican Tyrant's threat of a GRAND INVASION. We

6

understand the Admiralty is confident that his Lordship will soon send the French invasion craft now gathering in Calais and Boulogne to WATERY GRAVES.'

Hmm . . . the Government must be very worried if they thought it necessary to give Lord Nelson such a job: badgering barges in the Channel ports was more of a task for young frigate captains. Still, agents might have just discovered that Bonaparte had set a date for his great attempt, though it was more likely that the Government was trying to reassure the people.

As he read the next news item he knew it would make unwelcome reading for everyone living within twenty miles of the Kent and Sussex coasts:

'The latest intelligences received in London report that Bonaparte has given orders for the construction of ANOTHER one hundred barges and fifty gunboats. We estimate that the fleet for the *grand invasion* now lying at Calais, Boulogne, Wimereux, Ambleteuse, Etaples, Havre de Grace, St Valery, Gravelines, Dunkirk and Ostend now totals more than three hundred large barges to carry men, horses, artillery and provisions, and two hundred gunboats of various sizes intended to defend the fleet and attack the stout defenders waiting on the English beaches. Construction of camps for Bonaparte's Army of Invasion proceeds quickly and our patrolling frigates daily see more tents being erected on the heights around Boulogne.'

He pictured the frigates tacking and wearing along the French coast by day and by night, hoping to catch and destroy any enemy vessels daring to move from one port to another. The French would take full advantage of their shallow draft, keeping close in to the beach, and hoping that the frigates waiting for them like sharks would accidentally strand themselves on off-lying sandbanks.

The completed barges and gunboats were anchored off each port, exposed to gales but protected from the British frigates by batteries of guns. At low water the vessels would dry out, sitting on hard sand or shingle and protected by cavalry patrols from marauding seamen landed by boats from the frigates.

It was a complicated cat-and-mouse game: at high water a

frigate would tack back and forth close to an anchorage but beyond the range of the batteries and, when it judged the French gunners had been lulled into inactivity, suddenly swoop, hoping to fire a couple of broadsides into the anchored vessels before the French woke up and began a withering fire. But it was a dangerous game: the whole of the French coast was usually a lee shore, and a lucky shot could dismast a frigate and the wind drive her up on the beach.

As they tacked offshore, the officers in the frigates would be balancing themselves against the roll as they trained their telescopes on the hills and dunes round the ports. They would be counting yet again the scores of tents arranged with geometric precision round flagpoles from which Tricolours fluttered. They would note new camps being set up; off many ports they would see hundreds of tethered horses scattered across the hills, and ammunition wagons, field kitchens and field guns drawn up nearby. And the men in the frigates – and brigs and cutters – knew they were watching not only for signs of reinforcements but for the first hint that the troops were preparing to board the barges for the voyage across *La Manche* to the beaches of Kent and Sussex.

From what he had heard, the frigates were having very little success in their attacks: the French had so many batteries on the cliffs over the anchorages that they could keep up a lethal fire by day or night.

Yet the French were not the only ones making preparations: a glance over the rest of the page showed that the British were busy preparing suitable reception committees. Lord Romney had just reviewed 3,000 men of the Kentish Volunteers at his estate at Maidstone; the King had reviewed 1,500 of the Surrey Volunteers on Wimbledon Common. One news item described joint manœuvres held in the streets of London by the Loyal Hackney, Royal Westminster, Whitechapel and Shoreditch and Wapping regiments. An advertisement at the foot of the column announced that, 'Members of the LONDON and WESTMINSTER VOLUNTEERS may purchase WARRANTED FIRELOCKS at 2£ each at G. RIPPON'S WAREHOUSE, No. 3, Ludgate Hill. Cartouche boxes, pistols and swords may likewise be obtained.'

Every hamlet and town in the south-eastern corner of England must be swarming with patriotic citizens clutching ancient fowling pieces or newly-purchased muskets or, perhaps, only scythes or sickles, and eyeing strangers with suspicion since they expected to find Frenchmen lurking behind each hedge and thicket. Every poacher in the Weald of Kent and on Romney Marsh and Pevensey Level now had a perfect excuse for the magistrates when found on the squire's land with a fowling piece under his arm (though he would still be hard pressed to explain away a ferret in his pocket and nets over his shoulder).

For a moment Ramage imagined Gianna on one of her wild rides over the countryside suddenly reining her horse as a group of Volunteers emerged from a hedgerow, muskets at the ready, and Gianna explaining in her exuberant English that she simply enjoyed riding alone. Rustics, unable to distinguish an Italian accent from a French, and full of the wild stories the newspapers had been printing about Bonaparte's secret hot-air balloons and rafts driven by windmills, might think she was Bonaparte's modern equivalent of Joan of Arc, riding through the countryside intent on rousing innocent folk into bloody riot and vicious rebellion . . .

He turned the page to skim through the rest of the news. A gale of wind had put four ships ashore at Plymouth, scattering the fishing fleet just returning to harbour, and knocking down trees and chimney pots. A 'new stein is to be built at Brighton, with the Duke of Marlborough and others patronizing the undertaking'. The King would not after all be attending the ball being given tonight by the Duchess of Manston, because the Queen was still indisposed and remaining at Windsor. That would disappoint Gianna.

There was a section he would point out to Gianna. Headed 'The Fashionable World', it began by announcing that, 'The female fashion is every day encroaching on the male costume.' The article explained that with dozens of volunteer units being formed all over the country and their officers designing the uniforms as well as buying the necessary muskets, powder and shot, it was inevitable that 'the ladies would soon follow the fashion.'

Ramage smiled to himself at the descriptions that followed. The fashionable colours for the Summer of 1801 were purple, puce, yellow and scarlet, and beads and feathers were becoming popular along with spangled nets for the hair. Morning hats and bonnets of velvet, plain and trimmed, 'are among the latest inventions.'

Walking and full dress for ladies, the *Morning Post* assured its readers, were in two styles. One was of yellow muslin

9

trimmed with black ribbon and tassels and full epaulets; the other a round dress of white muslin with a spencer of scarlet satin trimmed with black lace, and topped by a small, round hat with a deep veil.

Certainly the military influence was obvious, Ramage thought sourly; he could just imagine all the general officers wearing small, round hats with deep veils and scarlet spencers as they reported to the Duke of York at the Horse Guards. (Now he came to think about it, why were those short jackets named after the man who had just resigned as First Lord of the Admiralty?) Complexions would be puce, and a general liverishness would probably turn the whites of their eyes to the fashionable shade of yellow. Gianna would find the prospect as amusing as he did. He pulled out his watch – nine o'clock. Well, no elegant young lady could take less than an hour over her toilet . . .

He turned to the back page, which was mostly advertisements. The first was intriguing. 'Two hundred guineas will be paid for a commission appointing an ensign to one of His Majesty's regiments (an old fashioned regiment) now serving in the East or West Indies.' Obviously some poor fellow was trying to escape a fate in England that he considered worse than the prospect of death in the Indies from any one of a dozen vile tropical diseases. The vengeance of a jilted woman? The threats of his creditors? Ramage shrugged his shoulders: from what he had recently seen in the West Indies, the poor fellow would be wiser to stay in England – better the devil you know . . .

The next advertisement claimed that the new magic lanterns were 'a pleasing family amusement . . . They are complete in boxes, each lantern with twelve glass slides, on which are finely painted about sixty grotesque figures which, by reflection, are magnified from a miniature to as large as nature, according to the size of the lanterns.'

The rest of the advertisements offered no scope to an imaginative mind, and he looked at his watch again – a quarter past nine. The room was brighter now, and through the window he could see that the cloud was breaking up. With luck it would turn out to be a warm summer's day – and, judging from the noise outside, the prospect was putting new vigour into the street hawkers. He could hear the distant call of an approaching pieman, although Mrs Hanson's pride in her cooking meant that there would be no custom for the poor

10

fellow at Blazey House.

The sheer noise outside! The cries of pedlars and hucksters all trying to outshout each other; the clatter of horses' hooves and the drumming of coach and cartwheels. The fiddler on the corner of Palace Street was tuning up with what sounded like lethargic melancholy. Ye gods and little fishes, how he hated cities in general and London in particular: he was more than irritated by the social obligations that had forced the family to come to London, and his father had been testy from the moment he stepped into the coach. His mother had long since resigned herself to the fact that both the men in her life had had their characters moulded by long periods of watching distant sea horizons, whether looking for an enemy or a landfall, and making decisions in the isolation imposed by command. She was one of the few people who came near to understanding that it made both of them impatient with the triviality and shallowness of London society.

The Admiral enjoyed his life of retirement at St Kew and begrudged every moment spent away from Cornwall, since there was nothing in London that could compensate for giving up his daily ride across land which had belonged to the Ramage family for three hundred years. So far as the old Earl was concerned, there was no drawing-room conversation to equal the chats he had with his tenants and neighbours at St Kew, sharing their good news and their bad. There was not a bunion nor a bad back, a feeble grandmother or a sickly child, that John Uglow Ramage, tenth Earl of Blazey and Admiral of the White, did not know all about and, if sympathy or guineas were needed, had not done his utmost to help or cure.

As his son and heir, Ramage hoped he would prove as good a landlord and neighbour when the time came, but since he was just past his twenty-fifth birthday and the Admiral was as lively as a frigate in a Channel lop, it would be a good many years before he was put to the test.

Ramage had been relieved to find that, in the year and a half he had been away in the West Indies, his mother seemed to have grown younger while his father had certainly held his own. The reason, his mother had confided in a whisper one evening (touching the side of her nose with her index finger in the conspiratorial gesture used by Italians to indicate secret knowledge), was having Gianna staying with them: her

11

youthful exuberance was infectious, even though, she had added with affection, 'The Marchesa di Volterra Has Settled Down!'

Well, he had to take his mother's word for that. Certainly Gianna's tiny figure no longer shook with hatred and anger when anyone mentioned the name Bonaparte, and she no longer wept at the thought of her little kingdom of Volterra and its cheerful people, which she had ruled until Bonaparte's approaching Army of Italy forced her to flee rather than collaborate with the French like her neighbour, the despicable and weak-willed Grand Duke of Tuscany.

His mother's verdict had been especially welcome because he had been doubtful whether Gianna would like staying at St Kew. The rambling old house was big enough by English standards, but the rulers of Volterra had lived for centuries in a palace of which the Medicis might have been proud.

Gianna had left behind in Italy more personal maids than the entire indoor and outdoor staff at St Kew. Perhaps part of the 'settling down' process was that the single maid she now had was a stolid local girl, and likely to say, 'Oooh, ma'am, you'll go into a decline if you carry on like that,' when Gianna threw a tantrum which would have left her Italian maids white-faced and trembling.

The fact was he had fallen in love with a girl who was as wilful and unpredictable as a puppy in a flower garden. Any man who provoked her anger might as well spend a quiet Sunday afternoon making sparks in a powder magazine. He should know, he admitted wryly. Hot tempered, yet generous; occasionally imperious but always (eventually) understanding; impatient yet – the list was long: any description of Gianna tended to be a list of synonyms and antonyms.

She certainly did not include punctuality amongst her virtues, he thought crossly, pulling out his watch, and then picking up *The Times* which also reported Lord Nelson's 'secret mission' with much the same wording. This almost certainly meant that it was true and not a wild or hopeful report by one of the *Morning Post*'s journalists.

At that moment the door was flung open and Gianna came into the room, offering her cheek to be kissed as Ramage stood up. She smiled mischievously, gesturing at the empty place at the table where Ramage had sat and at the newspapers he was holding.

'What a wonderful way to start the day! The man of the

house has eaten his breakfast in peace and quiet and read enough newspapers to be fully informed about what is going on in the world. Don't go back to sea, *caro mio!*'

'Someone has to defeat Bonaparte,' he said lightly, knowing he was joking about a dangerous subject.

'Leave it to the others,' she said airily. 'You've done enough already – ' She broke off as Hanson came in with the large tray, and after one look she said firmly: 'No oysters, Hanson! Take them away and keep them for the Admiral.'

The butler's face fell as he walked to the table, carrying the tray with the forlornness of a man trying to sell bruised apples in Covent Garden market.

'Do *you* like oysters, Hanson?' Ramage asked innocently.

The butler glanced nervously at the door, as if fearful his wife was waiting outside to pounce on him, and then shook his head expressively.

Gianna sat at the table and motioned Ramage to a chair opposite her. 'What have the newspapers to say today?'

'It seems My Lords Commissioners of the Admiralty have given Lord Nelson a new job.'

'As long as Their Lordships don't find one for you,' she said sharply. 'The Admiralty must let you have a holiday.'

'I have a month's leave,' he reminded her.

'But only eleven days are left.'

Ramage's eyebrows lifted. 'You keep a tally?'

'Yes,' she said quietly, 'though I don't know why: you can't wait to get to sea again and leave me all alone, and – '

'If there's no ship for me, I'll be able – '

'There'll be a ship,' she interrupted angrily. 'You are famous now! Why, even your father says you should be made post very soon. "Captain Ramage" – how does that sound? And you'll wear an epaulet on your right shoulder, and after three years you can put one on your left shoulder as well. You see,' she said, her eyes sparkling, 'I'm learning about naval etiquette. I've read the King's Regulations and Admiralty Instructions, and the Articles of War, too. Soon I – '

'The change of Government,' he said soothingly, alarmed at the way her voice was rising and startled at what she had been reading. 'Lord Spencer is no longer First Lord of the Admiralty . . .'

'But the new First Lord knows you well – why, Lord St Vincent was your Commander-in-Chief in the Mediterranean when Lord Nelson was still only a commodore.'

'He'll have forgotten me – there are hundreds of lieutenants in the Navy!'

'Thousands!' a voice boomed from the doorway. 'All of them scoundrels, with a girl in every port!'

The Admiral strode into the room, a tall man with aquiline features and silver-grey hair. He had the same deep-set and penetrating brown eyes as his son and the stance and walk of a man used to exercising authority; the lines on his face showed that he laughed readily and frequently. 'Good morning to the pair of you,' he said, noting Gianna's tight lips and wondering what they had been quarrelling about. 'You've already eaten, Nicholas?'

'Hours ago, sir,' Ramage said lightly.

'Left some oysters for me, I hope.' He saw Ramage's expression. 'I forgot you don't like 'em. Pity – oysters and cold tongue; the finest breakfast there is. Don't you agree, m'dear?'

'No,' Gianna said flatly, 'oysters *sono horribile*.'

The Earl grinned cheerfully as he sat down and rang the bell. 'You know, Nicholas, I've noticed that Gianna always lapses into Italian when she's on the verge of mutiny. Ever have the same trouble with Italian seamen?'

'Only that fellow Rossi – I was telling you about him.'

'But he's a *Genovese*!' Gianna exclaimed.

'Good seamen come from Genoa. Anyway, he helped save your life,' Ramage pointed out.

'And yours, too!'

The Admiral rang the bell again. 'Children, stop bickering.'

'I'm not bick – '

'You are out of fashion, though,' Ramage interrupted, raising the newspapers. 'At least, according to the *Morning Post*.'

Gianna glared at him, knowing he was trying to keep her off the subject of him getting a new ship. 'Let me see.'

He passed over the newspaper. 'Yellow muslin trimmed with black lace, scarlet spencers, and little round hat with deep veils . . .'

She read for a few moments and then sniffed. 'Rubbish – that's for innkeepers' wives. Anyway,' she added less emphatically, 'it's for walking-dress.'

'The feminine fashion is to copy the military,' Ramage murmured to his father.

'Ha!' the Admiral snorted, 'I can just see the ladies stamping along in heavy boots, leather crossbelts, and battered shakoes. Most becoming!'

'Tea, my Lord?' Gianna asked sweetly. 'You notice,' she added when he nodded, 'that the ladies are copying the Army, not the Navy.'

'Should think so, too,' the Admiral retorted. 'You'd look dam' funny in white knee breeches, frock coat and a cocked hat. You ought to borrow one of Nicholas's uniforms and wear it to the Duchess of Manston's tonight. New fashion – why, you'd set London by its ear!'

'Board 'em in the smoke,' Ramage said. 'Father will lend you his best dress sword.'

'What are *you* going to wear?' she asked icily. 'You haven't seen your tailor for years, so it'll be something old-fashioned and dowdy. Russet and green, no doubt, and everyone will take you for a gamekeeper.'

Ramage said: 'The newspapers say the King will not be there: the Queen is ill, and he's staying at Windsor. Anyway, I'll be wearing uniform.'

Gianna looked disappointed at the news of the King's absence and then exclaimed: 'Uniform? Oh, Nicholas! Please wear something more *elegante*.'

'He has no choice, my dear,' the Earl said. 'Lord St Vincent will be there, and he's very fussy about that sort of thing.'

'This Manston,' she said with the disdain of the head of one of the oldest families in Italy, 'who is he?'

'A comparative newcomer,' the Earl said lightly. 'His father was of some service to the present King's father.'

'Political service,' Ramage added. 'Rather a clever politician.'

'The Duchess,' Gianna said darkly. 'I hear strange stories about her.'

'Quite so,' the Earl said hurriedly, 'but one mustn't believe all one hears.'

'Makes for jealousy, too,' Ramage said, winking at his father.

Gianna tossed her head scornfully and picked up her cup. 'Even if one does believe, that woman hasn't achieved in a lifetime what some Roman women I know accomplish in a week. Why, the Duchess of Ravello had – '

'Gianna!' the Earl said sternly, 'no more of your detailed stories of light women – not at breakfast, anyway!'

'Later, then, when you feel stronger,' Gianna said nonchalantly. 'I don't know what has happened to Hanson.'

She rang the bell and pointed to the big silver urn. 'More tea? It will be cold in a few minutes.'

The Earl moved his cup towards her, and when a distant clatter in the kitchen startled both men, she noted how physically alike they were. The sudden noise made them both turn, reminding her of hawks poised to attack. They resembled so many of those forebears whose portraits hung from the walls of the St Kew house. Both had the Ramage face in full measure: high cheekbones and a thin nose (how did they say it in English? Aquiline?) and eyes like brown chestnuts and deep-set under almost fierce eyebrows. Full mouth, hands with long fingers . . . In one or two of the portraits the artists had managed to catch that elusive look of amused detachment with which the Ramages had apparently surveyed the world through successive generations and which, in Nicholas, alternately infuriated her and made her want to hug him.

The look was a pose, a mask which hid their true feelings, because she knew Nicholas was far from detached. Nicholas could (and did, for she had seen him a dozen times) stand on the quarterdeck of his ship, apparently concerned only with the trim of the sails and the course being steered, and surveying the men as though they were sheep. Later he would speak to Mr Southwick, who was usually the Master, and ask if a particular man had hurt his arm, or another seaman's leg was troubling him, and suggest they should be given lighter duties. Often Southwick, as kindly an old man as she had ever seen, would be startled by his captain's sharp eyes, since he had seen nothing and the man had not reported to the surgeon. Lord Ramage – or Lieutenant Nicholas Ramage, as he preferred to be called in the Navy – was far from detached, and she loved him and was terrified when he went to sea. The Admiralty *deliberately* chose him for absolutely impossible and dangerous tasks – and she was going to tell Lord St Vincent so when she saw him that night – because he usually managed to do the impossible, although sometimes at a terrible cost of life and limb.

As he watched her pecking at her food, Ramage tried to guess her thoughts: she had become strangely, almost ominously quiet. Perhaps she was upset that he would be wearing uniform that evening instead of being rigged out in whatever sartorial idiocy passed for male fashion at this particular moment.

There must be some vast philosophical conclusion to be drawn from the fact that today both newspapers devoted more space to news of the military influence on feminine fashion than Bonaparte's invasion plans and Britain's defences, though he was damned if he could think what it was. A display of confidence in the nation's safety, perhaps, and therefore better than printing shrill alarms? A crude gesture of defiance? Or was it a genuine disdain of Bonaparte's plans, which was dangerous because it went hand in hand with apathy?

Merely being on leave was a change of fashion for Lieutenant Ramage! After months at sea it was a comfortable change to be sitting at a table in a room with ten feet of headroom instead of the few inches over five feet usual in the captain's cabin of one of the King's smaller ships. Instead of his uniform he was dressed in pearl grey breeches, pale blue waistcoat – although he disliked the fancy silver thread embroidery, it was one of Gianna's favourites – and a relatively comfortable dark blue coat which Gianna scorned as more suitable for an unfrocked priest.

Women were traditionally the slaves of fashion, but men were just as bad, with politics thrown in for good measure. Some of Mr Pitt's supporters were wearing scarlet waistcoats and Mr Fox's buff without their womenfolk laughing them out of court, and he had heard that the Tory ladies were now sporting patches on the right side of their foreheads while the Whig ladies stuck them on the left. The doxies of the revolutionaries from the London Corresponding Society presumably wore them on the tips of their noses . . .

Still, he was thankful that wigs were becoming less popular, because they were still devilishly expensive. It was hard to find scratches or bob wigs for less than twenty shillings, and good grizzle majors and grizzle ties cost a couple of guineas and often more.

CHAPTER TWO

With his head thudding inside a tight band, his mouth dry and his feet swelling so much it seemed they must burst out of his new shoes, Ramage took Gianna's arm the moment the orchestra finished playing and began to steer her off the ballroom floor. 'Let's sit and watch the next one,' he said.

The ballroom in Manston House was said to be the largest in London, and he could well believe it: dancing round it once must equal a circumnavigation of Hyde Park. The Duchess had recently had it redecorated in pale blue and cream, with the complicated ceiling patterns picked out in gilt. There were so many chandeliers it was a wonder the weight did not pull the ceiling down on their heads, and the light was brilliant, emphasizing all the colour and gaiety of the women's dresses and bringing a sparkle to tiaras and bracelets. But all the scores of candles made the great room as hot as the Tropics, and Ramage longed for a cool breeze.

Gianna finished her survey of the hundred or so other women waiting with their partners for the orchestra to strike up again. 'Oh, Nicholas,' she pouted, 'four dances and you're exhausted! Yet you dance exquisitely.'

'Out of practice,' he said, holding her arm firmly and leading her towards a settee. As he walked he watched a young naval lieutenant in uniform come into the room, pause a moment to whisper something urgent to the major domo, and then hurry off in the direction the man pointed to, weaving through the waiting dancers to reach a group of ministers talking at the far end of the room.

'The orchestra is *wonderful*,' Gianna protested as the music started.

'The orchestra is wonderful, you look wonderful, and it's a wonderful ball, but I feel as though I've been in action for three hours!'

'Well, *I* don't,' Gianna said crossly, reluctantly sitting on the settee. 'Let's watch the Duchess dancing,' she said, arranging her flowing skirt. 'She must be at least thirty, but what energy!'

'At *least* thirty,' Ramage said gravely. 'She'll be a grandmother soon.'

'But she has no children!'

'Then she'd better hurry,' Ramage said vaguely, turning to watch the lieutenant reach Lord St Vincent, open the small leather pouch he was carrying, and hand over a letter. 'The Duke will want a son and heir,' he added lamely, realizing that Gianna was staring at him. 'It's only natural . . .'

'Is she pretty?' Gianna demanded.

'What – the Duchess?'

'Don't be exasperating! The woman you keep staring at.'

'I was watching that officer delivering a dispatch to the First Lord,' Ramage protested, turning to face her. 'Anyway, if there was a woman here more beautiful than you, I'd look at her out of curiosity, but since there isn't you can relax and stop stabbing me with those hatpin looks.'

She gave him a conspiratorial smile. 'You Englishmen tell lies so gracefully. Still, you're forgiven and I'll act as lookout to save you turning round. How do they say it – Deck there, masthead here: Lord St Vincent is reading the letter . . . Ah, he waves to Lord Nelson, who walks over to join him . . . Lord Nelson reads the letter – and hands it back: it must be a short one . . . They talk together, both frowning. Bad news? The poor lieutenant – ah, Lord St Vincent waves him away. They keep looking over their shoulders – making sure no one can overhear, I suppose. Lord Nelson may have only one arm, but he waves it about a lot!'

She paused and clapped politely as the orchestra stopped and, almost without pause, swept on to the next tune. As the dancers resumed, Ramage noticed that Gianna had suddenly tensed. 'What's the matter?' he said in alarm.

She made a placatory gesture with her fan. 'It's nothing. Lord Nelson waved, as though referring to someone over here, and now Lord St Vincent is quizzing everyone. He looks so stern!'

Ramage shrugged. 'Half the King's ministers are here tonight . . . Perhaps they've just received a dispatch saying that Boney's coming!'

Gianna shivered. 'Don't make jokes about it!' She began reading the card that she had taken from her tiny handbag. 'Ah, for the next dance my partner –'

But Ramage was not listening; instead he turned again and watched as the First Lord spoke abruptly to a tall and elegant young post captain, who then began walking round the edge of the ballroom after a quick glance in Ramage's direction. He took a short cut across the corner of the floor, where there were few dancers, and Ramage saw that both Lord Nelson and Lord St Vincent had deliberately drawn apart from their group and were waiting impatiently.

Perhaps this was a common occurrence at a great ball attended by more than half the Cabinet: the sudden arrival of an urgent dispatch requiring some equally urgent decision and action. He turned back to Gianna and envied whoever was being summoned to the First Lord's presence; it might spoil the rest of the ball for the fortunate man and make him unpopular with his partner, but it would mean employment. At sea with a good ship and orders for detached service.

'I'm a dull fellow at a ball,' he said apologetically to Gianna. She was not listening but staring up at someone. He glanced up too and was startled to find the post captain looking down at him.

The man bowed gracefully to Gianna and after a perfunctory 'By your leave, Ma'am,' said to Ramage: 'Lord St Vincent wishes to speak to you for a few minutes: his Lordship told me to remain with the Marchesa.'

'Most necessary, sir,' Ramage said, nettled by the man's disdainful manner, 'it says on the map, "Here be lions," ' He turned to Gianna, childishly gratified by the puzzled look on the captain's face. 'If you'll excuse me – I'll hurry back.'

Gianna smiled politely but she said firmly: 'No ship. Not for another eleven days, anyway. You tell him.'

Lord St Vincent had not changed in the two years since Ramage had last seen him: he was still the ramrod-stiff figure with a bowed head who spoke as crisply and as frankly as he wrote.

'Ah, Ramage, 'fraid I have to interrupt your social life for a few minutes. Pity the King isn't here tonight; intended to present you. His Majesty likes to meet the young officers he reads about in the *Gazette*. Still, there'll be another opportunity – as long as you don't blot your copybook, eh?' His Lordship gave a wintry smile. 'You understand me, eh?'

'Aye, aye, sir,' Ramage said, and realized the First Lord had a better memory than he had thought.

'Mr Ramage!' the First Lord said sharply, raising his voice above the orchestra, which had reached an exuberant passage, 'that's a very knowing smile you've rigged across your face. I've read all the correspondence concerning your recent actions. You're a brave and resourceful fellow, but make no mistake; I know you'd sooner disregard orders than obey 'em. Once in a thousand times that's justified – perhaps once in a lifetime. You've done it half a dozen times already. Remember that – and remember that the Navy List is full of brave and resourceful young officers.'

Only a fool would disregard the warning note in what was, for Lord Vincent, a long speech. 'Aye aye, sir,' Ramage said, hoping those three normally safe words would not get him into more trouble.

'My compliments and apologies to the Marchesa,' St Vincent said gruffly. 'Looks as beautiful as ever. Going to marry her?'

The First Lord was famous for his often stated view that the moment he married an officer was lost to the Navy, and Ramage was thankful he could answer honestly: 'It's never been discussed, sir.'

Lord St Vincent snorted and said suddenly: 'Just remembered something his Majesty mentioned. He noticed that they don't use your title in the *Gazette*.'

Ramage was not sure if it was a statement or a question, but Lord Nelson, who had been standing quietly in the background, moved closer and nodded a greeting as he said: 'I think it goes back to the Lieutenant's early days in the Navy, sir. Makes a pretty problem for a hostess seating her guests – does Lieutenant Lord Ramage take precedence over Rear Admiral Sir John Smith ...'

St Vincent nodded understandingly. 'Well, Ramage, hurry up and get your flag and stop being a problem for the ladies, eh? Now, let's find some privacy in the Duke's library.'

With that he turned abruptly and with Lord Nelson walked towards a corridor leading from the ballroom. A puzzled Ramage was just going to rejoin Gianna when he saw St Vincent glance round and beckon him impatiently. 'I'm sure His Majesty would be grateful if he knew you could spare his First Lord of the Admiralty a few minutes of your valuable time, Ramage,' he growled, 'and I'm equally sure that the Marchesa will be flattered that a couple o' hundred fellow guests saw you leave the ballroom in the company of one of the King's ministers and one of his most famous fighting admirals.'

'Quite so, sir; I – er ... didn't ...'

'Step lively and don't talk so much.'

The library was a book-lined cavern, and Lord St Vincent went straight to a table and sat down, gesturing to Lord Nelson and Ramage to be seated opposite.

Lord Nelson looked across at Lord St Vincent. 'There's no doubt about this report, sir?'

'None. Wish there was.'

'But I don't trust these French agents,' Nelson said querulously. 'No patriotism; they're doing it for money.'

Ramage wished he had heard the earlier part of the conversation, and was just reflecting that the question of allegiance depended upon whom you regarded as your leader, when the First Lord said: 'This man is Scots born. Lived most of his life in France. Our best agent, I'm told.'

'Apparently the Secretary of State has heard nothing,' Nelson said doubtfully. 'I'd have expected – '

'Lord Hawkesbury will have received the report half an hour ago,' the First Lord said impatiently. 'This man's an Admiralty agent: reports directly to us, and we send copies across to the Secretary of State.'

'That can't make him popular in Downing Street,' Nelson commented. 'The Secretary of State's office like to deal with all intelligence activities.'

'Quite so,' St Vincent said acidly, 'but they didn't have any choice with this fellow: he's highly placed in Bonaparte's circle, so his life hangs by a thread.' He looked up and saw Nelson's puzzled expression. 'He's the son of a former naval officer, and his reports reach England by – well, unusual seafaring routes. More convenient if the Admiralty handles them.'

Nelson reached out his hand. 'Perhaps I could read the report again?'

At that moment there was a double knock on the door and a man Ramage recognized as Lord Hawkesbury walked in.

'Ah! There you are,' he said, sitting down at the table. He glanced at Ramage, gave him a perfunctory nod and then said pointedly to the First Lord: 'I want to discuss this report we have just received.'

'It's all right. Ramage here knows nothing about it yet, but he is likely to be involved. You know him, I see.'

The Secretary of State nodded absent-mindedly. 'I guessed I'd find you here and came at once. What do you think about it?'

'I believe it,' St Vincent said firmly. 'I've been expecting something like this. That's why his Lordship,' he gestured towards Nelson, 'has been given this "Squadron upon a Particular Service."'

'Quite so,' Lord Hawkesbury said. 'But the agent makes a very bald statement!'

St Vincent shrugged his shoulders. 'He could have used a thousand words to say the same thing, but mercifully he didn't.'

'But he gives no proof,' Lord Hawkesbury complained. 'He never does. He is a member of Bonaparte's staff, and he knows we are aware of that. But if you'll look at the report again –' he motioned to Nelson to pass the sheet of paper, 'you'll see it's so worded that no one reading it could guess. It'd be a death sentence for him if it was intercepted.'

'Very well,' the Secretary of State said reluctantly, glancing at the page. When he had finished reading it he said querulously: 'The more I read it, the less it seems to tell me!'

'There are two separate items,' St Vincent said patiently, controlling his notoriously short temper. 'First, the troops. The fact that another 50,000 men are at this moment marching towards Boulogne and Calais means a considerable reinforcement: we know Bonaparte has 100,000 there already.'

'But is that *likely*?'

'Why not? Since he signed the Treaty of Luneville and put the Austrians out of business, Bonaparte isn't fighting anyone on the Continent of Europe –'

'I know that,' Lord Hawkesbury interrupted impatiently.

'I know you know that,' St Vincent said calmly, 'I mention it as a foundation for the point I am about to make, not as fresh news.'

' 'Pologies,' Hawkesbury said, 'I've had a tiring day.'

'Well, Bonaparte has had three or four months to re-equip his armies and make new plans –'

'And he's decided Great Britain is his last enemy,' Hawkesbury said in a return of his impatient autocratic manner.

'That's reasonably obvious,' the First Lord said, clearly controlling himself with difficulty, 'but until now, until the early summer, he lacked allies.'

'What allies?' Hawkesbury was puzzled, as St Vincent had intended him to be.

'The east wind and a calm sea,' St Vincent said grimly, 'and a new moon.'

'When can you anticipate that trio coinciding?'

'The new moon is predictable enough – three weeks' time. The east wind – anyone's guess. We've always anticipated that Bonaparte would have to pick a new moon period, but we need more specific intelligence, otherwise we'd have to bring the Channel Fleet up to the Strait of Dover once a month.'

'An east wind, eh?' Hawkesbury mused. 'What if Bonaparte can't wait for it? Can he risk sailing his Invasion Flotilla in a west wind?'

'He could, but ideally he wants if not an east wind then some wind with east in it, because his barges won't go windward. They need a following wind.'

'Are you saying we're safe with a west wind? I've never heard that view before.'

'A *strong* wind with any west in it will keep 'em in port; but we aren't completely safe in a light west wind or a calm; the small barges and gun boats could be rowed across. Hard work but possible.'

'A long row, eh? That'll give your frigates and line-of-battle ships a chance to get amongst them!'

St Vincent shook his head. 'I'm afraid a sea as calm as that would mean no wind, so the fleet and the frigates would be becalmed.'

'Of course,' Hawkesbury snapped, annoyed with himself for not realizing that. 'Very well, the agent hasn't told us much, then.'

'We've only discussed the first item,' St Vincent said sourly, 'which is that 50,000 extra troops are making for Boulogne. The second item – ' he picked up the paper, 'says less but tells us more: Bonaparte is about to ask Bruix – he's the admiral commanding the Invasion Flotilla, as you know – how soon the flotilla can sail.'

'Hmm – I can't see *that* tells us much,' Hawkesbury said.

St Vincent folded the paper with great deliberation and put it down on the table. 'On the face of it, it tells us that Bonaparte the General considers the Army is ready to cross the Channel, and he's asking Bruix the Admiral for the earliest date the Flotilla can embark it. The question is urgent only if the Flotilla can be made ready fairly soon. In three weeks' time,' he said ominously, 'or a month after that.'

'Quite so,' Hawkesbury said, 'so that narrows the date down to two periods of a very few days – I gather a full moon is no use?'

'No. The French want a new moon – setting two or three hours after it is dark – to get their vessels safely out of harbour without collisions and too much confusion. After that they want darkness for the crossing, to put our ships at a disadvantage, and dawn should see them just off our beaches.'

'If the wind is right.'

'As you say,' St Vincent agreed.

'Then what more do you want to know, my dear Admiral?' Hawkesbury asked, obviously puzzled.

'Well, sir, the problem is – we think . . .' he broke off and gestured to Lord Nelson, who put his hand down on the table and leaned forward slightly in a movement that reminded Ramage of a spring being wound up taut.

'Bonaparte may have marched the troops and asked Bruix when he will be ready just to spur on his generals and admirals, sir,' Nelson said quietly. 'He has another three months of summer left, another three suitable moon periods, and we can't be sure he won't postpone it at the last minute. If we assume the next new moon period is the real date and start moving the fleet round to the Strait of Dover and mobilizing our defences, should Bonaparte then postpone the attempt for a month he is bound to conclude that we knew of his plans, since we made no such move at the last new moon.'

'But surely preparing ourselves at each new moon is a logical reaction?' Hawkesbury asked.

'Yes – but we would rather that Bonaparte does not discover what our precise plans are.'

'But,' Hawkesbury protested, 'if he knows the Fleet is ready, he's less likely to sail!'

Now Ramage saw Nelson in a fresh light: he was a new man, his single good eye shining, his face flushed, the fingers of his hand drumming on the table.

'We can't smash Bonaparte's invasion plan if he keeps his ships and men safe in harbour, sir. We want his Army out on the open sea, so that we can sink or burn every ship. It takes a great army – and heavy losses – to destroy another army of 150,000 men on land: an army we can't muster. But our fleet can destroy such an army at sea – can and *will*, providing it sails.'

Hawkesbury was worried. 'It's a deuced risk: something the Cabinet ought to consider. Better keep the devils bottled up in Boulogne and Calais, I say.'

'Not while I occupy the office of First Lord,' St Vincent interrupted. 'I have a great respect for Mr Addison, but I only joined his government on the clear understanding that I was given a free hand.'

'Oh, I agree,' Hawkesbury said hastily, realizing he had stepped beyond his professional responsibility, which was foreign affairs. 'I was expressing a personal view, you understand; my colleagues probably would not agree with me.'

'Be that as it may,' St Vincent said uncompromisingly, 'I

assure you the Admiralty want the French to sail because it is confident that they can't land in England, so – '

'Very well,' Lord Hawkesbury interrupted. 'Now, why can't we rely on our agents – especially this man in Paris – to warn us in time enough if and when Bonaparte decides to sail his flotilla?'

Nelson glanced at St Vincent before replying: 'It is not the kind of information our agents in Boulogne – such as they are – will discover. That throws the responsibility on to the man in Paris. Unfortunately he never travels with Bonaparte. It seems that Bonaparte has a special staff that travels with him, and his regular staff remains in Paris.'

'How does that affect this situation?'

'I think we can assume that Bonaparte will leave Paris and travel to Boulogne fairly frequently from now on. We have no way of knowing – unless our man gets some hint – if he is simply going to review the troops and cheer 'em up, or get 'em to sea.'

Lord Hawkesbury turned to the First Lord. 'Well, what are you going to do about this report?' He pointed to the paper on the table. 'Mr Addison will be asking me.'

'I'm sending a man to Boulogne,' St Vincent said. 'This man,' he added, pointing at Ramage.

'Are you, by Jove?' Hawkesbury said. 'What do you think about that, young fellow? You look a bit startled. What are you going to do when you get there, eh?'

Ramage swallowed hard, hoping one of the admirals would come to the rescue, but when they remained silent he said, in a wild guess, 'Find the answers to His Lordship's questions, sir, and send back a report.'

'Speak much French? Spying is a dangerous job.'

'Enough, sir. I – ' suddenly the idea came. 'I can pass for an Italian, sir; it lessens the risk.'

He was aware that both the admirals were looking at him, and Lord St Vincent said gruffly, 'No need to worry about Ramage; he's used to this sort of thing.'

Ramage knew the remark was made to reassure Lord Hawkesbury and divert him, but the Secretary of State persisted. 'What is he going to find out?'

'Just how many vessels of the Invasion Flotilla are ready to put to sea – and give us some better estimates than we have at the moment of how many soldiers the various types can carry.'

'I fail to see how that information helps us much,' Hawkesbury said.

St Vincent managed to cut off a sigh. 'If he sees five hundred vessels are ready, and estimates that each can carry a hundred men, then we know Bonaparte can embark an army of 50,000.'

'Quite so,' Hawkesbury said.

'In other words, sir,' Nelson said, 'the fact that Bonaparte has sent another 50,000 soldiers to Boulogne need not worry us if we can be sure he has no ships to carry them across the Channel.'

'But what makes you think Bonaparte would send 50,000 men to Boulogne if he hadn't the ships to carry them?'

St Vincent pulled his nose impatiently. 'I don't think one way or the other. I learned only half an hour ago that another 50,000 men are marching there. I'm now taking steps to find out if Bonaparte has enough ships for them – and for the army he already has camped there. Until I get young Ramage's report I'm not thinking anything,' he added coldly.

'Excellent,' Lord Haweskury said, as if at last convinced the Admiralty planned to do the right thing. 'I'll report that to the Cabinet tomorrow morning. Most satisfactory – providing this young man can furnish you with the answers.'

'He'd better,' the First Lord said with a ghost of a smile. 'If he escapes Bonaparte's guillotine but comes back without the information he'll have me to contend with!'

The Secretary of State laughed as heartily as his normal cold and scholarly manner allowed. 'I'm told that sailors face the greatest peril,' he said dryly to Ramage, 'when they come on shore.'

'It seems so, sir,' Ramage said, and wished his laugh sounded more convincing.

St Vincent gave another of his wintry smiles and took out his watch. 'Mr Ramage will be waiting on me in the Admiralty at seven o'clock tomorrow morning, sir, and I've no doubt he would like another dance or two before getting to bed, so . . .'

CHAPTER THREE

As he waited in the ante-room to the First Lord's office the next morning, Ramage reflected that although a woman's tongue was reputed to be her only weapon, it was often most effective when she did not use it. When he had rejoined Gianna on the ballroom floor last night and finally got rid of that damned post captain – who seemed hypnotized by her – she had turned to him, her face expressionless and her eyes cold.

'Well,' she had said, 'I trust Lord St Vincent and Lord Nelson have accepted your advice.'

He had shaken his head helplessly, scared that if she had even a hint of what was happening she would sail over to Lord St Vincent like a frigate hard on the wind and make a scene. He had taken the cowardly way out, merely telling her that he had to be at the Admiralty early next morning. She had then lapsed into silence: a noisy, echoing and hurt silence that left him punishing himself more harshly than she could have done with her tongue.

They had danced twice more, but they were stiff and distant. She had made excuses to four other men who had requested dances and whose names were noted on her card, and then asked to be taken home. Ramage was thankful his father and mother had been too preoccupied with their own circle of friends at the ball to come over to them for a chat: he was sure Gianna would have involved his father – who must have seen him going off to the library with the two admirals – in the iniquity of officers having their leave cut short.

Now, sitting in this cheerless and chilly room, the skin of his face sore from a razor whose edge was quite unresponsive to the strop, he found he was getting frightened.

Last night he had been too preoccupied with Gianna's behaviour to have second thoughts about what he had been told in the Duke's library, and he had climbed into bed so weary that the next thing he knew was Hanson waking him with the news that it was half past five and time to get up.

Hellfire and damnation, this room was cold – and why, like almost every other room in the Admiralty, was it painted in this ghastly dark green and buff? The one tiny window opened on to a nearby wall so the sun never managed to find its way in. He shivered and a moment later wondered whether it was the temperature or the thought that within the week he would be in France acting the part of a spy. Acting! He would *be* a spy, a man who once caught would be executed after ruthless questioning and, if he did not provide the required answers, would probably be subjected to imaginative torture.

Had Gianna somehow guessed that not only would he be under Lord Nelson's orders and therefore involved in the preparations concerning Bonaparte's invasion plans, but that he would have to go to France? It seemed impossible, yet surely she would have behaved differently if he was simply being given another ship. She would have complained loudly – that was it: the chilly silence was unlike her. It was as though there was a genuine fear for him, not just disappointment that he was going to sea again after such a long absence.

He shrugged his shoulders. She might have connected the arrival of the messenger with the sudden activity involving Lord Nelson as well as the First Lord: and she had read of Lord Nelson's new appointment in the newspapers that morning. That would have led her to think of the invasion threat, and she could have fitted the rest of the puzzle together. She, of all people, knew that three years ago both admirals were involved when he ended up leading the landing party that rescued her from the Tuscan beaches with the French cavalry hunting her down only a few yards away. Lord Nelson knew that he spoke good Italian and French. In other words Gianna had instinctively reached the conclusion that he had only just reached by disjointed thinking: Lord Nelson had suggested him because he was the only naval officer readily available at one minute's notice who had a chance of working successfully behind the enemy's lines.

Spies must be either unimaginative people, or able to shut off their imaginations at will. He wished he had the knack, because his imagination would almost certainly be too nimble to allow him to sleep comfortably when French soldiers roamed the streets outside. He shut his eyes and pictured himself listening to a church clock striking three o'clock in the morning, and hearing the tramp of a French patrol and the orders and oaths shouted in French. It was bad enough in battle; up to now he had been able to fight off fear that made him want to run below when he saw the guns of an enemy ship's broadsides winking their red eyes . . .

The door opened and Lord Nelson beckoned him into the next room.

The First Lord, sitting at the table which was bare except for an inkwell, penholder, sandbox and two single candlesticks, looked up and nodded. 'From today you are under Lord Nelson's orders. I should warn you that secrecy is vital, so don't gossip.' He looked up and smiled, as if to take the edge off his harsh words. 'Don't look so hurt; you'll be the one that Bonaparte guillotines, not me.'

Lord Nelson ran a hand through his wavy and greying hair. 'It is too early in the morning to talk of guillotines, eh Ramage? Come along, the First Lord has given me my orders concerning you, so let us leave him with the rest of his day's business.'

The Admiral led him to a room along the corridor and sat down at a small table, reaching for a leather portfolio. As he fumbled with the straps Ramage reached forward to help, but Nelson shook his head. 'I've been without a second arm so long now that I'm used to it. This is the only thing that bothers me.' He pointed to his sightless eye. 'I think I'd sacrifice the other arm to have the sight back.'

He tipped the contents of the portfolio on to the table, and Ramage saw that much of it comprised pages cut from French newspapers and journals. The Admiral selected several sheets of notepaper, pushing the rest towards Ramage. 'Glance through those,' he said, 'then you'll know as much about Bonaparte's intentions as the regular readers of Le Moniteur.'

The pages, covering nearly a year, contained dozens of newspaper reports of Bonaparte's invasion plans or rather, as much of them as he wanted revealed by allowing them to be published. Some of the reports referred to orders that Bonaparte had given to his admirals and generals – these were in suitably flowery language and gave nothing away. Others showed how the Army of England, as it was hopefully called, had been assembled along the Channel coast over the past few months. But the most remarkable described how France's inventors were helping in the task of transporting the great Army to England.

Here were the original reports from which the British

newspapers drew their accounts and people like Gillray drew their cartoons: huge, hot-air balloons which could carry a hundred men in gondolas slung beneath for the 'Descente en Angleterre'; great rafts propelled by sails, oars and huge windmills with their blades somehow geared to paddlewheels mounted on the side of the rafts. The actual invasion barges were described in enough detail for Ramage to guess they were designed by men used to Mediterranean galleys and who over-rated the choppiness of the Channel in anything of a breeze. Little more than great boxes, they must be so heavy that they would need half a gale o' wind to move them under sail. Likewise the gunboats intended to protect the barges seemed more suitable for operation on a large lake than in the Channel, with its treacherous weather and strong currents.

Lord Nelson glanced up as he put down the last page. 'Well, what do you make of it?'

Ramage hesitated: what comment could a mere lieutenant make to the Navy's most successful fighting admiral that would not sound stupid, impertinent, banal – or all three?

'Tell me,' Nelson said sharply, 'if you commanded three hundred of those barges laden with troops and artillery, and two hundred gunboats fully armed, how would you rate your chances of making a successful landing on the Kent or Sussex coast?'

'If I had a brisk easterly wind and a dark night sir,' Ramage said diffidently, 'and the Royal Navy was not around, I'd hope to get fifty, perhaps a hundred, of the barges ashore in England. But they'd probably be scattered along miles of the beaches: it would be impossible to keep them concentrated.'

'Why?' Nelson demanded querulously. 'Doesn't say much for your skill as a commander, does it? Unless you kept the barges together you wouldn't stand a chance: a hundred seasick Frenchmen landing from a single barge in one place, and another hundred getting ashore a mile away – why, even the local Sea Fencible companies could mop them up!'

Ramage flushed but stuck to his opinion. 'The French won't have enough trained men to command the barges, sir. They would scatter from the moment they left port. Apart from Calais and Boulogne, the other French ports are tiny and dry out at low water, so at least two-thirds of the barges will come from those two ports. Even a hundred barges – not

31

to mention gunboats and sloops – leaving Calais on one tide: why, the confusion would be enormous. They seem to be so cumbersome that with anything but a soldier's wind they can't manœuvre. So they'd leave the French coast scattered, and I doubt if they could get into any sort of formation in the darkness before they reached England at dawn.'

'Where would you lose the two hundred, then? You said only a hundred would arrive.'

'Collisions, sir. That would bring masts tumbling down like corn before a scythe. And if they are being rowed, it needn't be an actual collision: one barge getting too close to another one means all the oars are ripped away and the rowers injured.'

'Two hundred lost like that?'

'No, sir: perhaps a hundred. Another fifty or so would be lost on sandbanks by navigational mistakes and poor seamanship while leaving the harbours in France – or hitting rocks and reefs on the English coast. The rest would probably sink because the planking opened up – poor construction, gun carriages breaking loose from their lashings, horses stampeding . . .'

'You're a damnably depressing fellow, Ramage! Are you always as gloomy as this?' The Admiral's expression made it clear he was teasing.

'No, sir, just that the barges and gunboats described here don't seem to have been designed by the French Navy – they have fine ships – and ninety per cent of the men on board will be landlubbers. Why, Bonaparte hardly has enough officers and men for the Fleet. And I was only answering your question, sir; I'm not counting losses caught by the Royal Navy.'

'Very well,' said the Admiral, 'another hypothetical question. You are allowed to pick your weather – and Bonaparte's only orders are that you have to concentrate the barges along a ten mile stretch of the Kent or Sussex coast. But now the Royal Navy is at sea. How many barges will you get ashore?'

'A few dozen, sir, and they'd be even more scattered,' Ramage said promptly.

'I'm glad Bonaparte can't hear you; he'd be dismayed!' The Admiral flattened the sheets of paper he had been holding. 'Now, the point of all this is that I want you to read and remember every scrap of information in the Admiralty's possession about Bonaparte's plans for his invasion, and forget everything you know about our defences. In case you are captured,' he added.

'I have a very poor memory, anyway,' Ramage said apologetically, appalled at the thought of learning facts and figures by rote. 'I mean, for learning and remembering numbers.'

Lord Nelson shook his head and said grimly: 'There's nothing to alarm you here –' he tapped the papers, 'because we know precious little about the barge and gunboat flotillas, apart from what has been published in the *Moniteur*. What we know from our agents – mostly emigrés, and their information out of date – is written down here. All the items of interest from the *Moniteur* are there – the ones you've glanced at. Put it all together and it doesn't make a big pile, does it?' he noted ruefully. 'Now, I want to run through what's written here; then you can spend the rest of the day digesting it.'

Quickly he read aloud from the written notes, which were the totals of barges and gunboats reported to have been completed and launched at each of the ports, the numbers actually under construction at the same ports, and the numbers believed to have been ordered but not yet started. Another list gave sites of army camps round Boulogne and Calais and some details of the troops and artillery occupying them, with possible sites for further camps. A third list gave the names of the senior French military and naval officers and their roles in the invasion plan.

As Lord Nelson spoke, occasionally making shrewd comments on the abilities of those French officers he had encountered in the past, Ramage became more and more appalled at the magnitude of the task he was being given, even though he did not yet know the exact details. How on earth was he to land in France and, within a very few days, start worming one of the greatest secrets in France out of generals and admirals? The whole thing was ridiculous, and he began to feel resentful at being singled out. He had been trained to command ships at sea; it was unreasonable to involve him in this hole-in-the-corner spy business.

At that moment he glanced up to see the Admiral looking at him. It was disconcerting because he was more than conscious that the right eye was almost opaque, as though a thick film had grown across it. But the left eye was sharp enough; Ramage had the uncomfortable feeling that the Admiral had just looked into his innermost thoughts.

'Unfair, isn't it,' he commented. 'Damn' fool admirals expect you to land in France and winkle out secrets within a week or so. Was that what you were thinking?' He suddenly smiled, a friendly and understanding smile, and nodded before Ramage could answer. 'I should hope so; anyone with enough imagination to succeed should have decided fifteen minutes ago that the whole thing is impossible. No, don't look so surprised; the fact is – and I'm speaking from a few years of experience – that the task that looks utterly impossible is often the easiest to accomplish. The tallest mountain isn't always the hardest to climb, you know; it's often the smaller ones that have vertical faces.'

Ramage realized he had just been given a revealing insight into the man who had destroyed the French fleet at the Nile, saved the present First Lord from disaster at the Battle of Cape St Vincent and turned it into a narrowly-won victory, and more recently, smashed the Danish fleet at Copenhagen in a battle that hung on a knife-edge for a couple of hours. Tall mountains aren't always the hardest to climb, he repeated to himself. He must remember the phrase: his father would be more than interested since Nelson, as a young post captain, had served under him.

'Very well, Ramage, that's all the information we have from our agents. I want you to have a complete understanding of it for a particular reason: whatever you pick up in France, you must be able to estimate its importance at once: whether we know it, whether we ought to know it and how urgently, and its significance. You'll also know what to ignore. But there's another reason. Frankly, I have my doubts about the accuracy of most of this – ' he tapped the written notes, 'because I have no great faith in the reports of agents and emigrés. It'll be useful to be able to check as much of it as we can when you get back. As far as the *Moniteur* reports are concerned, you must bear in mind that it is the most convenient way that Bonaparte has of providing us with misleading information.'

'Which in itself might provide positive information,' Ramage thought to himself and as Lord Nelson looked up suddenly realized he had said it aloud.

'Exactly, my dear Ramage, two negatives make a positive, and that's something you can bear in mind as you read those *Moniteur* reports – which I only obtained late last night from the Secretary of State's office. My French isn't good enough to make all that easy reading, but see what you can find out. Make notes. Mention anything you think might interest me. Anything,' he reiterated, 'however unimportant it might seem.'

'Aye aye, sir. But how am I to get to France?'

The Admiral laughed; a short, almost mirthless laugh. 'That's your problem. You can be put on shore by boat from any one of my cutters; or you can find out how the smugglers travel back and forth. Now for your specific orders. As the First Lord mentioned last night, it is essential to find out how many of each type of vessel the French can put to sea at the next new moon period. Barges, gunboats, fishing craft and so on. I'd like some estimate of how many more can be commissioned by the following new moon. So that is the first part of your task, and the most dangerous. The second part you can do by keeping your eyes open: accurate estimates of the number of troops, guns and horses and amount of provisions the vessels can carry.'

'And the sailing date . . .?' Ramage asked cautiously.

'The chances of your discovering that are slight, even if Bonaparte knows it, which I doubt very much. We can be certain of one thing, though: the French won't risk having the troops and horses on board for more than twenty-four hours before sailing. Most of those vessels are anchored in such exposed places that the soldiers will become seasick within fifteen minutes.'

The Admiral stood up. 'You can stay here and go through those papers. Put them in the portfolio when you've finished and return them to the Board Secretary. I'm going down to Dover now, and you can report to me there tomorrow evening. Is there anything you want to mention now that won't wait until then?'

Ramage nodded hurriedly, since he had been wondering how he could raise the point. 'Men, sir. At the moment I don't know how I'll be handling all this, but – '

'But by chance,' Nelson interrupted, 'you happen to know the ships in which some of those scoundrels from your last ship are now serving . . .'

Ramage grinned. 'Purely by chance, sir!'

'Very well, I'll speak to the First Lord, and you can leave a list with the Board Secretary when you give him the portfolio. No more than a dozen, and I don't know what the deuce you need them for.'

He had written the names of the three men he wanted before he realized that only one of them was British. The first man was Thomas Jackson, the American who had served as his coxswain in all the ships he had commanded. 'All' included the *Kathleen* cutter, which he lost at the Battle of Cape St Vincent, the *Triton* brig, which he lost after a hurricane in the Caribbean, and more recently the *Lady Arabella* brig. The second name was the Briton, Will Stafford, a Cockney who had been a locksmith and burglar before being swept up by a press gang. His former trade might come in useful. The third man was an Italian, Alberto Rossi, whose presence in France would not arouse suspicion.

He put the list to one side and began reading through the notes he had made while going through the dozens of pages taken from various issues of *Le Moniteur*. 'Two negatives make a positive,' Lord Nelson had said, and a pattern was certainly emerging. The Sussex coast was mentioned twenty-three times as a destination for the invasion and Kent only thrice; each time it was a passing reference to the white cliffs of the South Foreland at Dover. Essex was mentioned nineteen times, Ipswich seven and Colchester nine. London was never named, except for one reference to Napoleon holding a victory parade in St James's Park.

Providing it was not all a wild coincidence, there was someone on the staff of *Le Moniteur* whose job was to make the British believe that the French would land on the Sussex coast – using the vessels at Calais, Boulogne and nearby ports – and in Essex, using those at Ostend and Dunkirk. He was doing his best to make the British think there was no interest in landing on the Kentish beaches, and that London would not be the main objective.

Ramage shrugged his shoulders: Lord Nelson could draw what conclusions he liked, once he had the facts. He arranged the pages in sequence and found himself trying to look at it through the eyes of Admiral Bruix and Marshal Soult, who were in command of the French Invasion forces. Did Bruix know the English coast well? Had Soult ever visited England? Well, they had advisers, that was certain enough.

Forget visits and forget advisers: Lieutenant Nicholas Ramage is now a French admiral whose sole concern is to get at least 100,000 troops on shore and ready to fight. Where would be the best spot to land them?

Romney Marsh: somewhere along the dozen miles of flat coast between Dymchurch and Dungeness!

He reached for his pen and began writing:

'1   Landing troops from flat-bottomed barges requires (ideally) a smooth, sand or pebble beach. The barges should arrive near high water so they dry out as the tide falls and their cargo can be unloaded on to the beach.

2   The beach should not have off-lying rocks or sand-banks on which barges could strand themselves, but must be reasonably well sheltered from prevailing westerly winds.

3   The countryside inshore of the beaches must be reasonably flat so that large numbers of cavalry and troops can deploy immediately.

4   The beaches must be readily identifiable from seaward because navigation in the barges will vary from poor to non-existent.

5   The stretch of coast from Dungeness to Dymchurch, about eight miles, fulfils all these requirements, and barges would need only to steer for the southernmost piece of land (Dungeness itself).

6   It also provides the shortest practical sea crossing for the Boulogne ships and adds only a small distance for those from Calais.'

He put down the pen and read over what he had written. As far as he was concerned, if the French troops managed to land, they would march first towards London. They would cross Romney Marsh, that strange, secretive part of Kent, absolutely flat for miles, much of it below sea-level and only saved from flooding by the sea wall, and laced with more canals and drainage ditches than there were hedgerows. They would find scattered hamlets built round squat, square-towered churches, and peopled by the dour Marsh folk, men who smuggled, fished, bred sheep and kept their own counsel. They would find few trees on the Marsh and those there were bent by the wind. The Marsh had precious little but mutton for an invader to plunder . . .

He put his notes in his pocket and replaced the papers in the portfolio. A day spent shut up in an airless room, poring over *Le Moniteur*'s fine print, had left him with a headache and, for that matter, an empty feeling in his stomach as he contemplated the enormity of the task ahead. The whole thing seemed absurd until one realized that the Admiralty had no choice: their only chance of discovering the answers in good time was by sending a man to Boulogne, the port which was obviously the French headquarters. The Admiralty had nothing to lose and everything to gain; the man had nothing to gain and his life to lose. They needed to send that man at once, so although they might just have the man – fluent in French, with plenty of experience of working in France as an agent – obviously if he was not available they had to pick the least unsuitable man, and he happened to be called Ramage. The devil take the Duchess of Manston, he thought sourly; but for her damned ball I'd still be down at St Kew, out of sight and probably out of mind as far as the Admiralty, Lord Nelson and French invasion plans are concerned . . .

CHAPTER FOUR

As the carriage stopped at the top of Wrotham Hill to let the coachman push a metal shoe under each of the rear wheels, so that the drag would prevent the carriage careering down out of control, Ramage walked round to stretch his legs. Almost the whole of the Weald of Kent was laid out before him, the hop fields, meadows and orchards fading into the distance in geometric patterns that were softly-coloured exercises in perspective. The clouds threw fast moving shadows which, from this height, reminded him of wind shadows across a green sea, with the red-brick hop kilns and their stubby wooden spires looking like buoys marking roads and byways.

So far the war against France, fought for almost a dozen years, had left no marks or scars on the countryside of England. Prices were much higher in the shops and markets, and there was hardly a village which did not boast a son or husband away in the Army or at sea in one of the King's ships. But unlike the Low Countries, Spain and Italy, there were no ruined or burned-out houses, no empty hamlets and fields overgrown because people had fled or been killed or left impoverished by Bonaparte's invading troops, who reckoned to live off the land.

'Living off the land' was a polite way of describing how an army looted its way across a continent, stealing food for its stomach and valuables for its pockets. A hundredweight sack of grain, a pair of silver candlesticks from the church altar, a peasant's store of wine which was maturing before being sold in the autumn to pay all his bills, a woman's honour and her man's life if he tried to defend it – Bonaparte's Army took it all and thought nothing of it because it was done in the name of *Liberté, Egalité et Fraternité*. Ramage shivered when he thought of the Invasion Flotilla preparing for sea in Calais and Boulogne within sight of the English coast.

The coachman called and Ramage walked back to the carriage, reluctant to climb inside and settle back on the seat whose padding exuded a damp and musty smell with every movement he made. As the horses moved, the metal shoes began to grate and occasionally screech as one or other dragged over a sharp stone. The second coachman, now sitting behind ready to lean on the brake lever, shouted across the roof to the man at the reins.

How did the Men of Kent and the Kentish Men – the former living on the east side of the Stour, the latter to the west – regard the prospect of Boney coming? The innkeepers and potmen and porters on the road up to London from Cornwall seemed blissfully unaware or blithely unconcerned, and he guessed that most of the folk on the sixty-five miles of road from London to Dover had the same attitude. He was well over a quarter of the way to Dover and had yet to hear Bonaparte's name mentioned, and so far not a sign of soldier or volunteer on sentry duty; not an Army camp or field headquarters.

The journey was tedious enough, but everything about it felt unreal. At first he thought it was the effect of having spent so much time at sea: the rolling green countryside made such a contrast that it seemed separated from him by a pane of glass. But as the carriage arrived at the bottom of Wrotham Hill without mishap and the metal shoes were removed and hooked up under the axle, and the horses whipped up so that the carriage soon reached Maidstone, he began to have second thoughts.

By the time they arrived at Lenham, where the horses changed once again, he was feeling sleepy and numbed – the result of such an early start from Charing Cross and the drumming of the wheels – but still trying to analyse his feelings. Finally, when the carriage stopped for fifteen minutes at Ashford, giving him time to eat a hurried cold meat pie at the Saracen's Head while the coachmen changed horses in the yard, he realized that he had not felt the unreality on the journey up from Cornwall: he first sensed it, he now remembered sheepishly, after the carriage left Charing Cross and clattered out of London on the Dover road.

Again the coachman was calling and Ramage, after paying his bill, had hardly settled comfortably in his seat before the carriage had left Willesborough behind and the horses were alternately galloping down one long hill and struggling up the next as the road rose and fell through Mersham, Brabourne, Smeeth and Sellindge. The hop fields were becoming scattered now; more frequently sheep were grazing and bare patches of soil sometimes showed whitish-grey chalk streaks, reminding him that the road ran parallel to the North Downs a few miles away on his left and which would reach the sea at the South Foreland between Folkstone and Dover.

The explanation floated into his mind in the same insidious and invisible manner that the musty smell of the carriage upholstery entered his nostrils. The sense of foreboding, that he was being carried along helplessly in a strange current whose direction he could not begin to guess, had really started when he finally digested the orders and information given him by Lord Nelson. At first the prospect of landing in France had been exciting and not a little frightening, but the more he had thought about it the more it seemed an ominous journey into a long, dark tunnel.

His body gave a spasmodic twitch of annoyance as he sat up squarely, irritated that he had taken so long to understand. Not a dozen men in the whole of Britain knew that Bonaparte finally had a huge army ready which, given the order to sail, could leave every house in these hamlets a smoking ruin, and the fields – where sheep and cattle now grazed or men with weather-beaten faces were swinging scythes and sickles – littered with corpses of cavalry and infantry. The body of a burly Gascon from a regiment of Chasseurs who had fought the length of Italy and Spain could be lying beside a weaver in the Brabourne Volunteers who had been called to arms only a few hours earlier and killed by one of the first few shots he'd ever heard fired in anger.

He shrugged his shoulders and was once again thankful that he was the only passenger in the coach. The sighs and shrugs and grunts that he had been giving as he struggled to sort out his thoughts would have alarmed even the most phlegmatic traveller – and probably reduced a woman to hysteria.

He dozed off but was awoken almost immediately by shouting and the carriage coming to a stop. Thinking it might be a highwayman he looked sleepily through the window and saw they were on the high ridge above Saltwood. He opened the door and scrambled out, suddenly conscious that his whole body ached because rarely-used muscles were tired from bracing him against the swaying carriage. Just along the road several men were grouped round a capsized cart: a wheel had come off, spilling a whole load of cordwood. The men had to shift the cart before clearing a pathway through the logs, and Ramage cursed at the delay: already his mouth was dry and dusty – the snack at Ashford had done little more than emphasize his hunger.

The coachman, cooling down after delivering himself of a stream of blasphemy at the delay, had retired to his seat and was holding a bottle to his lips with an assurance born of long practice. The second coachman joined him and waited patiently for his turn.

Saltwood! Ramage suddenly remembered why the name was familiar. Some six hundred years ago, four knights had slept the night in the little castle which he could just see through the trees below. Then they had ridden on to Canterbury to find the Archbishop, Thomas à Becket, and cut him down with their swords.

Daydreaming as he waited, Ramage pictured them galloping up the hill from the castle, the early sun sparkling on their light chain mail. The quartet would carefully pace their horses to pick up Stone Street, the old Roman road running northwards in an absolutely straight line for ten miles before curving to the right to join Watling Street for the last mile or two into Canterbury itself. Surely there would have been pages and attendants for knights so close to the King that they heard his angry, 'Who will free me of this turbulent priest?' The history books were as silent on the point as they would be in a couple of hundred years' time about the British agent in Paris who was at this moment working in Bonaparte's headquarters. Yet people remembered the four knights long after they could recall the name of the King (was it Henry II?) and the reason why Becket had so enraged him that his life was forfeit.

A shrill whistle indicated that the men had cleared enough

for the carriage to pass, and Ramage climbed in and sat back, feeling sleepier than if he had stood watch for a whole night. He woke with a start as the carriage suddenly swung to the right, and stared blearily out of the window to see the sun had almost set and they were now running down into the town of Dover, nestling in a valley below Dover Castle, the massive and menacing great citadel of grey stone standing four-square and high on the side of the Downs, its guns protecting the town and covering the harbour. Covering the seaward end of the Roman road known as Watling Street, in fact: the Romans were probably the first to make use of Dover as a haven, and they had built their road straight to London, nearly seventy miles with only a few small bends, and the surface still good today – except where local folk had stolen the small, rectangular stone blocks to build their own homes.

As the carriage clattered down the steep hill Ramage found himself thinking more about the Romans. They would have sailed for England from France using landing places which eventually became Calais and Boulogne, Étaples and Wimereux, the very ports in which Bonaparte's invasion flotilla was now assembling.

They would have landed within a few hundred yards of where Dover now stood, pitched their tents for the night, and then marched off up Watling Street. Over the years Dover – they called it Dubris – became so important that they built a stone *pharos*, on top of which they burned bonfires at night, and which was still standing, the oldest lighthouse in the country. Claudius's invasion in AD 43, and William the Conqueror's in 1066 . . . Well, the country was better prepared now to resist whatever Bonaparte would attempt.

Arriving at the castle that evening, Ramage found Lord Nelson in high spirits and surrounded by young post-captains and lieutenants. This bore out all the stories he had heard about His Lordship doing everything he could to promote the careers of deserving young officers.

The Admiral's temporary office was sparse and windowless, the walls whitewashed and the only furniture a long, deal table, half a dozen chairs and two forms. The light from two lanterns was reinforced by candles stuck in the necks of empty bottles, and Ramage saw that His Lordship was bent over a chart of the Strait of Dover. He glanced up and smiled when Ramage was announced and gestured to the chair opposite him across the table.

'Ah, Mr Ramage – come and meet these gentlemen!'

He obviously had an affection for them: as he introduced each one, Lord Nelson made a little joke about some aspect of the man's personality. One otherwise meek and mild looking captain whose name Ramage did not recognize suddenly gave an almost Satanic grin when His Lordship said, 'He's almost as bad as you, Ramage, when it comes to stretching or even disobeying orders. Still, he's been as lucky as you have – so far.' With that the grin vanished and the captain and Ramage avoided each other's eyes: the Admiral's warning was unmistakable.

With the introductions completed, Nelson eyed the canvas pouch that Ramage was carrying. 'You've brought your notes, I hope?' When Ramage nodded, the Admiral said: 'These officers form part of my Squadron, and they'll be interested to hear what you learned from the latest issues of *Le Moniteur*. There's no need to discuss your orders, though,' he added quickly.

Ramage took his notes from the pouch. 'There *is* a pattern, sir . . .' He took a page and put it on the top. 'It seems they want us to believe they intend landing in Sussex and Essex, but not in Kent. They mention the Sussex coast in connection with the invasion twenty-three times and Essex nineteen times, while Kent is named only three times. Only one mention of London – and that in a reference to Bonaparte holding a victory parade. They refer to Colchester nine times and Ipswich seven, as if they want us to think of the east coast. No mention at all of Canterbury, Ashford or Maidstone, but with the exception of Hastings they refer to each of the main Sussex coastal towns – Bexhill, Eastbourne, and Newhaven, Brighton, Worthing and Selsey – a dozen times or more. No mention of Rye, either, which might be significant.'

He handed the page to the Admiral. 'Nothing else of any consequence, sir: there's no pattern in the mention of French ports. They make no secret that their headquarters, both Navy and Army, are at Boulogne. I noticed they often publish the latest number of boats ordered to be built, but there's never a hint of the number of troops arriving or expected there, nor of the number of boats actually completed and launched.'

Nelson had been glancing at the notes, cocking his head to

one side as he held the paper to catch more light from a lantern. He looked straight at Ramage and said quietly: 'I have asked all my officers, at one time or another, a simple question. Now you know as much about the French preparations as anyone on this side of the Channel, I'm going to ask you.'

Ramage, remembering the Admiral's questions at the Admiralty and guessing he had a very good reason for asking more now, noticed that all the other officers were now watching him closely, and there seemed to be a vague tension in the room. No, not tension exactly; perhaps a quickening of interest, as though they were waiting for him to read out the number of a winning lottery ticket.

'Take your time in answering,' Nelson said, 'and make all the qualifications you want. Now, if you were Bonaparte, where would you land your Army?'

Ramage grinned and thumbed through his notes until he found the page on which he had written down his own invasion notes. 'I'd favour Romney Marsh, sir; along about seven miles of the coast between Dymchurch and Dungeness.'

He noticed that four or five of the officers had looked away when he mentioned Romney Marsh, but three others had walked to the chart on the table. Three captains, he noted, all with less than three years' seniority since they wore epaulets only on the right shoulder.

Nelson, looking at Ramage, gestured at them. 'You've pleased my Marsh Men but disappointed my two Pevensey Level Loyalists – they favour a spot between Bexhill and Eastbourne – and my two Maplin Sands Stalwarts, who think Boney will favour the Essex side of the Thames Estuary.'

'And you, sir?' Ramage asked nervously. 'Might one ask . . .?'

'I'm not a betting man, Ramage; I hope my young men can pick the winners. Now let me look at those notes of yours.'

Ramage gave him the paper and as Nelson took it he said to one of the three captains, 'Carry on, Lacey; I know you have some questions for him!'

Captain Lacey, the meek and mild looking man with the surprisingly Satanic grin, gave a slight bow and then turned to Ramage. 'You know the Kentish coast well?'

'The landward side, sir. I spent some time on the Marsh when I was a small boy – an uncle lives at Aldington, overlooking the whole area. He also owns a farm or two round Old Romney and some land out on the 'Ness.'

'How many acres altogether?'

'A few hundred, I believe.' Since none of the officers seemed to be from land-owning families, Ramage guessed it was not the time or place to say that the total was counted in thousands and that his uncle – his mother's brother – was one of the biggest landowners in the county, a man reputed locally to graze more sheep than the King fed soldiers.

'Is that why you favour the Marsh?'

'Hardly, sir; my uncle would be one of the first the French strapped to the guillotine – if they caught him alive!'

The Admiral slid Ramage's notes across the table. 'Look at that Lacey; we have a budding Marshal Soult here.'

Lacey read quickly and grunted when he came to the end. 'Good point about Johnny Frenchman steering his barges for the southernmost point of land, Dungeness itself. Have to keep it a bit to larboard if he's landing on the east side,' he added, as though thinking aloud, 'then on the flood tide the current would set him nicely into the bay.'

Another of the captains – Ramage recognized him as one of the Pevensey Level Loyalists – said evenly, 'A special case can be made out for almost any suitable stretch of coast, sir, be it in Sussex, Kent or Essex.'

'Quite so,' the Admiral said, 'and that's why you've been here with me all day. By the way, Ramage, we spent the morning in discussions with our military friends, getting the benefit of their views and giving them the benefit of ours –' he paused as Captain Lacey gave a derisive snort, 'even if they listened with less patience than we did. I told them that we intended – if humanly possible – to destroy the French at sea. I had the impression the soldiers regarded us as rather unsporting – wanting to shoot their bird, as it were.'

'They'd miss it anyway,' Lacey said crossly. 'If the French don't land at Shorncliffe Camp, I can't see how the Army'd march in time enough to find 'em.'

'Have the soldiers any ideas on suitable landing places, sir?' Ramage ventured.

Again Captain Lacey snorted while Lord Nelson permitted himself a wry smile. 'We have the impression they were catholic in their choice. Anywhere from Essex to Hampshire, although they didn't rule out Suffolk, the Isle of Wight, Hampshire or even Dorset, though I presume they mentioned

45

that out of deference to Captain Lacey, who is as stout a champion of the county of Dorset as any man alive.'

'They rule out Norfolk then, sir,' Ramage said with exaggerated innocence.

Nelson laughed and slapped the table with his hand and when he spoke his Norfolk accent was more pronounced. 'Yes, though I'm not sure whether they think Bonaparte fears the men of Norfolk would toss him into the sea or whether he can't be bothered with them!'

'One night, just one night,' Lacey said crossly. 'If only those soldiers would get it into their heads that the French have to cross the Channel under cover of darkness. Eight hours at the most. That limits where they can land. Any wind that pushes those barges along at more than five knots will kick up too much sea for them to land, so that limits them to forty miles from Calais and Boulogne.'

'Don't forget Dunkirk and Ostend,' murmured one of the Maplin Sands Stalwarts. 'Two separate landings, you know, with the Dutch Fleet covering them. Just a token force from Boulogne and Calais to land on Romney Marsh, but the main force from Ostend and Dunkirk to tackle the Essex coast. Shortest route to London, by Jove; even the soldiers admit that.'

'We won't go into all that again,' Nelson said impatiently. 'Well, gentlemen, that completes our business for today. You've heard what the soldiers think; I've had the benefit of your views on the suitability – from the French point of view – of the stretches of coast you are patrolling; and we've all heard what a newcomer to the Squadron thinks.' As if realizing the ambiguity of the remark he turned to Ramage and added: 'Your reasoning is good. I find it most stimulating to hear the views of imaginative and practical young men. It makes sure I don't overlook anything.'

'Not much chance of that, sir,' Captain Lacey said, his voice betraying both disappointment and irritation. 'I don't think any of us have said anything you haven't already thought about.'

Ramage knew that Lacey was not a flatterer; his comment probably expressed a genuine fear that some possibility might still have been overlooked. A moment later the Admiral made the same point. 'I don't want any of you to relax just because I've held this discussion. Your views may be modified later as a result of hearing other men's opinions, and you might develop new ideas. If so, I want to hear them in good time: my flagship is anchored in the Downs, as well you know. Very well, I bid you all good night. Ramage, stay behind: I still have some matters to discuss with you.'

As soon as the other officers left, the Admiral said briskly: 'Tell me how you are going to get to France.'

'I haven't had time to find a way, sir,' Ramage said apologetically. Then, worried that Lord Nelson might have forgotten that he had arrived in Dover only an hour earlier, he added: 'But I'll be in Boulogne within twenty-four hours.'

'I'm less concerned about how and when you get there than about the arrangements you make for getting information back to me.'

'Exactly, sir,' Ramage said quickly. 'That was what made me rule out getting on shore from one of our own ships –'

'I can't see Bonaparte sending out a frigate to fetch you,' Nelson interrupted.

Ramage managed to choke a laugh: sometimes it was hard to know when His Lordship was serious and when he was teasing. 'I had in mind that it's still easy to buy French lace and brandy on this side of the Channel, sir, providing you know who to ask for it.'

The Admiral nodded. 'I have an idea that more is being smuggled across the Channel now there's a war than was brought over legitimately in time of peace.'

'Forbidden fruit, sir. Our people like brandy and enough Frenchmen still like whisky!'

'I hope you find our smugglers co-operative. They're a dour crowd, you know.'

'With Preventive officers in nearly every village and Revenue cutters at sea most of the time, they have to watch their tongues, sir. A bit of idle gossip could mean the noose for them.'

'You speak with all the feeling of a man who has money invested in the business,' the Admiral said dryly.

'Wish I had, sir,' Ramage said with a grin. 'Then there'd be no problem about getting to France!'

Nelson began folding the chart. 'You're quite clear what you are after?'

'Aye aye, sir.'

'Well, look'ee here young Ramage, I'm going to tell you more than I originally intended because it's obvious the French would never dream you'd know this sort of thing,

47

and I'm anxious you should understand precisely what information would be of use to me.'

He picked up Ramage's pages of notes. 'You know we do not want to bring the Channel Fleet round to the Strait of Dover unnecessarily, for fear we frighten Bonaparte. It's a risk leaving it down to the west, and for that reason it is absolutely vital that I get forty-eight hours' warning if the French are going to sail. That will give the Channel Fleet plenty of time to get round.

'That warning would most probably come first from you. I might hear later from the frigates if they see any unusual activity, but you will be in Boulogne. Use your common sense: don't pass the word when you're not really sure – but don't be over-cautious so that you pass the word too late.'

'If the French saw the Channel Fleet close in off Boulogne, sir,' Ramage began cautiously, 'they'd be frightened –'

'Exactly! That's just what I *don't* want!' Nelson exclaimed. 'It's no good frightening them back to their holes, so that they can attack us again the moment they've rested. We must *lure* them *out* and *destroy* them,' he said, emphasizing each word by slapping the table. 'We've nothing to fear from Bonaparte at sea – so that's where we can beat him. But he has such a vast army that we don't stand a chance against him in the field – sheer weight of numbers.'

By now Nelson's single eye seemed to be looking at some remote spot beyond Ramage; the little Admiral, as though still trying to persuade ministers and generals (and perhaps some admirals, Ramage thought sourly), said emphatically: 'Stalemate – that's the biggest threat. The moment Bonaparte realizes it's stalemate he'll offer us peace, and our wretched politicians will accept it. But any peace treaty with Bonaparte will be as good as a draft on Aldgate Pump – as worthless as a gallon of cold water.'

He gave a start, as though surprised to find himself in the stark castle room talking to a young lieutenant. 'Hmm, I was carried away. My sermon for the day. Now,' he said with his customary enthusiasm, 'you'll very soon be in France. What about those men of yours? Did you give their names to Mr Nepean?'

'Yes, sir, three of them. The Secretary said you had spoken to him, and they've been ordered up from Portsmouth by the telegraph. They should be here early in the morning.'

'Three?' Nelson frowned. 'I thought you wanted more.

Still, you've probably thought about the danger of marching through the streets of Boulogne with seamen who speak no French.'

'I'll keep them well hidden sir,' Ramage grinned. 'They'll be my insurance – and messengers, if I need men to bring back reports to you. Smugglers might not be too reliable.'

The Admiral nodded as he picked up a sealed packet. 'Well, Ramage, here are your orders. You have wide discretion: I've simply instructed you to proceed in pursuance of verbal orders. Don't be alarmed; no one is going to say afterwards that you were told to do something you never in fact heard about. I don't want orders lying around that might compromise your neck in France. And you've already received enough verbal orders. Get to France as best you can. If you want a cutter, apply to me. If you want to make your own arrangements, just carry on. I'll give you a letter so you can draw money.'

'I'll manage, sir. It'll probably take me most of tomorrow to make arrangements, but I hope we'll be on our way tomorrow night and land before dawn the next day.'

Nelson held out his left hand. 'Good luck, m'boy,' he said as Ramage shook hands awkwardly, and he looked away as he said quietly, 'I hate giving orders like this – I'd sooner order you to attack a brace of frigates with a rowing-boat. That sort of thing is out in the open. I don't like this hole-in-the-corner spy business, but it has to be done.'

CHAPTER FIVE

After seventeen miles in the darkness on a hard-mouthed horse borrowed from the squadron of cavalry stationed at Dover Castle, Ramage reined in at his uncle's house at Aldington. He guessed it was little short of one o'clock in the morning. His eyes seemed full of sand, his leg and arm muscles were pulled into knots; he felt so weary his brain seemed disembodied, floating in the darkness.

He dismounted and, holding the reins in one hand, walked to the front door and jerked the bell. Several minutes seemed to elapse – but probably only two or three – before the door swung open and a bleary-eyed and surly manservant with a lantern demanded to know who was bothering Mr Rufus

Treffry at this time o' night. As Ramage said his name there was a bellowed welcome from the stairs, 'Hello there, Nicholas! What brings you to the wilds of Kent – is Boney coming?'

'No, only me,' Ramage said with a weary attempt at humour as he shook hands with his uncle. 'You look fit, sir: how are the rest of the Treffry family?'

'Well enough, well enough. Your aunt will be down the moment she knows it's you. Have you eaten?' Before he could answer his uncle was peering out through the door. He took the lantern from the manservant and held it so the light shone on the sweating horse. 'Humph, where d'you get that nag, eh? Looks more like a remount!'

'It is – I borrowed it from the cavalry at Dover.'

His uncle stared at him from under bushy eyebrows and then snapped at the manservant. 'Come on, jump about! Get his Lordship's horse stabled and rubbed down. Feed and water it. Now, Nicholas, we'd better get you fed and watered, too.' He watched the manservant scurry out of the front door and then said quietly, eyebrows raised, 'Not a social call, I imagine?'

Ramage shook his head. 'I need your help, uncle.' Then, seeing the bewildered look on the old man's face and guessing at the questions that must be running through his head, he grasped him by the shoulders. 'Don't worry, I haven't "run". You haven't a deserter on your hands! I'm on the King's business.'

Treffry chuckled and led Ramage into the drawing-room. 'Even if you were being hunted down by the Admiralty, the Preventive officers or a dozen scheming women you'd always be welcome in this house.' He held the lantern higher and looked at Ramage. 'You look worn out. Sit down a minute – what do you want to eat? Let me rouse out the rest of the staff – '

'I had a meal before I left Dover. I'd like – ' he glanced at his watch and slipped it back in his pocket, 'five hours' sleep. Could we have a talk at six o'clock – over an early breakfast?'

'Of course, of course! But give me a hint of what it's all about, m'boy; otherwise I'll never get to sleep again!'

Ramage laughed, though he was so weary the room was beginning to blur. 'I need some help from the smugglers, and

I thought you might introduce me to them.'

He woke next morning to a sudden clinking of metal and sat up in bed, trying to remember where he was, to see the curtains being drawn back. The sudden light made him rub his eyes and a voice said, 'Them metal rings is noisy, m'Lord. There's a tray with hot tea and biscuits on the table beside you. I'll bring up a jug of hot water in a moment.'

The man was dressed in servant's livery but a long, wide scar across his left cheek had tightened the flesh to make the face sinister. Ramage pictured the man without the scar, and the features seemed familiar.

'Remember me, M'Lord? Raven, Mr Treffry's butler.'

Memories came tumbling over each other: boyhood memories of holidays spent in Aldington, scrambling along sunken lanes with rabbit nets and Raven handling his ferrets, and galloping across the rolling fields to Kingsnorth on a pony his uncle selected for him. Exploring thick woods of oak and beech and ash, and being frightened by the silence and shadows in the undergrowth; using one of his uncle's fowling pieces and getting an occasional partridge.

'Yes – you used to take me fishing in the river down by the mill. We used to catch roach and cook them on a bonfire. But . . .'

'I didn't have this in those days,' Raven said, touching the scar. 'Changes a man's appearance. You've collected a couple, too,' he added, tapping his forehead, where Ramage had two scars above his right eyebrow. 'Clean cuts, like from a sword. m'Lord?'

'Boarding parties,' Ramage said. 'What happened to you?'

'Misunderstanding with a Revenue officer a few years back,' he said briefly. 'I'll fetch up your hot water, m'Lord. I've unpacked your bag and set out your razor. Your linen's been washed and should be dry in half an hour – it's hanging over the kitchen stove. I took it down last night. Your fresh clothes is hung up.'

Ramage muttered his thanks and remembered the sealed orders in his coat pocket. He had not bothered to read them, and he waited until Raven left the room before jumping out of bed and reassuring himself that the seal had not been broken. Not, he realized, that the orders would give away any secrets – Lord Nelson made sure of that.

He stripped off his nightshirt and tossed it on the bed. It was chilly, and every muscle in his body seemed to ache, but five hours' solid sleep – much more than he could usually manage at sea – had refreshed him. Raven had hung up his uniform – well, he would not be wanting that for a while. He would wear the grey breeches and brown coat, and take an old pair of trousers and a jersey with him.

He walked over to the large window and looked down over Romney Marsh. It was as though a great wedge of low and utterly flat land measuring a dozen miles by almost twenty, with Dungeness its apex, had been arbitrarily stuck on to the high land stretching from Hythe through Aldington and in a gentle sweep on to Appledore and finally Rye.

From anywhere along this ridge – his uncle's house was right on the edge of it – one could look right across the Marsh to the Channel, which formed the distant eastern horizon. Even in the early sunlight the Marsh seemed mysterious and brooding. He had forgotten just how flat it all was. The canals and drainage dykes, which also served as hedges, now seemed as they reflected the rising sun like narrow ribbons of shiny metal criss-crossing the green fields and spanned here and there by small, hump-backed bridges which allowed the sheep to move from one meadow to another.

If there were few villages, there were fewer towns: he could just make out the buildings of Dymchurch round to his left, their west walls just black shadows, with Old Romney almost due south and the long point of Dungeness – known locally as 'the Ness' – beyond.

Fifteen minutes later, washed and shaven, he joined his uncle at the breakfast table. Rufus Treffry was a stocky man of sixty who did not carry an ounce of fat. His face was round and cheerful, and although his once sandy hair was now thin, his eyebrows were bushy, bristling out over startlingly bright blue eyes.

While Raven served at the table with a remarkable economy of movement, Treffry said: 'How is my sister, and that sailor she married?'

'Both very well. They didn't know I'd be calling, otherwise they would have sent greetings.'

'And what's the news from Dover Castle? They expectin' Bonaparte?' He spoke lightly, but Ramage detected his concern.

'Everything is quiet in Dover. I don't think there's more

52

news than is reported in the newspapers.'

Treffry grunted doubtfully as he helped himself to fried eggs and thick slices of gammon from the dish Raven was holding. 'One day they'd have us believe Bonaparte is due any moment, and the next they're laughing at him!'

Ramage grinned at the cross, almost aggrieved tone of voice and, catching his uncle's eye, glanced at Raven, indicating he would say more when they were alone. For two or three minutes the men ate in silence while Raven replaced the covers on the hot dishes and left the room.

'Well, what's all the mystery, m'lad?' his uncle demanded.

'I have to get to France in a hurry – and perhaps return in even more of a hurry . . .'

'What's wrong with landing by boat at night from one of the King's ships?' Treffry asked, his voice showing he accepted there was a reason and was merely curious.

'I'd probably land all right from a cutter, but the chances of getting away again – a rendezvous has to be arranged, and depends on weather. And I have to send reports back to England . . .'

Treffry frowned. 'Is this some sort of spy business?'

There was no harm in him knowing that much; indeed, there could be no other reason for visiting France. 'Yes, I have to try and find out one or two things, and send some reports back. Then I can come home again! Do you know anyone who can help?'

'I know some folk who could help if they had a mind to,' his uncle said cautiously, 'but they've no reason to love authority: the Revenue men make nothing but trouble for them.'

Sensing a reluctance on his uncle's part, Ramage said: 'Surely running foul of the Revenue men now and again doesn't turn them against the King, does it?'

'Dear me, no,' Treffry said agreeably, 'but you must remember that the war has made their – ah, profession – ten times as dangerous. So many of our own Navy ships at sea, and all on the watch for anything suspicious.'

'Very well, so smuggling is ten times more dangerous,' Ramage said sourly, 'but I'll wager it's also twenty times more profitable, thanks to the war.'

'Very probably,' his uncle said, his eyes twinkling, 'and no doubt Bonaparte's *douaniers* want ten times bigger bribes. I must admit I know very little about it; I must be one of the

53

few around here not involved. I hear some of my neighbours grumbling at the risks their men run, and they usually send me a case or two of brandy at Christmas, Easter and Michaelmas. Still, when I see a string of packhorses being led across my land in the middle of the night, I must admit I look the other way; and when I see a shielded lantern shining from a high window facing the Marsh I assume it is a curate working late on his church accounts, although no doubt the Revenue men would claim it was a signal to smugglers that the coast was clear for their packhorses to make a delivery.'

'I'm not judging them,' Ramage said hastily. 'I just want their help!'

'Yes, I know all that, my lad; but I'm trying to warn you it's not going to be as easy as you think. First, you have to understand these men haven't been smuggling just for the last seven or eight years – since the war began. No, they've been smugglers all their lives, and their fathers before them. They – '

'I know all that, sir,' Ramage said impatiently.

'I doubt it,' his uncle said, unruffled, 'and if you want their co-operation it'll make your job a lot easier if you know more about 'em. I can see you're thinking in terms of a couple of men and a small fishing smack, but – ' he wagged an admonitory finger, 'remember the Marsh covers a couple of hundred square miles, and the Marsh Men control all the smuggling along the coast from Folkestone to Rye Bay, and that's some twenty-five miles. Why, I doubt if anything happens on the Marsh without them knowing about it – and not only on the Marsh. Did you notice any people on your way here last night?'

'I didn't see a soul after I got through Hythe.'

The old man shook his head and smiled. 'I'm sure you didn't; but people saw you: long before dawn they were trying to discover why a naval officer galloping full tilt along the Ashford road suddenly turned off southwards at Sellindge and headed for Aldington. Many people were roused from their beds, and didn't get back to their sleep until word reached them that Mr Rufus's nephew had arrived at Treffry Hall, and all was well.'

'But what – ' a startled Ramage began to say.

'Ask anyone on the Marsh the distance from one place to another, and he'll say so many miles, as the Rhee hawk flies.

If he gives an odd sort of grin as he says it, you'll know he's a Marsh Man.'

Ramage looked puzzled. 'Rhee hawk? What sort of bird is that?'

Treffry gave a dry laugh. 'Ah, you might well ask. An invisible bird that can carry a message in its beak and fly almost as fast as a galloping horse.'

'But "Rhee"? I don't remember –'

'Part of the sea wall that stops the Marsh flooding at high water . . .'

Ramage nodded. 'I remember. They say the Romans started to build it when they began draining the Marsh. Separates Romney Marsh from the next one – Walland Marsh, isn't it? Joins up with the Dymchurch sea wall.'

'Well, the hawk in question probably nests somewhere in the Rhee Wall,' his uncle said enigmatically. 'Anyway, you'd better forget all about it now, as long as you've grasped what I'm trying to tell you.'

Ramage glanced at his watch but his uncle shook his head. 'There's no hurry – yes,' he held up his hand to quieten Ramage, 'I know you're in a rush, but you can't do anything until Raven comes back.'

'Where's he gone? He was here a few minutes ago.'

'Gone to see a friend of mine. He'll be back within the hour – and then we'll know if my friend is going to be your friend, too!'

'You're talking in riddles,' Ramage protested mildly.

'Not really! Raven's gone to ask a man on my behalf if he can help you.'

'But Raven doesn't know what I want!'

'He knows all my friend needs to know – and anyway, he's carrying a letter from me.'

For the next ten minutes both men ate in silence. Treffry finally pushed his plate aside and said, 'Your aunt will be down very soon. She has a bagful of questions about the family – that's why I haven't asked any! – and she'll want you to look at the grapes.' Seeing Ramage's puzzled expression, he added, 'You've forgotten your aunt's big vine on the south wall – just about covers the lower half now. Lot of fruit on it – she's hoping for a mild summer.'

'So's Bonaparte,' Ramage said, irritated by the way the time was passing. Then, regretting his hasty remark, he added:

'I remember stealing a bunch of grapes when I was a small boy.' He grinned as he recalled more of the episode. 'They were sour as the devil, and you made me eat them all, as a punishment!'

'And you had colic for a couple of days. Your aunt played merry hell with me; said I was a wicked uncle.'

An hour and a half later, by which time Ramage had told an eagerly listening Aunt Henrietta all the family news he knew and all the London gossip he could remember, horse's hooves thudding up the long driveway signalled Raven's return.

Ramage repressed a smile when, five minutes later, once more neatly dressed in his butler's clothes, Raven came into the breakfast room with a letter on a silver tray. He glanced at the plates on the table, as if shocked that the family should still be sitting in the breakfast room, and delivered the letter to his master.

Ramage noted that his uncle played the role equally well: he took the letter as though Raven had just received it from a messenger at the front door, thanked him, and waited until Raven had left the room – after refusing a request that he be allowed to clear the table – before breaking the seal.

He winked at Ramage. 'Raven knows better than I what this letter says, but he's a stickler for appearances.' He fished around in a pocket and brought out a pair of pince-nez, which he jammed on the end of his nose. 'Hmm – from his handwriting you'd never guess this fellow has a cool quarter of a million in Consols and as much again in property. Ah . . . cautious into the bargain: I expected as much.'

He removed his pince-nez, put them in their case and stuffed them into his pocket along with the letter. Ramage tried to appear unconcerned but could think of nothing to say to his aunt, who was waiting for her husband to speak. Finally she said impatiently, 'Rufus – don't be irritating. I'm sure that letter says something that concerns Nicholas, and the poor boy is on tenterhooks!'

'Oh? By jove, Nicholas, I was daydreaming. Nothing to worry about. Wants to meet you. If he agrees to help, wants me to stand as surety.'

'Surety for what?' Ramage exclaimed.

Treffry gave a rich laugh. 'For your good behaviour. He's probably not yet convinced you haven't left the Navy and joined the Revenue Service without telling me!'

'And if I'm not well behaved?' Ramage asked sarcastically.

'I indemnify him for whatever he might lose,' Treffry said simply, 'and of course I accept. But don't worry, once he hears your story he'll do all we want.'

Your story . . . for a few moments Ramage had the feeling he was galloping across the Kent countryside and shouting at the top of his voice that he was going to France on a secret mission. His uncle seemed to sense his thoughts and said reassuringly, 'Never fear, these people know better than most how to keep their mouths shut. One careless word could hang them. And don't worry about informers – those that aren't Marsh Men know better than to look one way when they should be looking t'other, and they know what happens to men that look and gossip . . .'

Ramage pictured the bodies of past informers being put in sacks, weighted with stones, and dropped into one of the dykes. Or maybe not even weighted, but left to float, a warning to like-minded folk and over-zealous Revenue men; the smugglers' equivalent of a gamekeeper hanging up dead carrion crows outside his lodge. Yes, he would be a foolish fellow who saw packhorses laden with casks of brandy and leather panniers of French lace passing his door on a wet and windy night; the slightest hint that these unshod hooves were on the move would be enough to make men talk loudly to their wives, or put more wood on the fire; do anything in fact, except look out of a door or a window.

Treffry stood up. 'We'd best be on our way. I'll find you a decent horse.'

Ramage shook his head. 'Thank you, no; I'll use the one the soldiers lent me so that I can go straight back to Dover to collect my men. I'm leaving my uniform here,' he told his aunt, 'I'll collect it on my way back!'

'I'll tell Raven to get your luggage, then,' his aunt said and gave him an affectionate kiss. Although she obviously did not know where he was going and for how long, she assured him he would find Gianna staying at Aldington when he returned.

Fifteen minutes later Ramage was spurring his horse and following his uncle along the narrow road to Lympne and Hythe. The road ran eastward along the high land above the Marsh, dipping occasionally and running over a brook and through a copse of trees, then rising over a crest from which Ramage could look to the right across the Marsh and to the left where the land dropped into a valley and then rose and fell in ever increasing hills and valleys until it reached the North Downs.

As they rode at a brisk canter, passing a village every mile or so, Ramage remembered his uncle's comment about shielded lanterns and noticed for the first time that at least one house in each hamlet – usually the inn – had a tiny dormer window high in the roof, usually on the south side; a tiny window whose actual opening was shielded from the road but was visible for a long distance from the flat land below – and, he guessed, from pathways and tracks leading up from the Marsh. A train of packhorses coming up to an inn with contraband liquor, or to a grocer's with tea and tobacco, would watch for the light. There must be some code, so that the light – or its absence – told the smugglers that it was safe to make the delivery or that the Revenue men were out and waiting in ambush.

An old farmer standing at his gate, a fowling piece under his arm and a bulging game bag over his shoulder, gave a cheery wave as they cantered past; the ancient and rheumy-eyed driver of a heavy cart and pair, laden with soggy manure, raised his hat. A parson in black broadcloth, with the bright red complexion and bulbous, purple nose of a determined toper, reined in his apology for a horse, anticipating a chat, but Treffry called his regrets and they rode on.

'Another five minutes,' he told Ramage. 'Our fellow lives in the lee of Studfall Castle – the ruins of it, anyway.'

Who was 'our fellow'? Was he by any chance the leader of the Marsh smugglers? A quarter of a million in the Funds and a quarter of a million in land – one needed to have been a nabob to have that sort of money. A nabob, a West India planter – or a successful smuggler.

As they cantered on, Ramage found himself wondering about the sheer administration needed for successful smuggling operations; administration and capital, too, since presumably the French wanted cash for their brandy, tobacco, tea, mother of pearl, lace and other luxuries – and no doubt had to pay cash for the whisky, gin, wool and whatever else the Marsh men smuggled to France.

He knew the Board of Customs waged war on the smugglers with all the determination of the Board of Admiralty in its war against the French, and both boards always had the same complaint – too few ships and men to do the job properly. From what he had heard the last time he was in Portsmouth, the Customs people had a good case: the smugglers were now using such large and well-armed vessels that few of the older Revenue cutters could tackle them, and usually they escaped unless the Navy could lend a hand.

He wished he had paid more attention to the gossip, but he remembered talk of smugglers using fast cutters of 200 tons burthen, armed with a dozen or more 4-pounders and regularly running over to the Channel Islands and French ports. They carried their own boats on deck, enormously long and narrow (forty feet, with a beam of less than five feet, rowing ten oars or more). Frequently a cutter arrived a couple of miles off the coast, hoisted out a boat, loaded it with up to five hundred casks, and sent it off to some deserted beach, where carts and packhorses waited. By the time the alarm was raised, the horses had vanished inland with the contraband, and the boat was back with the cutter.

Sometimes the smugglers' cutters did not have to take even that risk: the Customs men were worried about a new trick, known as 'creeping.' A smuggling cutter roped a cask, leaving a very long tail which was lashed round a heavy stone, similar to those used for ballast. The cutter sailed – by prearrangement – near a fishing-boat and (as far as an innocent onlooker was concerned) tacked and at the same time threw some ballast over the side. Quite a normal activity, particularly before running for home. But each sinking stone would take a cask down with it, and at their leisure the fishermen would use grapnels to catch in the tail and 'creep up' both stones and casks, cutting the casks free of the stones as soon as they came to the surface.

Being practical businessmen, the smugglers had a scale of prices depending on the method of delivery: a four-gallon cask of brandy sold at sea (to fishermen loading it into an open boat for transfer to the smack, or sunk for 'creeping') would cost a guinea, while a similar cask landed would be thirty shillings or more. The buyers on shore were usually 'traders'; men who bought direct from the smugglers and distributed the contraband to those that wanted it – inn-keepers for the brandy, grocers for the tea.

The more he thought about it the more he realized that smuggling was a good deal more complex than one might think; a good deal more than desperadoes with black eye-patches thrashing their way across the Channel on a stormy night . . .

First, someone had to put up the cash for building a vessel, whether a small fishing-smack with a lugsail, or a big cutter carrying her own ten-oared boats. Apart from the greater carrying capacity, the big cutters had an advantage over the smaller vessels because they did not come within the Hovering Act and the later Smuggling Act, which were particularly aimed at vessels hovering off the coast, waiting for a chance to land contraband when there was no Revenue cutter in sight. Any small unlicensed boat found more than nine miles from the shore was, under the Acts, considered to be 'hovering' and liable to confiscation, but the big cutters came outside their provisions.

The regulations were strict but the Customs did not have enough vessels to enforce them. And if a privately-owned cutter sailed from Cowes bound for Dover, it was almost impossible – without catching her – to prove in a court of law that she had called in at a French port on the way, loaded contraband, sailed back and unloaded it secretly somewhere along the shores of the Marsh, and then gone on to Dover, entering as though she had come direct from Cowes.

All along the coast the Customs had their Riding Officers, men who patrolled on horseback and watched for unusual activity, usually a suspicious number of carts and packhorses close to a quiet bay or beach. But Riding Officers were responsible for long stretches of coast; often one man had to cover fifteen miles or more; and it was not difficult for a rowing-boat to slip into the beach on a dark and wet night after being given a signal that the officer had passed.

An amused 'Whoa there!' jolted him out of his daydreaming, and he reined in to find his uncle had stopped several yards behind. When Ramage rejoined him, Treffry waved his riding-crop towards a large, well-proportioned stone house set back half a mile from the road and sheltered from the wind by a circular copse of trees. It stood on the edge of the ridge of land over the Marsh; Ramage guessed from the windows on the east and south side there was an uninterrupted view of the coast from Hythe to beyond Dungeness.

His uncle coughed. 'We'd better keep a tight rein on our curiosity, heh?'

Ramage nodded. 'Simply a social call by Squire Treffry and his sailor nephew, I think. He knows what I want, so we can leave it to him to raise the subject.'

'Splendid – ticklish business.'

Ramage sensed that his uncle was uneasy at the prospect of the forthcoming meeting: the Marsh Men must have a fearsome reputation . . .

He might have a fearsome reputation among the Marsh Men, but Charles Henry Simpson (a director of the East India Company, Vice-President of the Westminster Lying-in Hospital, Vice-President of the Sea-bathing Infirmary, director of the British Fire Office, and elected trustee of the British Museum) had enough of the breezy assurance of the wealthy to thoroughly enjoy his last appointment.

'I'm the newest captain in the Romney Volunteers, my dear Treffry,' he said proudly. 'The newest and the most junior. And all my senior officers are tenants of mine!'

Treffry wagged a cautionary finger at the tall, silver-haired man who was standing at the sideboard removing the many-faceted cut-glass stopper from a sherry decanter. 'Mind they don't have you swimming dykes and doing extra drills because you charge 'em too much rent!'

Simpson gave an easy laugh as he poured two sherries, giving one of them to Treffry.

'Well, Lieutenant, you sure you won't join us?' When Ramage shook his head, Simpson sipped his sherry delicately, gave an appreciative sigh, and said: 'Your uncle tells me that I can be of service to you . . .'

Not knowing quite what his uncle had written in the letter, and irked by the question of a surety, Ramage said warily: 'I have to get to France in secret – on the King's business, you understand. Once there, I have to be able to send back at least one report, and possibly more. And then I have to return with –'

'You have proof that you are on the King's business?'

Treffry interrupted sharply: 'You have read my letter?'

'Of course, of course, my dear Treffry; it slipped my memory.'

Ramage stared at him coldly, slowly rubbing the older of the two scars on his right brow. It ill became one of the leaders of the Marsh smugglers – he was rapidly coming to believe that Simpson was *the leader* – to cavil about proof that he was on the King's business. How many French spies had made use of Simpson's services to land in or leave England?

Simpson was polished; his home was elegantly and expensively furnished. Yet for both man and house it was a studied elegance, an elaborately applied polish. The man spoke slowly – yet he thought quickly. It was a slowness that was deliberate; possibly the result of careful training, to ensure correct diction. But although Uncle Rufus had referred to the man's wealth, he had made no mention of origins: no 'son of . . .', or 'his brother is . . .' or 'father was . . .' – the normal, identifying remarks. No, it was unlikely that Mr Simpson would welcome any questions about his origins, and he was wealthy enough to stifle any in this part of the country.

'I had in mind hiring a fishing-smack. My purpose in trying to find a smuggler is that he will know his way about the French coast better than most . . .'

Simpson was nodding, an understanding smile on his face, as if wanting to make amends for his earlier tactless question. 'Not only would know, but would be assured of an understanding attitude on the part of the douaniers. The French are anxious to get their hands on sterling, since their own currency is worthless, so their Customs men do not consider that Frenchmen selling brandy and tobacco and tea to fishermen for sterling are dealing in contraband.'

'As long as I get to France, I'm not questioning anyone's motives,' Ramage said dryly.

'In that case,' Simpson said equally dryly, his tone of voice showing that he guessed Ramage's thoughts, 'my friends will be able to accommodate you. When do you want to sail?'

'Tonight, if possible. There'll be four of us.'

'Four? I thought you would be alone.'

'Myself and three of my seamen.'

'The fishermen who carry you across might be nervous at being outnumbered by – well, King's men . . .'

'Perhaps it could be explained to them.'

'That would not be possible.'

'But – '

'Take my word for it, Mr Ramage; I can't explain why at this stage, but believe me, you'll understand before you reach France.'

'There is no point in me going without my men: the whole business would fail.'

Simpson shrugged his shoulders. 'I'm sorry, Mr Ramage; I have to think of my friends.'

'So you won't help?' Ramage asked bluntly.

Simpson shook his head sadly. 'I daren't involve my friends . . .'

Half the morning had been wasted; he had to be in France within the next twenty hours. Yet there was not enough time left to start all over again. Simpson was too smooth, too suave, too sly for any honest man to trust him; but Ramage knew he had no choice. This man had to be persuaded. He glanced at his uncle, who was finishing his sherry in anticipation of leaving.

'Mr Simpson, I must tell you that the reports in the newspapers that Bonaparte is likely to invade within a short time are taken very seriously in London. In fact – '

'But such reports appear every week,' Simpson interrupted scornfully. 'We've been reading them for more than a year.'

'Quite, but there are reports which have just arrived and which you will *not* be reading in the newspapers. My orders are based on those.'

One could hardly tell a smuggler, even a wealthy smuggler who was one of the biggest landowners in Kent, that the First Lord of the Admiralty himself, and Lord Nelson, had decided to send him to France: that might start the fellow thinking that if the operation was as important as all that, then someone ought to be paying a lot of passage money. That in turn would mean that Lieutenant Ramage paid since the Admiralty would – officially, since such money had to be paid officially – refuse to have anything to do with smugglers.

Simpson shook his head and smiled; a disarming smile, Ramage felt, of the type he would use when gently refusing a parson's plea that he should pay for putting a new roof on the church in the next village but one.

'I'm sorry, Mr Ramage . . .'

'Very well,' Ramage said bitterly, 'I must admit I'm not surprised: my uncle was unduly optimistic.'

'Come now, Nicholas,' Treffry said gruffly, 'don't be hasty!'

'Hasty!' Ramage exclaimed angrily. 'With respect to Mr Simpson, we aren't asking much. If Bonaparte invades, there'll be no more smuggling: no more Mr Simpson, in fact, since he'll be one of the first strapped to the guillotine. What' – he held Simpson's eyes, his voice harsh but quiet – 'exactly what have you ever done for the country in this war, except make a fantastic profit? Yet you were born in the country. Two of the three men I'm taking with me to France, and whom you object to, are foreigners.' His tone now became contemptuous. 'One is American and the other Italian. Each of them has done more for Britain in the war than all the men that you employ!' He turned to Treffry: 'Come, uncle, it seems there's little honour among – smugglers.'

As Treffry stood up, his face flushed but obviously angry with Simpson rather than his nephew, Simpson gestured to the two of them. His face had suddenly gone white and strained; the nonchalant attitude had vanished. Ramage suddenly saw in his expression the face of a man with a bad conscience.

'Please sit down again, both of you. Mr Ramage, you put into words the thoughts that sometimes come to me in the sleepless hours before dawn. But' – he looked up, half-defiant and half-apologetic – 'I'm not apologizing for anything except my decision not to help you. I was wrong. All my resources – and they are not inconsiderable, as you have probably guessed – are at your disposal. You will be landed in France tonight. Where are your men?'

'At Dover. They will arrive –' he looked at his watch, 'in half an hour.'

'Very well. There's an inn close to the west quay at Folkestone called the Kentish Knock – named after the shoal in the Thames Estuary, I suppose,' he said with an attempt to lighten the tense atmosphere. 'Will you be there with your men by nightfall? A man will introduce himself to you. What should he say so you'll know he is not an impostor?'

'Have him say, "Do you remember me? I served with you in the *Triton*." '

'There's just one thing,' Simpson said, almost apologetically. 'Getting you to France is no problem, but you want to be able to escape again. I presume you won't know when you'll have either the opportunity – or the need. So I will arrange – no,' he said hastily, 'don't tell me anything about *your* plans; just tell me if mine don't fit in with them. So, I'm arranging for you to get to France, and for a fishing-smack to be waiting for you in Boulogne for as long as you want. It can pass from Boulogne to Folkestone without difficulty. That will make your escape less of a problem.'

'It will make it no problem at all,' Ramage said cheerfully, anxious to restore a better atmosphere.

'Good, but you must understand that the smack can wait because of – er, certain arrangements – made long ago, before the war, in connection with – er, certain contraband business . . . and, er . . .'

Simpson was having such difficulty that Ramage said helpfully, 'You want to be sure you can continue the operations long after I am back here.'

'Yes, exactly! I would appreciate it if you forgot all the details, should you have to write any reports for the Admiralty.'

'Agreed,' Ramage said. 'I shall be as anxious as your men to keep out of the hands of Revenue officers!'

Simpson stood up and held out his hand. 'Yes, our greatest danger – and I say "our" advisedly – is from our own cruisers. The French will be no problem. By the way, until you arrive in France, I must ask you to do exactly what the smacksman says, even though he may give you strange instructions. Their significance will become clear to you by the time you reach Boulogne.'

CHAPTER SIX

Although the new Army barracks at Shorncliffe were nearby, so few Scottish or Irish regiments marched through the streets of Folkestone that bagpipes were rarely heard in the town. Yet the deep-throated skirl of the Scottish and Irish pipes had a little in common with the thin and reedy yet lilting music coming from the Kentish Knock's bar parlour, in Piecrust Lane, one street inland from the harbour, so that passers-by paused to look in.

The young man standing by one of the tables and playing the pipes was plump and stocky with wavy black hair which fell over eyes now glazed from the effort of blowing and keeping the small bag full of air.

The tune, a strange one to English ears, was nevertheless haunting, and the dozen or so seamen in the bar had fallen silent, watching the piper, whose expression showed that the melody he was playing had momentarily carried his thoughts to a distant country.

Finally the tune ended and he snatched the bag from under his arm, cutting the notes off sharply. He sat down at the table, grinning at the three men already seated, and waving to other seamen who called their appreciation.

One of the three, a lean-faced, raggedly-dressed individual with thinning sandy hair, who was apparently more than a little drunk, pushed a mug in front of the piper. 'Have a pint of Kentish ale, Rosey, and play some more. Those Italian bagpipes kick up a nice tune.'

'You like, eh? *Sono doloroso* . . . I so sad now; is a long time . . .'

'You'll go back one day; Genoa has been there a long time – no one will steal it.'

'You don't know Rosey's mates,' a Cockney said. 'Like pursers, they are; steal it bit by bit, so's no one really notices 'til it's all gorn!'

'Is true, Staff,' the Italian said. 'This Bonaparte steal it all now, but one day we chase him out and go back, eh – Nick?'

There was a slight hesitation as the Italian (who until a few hours earlier had been noted down in the Muster Book of a ship of the line in Portsmouth as Alberto Rossi, born in Genoa, and rated ordinary seaman) used the name Nick: he was finding it hard to be familiar with Lieutenant Nicholas Ramage, the man who had for so long been his commanding officer.

Now, in common with the other two men who, when sudden orders had been received from the Admiralty by the new tele-graph linking Portsmouth and London, had travelled to Dover with him from the same ship in Portsmouth, he was doing his best to carry out Mr Ramage's orders. These were simple enough: they were all – including Mr Ramage – to behave like fishermen or seamen from a merchantman while in England. Once they reached France they would receive fresh orders.

France! He was hot and nearly winded from playing the pipes, but the thought of landing in Bonaparte's own country chilled him. Not because the prospect of a fight with a bunch of Frenchmen was frightening: no, it was more the idea that Bonaparte's armies now strutted like peacocks over most of Europe – the Low Countries, Spain, most of the states in Italy, Austria, maybe even Switzerland. In fact it was easier to remember that they were not in Britain and Portugal. Perhaps some of those places round the Baltic – Sweden, for example – had not been invaded, but Rossi knew that the only possible reason was that they were too insignificant for

Bonaparte to be bothered with. Russia? Probably too big . . .

Will Stafford, born in Bridewell Lane, within the sound of Bow Bells, and apprenticed to a locksmith before going to sea, had a wide-eyed naïveté about some aspects of life which contrasted with a remarkable knowledge of other aspects, most of the latter picked up while working as a locksmith at dead of night and usually without the owner of the lock knowing or being charged. Yet Stafford had an instinctive understanding of people; he usually sensed moods in his shipmates and recognized the sudden stab of nostalgia in time to murmur a comforting phrase or divert the mood with a quick joke.

As he watched Rossi fold the pipes before putting them down on the table, he saw that the Italian was brooding and knew he had to be brought back from the past of the hills of Piedmont and Tuscany to the present of the bar parlour of the Kentish Knock, with its low ceiling blackened round the fireplace from years of wintry evenings and smokey chimneys.

'Them pipes is more musical than the Scotch ones,' Stafford commented. 'Ain't got so much body, though.'

'*Accidente*,' Rossi said, 'I never hear the Scotch, but pipes *sono Romani*! The Romans have the bagpipes first. These Scotch – ' he waved, dismissed kings and clans contemptuously, 'they copy them. They eat the porridge and drink the whisky and blow hard.'

'Scots,' said the lean-faced man sitting on the form next to Ramage. ' "Scots" if it's people, "Scotch" if it's things.'

'That's why it's called "Scotchland", eh Jacko?' Stafford said sarcastically. 'Anyway, I've heard the Irish had 'em afore the Scots.'

Jackson gave an easy laugh. 'Don't expect an American to explain that. Why – '

He broke off suddenly as he saw a man come through the door from the street and stop, peering round at everyone in the bar. The man saw Ramage and began sidling over towards him, but he had not moved six feet before Jackson, in one catlike movement, had left the table to intercept him.

'Hello, Jacko,' the man said nervously, half-expecting to see a knife, 'it's all right, I'm expected!'

Ramage, equally startled, signalled reassuringly to the American and looked at the man, his face unsmiling and questioning.

'You remember me, sir?' the man said almost slyly, keeping his voice low so that only Ramage and his group could hear him. 'I served with you in the *Triton*.'

Ramage gestured to him to sit down and said icily, 'You did too, by Jove. Dyson, isn't it?'

'Slushy Dyson, sir, an' I want ter say I'm sorry, an' thank you fer puttin' me on board the *Rover*.'

'Two dozen lashes, I seem to remember,' Ramage said, his voice still cold. 'I logged it as drunkenness, I believe, not mutiny.'

'Yes, sir; I deserved to 'ave been 'anged, an' I know it. Lucky you was the capting, sir; anyone else would've made sure I was strung up by the neck from the foreyardarm.'

Ramage began to realize that Dyson's appearance might not be a matter of chance: at first he had thought that the seaman's 'You remember me, sir? I served with you in the *Triton*,' had been an extraordinary coincidence – the normal thing for the man to say, and not the password arranged with Simpson. Now Ramage remembered Dyson's reassuring comment to Jackson, 'It's all right, I'm expected.' Had Dyson come from Simpson? One thing seemed certain: Dyson was no longer in the King's service!

'So when I transferred you to the *Rover*, I suppose you deserted. Are you marked "run" in her books?'

He watched Dyson shaking his head half-heartedly and noted that Jackson, Stafford and Rossi were staring at the man with curiosity: their wary suspicion had vanished. Yet but for these very men, Slushy Dyson, cook's mate, would have led a mutiny in the *Triton* within hours of her sailing from Portsmouth for the West Indies. Dyson was not exaggerating when he said he deserved to have been hanged, and his gratitude at being let off with a couple of dozen lashes and transferred to another ship was genuine enough. If the Admiralty ever found out all the details, Ramage himself would probably be court-martialled as well, for failing to bring Dyson to trial. But he was curious to know why Dyson, having been in the shadow of the noose very briefly on board the *Triton*, should have deserted so that he was now in it permanently. His life was in perpetual jeopardy if he was now a deserter; his liberty was in perpetual jeopardy if he was now a smuggler.

Ramage decided that this must be Simpson's emissary and said: 'As I gather we are going to be – er, shipmates again, Dyson, you'd better tell us all about it, and clear the air.'

68

The bar was almost dark now and Dyson waited while the innkeeper put candles on the tables where customers were sitting. The innkeeper was used to sailors and did not try to press them into ordering more drinks: he knew they would shout loud enough when they were thirsty and were likely to turn truculent if they suspected they were being forced. The candle on Ramage's table flickered in the faint draught from the door, and Dyson's narrow, shifty face seemed even more haggard than Ramage remembered it nearly two years ago. Every wrinkle was shadowed by the weak flame, the eyes were still as shifty, and the ears oddly pointed, almost fox-like.

'Twas all right in the *Rover*, sir,' he said softly, his eyes dropped and yet apparently focused on a distant object, 'an' I reckoned you had told her captain all about it.'

'No,' Ramage interrupted, 'he was told you'd been flogged for drunkenness.'

'Oh,' Dyson said, obviously absorbing the information. 'Well, in Portsmouth I was sent to a ship of the line. The fellows saw the scars on m' back from the cat-o'-nine-tails, and one of the bosun's mates got it in fer me. Seemed to guess what really happened, but I don't know 'ow 'e could. Well, I couldn't move without gettin' a floggin'. Case o' give a dog a bad name, I reckon. That cat would 'ave killed me if I 'adn't run, sir, and that's the bleedin' truth.'

And Ramage believed him: he had heard at least one captain declare that flogging ruined a good man and made a bad man like Dyson much worse. But at the time there had been no choice: Dyson had quite deliberately planned a mutiny, and a couple of dozen lashes was an almost derisory punishment: a court martial would have hanged him or given him five hundred lashes – which would probably have killed him before they were all administered. Dyson's life had in fact been saved because Ramage's orders were to carry urgent dispatches to the fleet off Brest and to the West Indies: there was no time to land him, let alone wait for several days for a court-martial.

Dyson was a bad man; even in time of peace he would always have been on the run from the law, a clumsy pickpocket, a noisy cutpurse, a highwayman whose horse always went lame or whose pistols misfired . . . War had only hastened the process of dissolution.

Meanwhile they had to work with Dyson – and Dyson had to work with the three seamen who had forced a confession out of him, and the officer who had ordered his flogging. He was ideally placed, Ramage thought uncomfortably, to get his revenge by betraying them all in France.

'Who chose you to help us?' Ramage asked curiously.

Dyson glanced round to make sure no one else was within earshot. 'The leader of the Folkestone and Dover smacks – the contraband smacks, you understand? – had a chat with three or four of us skippers. Didn't say your name, o' course, 'cos he didn't know it, but when he said the password – mentioning the *Triton* – I straight away thought of you, sir. An' – well, I volunteered because I – well, you treated me all right, sir, an' I thought if I could 'elp you . . . I guessed it was summat unusual, so . . .'

Surprisingly, Ramage believed him: the story was so improbable that it had to be true. 'I understand, Dyson. We'll forget the past now because we've got a busy future ahead of us.'

He called for more beer, and was thankful that Dyson's story ruled out Simpson having had a direct hand in the seaman's choice. The man living in the shadow of Studfall Castle would have been capable of arranging it as a veiled threat: reminding Ramage that he was at the mercy of a former mutineer . .

'Well, when do we sail, Dyson?'

'You'd better call me Slushy, sir, while we're in 'ere, just in case one of the local lads 'ears us. Sounds less formal, like,' he explained apologetically.

Ramage nodded. 'Very well. How about your crew?'

Dyson looked up quickly. 'I 'aven't signed on a crew apart from two of me regulars' – he managed to avoid saying 'sir' – ''cos they said you 'ad three men. I –' he looked nervously at the three seamen, as though uncertain how they would react to what he was about to say, 'I sort of 'oped it'd be these three, and the five of us is enough for the smack, wot wiv the other two . . .' He stopped, confused and glanced round the bar, noting the group of seamen drinking at the far end. 'Mebbe we'd better get on board the smack where we can talk wivart whisperin'.'

It was difficult to distinguish the shape of the smack in the darkness, except that Ramage saw she had a squarish transom which made her look more French than English. But as he hauled himself on board from the heavy rowing boat he could see she was strongly rigged: the lanyards were freshly tarred, and the shrouds were hemp. Expensive stuff for a smack; at least if she had been a smack whose catch came in nets, not casks.

The name carved into the wood across the transom was *Marie*, with 'Dover' in smaller letters on a board beneath: small enough to be almost indistinguishable.

Dyson muttered sheepishly, 'Welcome on board, sir,' and led the way to the little cuddy, climbing down the hatch and hanging the lantern he had been carrying on a hook screwed into the beam over a small table.

Crouching because there was little more than sitting head-room, Dyson squeezed to one side of the companion ladder so that Ramage, Stafford, Rossi and Jackson could pass him and sit on the U-shaped seat built round the two sides and the forward end of the table. As soon as they were seated, Dyson leaned back, sitting partly on one of the companion ladder steps, his head at the same level as the others.

The wind was from the south-west, pushing just enough swell into the inner harbour to make the *Marie* roll at her mooring. The lantern swung on the hook, sending shadows dancing round the cuddy, but its long handle and the low head-room meant the flame dazzled Ramage, sitting at the forward side of the table, and prevented him from seeing Dyson's face. The suspicion that the seaman had deliberately placed him at a disadvantage vanished when Dyson reached over with an oath and put the lantern on another hook on a beam farther aft. 'Let's all shift round a bit so's I can sit here at the table; that bleedin' lantern's blindin' me.'

There was just enough room for him to squeeze on to the seat next to Jackson, with Rossi and Stafford facing him and Ramage to his right, as though at the head of the table. Dyson sat for a minute or two alone with his thoughts while the other four men wriggled themselves into comfortable positions.

Two years – it wasn't a long time, really, but a lot had happened in Dyson's life. Two years ago he had existed only as an entry in the Muster Book of His Majesty's brig *Triton*. All that the Navy wanted to know about him had been written in one cryptic line under several headings: Albert Dyson; born Lydd, Kent; age on entry 28; rating, cook's mate; pressed; served in the brig fourteen months before being discharged to the *Rover*.

Various other reports and returns now gathering dust on the shelves of the Admiralty and the various boards which administered to the Navy's needs recorded the rest of the brief and mundane history of Albert Dyson's efforts towards defeating France. The slop book recorded the clothes and other items issued to him when he first joined a ship ('1 shirt, 1 frock, 1 trowsers, 1 shoes, 1 bed, 3lb tobacco,' and the prices he was charged – 15s 8d for the clothing, 10s for the bed, which was of course a hammock and blanket, and 4s 9d for tobacco). He appeared once in the *Triton*'s log and in her Captain's journal: in the 'Remarks' column, next to the time, distance sailed, speed and wind direction, was noted the fact that Albert Dyson had been given two dozen lashes for drunkenness. But Albert Dyson's name appeared most frequently in the Surgeon's daily journal, not because he was ever really sick but because he was imaginative enough to invent aches and pains which at first had led the surgeon to allow him a day in his hammock from time to time. This had continued until Ramage's predecessor as captain of the *Triton* became exasperated and suggested to the surgeon that a few tots of castor oil might well bring about a miraculous and permanent cure of all the cook's mate's varied ailments. The Surgeon's journal eventually recorded – if only by the subsequent absence of Dyson's name – the captain's diagnostic skill.

As he sat in the *Marie*'s cuddy, Dyson for once found himself tense but not nervous. Normally the two went together because tension was caused by the fact he was usually engaged in some illegal act, and the nervousness came naturally since he knew the penalty. Experience had taught all the Dyson family that only quick wits, a smooth tongue and very careful planning could keep their bodies clear of gibbets and outside prison walls.

Albert Dyson had been eleven years old when the uncle after whom he was named was marched off to Maidstone Assizes, charged with sheep-stealing, and finally hanged. Albert's father had discovered that his brother was caught only because he had been almost blind drunk as he hurried a dozen stolen ewes over a narrow bridge across one of the Marsh dykes – indeed, it seemed more likely he followed rather than guided them. A pony and trap rattling towards him from the other direction had scattered the startled sheep, and an enraged Uncle Albert had whacked the pony across the rump as it passed and hurled a shower of abuse at the farmer driving it before realizing that the man was the rightful owner of the sheep and a magistrate driving to Romney to sit at the brewster sessions.

All that could have been put down to bad luck, but the Dysons had never been able to live down what followed: the farmer had eventually managed to quieten the horse after a mile's wild gallop, turned the trap on the narrow Marsh lane, and went back to the bridge to find Uncle Albert sitting on its low wall tippling from a bottle of contraband brandy and by then oblivious of what had just happened. The wrathful farmer was met with a splendidly vacant grin and an invitation to share the brandy, to which he had responded by shoving Uncle Albert over the wall and into the dyke and nearly drowning him.

Thus Uncle Albert had brought shame to the Dysons. His brother was so angry and disillusioned at having named his eldest son after such a man (and virtually apprenticed the boy to him) that young Albert was then unofficially apprenticed to a highwayman who worked the road from Ashford to Folkestone. Albert, who acted as lookout, had been present but managed to escape, when his wrong identification led to the highwayman holding up a carriage containing five Army officers instead of the carriage transporting the Bishop of Dover. Expecting to find a cringing prelate with proffered purse, the highwayman was cut down by a fusillade of pistol shots, the Bishop's carriage arriving in time for him to mutter a perfunctory prayer as the highwayman departed this life and young Albert, watching horrified from behind the hedge down the road, departed hurriedly for home.

By now young Albert was twelve, and he spent the next few years picking pockets, starting off by sampling the visitors to Ashford market on Tuesdays, Canterbury market on Wednesdays and Maidstone on Fridays. That produced next to nothing, since the farmers and their wives were not given to carrying much money, so he started working the fairs, where the visitors were more bent on pleasure than business, but the travelling and the need to watch the calendar proved too much. After all these years he could remember the dates.

The year began with Maidstone on the 13th January and Faversham on the 25th, then came a long wait for Great Chart on the 25th March and Biddenden on 1st April (better than Deal and Lamberhurst, which fell on the same day). Another long wait for Charing on 1st May (with the choice of Wittersham and Wingham the same day), Hamstreet or Winchelsea on the 14th, Benenden the next day, Ashford two days after that, and then nothing until Cranbrook on the 30th. And so it went on throughout the year. The life was feast or famine: either so many fairs on the same day or so close he could not visit them all even by riding half the night, or weeks with nothing except weekly markets which yielded very little.

But, Dyson recalled without bitterness, it was growing up that had done him in as a 'dip.' He had been small and skinny for his age and no one noticed him at work in a crowd, and he was agile enough to dip his hand into a pocket or pouch without much risk. A night ride from one fair to another, or sleeping under a hayrick or in a barn, did not matter until he was old enough to shave. Then, and he was the first to admit it, a couple of days' growth of beard on his face made him look just what he was, and if he was also a bit red-eyed from drinking and wenching and lack of sleep – well, the sight of him made wise men keep their hands on their guineas and mothers call their children and clutch their purses . . .

His last year had been a disaster when his father worked out the tally. It was the year the damned spavined horse broke a fetlock and had to be shot, miles away from anywhere so he could not even sell the flesh and had to walk eleven miles with the saddle over his shoulders, and he had 'lifted' under twenty guineas from seventeen fixed fairs. Then Dad, who had long since given up trying to keep a calendar on the moveable fairs, swearing one needed to be a parson to do it properly, got in with Mr Simpson up at Studfall, and young Albert had become a fisherman. Not a fisherman who caught fish, but a fisherman who went out in a boat with nets and lines and hooks and bait, in case a Revenue cutter became nosey, and who came back long after dark . . . Bottle fishing, some folk called it, even though the haul was in casks.

For a few years the Dyson family flourished, thanks to Albert. Everyone was proud of Young Albert – until one rainy night he and five others in the boat stepped ashore at Camber to land some casks and the pile of rocks at the back of the beach turned out to be Customs men crouching down, waiting for them. Five years in gaol, the judge had said, or they could walk out of court, with a Navy press gang waiting in the road.

After a month in a receiving ship, a hulk at Sheerness, and six months in a ship of the line, Albert had decided that the galley was the safest and warmest place in any ship, and got

74

himself rated cook's mate. Everyone sneered at the job, which meant keeping the galley fire stoked or clear of ashes, and cleaning and polishing the big copper kettles, but there was money in it. When the great chunks of salt pork or salt beef were boiled in the kettles, gobs of fat (known as slush) floated to the surface, and the cook's mate skimmed it off and put it to one side. Later he sold it illicitly to the seamen, who spread it on the biscuit which passed for bread. The slush not only softened it, if it had grown hard, or bound it together if it had begun to crumble, and suffocated the weevils, but it gave Slushy Dyson his nickname and put money in his pocket.

Slushy Dyson knew better than most men that all good things come to an end, whether because of the drunken carelessness of an Uncle Albert, the thoughtless dating of fixed fairs, the sprouting of the whiskers of adolescence or the mischance of the ship of the line in which he was serving being paid off, resulting in the transfer of Albert Dyson, cook's mate, to the *Triton* brig where he had less than sixty customers for his slush, instead of five hundred or so. It hit a man cruel hard, that sort of luck; indeed there were times when Slushy almost gave up hope. In the end he had realized that this run of bad luck, extending over several years, was the best thing that had ever happened to him. Just before Mr Ramage came on board to take command and sail for the West Indies, the whole of the Fleet at Portsmouth had mutinied. Albert Dyson had been caught organizing a mutiny on board the first night out of Portsmouth. The three seamen now sitting round the table had captured him but he had got away with a couple of dozen lashes, been transferred to an inward bound ship, and had later been able to desert.

Three years at sea in the King's ships had taught him a lot. When he had called on Mr Simpson at Studfall and told him the tale, he had been welcomed back into the Trade. Within a couple of months a clerk at the Navy Office had passed the word to Mr Simpson that the Two-monthly Book from Dyson's last ship – which was a copy of the Muster Books – had been received, and one letter against the name of Albert Dyson had been carefully erased and two others written in. The changes were simple: originally the letter 'R', for 'Run', the Navy's word for deserting, and the date, had been written in the appropriate column. The clerk had carefully changed 'R' to 'D.D.', which was the only legal way of leaving the King's service apart from being so badly wounded or permanently sick as to be no use on board a ship. The record therefore showed that Albert Dyson, cook's mate, had died on the date shown, and been 'Discharged Dead.'

Dyson knew that there were too many other reports and logs coming in from the ship during the next few months for that single change in the Two-monthly Book to make him vanish altogether as far as the Navy was concerned. However, the clerk was sure that the general inefficiency in the Navy Board, which had to deal with a Navy which now comprised more than 100,000 men, meant that he was safe enough: clerks tended to deal with discrepancies or contradictions by ignoring them, particularly if there was no widow asking awkward questions. And then, as an insurance, Mr Simpson had obtained a Protection for him: a regular Protection made out in his own name and describing him as a regular waterman. With that Albert Dyson could not be taken up by a naval press gang: watermen, along with masters, mates and apprentices in merchant ships, and a few others, were admitted by the Admiralty to be better left alone rather than swept into the Navy.

Dyson reached under the seat and pulled out a box, extracting a bottle carefully wrapped in a piece of cloth, and several tin mugs so dented from use they looked like carelessly hammered pewter.

'Best brandy,' he said, pushing a mug across to Ramage. 'How about you, sir: a "welcome on board" tot?'

Ramage had an inflexible rule that he never drank at sea in his own ship; but the little *Marie* was far from being his ship, and before they sailed he was anxious to find out a great deal more from Dyson than he knew already. Refusing a drink might upset the fellow, who had all the touchy pride of a real rogue.

'A small one, then; just enough for a toast.'

Dyson poured a little into five mugs and passed them round. 'Won't do to get drunk; we'll need our wits about us a'fore the night's over.'

Jackson felt the pressure of Ramage's knee and immediately took the hint, asking: 'How so, Slushy?'

Dyson lifted his mug: 'Here's to a successful cruise.' When the other four had echoed his toast he put his mug down with an exaggerated gesture, as if to lend weight to what he was about to say. 'We have a lot of dodgin' to do, an' we're due to meet another smack . . . let's 'ope it ain't too rough.'

Jackson knew Mr Ramage must have his reasons for wanting him to question Dyson. 'Aye, dodging the Frogs is going to be difficult . . .'

'The Frogs?' Dyson exclaimed, obviously startled and with more than a hint of outraged indignation in his voice. 'T'ain't the Frogs we got to worry about; it's our own bleedin' Revenue cutters first, then 'is Britannic Majesty's frigates once we get near the French coast.'

'Why?' Jackson asked innocently. 'What harm will they do us?'

'Come orf it,' Dyson growled. 'Just give a sniff. Go on, sniff 'ard.'

Jackson sniffed and shrugged his shoulders. 'Can't smell anything odd. Tarred marline – Stockholm tar, from the nets I suppose. Bit musty – some rot around in the planking or the frames . . .'

'Nothin' else?'

'No-o,' Jackson said cautiously. 'Whiff of fish, perhaps.'

'Just a whiff, eh?'

When Jackson nodded, Dyson said contemptuously, 'You wouldn't make much of a Customs searcher, Jacko! Just a whiff o' fish in the cuddy of a smack – why it should *stink* o' fish!'

Stafford gave a tentative sniff. 'S'fact. What 'appened, Slushy – all the fish swum away, or you gettin' lazy?'

Dyson looked round the group suspiciously, as though suspecting they were teasing. Then, deciding they were not, he leaned forward and said mysteriously. 'It's a special sort o' fishing.'

'Ah, bottle fishin',' Stafford said scornfully. 'You're a bleedin' smuggler, Slushy! I couldn't see you 'auling in 'alibut, I must say.'

Dyson's face fell and he drank from his mug to hide his disappointment at not being able to reveal his secret with a flourish.

Jackson had been waiting patiently. 'You said we have to meet another smack tonight, Slushy, and you hoped the sea wasn't rough . . .'

Instead of answering the American, Dyson turned to face Ramage. 'They left it up to me how much I tell you, sir. They're worried about when you get back: you – well, they –'

'They're frightened I'll inform the Revenue men, eh? Tell me, Dyson, if you get us over to France and back again, do

77

you think I'd be so ungrateful that I'd give you away? Be honest, man; this is your ship and you're free to say what you think.'

Although the anguished look on Dyson's face told him all he needed to know, Ramage waited. The man sipped from his tin mug – whatever else he might be, he was not a heavy drinker – and, suddenly setting the mug down, he said simply: 'I owe you my life, sir: any other capting would 'ave brought me to trial and made sure I 'anged. I don't forget that in a hurry; in fac', I'll remember it to me dyin' day. No, the trouble is the uvvers, sir; they don't know you and they 'ave to take my word for it – ' he broke off embarrassed.

'Don't they trust you, Slushy?' Jackson asked.

'Well, yus and no. They do as far as bottle fishin' goes – I've proved meself long ago. It's just they're a bit suspicious 'bout what went on while I was – well, was in the King's service.'

'Why the distinction?' Ramage asked.

'It's like this, sir. When I heard what the password was goin' to be and guessed it was you, I got so excited I told 'em all about – well, the *Triton* brig business. Instead of that 'elping, it made 'em suspicious, on account of them thinking it gave you a sort o' twist on my arm: you'd know I was a deserter, an' you could threaten to hand me over to the authorities if I didn't tell you everything you wanted to know about 'ow contraband is landed on the Marsh – all that sort o' thing.'

'But nevertheless you managed to persuade them?' Ramage asked quietly.

Dyson looked uncomfortable. 'I made a bargain. I can use the *Marie*, but I had to put up a sort o' guarantee. It's all arranged, sir; there's nothin' to worry about.'

'What was the guarantee?' Ramage said.

'Just some money as security for the *Marie*, and my young brother – he usually sails with me as mate. I had to leave him behind.' Dyson saw Ramage's raised eyebrows and added uncomfortably: 'Better security than money, my brother, an' they know it.'

Was the brother literally a hostage? Ramage was not sure and phrased his next question carefully: 'What does the money and your brother's life guarantee, exactly?'

The seaman shrugged his shoulders. 'Hard to say, come to think of it. Our good behaviour, I s'pose. That you don't

78

interfere with the contraband trade and don't hand me over to the authorities; and – well, that I get you there and back and don't take risks with the smacks.'

So the smugglers were quite ruthless: Dyson's brother would get his throat cut if Slushy put a foot wrong. Ramage also pondered over 'smacks.' Was another one due to sail with the *Marie*, or was Dyson referring to the one they were supposed to meet? He decided to wait and see: at the moment Dyson seemed angry with his smuggler friends and genuinely anxious to repay what he regarded as a debt to Ramage himself. Yet Ramage was curious at the way Dyson had been treated – it contradicted Simpson's airy and open-handed behaviour of a few hours ago.

'Tell me, do you have much to do with – well, no names, but he lives near Studfall?'

'The gentleman you went to first,' Dyson nodded. 'No one sees 'im. Like the Navy, it is. If he's the Commander-in-Chief – and I ain't sayin' he is,' Dyson added hurriedly, 'then the like o' wot I deal wiv is bosuns, and me a bosun's mate.'

'A big organization,' Ramage commented. 'But when I talked with the man at Studfall, he promised me everything I asked.'

'I'm sure he did, sir, and meant it too. The trouble starts among the men under him. It's money, Mr Ramage; contraband round the Kent coast brings in a great deal of money, and where there's that kind of money men get greedy and suspicious o' each other. Money never bought loyalty, sir. The gentleman at Studfall won't have any idea about the guarantees I 'ad to give; fact is, I dare say 'e'd get very angry. But 'e'll never know; not from me, anyway: more than my life'd be worth, to make any complaint. An' I ain't complaining, reelly; you was askin' me. Fact is, no man's yer friend as far as bottle fishermen are concerned.'

Rossi tapped the little table with his mug. 'So sad, Slushy; I cry for you. *Poco tempo fa* – not so long ago – you sell off the slush from the *Triton*'s coppers to make the extra *soldi*; now you are the *grand signor*. Of course is dangerous; of course is not many friends. But the Navy, *amico mio*, is short of friends, too. The *Triton* after you waved goodbye – two, three times we are in battle. And a hurricane – Madonna! such wind – and we lose our masts and run on a reef. Yes, Slushy, I cry for you – on your saint's day.'

'Thanks,' Dyson grinned. 'That'll be a great comfort to

my old mother, p'ticularly since she reckons the Devil's a Catholic. You want some more brandy in that mug?'

Before Rossi could reply, Ramage interrupted: 'What time do you intend sailing, Dyson?'

The seaman pulled out his watch. "Bout eleven, sir – in fact, won't 'arm any to leave earlier. We can go now. If you'd let my men pass down your seabags we can stow 'em and then get under way.'

He made no move as he put his watch away, and Ramage looked questioningly. 'Do you have any special orders for me, sir? I mean, is there anything I need to do a'fore we get under way?'

'Is anyone going on shore before we sail?' Ramage asked cautiously.

'No, sir; my two lads are coming with us – part of the trip, anyway.'

Unsure whether Dyson was deliberately talking in riddles or assumed he had guessed more than he had, Ramage decided to wait before asking any more important questions: Dyson seemed to be the kind of man of limited intelligence who thrived on mystery; who for various devious reasons made secrets from what others would regard as idle gossip or the kind of information imparted when passing the time of day.

'What exactly were you told had been arranged with the man at Studfall?' asked Ramage.

'No one seemed right to know. Take you and some men to Boulogne; stand by to bring you out again; mebbe bring some things back in between – reports and the like.'

Ramage felt relieved. 'That covers everything,' he said. 'How will you be able to stand by?'

'Smack'll be waiting in Boulogne 'arbour, sir,' Dyson said, his voice showing surprise that Ramage did not know that. "Ow else can I be standing by?'

Ramage shook his head, trying to stifle his exasperation. 'Dyson, I don't know a dam' thing about how you people run your affairs, so you'd better –' He broke off. The devil take it; he had neither the wish nor the patience (and too much pride?) to squeeze Dyson like a lemon for drops of information.

CHAPTER SEVEN

By midnight the *Marie* was heading for Boulogne with the wind comfortably on the starboard quarter. Comfortably as far as steering her in the darkness was concerned, because the wind was far enough round that a few moments' inattention by the helmsman or an unexpectedly large swell wave coming up astern would not gybe her all standing, the heavy boom and gaff crashing over as the wind filled the mainsail on the other side.

As far as the Revenue officers in Folkestone and Dover were concerned, the smack *Marie* had sailed for a night's fishing and, as usual, was under the command of Thomas Smith, who was noted down in the Register of Ships in Dover as her owner and to whom had been issued, under the recent Smuggling Act, a special licence.

As its name indicated, the Act was intended to stamp out smuggling; but like most acts which Parliament in its wisdom passed with much talk and eventual self-congratulation, it was only a partial success (the Government's view) or an almost complete failure (the view of the Inspectors of Customs stationed round the coast). Thus the judgment of the Government and of the Customs was really the same, but a politician prefers to describe an almost complete failure in more positive terms as a partial success. Men under orders to enforce the law had to take a more realistic and thus more negative view.

So as far as the law was concerned, the *Marie* was going about her lawful business of fishing. She was more than a certain length and had a fixed bowsprit, so under the Act Thomas Smith, her registered owner, had to have a licence. He had a licence and was at all times ready to show it to any official duly authorized to demand its production.

The Act was an almost complete failure because the various experts concerned in drafting it would not (the view of the Inspectors of Customs) or could not (the subsequent excuse offered by the Government) interpret the appropriate requirements set out by the Board of Customs. Instead, Parliament passed an Act which was, as usual, a legal redundancy, and superbly upholstered with 'whereby', 'notwithstanding', 'here-tofore' and other such words so beloved of anyone who ever used a heavy legal textbook to prop open a door on a windy day.

One did not have to be a boatbuilder to find the loopholes. The fixed bowsprit, for example. One boat could have a sliding bowsprit, which meant it could be run in (slid back out of the way, as a Customs Board member had patiently explained to one of the legal draftsmen working on the original Act), and put her into a certain category. Her other-wise identical sister ship could have holes drilled for a couple more bolts and, providing the nuts were tightened up, the bowsprit could be classified as fixed, putting her into another category requiring a licence.

To a boatbuilder it was a distinction without a difference – an hour's work with an awl and the supply of two long bolts, washers and nuts meant the owner decided whether his vessel had a fixed or a sliding bowsprit: it took only a matter of minutes to change from one to the other.

In the case of the *Marie* the real owner was a wise man: he knew the value of having a document to flourish at an official, whether the commander of a Revenue cutter or a naval frigate. 'What are you doing?' 'Fishing.' 'Prove you're not out here for smuggling!' 'Here's my licence allowing me to fish nine miles offshore . . .'

So the new Act modified an earlier one, the Hovering Act, which had at least given the Revenue men an excuse to act on suspicion. Any vessel waiting some distance off the coast was assumed to be 'hovering for an unlawful purpose.' Now, under the new Act, licences had to be issued to applicants unless a very good reason could be found for refusing them, and the effect was to legalize hovering, to the delight of men like the owners of the *Marie* and the chagrin of the Revenue officers.

Previously it had been enough to sight a vessel; the owner could later be charged with hovering. Now a vessel had to be caught smuggling – a far from easy job, since the larger smug-glers were usually faster than the Revenue cutters – and searched for contraband, with the certainty that during the chase the smuggler would, if there was a risk of capture, quietly dump the contraband over the lee side, thus destroying any evidence and leaving himself with the excuse – should anyone claim that flight was proof of guilt – that he had fled because he thought the Revenue cutter was a French privateer.

At midnight Ramage knew very little more about Slushy Dyson's immediate intentions than he did before they slipped the mooring in Folkestone harbour. The two seabags of spare clothing and Rossi's bagpipes were in the cuddy, and Stafford and Rossi were already stretched out on the seats, fast asleep, along with the third man in Dyson's crew.

Thomas Smith, officially the owner and master of the *Marie* but, from the way he was treated by Dyson, no more than a hand, was at the tiller and to Ramage's surprise (until he remembered Dyson's reference to meeting another smack) steering a very careful compass course, cursing all the while that the wick of the tiny binnacle light had not been properly trimmed.

Dyson had muttered something about the chart and gone below to the cuddy and lit the lantern, leaving Ramage and Jackson sitting on the deck, using a bundle of the smack's nets as cushions.

As far as the *Marie* was concerned, she might have been the only British vessel at sea. Jackson commented that if the people in England who worried about Bonaparte could see the Channel now, they would lock their doors, hide under their beds and pray to be spared to see the dawn.

Thomas Smith lifted his head from the binnacle long enough to reveal that his mind was on Revenue cutters rather than invasion flotillas. 'The Rev'noo won't be takin' a night orf, you can rely on *thaat*,' he said bitterly.

Ramage suddenly jumped up with an oath: a dark red glow flickered up from the cuddy, as though the smack was on fire and about to explode. But even as Thomas Smith said phlegmatically, 'S'only Slushy wiv the lamps,' the flickering stopped and Ramage realized Dyson must be preparing a signal lantern with a red glass. The light dimmed as Dyson turned down the wick and a moment later began to flash rhythmically through the open hatch, in time with the rolling of the smack, as Dyson hung it from a hook on a beam.

'Shut the bleedin' 'atch, Slushy,' Thomas Smith growled. 'The sentries at Dover Castle'll see that light in a minute!'

Dyson climbed up the ladder and slid the hatch closed, leaving a small gap for air to get below. 'Just hanging the lamps up ready,' he explained. 'Quarter of an hour to go, I reckon, then we'll spot 'er.'

'Just one of the local whores or someone we know?' Jackson asked innocently.

Dyson glanced at him in the darkness, his eyes as red as a ferret's in the chink of light escaping from the hatch. 'Our opposite number, o' course!' he said scornfully. 'Wotcher fink'd 'appen if the *Marie* stayed out fishin' for a month, or 'owever long you want ter stay in France?'

'I was wondering,' Jackson admitted.

'Nah,' Dyson said patronizingly. 'The *Marie*'ll be back on 'er mooring in Folkestone 'arbour time enough for the early market this morning.'

'Won't have much of a catch, though.'

'Enough,' Dyson said airily. 'Already caught and sorted and boxed by now, it is.'

'So I see,' Jackson said lightly.

'I should think so; you seem to be very slow sometimes.' With that Dyson lapsed into silence and a frustrated Ramage was left little the wiser. At least he now knew they would be transferred to the vessel they were going to meet, and the *Marie* would return to Folkestone. It was the obvious way of doing it, but would only work if there was a prearranged rendezvous. How would they be able to get back from France? How long did it take to arrange a rendezvous – two or three days? It was going to be a devil of a job sending back reports, and if things went wrong in France there was no chance of a hurried escape.

All of which, he told himself, angrily, was his own fault: he should have forced Dyson to explain everything before they left Folkestone; explain while there was still time to change his plans. Because of his own carelessness, he was in Dyson's hands. Carrying out the intentions of the First Lord of the Admiralty depended on the whim of a deserter, a former cook's mate and mutineer who had the marks of a flogging on his back and was now a smuggler . . . Afterwards, if the whole thing was a fiasco, he could imagine Lord St Vincent's questions, in that deceptively quiet voice. And Lord Nelson's, in that slightly nasal tone, the Norfolk accent unmistakable. 'You planned the whole operation so that its success depended on the actions of a deserter, eh Ramage? . . . You stand there and admit that halfway across the Channel you still didn't know what the devil this fellow intended to do? . . . You didn't plan the operation?' The voice would be incredulous. 'You just met this smuggler in a bar and went on board his smack without making any arguments whatsoever?'

If he was honest with himself, he had to admit that he could hardly believe it either. In giving him these orders, Lords St Vincent and Nelson had made it more than clear that the safety of the whole nation might depend on his success. Both of them had anticipated that the difficulties and dangers would be in France. Instead, the crisis seemed to be coming in mid-Channel . . .

Dyson hauled a watch from his pocket and bent over the binnacle to catch some light. 'Not a bad guess: quarter past midnight: time for the lanterns.' With that he opened the hatch to the cuddy.

'You'd better rouse Stafford and Rossi,' Ramage said, 'and tell them to bring up the seabags.'

'They'd better stay there out of the way – men and bags,' Dyson said as he climbed down the ladder. 'My fellow and Tom, an' if Jacko'll bear a hand . . .'

While a puzzled Ramage was digesting that, Dyson popped up at the hatch again, holding the red lantern. ''Ere, Jacko, 'old this a minute while I get the other one. Watch out, Tom; shut an eye when I call, or you'll be completely dazzled.'

Ramage had already turned away to keep his night vision and blinked as he saw a red and then a white spot of light. 'Dyson – red light over white, fine on the larboard bow, less than a mile away.'

The seaman grunted as he scrambled up with the second lantern. The red lantern had lit the *Marie*'s deck and mainsail with a soft glow; the harsh white light showed every seam and made the shadows of the rigging dance on the canvas.

'Red above white, eh?' Dyson murmured. 'Ah yes, I see 'er. Jacko, hold that red lantern as high as you can.' With that he held the white lantern below it. Immediately the distant red and white lights were changed so the red was above. Dyson then held the white lantern so that it was level with the red. The distant lights once again reversed position.

'Challenge and reply,' Dyson muttered, opening the door of the red lantern that Jackson was holding and blowing out the flame. 'That's the fellow we're looking for. Put the lantern down below, Jacko and rouse out my man, will you? Time he woke up.'

As soon as the third man emerged from the cuddy, Ramage saw a new Dyson: a man snapping out orders which had the *Marie*'s heavy mainsail lowered and furled, followed by jib and staysail. The thumping of the boom and rattle of the mainsail hoops brought a sleepy Rossi and Stafford on deck. Within ten minutes the other vessel had sailed down close enough for Ramage to identify her as another smack and as she luffed up and dropped her sails he was puzzled by the fact that her shape was familiar. She had the same curious stern as the *Marie* – neither typically Kentish nor typically French, but reminiscent of both.

Thomas Smith and the third seaman had by now hauled up the small boat which they had been towing astern. The third man jumped into it, put in the thole pins and then unlashed the oars.

Dyson said to Smith: 'You got the papers in your pocket? Right, off you go, then.'

With that Thomas Smith climbed down into the boat and Dyson let go the painter.

'Time now for a bite to eat,' Dyson muttered as he lashed the tiller which was slamming back and forth as the *Marie* pitched. He took the lantern and climbed down to the cuddy. A couple of minutes later he pushed a small basket up through the hatch, calling to Jackson to grab it, and followed with the lantern.

'Cold chicken, cold potatoes, bread and' – he put a bottle down beside the basket – 'some good red wine I had stowed in the bilge. May be vinegar by now, what with all the shaking up, but usually it lasts well. I'd like your view on it, sir.'

Ramage almost laughed: Dyson's comment on the wine was spoken with all the proud authority of a gourmet inviting an opinion on the first case he had received of a vintage wine.

As Dyson began unpacking the basket he suddenly swore. ''Ere Rosey, nip down and get the mugs, will you? Give 'em a wipe out with the tail o' yer shirt, else the wine'll taste 'o brandy.'

The five of them squatted round the lantern and began eating thankfully as Dyson tore cold roast chicken apart with his fingers and shared it out. The cold potatoes had been roasted in their skins, sliced in half when cold and a piece of butter put inside.

'Greasy p'tater, my mother calls it,' Dyson said as he offered one to Ramage. 'But don't eat it too fast, sir, else it lodges on the breastbone an' gives yer what for.'

They had just finished eating and were wiping greasy fingers on their trousers when there was a hail from the darkness.

'Here 'e comes,' Dyson said matter-of-factly. 'The new master of the lerbong b'tow *Marie*.'

It took Ramage a moment to realize that Dyson was merely massacring the French language. Would the new master of *le bon bateau Marie* be French?

The man who scrambled up after throwing the painter on board and pausing only a few moments to lash the oars was indeed French; and as his face was lit up by the lantern on the deck, throwing the eyes into shadow, Ramage saw that by comparison Dyson's face was one which inspired confidence and trust, but only by comparison.

It was as if a wilful Nature had created a face which was the exact opposite of Dyson's: the Frenchman, introduced to Ramage with a brief, 'This 'ere's Louis,' looked like a pumpkin into which had been pressed, too far apart, two black buttons for eyes, two holes which were nostrils – no nose as such was apparent – and two narrow sausages which were his lips, and between which a furry tongue popped out in a grotesque circular motion every minute or so. Occasionally the lips parted to reveal uneven and blackened teeth.

Louis was about five feet four inches tall and his body, a barrel stuck on two short legs, reminded Ramage of a performing bear sitting up and begging while his master played a fiddle. Louis gave the impression of enormous strength. In contrast to his short legs, his arms were long, and he stood with a thumb jammed in his belt, arms akimbo, tongue appearing to circle briefly, like an obscene rodent poking an inquiring head out of its lair.

The Frenchman stared curiously at Ramage for a few moments, and then said to Dyson in heavily-accented English: 'We get the mainsail up, eh?'

From the way he spoke, it was clear that Louis, if not Dyson's superior in the smuggling hierarchy, was at least an equal, but it was equally clear that Dyson resented the fact.

'Got the papers?' he demanded.

The Frenchman tapped a pocket and repeated, 'We get the mainsail up, eh?'

Dyson swung round and walked towards the mainmast. 'Give us 'n 'and,' he said to Stafford and Rossi. 'That throat halyard just about creases me up.'

Jackson threw off the gaskets and as the mainsail was hoisted Ramage noticed that Rossi was hauling down on the throat halyard and Stafford the peak, while Dyson was standing back encouraging them. And that showed more clearly than anything else that Dyson, the Marsh Man, was considerably more artful than Stafford, the sharp-tongued Cockney. With those two vying with each other to avoid the hard work it was inevitable that the good-natured Rossi should end up with the throat halyard. But all the native shrewdness and tricks learned during a childhood spent in Genoa emerged the moment Rossi thought he was 'being took advantage of', a phrase he had learned from Stafford. With the main halyards belayed, Ramage was not surprised to see that Dyson and Stafford found themselves hoisting both staysail and jib while Rossi walked round, explaining loudly that he was 'tending sheets'.

Louis, hunched over the binnacle, pushed the tiller over as soon as the *Marie* had steerage way, and grunted his thanks as Ramage trimmed the mainsheet.

Dyson came aft and squatted down on the deck with an exaggerated sigh of weariness. Ramage thought for a moment and then asked: 'Well, what do we do when the *Marie* goes into Boulogne?'

Dyson glanced up in surprise as he opened the lantern and blew out the flame. In the sudden deeper darkness he said: 'Do sir? Why, we let Louis go on shore and shout loudly there's no fish, an' he takes the papers to the port captain. Then, when it's dark again, you all go on shore. You'll have to stay down in the cuddy while it's still daylight.'

Steady, Ramage told himself; the tone of Dyson's voice made it clear the man was stating what he considered to be obvious.

'I thought you said the *Marie* had to be back in Folkestone by dawn . . .'

'But she will be, sir!'

Ramage struggled to speak quietly; to keep the edge out of his voice – an edge which Louis, if his English was bad, might well misinterpret.

'Dyson, one ship can't be in two places at once. The *Marie* can't be in Boulogne *and* Folkestone at the same time.'

'But she can,' Dyson protested and then, as Jackson began to laugh, hastily explained: 'There's two *Maries*, sir; habsolutely hidentical they are. See, it don't matter which one goes into what port, perviding the master's got the right set of papers. The authorities don't know, o' course!'

88

'Of course,' Ramage said casually; so casually that only Jackson knew how angry he was with himself. 'So Louis will have caught enough fish for Thomas Smith to run into Folkestone market.'

'Five stone,' Louis grunted, revealing his knowledge of English.

'But – you said Louis reports we caught nothing when we get to Boulogne. You don't intend to try on the way in?'

'What, an' get the stink of fish all over us?' Dyson made it clear that as far as he was concerned, the idea was unthinkable, but he added: 'Mind you, if Jacko or someone wants to try his 'and with an 'ook and line . . .'

'The French port authorities – won't they get suspicious?' Ramage asked cautiously.

'Never 'ave so far; we pay 'em enough to take their suspicions somewhere else. It's only the English Revenoo men we 'ave to worry about. They're all too stoopid to take bribes.'

'Or too honest,' Ramage said.

'Same thing,' Dyson said bitterly. 'Gawd save us from 'onest fools. 'Ere, Jacko, in that locker there you'll find a board with 'Boolong' written on it. Take it out and change it for the one that says 'Dover' on the transom. Just slips up and down vertical, like a sliding window.'

Dawn found the *Marie* running into Boulogne with a Tricolour flying from the leech of the mainsail and only Louis and Dyson on deck. For the previous hour both men had taken it in turns to search the horizon carefully with a night glass.

'It can get like a main highway out here,' Dyson had explained. 'So many of our frigates and cutters keeping a watch. We usually time it so we've got 'em east of us as dawn breaks, so they show up against the lighter sky. That gives us a chance to dodge. Still, quiet enough this morning.'

Louis invited Ramage to watch at the hatch so he would recognize Boulogne from seaward again: there had been many changes, he said, pointing out the stone forts of Pointe de la Crèche and Fort de l'Heurt, and several batteries round the harbour and on the cliffs and hills surrounding it.

'Barges,' he said, pointing at the rows of vessels anchored close inshore and almost hidden in a gloom only lightly washed by pink from a sun still below the horizon. 'Gunboats, and sloops too. More there – and there. They build

89

there – ' he pointed at the shore, where what seemed at first to be several wooden buildings on the sloping foreshore proved to be vessels under construction on crude slipways. 'Very slow. No money, no wood, no shipwrights. No sails and no ropes either. Even when money and wood, still slow. Butchers' and bakers' apprentices is all they have, twenty old men and boys to every shipwright, and sometimes conscripts. The Admiral – he goes crazy. Much trouble when the Corsican makes a visit . . .'

He pushed a hip against the tiller and pointed again: 'You see the camps? Five so far – have you ever seen so many tents?'

Boulogne seemed as martial as Folkestone was peaceful, and Ramage felt a brief dismay. This was what the lists had said, but somehow he had not actually pictured what they had told him. Twenty barges – yes, it didn't seem much when written down, but the devil of a sight it looked, with them moored bow to stern! The Norman – for Ramage had at last managed to identify his accent – made no secret of his contempt for Bonaparte, a contempt that seemed both deep-seated and genuine. As he stared at the rows of barges, Ramage said: 'Do you think Admiral Bruix is ready to sail his flotilla to England?'

Louis shrugged his shoulders. 'They brag like Gascons; all the invasion talk is gasconade. Yes, he *could* sail a flotilla . . .' But there was no mistaking the contempt in his voice. 'Anyone could sail a flotilla from Boulogne. But to reach the English coast – *that* is another question! Boxes, these barges; they are beyond management.'

He gestured to Ramage to get his head below the level of the hatch. 'We pass close to the watch tower in a few minutes. You stay down now.'

Dyson, anxious to seem well informed, said: 'Once you go on shore you'll be able to walk around and look for yourself, sir; they don't have guards or nothink, just patrols roaming the streets like stray dogs.'

'Dogs can bite,' Ramage heard Stafford mutter from the forward end of the cuddy.

Louis said sharply: 'Mainsheet, Sloshy!'

Dyson hauled the sheet hurriedly. 'Enough?' he asked hopefully.

'You are too lazy to haul in too much,' Louis said sarcastically. 'Now the staysail sheet. Then you drop the flying jib.'

The Frenchman was a good seaman who obviously took a delight in keeping Dyson running about the deck. The flying jib had not been down five minutes before he wanted it hoisted again and sheeted home, explaining that the wind was falling light, and a puffing Dyson had only just completed that task before Louis wanted the boat painter shortened in.

'Give us a luff,' Dyson gasped as he tried to haul the boat closer to the smack, 'there's too much weight: I can't haul in an inch wiv you racin' acrorst the 'arbour.'

'I'm not loffing,' Louis snapped crossly. 'You haul him in, and make the rush; we are alongside the quay in two minutes, and then you 'ave the 'urry.'

Jackson called up through the hatch: 'You were better off in the *Triton*, Slushy.'

'At least I could mutiny and only get a couple of dozen lashes,' Dyson gasped glumly. 'I don't fink Louis'd let me off as lightly.'

'No one else would, either,' Jackson said. 'You were lucky to pick the only captain that would.'

'I know, I know,' Dyson said impatiently, 'an' that's why I'm here, trying to 'elp 'im.'

Ramage felt the *Marie* heel sharply and then come upright again. 'Leave the boat painter,' snapped an exasperated Louis. 'Drop the jib, then the staysail. Then stand by the main halyards.'

By now the sky was lightening, and down in the cuddy they heard the jib halyard squeaking through the block, and then the rope slatted against the mast. That was followed by the rattle of the staysail halyard, and the sail thumped the deck for a few moments before Dyson stifled it.

A couple of minutes later Louis's order to lower the mainsail turned into a stream of virulent French curses softly spoken but punctuated by grunts of exasperation. Then the light moving round the cuddy warned of a change of course and the water gurgling more slowly told Ramage that the *Marie* was losing way. There was a gentle thump as Louis put her alongside the quay and Ramage saw him move swiftly across the open hatchway, obviously not trusting to Dyson's alacrity with the dock lines.

'Wish it was always like this, comin' into 'arbour,' Stafford muttered. He turned to Ramage with a grin. 'I'm a born passenger, sir.'

'I noticed that a couple of years ago,' Ramage said sarcastically, 'though I never thought I'd hear you confess it. Still, if you ever serve with me again . . .'

Dyson stuck his head down the hatch. 'Welcome to Boolong, everyone. No Frenchies about, so you can talk, but don't come up on deck. Louis is going up to the 'arbour capting's orfice with the papers.'

'Any food on board, Slushy?' Stafford called. 'If we gotter spend the day down 'ere . . .'

Dyson swore and leapt on to the quay, returning in two or three minutes. 'Good job you remembered. Louis is going to buy some grub on the way back. There's still some wine in the bilges.'

'We need some water, too.' Ramage said sharply, using the opportunity to warn his men that they were not going to spend the day drinking wine as they waited for darkness.

'Quite so, sir,' Dyson said. 'There's a full water breaker up forward there – somebody'll have to climb over the athwartship seat and haul it out.'

The day's waiting in the *Marie*'s crowded cuddy was one of the longest and most tedious that Ramage could remember, and as the sun rose higher the atmosphere became stifling. The water was a good deal less fresh than Dyson thought, and the food brought back by Louis was the only bright spot in the day. The bread was coarse but the cheese excellent, the taste enhanced by the fact it had been a long time since Ramage had tasted fresh French cheese.

Dyson produced a greasy pack of cards and began what seemed to Ramage interminable games with Jackson, Stafford and Rossi, most of which he lost with ill grace. When Louis returned after an absence of several hours and squatted at the top of the hatch, Ramage suggested that if he came on deck and hunched over some rope, pretending to be splicing it, prying eyes would assume it was Dyson. Louis readily agreed though, he said without a smile, the sight of Dyson working was more likely to arouse suspicion than allay it.

As Ramage sat down, the bright sun on grey stone walls and slate roofs emphasized that this was France. In the distance fishermen walking along the quay wore the blue trousers and smocks that were almost a uniform, and the fishing-boats nearby all had the distinctive French transoms. For the moment it was hard to believe this was the enemy's land, and he knew it would take a few hours for his mind to absorb the fact: the transition from Folkestone to here had been too swift.

He talked to Louis for more than two hours, slowly building up the picture of how, in the past year, the tempo of ship-building had increased. For years before the Revolution the two local shipyards had built for local owners: anything from small fishing luggers to large *chasse-marées*, the two- and three-masted vessels that became privateers as soon as war began.

The yards were family affairs, Louis explained; sons and nephews served their apprenticeships with fathers and uncles. And the brothers who owned the yard at any given time were building boats for owners whose fathers and grandfathers had had boats launched from the yards. Just as boat-building stayed in a family for generations, so did fishing – and smuggling.

One of the yards had built one of the *Maries*, though Louis admitted that after all this time, with scores of Channel crossings, he could not remember which smack was which. He thought the one they were in was French-built, but he was far from sure. The idea for the identical ships, he explained, came originally from a wealthy Englishman. Not a *milord,* but not far from it. He had the first *Marie* built at Folkestone, and as soon as she had been launched and registered, and her number was carved in the mainbeam – 'before the war, you understand' – he announced that he was going to visit France in her; go for a cruise, in fact. And what more natural than that she should spring a leak while in Boulogne harbour – Louis gave a broad wink – so that she had to be hauled out on one of the slipways for repairs.

And what more natural than the yard foreman taking the lines off her while caulkers banged away with their mauls? Various internal dimensions were measured, the exact way the number was carved on the main beam – all these things were noted. And one night when it was dark a British-made compass was handed over, still in the maker's box, and several bolts of British-made sailcloth. And while repairs were being done, what was more natural – again Louis winked – than the owner sending his sails round to the local Boulogne sailmaker while waiting for the caulkers to finish their work? Just a matter of some re-stitching. And what more natural than the sailmaker sewing a new suit of sails to the same pattern, including storm canvas, and storing them away in his loft?

Anyway, the British smack *Marie* left, and everyone had forgotten her by the time the yard – which had been kept busy building many other boats of about the same size – launched a smack which had the name *Marie* carved on the transom. It was a common enough name, and because the French authorities used a different system of measuring and marking tonnage, and numbering, and anyway French officials are much more understanding – Louis winked for the third time – perhaps it was not surprising she had the same number and tonnage carved on her main beam as the *Marie* that once visited Boulogne from Folkestone. Indeed, by a curious coincidence the Boulogne-built *Marie* also had a copper tingle on the starboard side just forward of the chainplates, matching the one on the Folkestone *Marie* (she had sailed into the quay soon after being launched, and her builders had nailed on a piece of copper sheathing). So if both smacks had anchored near each other – not that they ever had, and very few people knew of the twins – it would have been impossible to tell them apart. And of course the French owner was a law-abiding citizen; naturally he had all the necessary papers providing that the Boulogne-built *Marie* was a regular Boulogne-based fishing-smack – just as the owner of the Folkestone-built *Marie* had papers proving she was a regular British smack.

The only thing was – and now Louis tapped the side of his nose – the British *Marie* with French papers and the French *Marie* with British papers, could cross the Channel in opposite directions at the same time, meeting briefly in mid-Channel to exchange documents and the British skipper, and visit each other's home ports without anyone being the wiser. The only physical difference was that the board on the transom showing the port of registry was changed – each smack carried both names. Regulations about having the abbreviation for the port of registry painted on the bow and sewn on the sail were ignored . . .

Nor did the English Revenue men pay much attention. For years, in peace and war, they had seen the *Marie* sail late in the evening to go fishing and return at dawn, time enough for the early market, and everyone knew she could never sail to France and back in that time, so she couldn't be carrying contraband. Maybe a cask or two occasionally, bought from a passing smuggler on a dark night – but certainly not bales of silk and lace lashed up in canvas, boxes of tobacco, cigars and tea, casks of brandy and pipes of wine. Obviously, the Revenue men thought, smuggling contraband on that scale could only be done by the bigger vessels which were away for several days; even the greenest young Customs searcher knew that. So no one ever bothered to see how thick was the layer of fish caught by the *Marie*; no one ever compared the probable amount – judging by the quantity in the fish hold – with the amount boxed and taken to Folkestone market . . .

It was an ingenious system and, Ramage noted, like all good systems it was simple. Only one lot of bribes had to be paid – to the French officials in Boulogne. Since the French authorities did nothing to hinder smuggling to England, the only risk was from greediness rather than informers. In fact, from what Admiral Nelson had said, it was highly unlikely that bribes needed to be paid: with French currency worthless outside the country, Bonaparte needed foreign currency to pay for goods he bought abroad, and the guineas and shillings paid by the English smugglers for the contraband would fetch a good rate of exchange . . .

'Do you carry contraband only one way – to England?' he asked Louis.

The Frenchman shook his head vigorously. 'No, usually we bring back woollen things (very short of clothes here, unless you wear only silk and lace), rum – the only supply from Guadeloupe is very small these days – and often whisky.'

When Ramage raised his eyebrows in surprise Louis laughed. 'No, the French are not suddenly changing their taste – except to drink more gin from Holland. The British *détenus* – there are hundreds held at Verdun and such places – like whisky and still have the money to pay for it.'

Ramage wondered if Bonaparte knew that one section of his British prisoners – the hundreds of civilians trapped in France when the war began and since treated as prisoners of war – had a regular supply of their favourite drink smuggled in through his main invasion port . . .

Well, it was all very interesting, but smuggling was only indirectly involved with the job in hand. The question was how much could he trust Louis? The man must know Boulogne very well. If he did not know something, he would know where to find out. Ramage had to balance the need for secrecy with the fact that he had to start gleaning information from somewhere. He thought for a moment of Dyson, who already knew a certain amount and was probably shrewd enough to guess most of the rest of Ramage's task. Anything Dyson knew or guessed must be regarded as information shared with Louis – although Ramage was doubtful if Louis shared much with Dyson.

Thinking that he might one day have to justify his decision to enlist Louis's help to the Admiralty, he realized that it would be almost impossible to put his reasons into words. Louis was rough, though clearly not uneducated, and officially the subject of an enemy nation. But he was a smuggler – and probably had been one for most of his life, and perhaps his father before him. Smuggling was an international calling or, rather, smugglers acknowledged no flag; their allegiance was to money.

He found he could almost argue the smuggler's case. In a Britain where almost everything was in short supply, what shopkeeper could refuse a lady a few yards of French lace for her new ball dress, a bolt of silk, pearls, mother-of-pearl? What shopkeeper could refuse to sell the lady's husband a few pounds of choice tobacco or cigars? What wine merchant could refuse an old and valued customer a pipe of wine, a cask of brandy, a puncheon of port, a couple of dozen of fine sherry? The smuggler knew the answer only too well: shopkeepers, vintners, tobacconists and the like usually had to refuse because they could not get the items, but the smuggler could, and who was to blame him for supplying them at a price which rewarded his risk but was still far below the price when duty was added?

Because of the war, these items could not be imported legally, since they came from the enemy's country. Law-abiding businessmen could not import them even if they paid all the duties in hard cash and with a smile on their faces: that would be trading with the enemy and akin to treason.

So, the smuggler would argue, who can blame me if I risk my life and liberty to go to France and get these items, and risk my life and liberty once again on my return to England? If I declared them so that I paid the regular duty, I'd be put in jail, so I land them on a dark night (thus adding more risk to the whole venture) and satisfy the ladies and gentlemen: the ladies can dress in beautiful clothes and cheer up the gentlemen; the gentlemen can puff a pipe or a cigar after a good dinner which was helped down with a fine wine topped off with a good port. The gentlemen were

– however briefly – cheerful enough not to curse the government or bully their wives; the wives were so happy in their new finery they did not nag their husbands.

Ramage chuckled to himself: there was an equally good case for arguing that smugglers should be honoured like other worthy citizens: he could just imagine the announcement that so-and-so had been created a Knight Commander of the Order of the Bath 'for distinguished services to smuggling'. One did not have to be very sophisticated to consider it better earned than the knighthoods, baronies and the like that were handed round like buns and ale at a cockfight in return for money paid to a political party. Better if a man earned a knighthood after risking his life than bought it in the same furtive way he would a puncheon of brandy . . .

Anyway, there's nothing like sitting on the deck of a smack in the sunshine in the middle of an enemy harbour for getting a fresh perspective. And not only a perspective – the hot sun was doing nothing to disperse the sickly smell of garbage, boiled cabbage and urine that seemed to lie over the quays in an invisible layer many feet thick.

So a smuggler's allegiance was to money rather than a flag, and he was lucky because Louis also had a deep and apparently genuine contempt for the Corsican who, to many Frenchmen, typified France even more than the Tricolour; who so believed in *Liberté, égalité* and *fraternité* that apparently he wanted to conquer and rule the whole world.

The first move was to see if Louis was willing to help; after that the price could be settled. So much easier to deal with men whose consciences were uncluttered with complicated loyalties . . . 'Has Slushy told you why I've come to France?' Ramage spoke in French, since there was no need to disguise the fact he spoke it.

'No – all I know is what Thomas Smith said when he came over with the papers in the middle of the Channel: that there was no contraband this voyage, only four passengers.'

'Do you often carry passengers?'

Louis shook his head. 'Not to France. Occasionally one of the leaders – one of the chief smugglers, you understand – visits France to check the accounts and pay or collect money. Twice a year, perhaps. To England? Very occasionally, and usually they are British prisoners of war who have escaped from Verdun or Bitche or one of the other fortresses. A very dangerous traffic for us: it's asking a lot to risk having the authorities here in Boulogne forbid all smuggling to England just for the sake of helping an escaped prisoner.'

'But they pay you well, surely?'

'They offer to, but if we carry them, then they pay only for a small rowing-boat: we take them to within a mile or two of Dover and let them row the rest of the way in the boat. They tell the authorities in Dover they stole or bought the boat and rowed all the way. They say nothing of the *Marie* or anyone they met. That is the price of our help: silence!'

'It's a price anyone can afford!'

'I have too much imagination,' Louis confessed unexpectedly. 'I just think of myself escaping from a prison fortress, being hunted across two hundred miles of countryside, and then reaching the coast to find I can see my homeland but cannot get across. The fisherman or boatman that drives a hard bargain in such circumstances ought to have a taste of prison . . .'

'What else did Thomas Smith tell you?' Ramage asked casually.

'Just that a gentleman with three attendants was being taken to Boulogne.'

'Attendants?'

Louis laughed, explaining, 'Thomas Smith is proud of his French and practises it on me. I think he liked the sound of "jonty-yomm" ' – he made an exaggerated gesture as he imitated the Marsh man's pronunciation, 'whereas "lieutenant" sounds more or less the same (the way Smith pronounces it) in either language. You are a lieutenant, I think?' When Ramage nodded he added: 'I thought so, and these three men served with you?' Without waiting for Ramage's answer he said: 'One can tell there is a rapport between men who have faced death together, no matter what their rank. Well, the fact that the Chief arranged your passage is enough for me to say, if I can be of service to you . . .'

'Thank you, but was that the British chief or the French?'

Louis chuckled, thought for a moment and then said: 'There's only one chief, and although I have never seen him, I am sure he regards himself as a citizen of both countries.'

'A man of two worlds, eh?'

Louis repeated the phrase, as though savouring it. 'All of us concerned with contraband have to be. However, contraband is the least of your worries. When you go on shore tonight, have you lodgings arranged?'

'Not yet. Will they be difficult to find?'

'I will help you. The main difficulty is moving about after dark.'

'Is there a curfew?'

'Only for the soldiers, but there are patrols everywhere. Everyone challenged has to show a passport, unless he can prove he lives in Boulogne. A man without a passport or a home in Boulogne goes straight to jail . . .'

Which shows, Ramage thought to himself, the dangers of not planning an operation carefully. But there had been no time to do more than get to France; there was no way of finding out what conditions were like. One day a government department might make itself responsible for collecting all that kind of information, so that it was available to the Admiralty and War Office, and even the Secretary of State's office. But since captains were having difficulty in getting the Admiralty to agree to print charts because Their Lordships expected captains and masters to have their own (though not specifying where they were to come from), it was unlikely that the Government would ever show any interest in what went on in an enemy country.

'Such documents provide no problem,' the Frenchman said. 'I'll get them before you leave. I need to know what trades you follow though, and you must decide on your names – or what names you want to use, rather. One of the men is not English, I think.'

'One is Italian, one British, and one American. The Italian speaks English and some Spanish. The American speaks a little Spanish – perhaps enough to fool a gendarme. I speak some Spanish, too. The American also speaks some Italian, and so do I.'

'Your Spanish and Italian – is it as good as your French?'

'Better – I've spoken both fairly recently. I haven't used my French since I learned it, unfortunately.'

'You have nothing to worry about. The accent of Paris – it shows. Your teachers made you work hard! But the Englishman – he speaks only English?'

Ramage nodded. 'His own particular brand of it!'

'Then he must be the dumb one, while the two of you must be Italian or Spanish. Italian would be better – the Spanish are not popular in France at the moment, as you probably know.'

'Yes, that gives us one native Italian – a Genovese – and I can pass for a Tuscan. If the American just grunts and the Englishman holds his tongue . . . But trades – what do you suggest?'

'It depends on your task. I'm not prying,' Louis added hurriedly, 'but one trade might be more suitable than another for your –' he broke off, embarrassed and obviously unable to find the right words.

'My masters are worried that Bonaparte's Army of England might suddenly arrive one morning . . .'

'It worries my masters too,' Louis grunted nodding as though Ramage had confirmed his guess. 'That would put every smuggler out of business along the whole French coast. The interests of our respective masters therefore coincide, which makes our task easier.'

Suddenly Ramage remembered the moment when Simpson had changed his mind and agreed to help when, in the comfort of his study, he had finally guessed the substance of Ramage's orders and realized that, with Bonaparte's threat of invasion, the smugglers' and the Admiralty's interests were perhaps for the first time in history the same.

'Carpenters!' Louis said suddenly. 'Carpenters sent to Boulogne from Italy to help build the ships. You have just arrived. In Italy the French officers – blame the Army – promised you high wages if you went to work on the barges in Boulogne. With your tools – yes, that would help because they are short of tools here –' he saw Ramage's face fall and said reassuringly, 'don't worry, you are poor men and cannot be expected to have a lot of tools, not more than I can provide.'

'All we need is some skill with wood; it looks as if you can provide everything else!'

Louis shrugged his shoulders. 'You and your men know enough about the way ships are built to bluff questioners – and that is all it would be, questions. I doubt if a gendarme would give you a plank of wood to make you demonstrate! And if you want to work in the shipyards for a day or two – well, there is so much chaos there that if each of you carries a piece of timber and some tools and you look busy, you could walk for many hours without anyone asking questions – long enough for you to find out whatever you need to know.'

Ramage looked at his hands. Despite the last few hours spent in the *Marie*'s grubby cuddy, his hands were still soft and well-manicured.

'Don't worry,' Louis said cheerfully, 'you are the foreman, and anyway it has taken you a month to get to Boulogne from Italy: time enough for any man's hands to get soft. Your men's hands are harder, I noticed. Well, you all had to stop from time to time to do some carpentry to pay for food. You found the business, since you speak some French – not very good French,' he warned, 'in fact only just sufficient to make yourself understood – and you made the men do the work, as all good foremen should.' He chuckled at his own joke and added: 'If I wasn't so well known here I would act as the entrepreneur!'

He stood up. 'I will go and arrange the papers and hide some tools where we can pick them up later. We must make up names for all of you, and you must practise signing them. If gendarmes stop you and are suspicious, the first thing they do is make you sign your name. Then they compare it with the signature in the passport.'

'Tell Rossi to choose short and easy names then,' Ramage said, visualizing Stafford stumbling over something like 'Giuseppe di Montefiore'. 'In fact let me look at the list. But – how can they practise the signatures before they see what names are written on the passports?'

Louis grinned and shook his head slowly. 'You under-estimate us, Lieutenant,' he said. 'I shall bring passports complete in all but three details – the owner's name, trade and address. And official paper so that we can draw up a travel document for the four of you. Something impressive to introduce you to the master shipwright at Boulogne.'

'He's the man we must keep away from,' Ramage said cautiously.

'Don't worry, the introduction is only for you to show an inquiring gendarme.' Louis thought for a moment. 'Money – you have money?'

Ramage nodded. 'Sufficient, I think, but if not . . .?'

'If not, a draft on London . . .'

CHAPTER EIGHT

By eleven o'clock that night Ramage and his three men were comfortably installed at a small inn midway between the quay where the *Marie* was alongside and the eastern side of the harbour, where barges and gunboats were secured several deep, waiting to be fitted out with sails and guns.

Louis had warned them that the innkeeper was a revolutionary: a former corporal who had lost a leg in Spain, though it was generally believed among his customers that it happened during a fracas in a brothel rather than in a desperate affray with the enemy. But the smuggler had also explained that quite apart from the fact that it was cheap, clean and known for its good plain food, it was also just the place that Italian carpenters working at either of the shipyards would choose. More important still, no one would ever dream that a British naval officer and three of his men – spies, no less – would dare to stay under his roof. The regular twice-weekly inspections of inns carried out by gendarmes all over the country were cursory; at the sign of *Le Chapeau Rouge,* merely an excuse for a glass of wine.

Rossi had startled Louis by declaring, with a straight face, that a man owning an inn with that name must be an agent of the Vatican, not a revolutionary, and Louis had begun a vociferous denial before Ramage, worried that their English might be overheard, explained Rossi's play on the fact that a Catholic cleric wore the *biretta,* 'the red hat,' and someone with a warped sense of humour could claim the inn's name referred to that, not the Phrygian, or red cap that was as much part of the Revolution as the Tree of Liberty – and the guillotine.

Ramage had negotiated the ritual of getting a room with no trouble. He had led his three men into the smoky and smelly bar, waved cheerfully to the half a dozen men sitting round the table and made a face in the direction of a customer stretched out across three chairs, his head hanging down in the total surrender achieved only by the dead or the drunk.

The innkeeper had been surly until Ramage, in halting French heavily larded with fluent Italian, explained that he and his men wanted accommodation 'for the many weeks' they would be working at the shipyard. As he spread passports and travel documents on the wine-stained counter in a gesture half-triumphant and half servile, as befitted the subject of a conquered state, he commented that Boulogne was indeed a long march from Genova.

'Italy, eh? I know Spain well enough,' the Corporal had growled, as though doubtful of Italy's existence, 'in fact I fought there, and lost a leg, too.' To underline the loss he banged the floor with his wooden stump. 'Corporal Alfonse Jobert, once of the 14th Regiment. You served in the Army of Italy,' he said, as though the fact that a man came from Italy made it obvious, and when Ramage shook his head apologetically he began glancing at the passports and said more sympathetically, 'Well, not everyone could have the honour of serving in the Army of Italy under General Bonaparte . . .'

He leafed through the papers with the uncertainty of an illiterate, and then reached under the bar for a pencil and a scrap of paper. 'Write all your names down there – for the gendarmes. Four of you share one room, eh? Two francs a night for the room and use of linen. Breakfast one franc and supper two – each that is. Good plain nourishing fare, and wine is extra. No going to bed with your boots on, mind you, and no women in the room – I know what you foreigners are like. Anyway,' he added in a man-to-man voice, 'there are plenty of "houses" round by the town hall.'

Ramage began writing, meekly assuring M. Jobert that they never slept with their boots on, not in a bed anyway, and that poor carpenters could not afford to entertain women in their room, even if they wanted to – not that they did, he said hastily, although the effect was almost spoiled by Rossi who, understanding enough French to follow the more interesting part of the conversation, muttered in Italian: 'This capon wants *castrati*, not carpenters . . .'

Ramage managed to turn a laugh into a snarl: the innkeeper bullied him, and he, as leader of the band of carpenters, was expected to bully them. 'Understand that, you miserable knots of wood,' he said in Italian, 'no boots in bed, no women, and two francs for supper!'

Jackson and Stafford looked suitably impressed although they did not understand a word, and Rossi was quick-witted enough to mumble a stream of Italian signifying grateful acceptance of the terms.

Finding that his new lodgers were docile, the innkeeper picked up a candle and stumped across to the stairs, beckoning to them to follow, and as he led the way he told Ramage confidentially: 'You can call me "the Corporal", like the rest of my patrons do. They like the idea of a military man on the premises, you understand.'

Ramage thanked him, and agreed that it was indeed a comfort to have someone of his military experience in the house; particularly with the damned English so close.

The Corporal stopped as suddenly as if he had walked into a sword blade and turned towards Ramage so quickly he almost overbalanced, the candle tilting and dripping wax on the bare boards. '*Merde!* You've nothing to fear from *them.* Why, with the Army that the First Consul is preparing here, the Tricolour will be flying over the –' he paused for a moment, obviously at a loss, and then the memory of the Bastille helped him, 'the Tower of London before we harvest this year's apples. Believe me,' he added, lowering one eyelid conspiratorially, 'I know what I'm talking about. My brother –' he dropped his voice and spoke slowly, to make sure the foreigner understood every word, 'my brother owns the inn which is patronized by Admiral Bruix's messenger; how about that, eh?'

Ramage looked unimpressed, anxious to learn more about the brother.

'Citizen Bruix,' the Corporal said heavily, 'is the admiral who commands the invasion flotilla – all the barges and gunboats and sloops and frigates that will carry the Army of England to – well, to England, of course. And he is stationed here in Boulogne, where he can keep an eye on things, and hurry your fellows along with your saws and adzes and planes – yes, and your hammers and nails, too.'

He paused dramatically, like an actor reaching the really dramatic speech in his act. 'Well, once a week Citizen Bruix reports to the First Consul on the progress being made at Boulogne in building the invasion flotilla – yes, and at the other ports along this coast that are privileged to build the ships for the Great Invasion. Every Friday night, as soon as all the returns are in from the shipyards, Citizen Bruix sits down in his house – it is the great white house at Pont-de-Briques, just before you enter the town, you must have passed it – and draws up his report with great care. Then can you guess what happens?'

Ramage shook his head dumbly, hoping that the Corporal would not get tired of perching on the stairs on his one good leg before he had finished his revealing story.

'Ah – well, he seals it up and calls for his messenger. Not an ordinary messenger, though; this man is a highly trusted officer, a *lieutenant-de-vaisseau*, no less, attached to Citizen Bruix's staff. The officer produces his special leather bag, Citizen Bruix puts his report inside, and then he locks the bag with a special key – a key which never leaves Citizen Bruix's possession – and then the lieutenant leaves for Paris before dawn next morning.'

'How do they open the bag in Paris?' Ramage asked innocently.

'With the duplicate,' the Corporal snorted contemptuously. 'That's the point, the duplicate key is kept at the First Consul's headquarters. No matter where in the world he is,' the Corporal said grandly, 'the duplicate key is always with him, ready to open the bag of dispatches from Citizen Bruix's headquarters.'

Ramage nodded his head wonderingly. 'The secret of success is careful preparation,' he said sententiously. 'I always tell my men, measure the wood carefully before you begin to saw, and then you –'

'Quite, quite,' the Corporal interrupted impatiently. 'Well, the lieutenant leaves immediately for Paris on horseback – note that; no comfortable, slow coach, as in the days of the *ancien régime*, but a galloping horse. For speed, you understand; so that the First Consul shall always know exactly what is going on all over the Empire.

'Off he gallops, whatever the weather, and he rides like the wind until it is too dark to proceed – the First Consul expects the report to be waiting on his desk first thing on Monday morning,' the Corporal explained, oblivious to the contradiction of the timing implied. 'In fact, the lieutenant usually manages to reach Amiens, and that's where my brother has his inn. A very comfortable establishment, you understand; one well equipped to attend to the wants of Citizen Bruix's special messenger.

'The lieutenant stays that night, dines well after such a ride, sleeps in his special room and at dawn he is off again. By nightfall he is in Paris with the report. So you can see why I know,' he added proudly. 'About the Invasion, I mean.'

'Indeed I do,' Ramage said, awe in his voice.

'Ah well, you will be wanting to get to bed.' With that he stumped up the two remaining stairs, led the way along a short corridor and opened a door. He handed the candle to Ramage and stood back to let him pass. 'I could tell some stories,' the Corporal said wistfully, 'but you'll be tired.'

'Oh no,' Ramage said eagerly. 'These men of mine are sleepy, and they can go to bed; but me – I would like the chance of talking with a man of affairs like yourself, and I have a few francs left to buy the wine.'

The Corporal winked and stumped back along the corridor. 'I'll see you downstairs then,' he called back over his shoulder. 'And tell your men not to worry about the English; they can sleep soundly in their beds. My brother already has plans to open an inn at Dover – how about that, eh?'

As soon as they were all in the room and the door was shut, Jackson whispered: 'I couldn't follow any of that, sir, but from the way you was listening it sounded as though it was useful.'

'It was,' Ramage said cheerfully, 'and there's more to come. I'm going downstairs to drink with him for an hour or two. You had better get some sleep, just in case we have to prowl around tomorrow night. Before you turn in just make sure you can hold the tools properly – ' he gestured at the canvas bags Rossi and Stafford had just put down by the foot of one of the beds. 'Try and look like professional carpenters – without cutting yourselves . . .'

He eyed the two large beds. 'I seem to remember you snore, Rossi. What about you, Stafford?'

The Cockney shook his head sadly. 'Me too, sir. Jacko doesn't – you'd best share a bed wiv 'im, and I'll doss wiv Rossi.'

'Very well,' Ramage said, and took the passports and travel documents from his pocket. 'You'd better look after these,' he said, handing them to Jackson. 'Who knows, I might get as drunk as that fellow stretched out on the chairs.'

The American grinned. 'That'll be the day, sir. You all right for money?'

Ramage took ten francs from the handful in his pocket and gave the rest to Jackson. 'You might as well look after these, just in case.'

He sat down on the bed for a few minutes. A ghost of an idea had appeared while the Corporal was telling the story of the *lieutenant-de-vaisseau*'s overnight stay in Amiens. And 'ghost', he reflected, was the right description: the more he thought about it, the more he saw it had precious little shape or substance. Well, there was time enough for him to look closer . . .

He found the Corporal waiting behind the bar, a bottle in one hand and the corkscrew ready in the other. 'Ah,' he began turning the corkscrew as soon as he saw Ramage, 'you can tell me if you have a red wine the like of this in Italy.'

'I'll be glad to,' Ramage said eagerly; so eagerly that the Corporal hastened to make it clear that Ramage was paying for it. 'It's not expensive, though, and you'll enjoy it!'

The bottle had gone and been replaced by another (the Corporal making sure that each bottle was paid for as soon as it was uncorked) before Ramage could get him back to the subject of his brother at Amiens, a man for whom the Corporal combined envy with pride.

'He has a fine position, right by the crossroads, Paris ahead, Rouen to the right, Arras to the left. That's the secret of a profitable inn, of course; you have to be where the traveller can find you. Great mistake I made, settling here. I was relying on the local people for custom but – ' he glowered at the half dozen men still playing dominoes at the table, two empty bottles and one half-full representing the entire evening's drinking for six men, 'well, you can see; they talk like wine cellars about how much they need, but half a bottle each sees them through the evening.

'My brother, though: there he is, on the main post road to Paris, tactically placed – ' he cocked his head a moment, as though the word brought back memories of a more martial life, 'yes, *strategically* placed for the travellers to Paris. Travellers have the money to spend. Generals are the best – at least six staff officers with them, and a dozen soldiers. Forage for the horses, a big dinner and an early breakfast and they're away, so you can get their rooms tidied up in good time for fresh guests.

'Ah, my brother knew what he was doing when he took over the Hotel de la Poste. He was telling me his plans for after the Invasion of England. He thinks he'll open his first place at Dover – after the travellers' trade again, of course. He's not sure from the map which is the most popular route to London, though. One road goes through – Canterbury, I think he said – and the other through Ashford. He'll wait and see which the Army favours and take over the best hotel at one or the other place. London – ah, he has big plans for London. The headquarters staff, that's who he has his eyes on in London.'

He filled his glass and drank deeply and, as if comparing the position of former Corporal Jobert in Boulogne with his brother M. Jobert in Amiens, he said almost spitefully: 'But he's not in England yet, and he has his problems in Amiens. Ah, I could tell you a thing or two about them, too . . .'

His eyes seemed to go glassy at the thought, and Ramage prompted him. 'We all have our problems, it's overcoming them that distinguishes the men from the boys!'

'Or the girls,' the Corporal said, almost absently. 'It's his daughter that is the problem, you see. My niece. A fine girl mind you; pretty and hard-working, but inclined to be wilful. My brother says that the minute the girl and the lieutenant first looked at each other, he knew there would be trouble.'

He drained his glass, and Ramage pushed the bottle towards him. 'Trouble? With the lieutenant on the First Consul's headquarters staff?'

'The Admiral's staff,' the innkeeper corrected him. 'Twice a week he rides into the hotel yard – on Saturday night as he goes to Paris, and on Tuesday night as he returns with orders and dispatches for Citizen Bruix from the First Consul. It all seems very romantic to a young girl, I suppose.'

'It would be a good match,' Ramage said, knowing that would provoke the Corporal into more confidences.

The Frenchman shook his head sadly. 'It might seem like it to you, because you are looking at it as a carpenter; but you have to consider it from the point of view of a man of property: a man like my brother – or me, come to that. She's his only child, you see, so what happens when he's gone? None of us live for ever. But a lieutenant's wife – will a naval man settle down to an innkeeper's life after the war?'

Ramage nodded his head vigorously, not liking the sad note creeping in to the Corporal's voice, which was already slurring as the new wine added its weight to that drunk before Ramage and his men arrived at the *Chapeau Rouge*. 'After all, you've settled down as an innkeeper after a military life.'

The flattery was so gross that for a moment Ramage thought he had overdone it, but the Corporal screwed up his eyes, as if examining the statement and liking what he saw. 'That is true,' he admitted judiciously, 'and I don't want you to think I'm against the young man. He is a smart fellow. Five years ago he was a haberdasher's assistant. He joined the Navy – and now look at him. Why, in a year or two who knows – he might be given the command of a sloop of war; a frigate, even.'

'He'll end up an admiral, you'll see,' Ramage whispered in a suitably awed voice. 'An admiral, think of that!'

'Not a chance,' the Corporal said firmly, 'the war won't last long enough. It takes time to become an admiral; another seven or eight years, I should judge, and the war will be over this time next year, you'll see.'

'Still, he has an interesting job now – and exciting, too: just imagine, galloping to Paris with urgent dispatches; sleeping with a pistol in his hand to guard them safely I expect . . .'

The Corporal laughed condescendingly. 'Not as romantic as that, I can assure you. Sleeping with a pistol in his hand – why, he would probably blow his foot off in his sleep! That's the thing you people don't understand. When you are handling secret dispatches all the time – as this young man is – you get used to it. Like you carpenters starting off with a plain plank of wood. Why, my brother says the lieutenant has even left the satchel behind on the dinner table – how about that, eh?' He nudged Ramage across the table. 'Mind you, my brother is a responsible innkeeper, and seeing the young man was lifting his glass a bit freely – it's a fault he has, I have to admit – he kept an eye on the satchel. After all, the First Consul's secret documents have to be safeguarded.'

'Indeed they do,' Ramage said. 'What about another bottle?'

Ramage was weary, jubilant but just sober when he finally returned to the room to find Jackson still awake but the other two snoring stertorously. After assuring Ramage that the passports and travel documents were safely hidden under the bolster, Jackson waited to see if he was going to hear an account of the talk with the Corporal. Ramage thought about it for several minutes and decided that their situation was precarious enough for the American, as the second-in-command of the little expedition, to need to know all the details, so that he could take over if necessary.

Keeping his voice down to a whisper, Ramage quickly outlined the orders he had received from Lord Nelson and the procedure he intended to adopt to get reports back to England.

'I'm hoping we'll get all the information at the same time, so we can all go together; but if not, then one of you will sail as necessary with Louis and Dyson in the *Marie* here, meet the Folkestone *Marie* – she'll be going to the rendezvous every night from tomorrow night onwards, Dyson was bright enough to arrange that – and return with her to Folkestone. Each report must then be taken at once to Dover Castle, so that it can be forwarded immediately to Lord Nelson.'

Ramage paused to rest his throat: whispering was extraordinarily tiring, and he wondered if he would end up with a sore throat.

'Now we get to this innkeeper. He wants us to call him "The Corporal" by the way: it seems he was once in Boney's Army, and lost the leg in Spain. He has a brother who owns an inn at Amiens called the Hotel de la Poste – remember that name. The brother's name is Jobert. Now, the French admiral in charge of the invasion flotillas along this coast – and that includes construction – is called Bruix. Every Friday night Bruix writes a report on the state of the invasion flotilla, including new construction, and sends it to Bonaparte's headquarters in Paris first thing on Saturday morning.

'In other words,' Ramage said slowly, 'all the information the Admiralty needs might be contained in that one report. It could be this week's, last month's – but the information it contains would take us six months to discover on our own.'

He could feel Jackson's body tensing as he grasped the significance of what Ramage was saying.

'The link between the Corporal's brother in Amiens and Admiral Bruix is a young lieutenant who rides to Paris, leaving Boulogne early on Saturday and arriving in Paris on Sunday night – '

'And spending Saturday night at the Hotel de la Poste,' Jackson whispered.

'Not only that, but he drinks too much, left the leather dispatch case behind on the dining-room table at least once, and is much enamoured of the innkeeper's daughter.'

'Does he spend the night with her?' Jackson asked bluntly.

'I doubt it; in fact the worthy innkeeper and his wife probably lock her bedroom door. They are considering him as a husband for the girl, and as she's the only child that means they are deciding whether or not he is worthy of inheriting the Hotel de la Poste when they die: probably in lieu of a dowry, knowing how canny their sort of folk can be.'

Jackson was silent for a moment, and then whispered cautiously: 'If we could get our hands on the bag . . .'

'We'd find it locked. Only two keys – Admiral Bruix has one; the other is kept at Bonaparte's headquarters.'

'But a *leather* bag,' Jackson said longingly. 'I can just see Staff's face. He's brought a set of picks with him, and those leather bags never have much of a lock on them . . .'

'Surprising how useful it is to have a locksmith in one's crew,' Ramage mused, 'and particularly one trained to work in the dark . . . Still, what bothers me is that it all looks a little too easy at the moment.'

'Well sir,' Jackson whispered cheerily, 'over the past two or three years we've had our share of jobs that looked impossible from the start, but we managed them.'

'That's what I mean,' Ramage said, unable to keep the sharpness out of his voice. 'The difference is that this looks so easy at the beginning that we can be sure it'll turn out to be difficult.'

'Ah, you're looking at it from halfway through, sir,' Jackson pointed out. 'We're already in France and halfway through carrying out the orders. I doubt if you thought they were so easy when Lord Nelson gave them to you.'

Ramage recalled the three meetings – in the library at the Duchess of Manston's, in that miserable room at the Admiralty with the green-painted walls, and in that cellar-like room in Dover Castle. Jackson was right; at the time they seemed the most impossible orders he had ever heard of, let alone received.

'I see what you mean, but don't let's get too confident, Jackson. And we need some sleep too.'

CHAPTER NINE

Ramage woke next morning with a start but knew he had not been roused by the daylight trying to penetrate the dirty window panes. Approaching footsteps – the heavy tread of boots on wooden planks; the measured steps of a man climbing stairs, not the thud-and-click of the Corporal and his wooden leg. He sensed that Jackson was already awake and looked round at the two men in the other bed. Both of them were watching him over the top of the blanket, waiting for a word or gesture.

'If he's coming here, we bluff! Pretend to be sleepy,' he whispered.

The man reached the top of the stairs and marched along the corridor. Ramage remembered two other doors, but the man was not interested in them and, even though he was waiting for it, the sudden heavy banging on the door made Ramage jump.

'Open the door! Police!'

Ramage forced himself to wait. One gendarme. Surely there would be two if it was trouble? But they might be intelligent enough to have surrounded the inn, or more could be waiting at the bottom of the stairs. Again there was a banging on the door and an impatient order to open it. Ramage forced a noisy yawn and, in the French heavily laced with Italian that he had used the night before, called out: 'Who is that making so much noise? Is breakfast ready?'

'Police,' the man called, 'open the door!'

'Open it yourself,' Ramage said in a surly voice, 'I am still waking up.'

The door swung open and a gendarme, one arm protruding from under the cape drawn round him against the early morning chill, slouched into the room. He flung the cape back over his shoulders, like a bird settling its wings, and rubbed a hand over the stubble along the side of his jaw, the rasping reminding Ramage of a holystone sliding along a dry deck.

'Out of bed!' he ordered, 'and show me your passports and lodging passes!'

Knowing the other three would be watching him for a lead, Ramage slowly got up, mumbling to himself in Italian, and Rossi followed, muttering a stream of Italian which more than made up for the silence of the other two. Ramage fished around under the mattress and Jackson, guessing what was needed, pulled the documents from under his side of the mattress and gave them to Ramage.

Handing the four passports to the gendarme, Ramage waited for him to read the details, but instead the man barked: 'Lodging tickets!'

Ramage shook his head dumbly. 'What are lodging tickets?'

'No lodging tickets?' the gendarme repeated incredulously. 'But you must have them! Why . . .'

They could knock him out and tie him up and leave him gagged under the bed. Providing he had been alone, they might be able to escape through the window – although Ramage realized that he had no idea what was outside: perhaps a yard with a high wall. Blast Louis for forgetting lodging passes: here they were, trapped and about to be arrested as spies, all because Louis had forgotten lodging passes. But – up to a point – time was on their side; a little judicious stupidity on his part might result in the gendarme revealing whether or not he was alone.

'Do not talk to *me* of lodging tickets,' Ramage said with a sudden show of anger. 'You tell that captain in Genoa!'

'What captain in Genoa?' the gendarme said warily, startled by the outburst.

'Captain or colonel, I don't know which,' Ramage said, taking advantage of the effect the rank had on the gendarme. 'Many promises he made when he gave us the passports and travel documents. "Plenty of work and good pay for carpenters," he said.' Ramage mimicked the precise voice of someone in authority. ' "Just take your tools there and turn the wood shavings into *soldi*!" So we walk and get rides in farm carts – mostly we walk – fifteen hundred kilometres, no less. And when we arrive in Boulogne, what happens? Ah, you see what happens; the first night we get a decent bed to rest our weary bodies, along comes a gendarme. Bang, bang on the door. "Open!" he shouts. "Where are your lodging tickets?" he shouts. A fine welcome that is for honest Italians who come to help fight the English but –'

'But for free lodgings you need lodging tickets,' the gendarme interrupted, trying to quieten Ramage, who had raised his voice to the pitch of a querulous washerwoman. 'You are conscripts – so you must –'

'Conscripts!' Ramage almost shrieked, and lapsed into a stream of Italian to give himself time to think, afraid that his French had become too fluent. 'Conscripts, are we? Ah, I see now, it is all a trick! That colonel – I thought he was a general – was no more than a recruiting sergeant, eh? All his soft talk about skilled carpenters – and we are skilled, I might tell you; you should see the furniture my brother and I have made. Why, when my brother's daughter (she is my niece, you understand) married the son of Giacomo Benetti, you should see the tables and chairs we made for her *dot*; even my brother's wife, for all her airs – she's no better than us, but

113

she walks with her nose high, like this – well, even she had to admit, they would have looked well in the Pitti Palace – '

He broke off, afraid he would burst out laughing, and hoping the gendarme would recover quickly from the outburst and say something, but the man just rubbed his jaw rhythmically and stared.

'What have you to say to *that*?' Ramage said, his voice full of indignation.

'You mean you are not conscripts?' the gendarme asked anxiously.

'Read the documents,' Ramage said with a great show of patience. 'Just read them. A man who can make furniture fit for the Pitti Palace taken up as a conscript? Why, even my brother's wife would – '

'Give me time to read,' the gendarme said hastily, obviously alarmed at the idea of hearing more of the niece's *dot*. He sat down on the edge of the bed, gripping the papers as though fearful they might be snatched away. Finally he let go with one hand and began following the writing with a forefinger, the nail of which was bitten almost to the quick. For more than five minutes he worked his way through every line of all eight documents. When he had finished he carefully folded the papers, stood up and gave them back to Ramage.

'Carpenters, eh? There is plenty of work for you here, helping to build the flotilla.' He looked round at the other three men and, as if anxious to reassert his authority, said sternly: 'See you don't get drunk. The wine of France is very strong; not like that coloured water you get in foreign places.'

'You need not worry,' Ramage assured him. 'I am their foreman; I'm a father to them. An uncle, at least. I bring them all this way. When they are sick I nurse them; when they are weary – '

'Quite so,' the gendarme said, 'and make sure they work hard in the shipyard.' With that he turned on his heel and walked out, slamming the door behind him. Ramage signalled for silence and listened to his footsteps as he went down the stairs.

'As soon as we have had something to eat,' Ramage said heavily, 'we'll have a look at the docks and the shipyards.'

By noon they had the layout of the port firmly fixed in their minds and were due to meet Louis at a café near their hotel, a rendezvous they had arranged by walking purposefully past

114

the *Marie,* their carpenter's tools over their shoulders and, with no strangers within earshot, calling to the Frenchman.

More important than the layout of the port was the size of the Invasion Flotilla. At first Ramage had been appalled by the number of vessels: those he had seen when he sailed in with the *Marie* only half-filled the outer harbour, but all the inner docks and muddy banks of the river Liane were crowded with a wide variety of craft. The largest were *prames,* obviously designed as barges to carry troops and cavalry but, as Jackson commented, looking little more than lighters rigged with inadequate masts, and obviously incapable of going to windward. Any progress they made would only be running almost dead before the wind.

All four men had estimated separately how many soldiers or cavalry the *prames* could carry and agreed on two hundred infantry with arms and baggage, or fifty horses and cavalrymen and a platoon of infantry, with all their rations, ammunition and forage.

There were sixteen *prames* altogether, though many were not rigged, and forty-one sloops, which were smaller and more weatherly, and would be crowded with a hundred men and their supplies and weapons. The most numerous vessels were the gunboats, sixty-one of them, but less than a score had masts and mounted the 24-pounder gun for which each of them was pierced. Like the sloops, they could probably carry a hundred men with stores and ammunition. There were fifteen large river barges, normally towed by horses. Presumably they were to be towed over by frigates.

One dock was filled with a variety of different craft: more than a hundred caiques (which could carry less than fifty men and were more suitable for carrying cattle or horses); thirty or so corvettes carrying about the same; and more than half a dozen different types of fishing-boat, their varied shapes showing they had come from such widely spaced ports as those on the shallow north coast of Holland, with its treacherous sandbanks, to the Breton coast, where fishing was in deep water with rough Atlantic seas. The hatches of the fishing-boats were so small and smelly – Ramage could detect the stench from five hundred yards to leeward of the nearest one – that they could not be used for troops, who would be seasick long before the craft cast off from the dock, let alone reached a mile offshore. The largest of them looked capable of carrying twenty horses with saddles, while the smallest might manage five. But alone in the flotilla, the fishing-boats could go to sea in almost any weather and be sure of reaching their destination.

It was curious how hard it was to relate totals written on paper with what you saw afloat: walking round the quays, it seemed Bonaparte had assembled a large flotilla, with the whole port seemingly full. Then when you wrote down the totals for the various types on a sheet of paper, it reduced in size. But this was only the Boulogne section: there would be many more in Calais, and perhaps as many again in all the small fishing ports. And he had no idea yet how many more were building – not just here in Boulogne, but at the other shipyards up and down the coast.

As they walked to the café, Ramage recalled the phrase Louis had used when he pointed out the first of the vessels – Bonaparte's *flotilla de grande espèce*, which was certainly a grand enough title. They reached the café and found a few workmen at one table, noisily drinking onion soup and pausing only to break pieces from small loaves of black bread. Ramage sat down at the largest empty table and gestured to the others to leave a chair for Louis. One look at the *patron* showed why Louis had chosen this particular café: unwashed, unshaven, the man was grossly fat, with the slack face and bloodshot eyes of a perpetual drunkard, and when he lurched over to take Ramage's order of soup for all of them he obviously did not trust his own eyes to focus.

'For how many?' he asked.

'For five,' Ramage said and a moment later Louis joined them, settling back in the chair facing Ramage, who saw that he had shaved and combed his hair since they last met. The Frenchman noticed the glance and grinned. 'I thought I had better tidy myself up, so that I look like a carpenter too! Tell me,' he asked quietly, 'is it an emergency.'

Ramage shook his head. 'Not an emergency, but a change of plan – ' He broke off as the owner arrived with plates, spoons and a large jug of soup, all of which he dumped in the middle of the table. He fished around in the large pocket in front of his apron and produced a loaf of black bread, which he put down beside Ramage and lurched back to the bar at the far end of the room.

Rossi poured soup into the plates and passed them round while Jackson produced a large knife and sliced up the bread.

As soon as they were all bent over their plates Ramage described, between spoonsful of soup, the Corporal's description of the lovelorn lieutenant and his weekly ride to Paris with the Admiral's dispatches. At the end of the story Louis was silent for several moments and then, picking up the jug to see if any more soup remained, he gave a prodigious belch. He sat back in his chair looking to his right, away from the group of workmen at the other table, and apparently bored or daydreaming. But Ramage noticed that no lip-reader could watch his mouth.

'So you wish to sample the food at the Hotel de la Poste at Amiens . . .' It was a statement, not a question, and Ramage waited as Louis mulled over the problems involved. '. . . Carpenters won't do – Amiens is the centre for velvet, and that sort of thing. And priests, too,' he added maliciously, 'with the largest cathedral in Europe. Priests are great travellers now, since the First Consul and the Pope signed the Concordat – always going to see the bishop. Not so long ago they were being hunted down by the *enfants de terreur* and their churches and cathedrals robbed and pillaged. Fashions change,' he commented. 'Passports will be needed, and different clothes. I shall want some money to pay for all this.'

'Of course,' Ramage said. 'And I need to be in Amiens by Friday night, so that I can spend Saturday arranging things at the hotel. The others could arrive on Saturday, if that would make it any easier.'

'It might be better to split into two parties of two,' Louis said, obviously thinking aloud. 'Two priests, two weavers, two masons . . . people travel in pairs. Four creates suspicion. Let me think about it. I'll see you in your room at ten o'clock tonight.' He called to the *patron* for wine and asked quietly: 'You had an interesting walk round the port?'

'Very interesting,' Ramage said, 'and a little frightening. Even the vessels completed so far could carry an army across the Channel . . .'

'They *could*,' the Frenchman said evenly, 'though whether they will is another matter. Would you bet on a week or more of easterly winds?'

'Not if I was a Bonaparte, but the odds seem shorter when you look at it from the British point of view.'

Louis shrugged his shoulders. 'Appear to shorten my friend, but an east wind is still an east wind, and this flotilla of sheep needs moonlight also or they'll all get lost. You have seen those *prames*? They need a gale of wind under them to make any progress . . .'

'If only half of them arrive on the Kentish beaches,' Ramage said, 'they might not take the country, but the devastation . . .'

Louis reached up and took the carafe of wine from the *patron* and reminded him they needed glasses.

'Yes, there would be much devastation. Indeed,' he grinned broadly, 'it would upset the contraband trade for a long time, too, which is one of the reasons why we are helping you. To tell you the truth, I'm beginning to enjoy it; running contraband three or four nights a week becomes boring.'

Ramage raised his eyebrows. 'I should have thought boredom was the last thing that troubled you.'

'Don't misunderstand me; a boring voyage means a safe one, and I have no wish to return home with wild stories of narrow escapes. We make a profit because we sail as regularly as the packetboat did before the war. But it is still boring!'

The *patron* arrived with the glasses, which Ramage saw were even dirtier than the windows at the Corporal's inn. He reached for the bottle and poured wine for them all and lifted his glass to Louis. 'War sees some strange alliances – here is to this one.'

The Frenchman drank to it and then put his glass down carefully. 'Not so strange, when you think about it carefully. I don't want to rule the world; I just want to be left in peace to follow my trade. You don't want to rule the world either, nor do these men; you just want to be left in peace, knowing your family and friends are safe from invaders. That is why we are allies against this Corsican . . .' He stood up. 'I'll see you in your room after supper,' he said.

That night while Ramage and his three men were sitting on the two beds in their room, talking in whispers as they waited with the flickering candle flame glittering occasionally on the shiny blades of the carpenters' tools stacked on the floor beneath the window, there was a faint double tap at the door, and before anyone could move Louis slipped into the room, closing the door silently behind him.

Stafford looked at him and said admiringly, 'Cor – didn't hear the coming of you! If you want a job when the war's over, just look me up in London: we could make a good living, s'long as you don't mind working at night.'

The Frenchman grinned and said to Ramage in his hesitant English: 'I think the heavy feet might alarm you, no?'

'It most certainly would,' Ramage said in French. 'We were woken this morning by a gendarme banging on the door. He wanted to inspect our papers – mistook us for conscripts.'

'I warned you: they check all inns and lodging houses for deserters two or three times a week. A matter of routine, but alarming if you have a guilty conscience!'

He sat down on the bed beside Ramage and took some papers from his pocket. After putting them down, he brought out a bottle of ink, and then carefully removed a quill pen which he had slid down inside his boot. He held it up to the candle flame to make sure the point had not split.

'We have to write in the details on the documents,' he explained. 'Who you are, why you are travelling . . . But first I must tell you some differences you will find on the road to Amiens – on any road, in fact. If you use a postchaise (the wagon is too slow), the posts are still the same: thirty-four between here and Paris, and usually ten kilometres (about six English miles) apart. They are well supplied with horses, although the postmasters no longer follow the old rule of one horse per person; you're lucky to get three horses for four people these days. The postillions can legally charge only fifteen *sous* per post, but if you do not pay them double they can make the journey unpleasant in many little ways.

'Now, listen carefully; there is now a new system by which the traveller has to pay a toll. The money is supposed to be for the upkeep of the roads, but no one has spent a *sou* on a road in France since the Revolution, let alone a *livre*: there are deep potholes every few yards. You pay the tolls at *barrières* which have been set up along the main roads. But watch out, they are not at regular intervals, and the toll varies between three and eighteen *sous*.

'All of this makes travelling expensive: before the Revolution you could take a postchaise to Paris for 213 *livres*; now you have to pay double. Still, there is a brighter side: before the Revolution you would be lucky to arrive in Paris without meeting a highwayman or a footpad. Now they are a rarity.

'They are a rarity,' he said, tapping Ramage's shoulder for emphasis, 'because – from your point of view – there is another pest on the roads: mounted gendarmes. They halt all carts and carriages and demand to see every traveller's papers. Anyone arousing suspicion is taken to the nearest jail. Oh yes, their favourite trick is to make you sign your name, which they compare with the signature in your passport, so remember that and practise it!'

After making Ramage repeat the details, Louis said: 'Now, the journey to Amiens. The route from here is through Montreuil (four posts, or about twenty-three miles), Nampont, and Nouvion to Abbeville –'

Ramage noticed the Frenchman tensed slightly as he paused and then continued.

'It is a wretched town now; half the people have left and the Revolution has ruined the damask industry. Reichord's Hotel is comfortable – by today's standards, anyway. Then you go on to Ailly-le-Haut-Clocher. There's a Red Cap of Liberty on top of the church steeple. It is stuck on the weathercock, so it swivels round with every change of wind.' He shrugged his shoulders. 'Perhaps others have noted the irony – to comment aloud in public would be to risk your neck. At the next village, Flixecourt, you will get your first sight of a Tree of Liberty; they are proud of the one set up in the square. You will change horses for the last time at Picquigny, and Amiens is only a league and a half beyond.'

'Abbeville,' Ramage said quietly, 'has some unpleasant associations for you.'

Louis looked down and was silent for a full minute, seeming almost to shrink, leaving his body behind while he went to some private place full of dreadful memories. Embarrassed at this unexpected reaction to his curiosity and regretting the question, Ramage was trying to think of a way of changing the subject when the Frenchman looked up.

'I will tell you about it – no, don't worry,' he said as Ramage went to speak, 'I want to tell you so you can understand better why I help you. At the moment I must seem to be a smuggler with no allegiances; a man whose loyalty can be bought – no, do not bother to protest, M. Ramage, you have all the doubts about me that I would expect in an honest man. In a minute or two you will understand and we shall be better friends.

'The name Joseph Le Bon means nothing to you. To me he is a former priest from Arras who almost made me believe in God. "Ah" you might say, "a saintly man, and wise, as befits someone who once taught rhetoric at the College of

120

Beaune, in Burgundy, and a man of great ability if he nearly succeeded in making an atheist like Louis believe in God and an after-life."

'You would be partly right: Le Bon made me *hope* there is an after-life because I want the comfort of knowing there is a Hell in whose flames Joseph Le Bon burns in agony for all eternity, for he is now dead. My only regret is that the Committee of Public Safety finally ordered his execution and cheated me of my revenge. But those who watched him on the scaffold – they saw him screaming with fear, groaning, wailing and begging for mercy before the blade dropped. I had planned that he would be begging *me* for mercy, but – ' he shrugged his shoulders ' – the Committee that set him on a path of mass murder eventually executed its own servant.

'I can see you are wondering why this man Louis should be hunting another man, a former priest and teacher of rhetoric, with a knife, with the intention of murdering him. Don't protest, *m'sieur*,' Louis said grimly, 'it is a reasonable question for a man whose country is not torn by revolution, who has never seen pork butchers set down their knives and become ministers of state overnight and use the guillotine to butcher their fellow men, and bakers and grocers made judges who listen only to the charges against the man, never the evidence for his defence, before sending him to death.

'You will learn what happens when I tell you of Le Bon. After the Revolution this man left the Church and entered politics, becoming the Mayor of Arras. He showed judgment; he was even moderate. Then, since he had also been given responsibility for the whole Department of the Pas de Calais, he was told to destroy any anti-revolutionary movement in Calais and the neighbouring towns.

'Again, he was moderate, even indulgent – so much so that one of his enemies denounced him to the Committee of Public Safety as a protector of aristocrats and a persecutor of patriots. He was recalled to Paris, escaped being put on trial for his life only because Citizen Robespierre liked him and accepted his promise to redeem himself.

'Redeem himself! He was sent back to Calais – a badly frightened man, with unlimited powers to crush the anti-revolutionaries. The problem was that Le Bon could not find any, so in fear of his own life he simply accused scores and scores of innocent people and sent them to the guillotine.

Within weeks hundreds met their death in Calais alone. He then went to other towns – Abbeville, Amiens, Arras, Boulogne . . .

'Two young ladies in Abbeville who taught the pianoforte, for example, were playing *Ça Ira* on the day a defeat by the Austrians was announced. Le Bon heard them and accused them of having an evil disposition towards the Revolution. They said quite truthfully they had heard nothing of the defeat, and in any case *Ça Ira* was a patriotic tune. Le Bon disagreed – playing *Ça Ira* in those circumstances, he said, meant that they wished the Austrians to advance and capture other French fortresses. If they were true patriots, he told them at the tribunal, they should have played *Le Rével du Peuple* . . .

'So he condemned them to death, and at the scaffold next morning, while the young ladies were in the tumbril at the scaffold, he delayed the public execution for a quarter of an hour, until some women of the town, in all their finery, had arranged themselves comfortably on a balcony overlooking the guillotine. You find the story hard to believe, I see . . .'

Ramage nodded and was about to add that that did not mean he thought it was untrue when Louis turned to look him straight in the eye, the strained look back on his face. 'Those two young ladies were sisters, *m'sieur*. The elder was my wife, who was staying in her mother's house while I was away at sea. Some might say it was punishment on me for being a smuggler,' he said bitterly. 'Anyway, when you get to Abbeville, ask about Joseph Le Bon, and they will tell you that story.'

'But you said he was executed – '

'I came back a few days after Le Bon had finished his bloody business and gone on to Paris. I followed him – and was arrested almost immediately, because my passport was for travelling only from Boulogne to Abbéville and back. They knew who I was but the gendarmes at Breteuil, where I was imprisoned, were sympathetic because of my loss. They never guessed I was following Le Bon; they assumed I was going to Paris to protest to the authorities. So they kept me in prison for a year, and during that time the mayors of several towns had protested to the Ministry of Police at Le Bon's wholesale murders. He was accused of public assassination and oppressing citizens of the Republic, found guilty of "an unlimited abuse of the guillotine" and sentenced to death.

Yet he was a craven man; I think he was always frightened for his life, and when they sent him back to Calais the second time he became so obsessed that he saw enemies of the Republic all round him. People told me that when the time came to dress him in the red garment which is reserved for murderers as they make their last journey in the tumbril to the scaffold, Le Bon said, "It is not I who should wear this garment, but those whose orders I obeyed." Ironic,' he added, 'that Fouché, the present Minister of Police, is also a former priest: a sea captain's son who was an abbé and a professor at Nantes university . . .

'I had a long time to think about the past while I was in prison. I despaired and grew fat – can you imagine that? I, who did not want to live, became ugly and gross; my teeth fell out, I began to grow bald . . . But in that time I came to understand what Le Bon meant. I would agree with him if he had said, "It is not I *alone . . .*"'

Louis stood up and walked over to the window, glanced out into the darkness, and then sat down beside Ramage, who knew the movement was not curiosity about what was outside but rather closing a door on his past which he rarely dared to open.

'I have been thinking about your journey to Amiens. It will be dangerous. In Boulogne people accept you as foreign carpenters because there are many of them working in the shipyards. The road to Amiens from Boulogne is different. Four Frenchmen might be suspected of being deserters. Four foreigners – well, I can only guess at what protection the possession of passports and travel documents would give you against suspicion.'

'Is the danger because there are four of us, or the fact we are young and not in the Army?' Ramage asked.

'The number. If you travelled in pairs it would be safer, but there is the language problem if you split up. You and the American, for instance; that would be all right because you can do the talking and if you met with difficulties would understand what was happening. But the Italian – his French is not sufficient, and if they found a translator to question him in Italian, I doubt if he could tell a convincing enough story of travelling up from Genoa.'

Louis was only echoing the doubts that had beset Ramage since he first heard the Corporal's proud boasts: he had too many men. He needed Stafford in Amiens, but he dare not leave Rossi and Jackson behind here at the *Chapeau Rouge* in Boulogne: if they were questioned they would give themselves away. Unless they hid on board the *Marie,* ready to sail to England with his reports! He was angry with himself for not –

'You need the man who is the picklock,' Louis said. 'If you could leave the other two behind, Dyson can hide them on board the *Marie*: they can be his crew if he has to go to the rendezvous. If you need a third man in case of trouble, I know the road well enough . . .'

Ramage stared at the Frenchman. 'But the risk for you would be enormous! I can't – '

'No greater than the risk you are taking,' Louis interrupted. 'One can be guillotined only once. I – '

'Once is enough,' Ramage said sharply.

Louis shook his head. 'I am content to share the risks that you take. We agree that our interests are similar – the smugglers' and the British Admiralty's – and I've just told you of *Ça Ira.* So listen to an idea which I'm sure will work and which is based on just you, the man Stafford and myself going to Amiens. You are an Italian who owns a large shipyard in Genoa. At the request of the French authorities there you came to Boulogne with your foreman to make arrangements to bring up all your carpenters and shipwrights – a score of them – and their tools.

'Very well, you arrived in Boulogne, made your inspection, and decided you and your men can help build the barges and gunboats – even improve and speed up the methods being used. But you are not satisfied with the wages or conditions you have been offered, so you want to return to Paris – you came by that route – to visit the Ministry of Marine and negotiate better terms.

'Now, we have to account for my presence. I am – ' Louis's mouth curved down in a wry smile, 'I am a representative of the Committee for Public Safety, making sure you do not get up to mischief! Of course you do not know I am your guardian; you think I am a representative of the Ministry of Marine. Yes, that story would go down well with the gendarmes; I wink at them confidentially and show my papers and whisper a few words about Italians so they think they are helping the Committee. Well, how do you like my little plot?'

'Well enough,' Ramage said slowly, 'except that it will not stand up to a moment's investigation in Boulogne or Paris.

If the gendarmes checked with the shipyard – '

'*No* arrangement we can make will stand such checking,' Louis said emphatically. 'The best we can do is to have such a good story that they accept it the moment we tell it, and accept our papers. There is no problem about papers, and our whole purpose is to have a story that is slightly unusual yet completely probable: something only just outside the limits of their experience, yet well within their comprehension. There is not a man between here and Paris who wouldn't understand and believe the story I am suggesting.'

'Supposing we met someone who knew you?' Ramage said doubtfully.

'What if we *did*? That is the advantage of choosing the Committee of Public Safety for me: they work secretly and use the most unlikely people – Joseph Le Bon was once a priest! And we have the papers' – he pointed to the packet he had put on the beds – 'with the correct heading and stamps.'

'You certainly have a variety of stationery.'

'We need it. Although the French government does not harass us when we smuggle French goods to England – they are only too glad to get English currency – they do not approve of us smuggling English goods into France. They demand a heavy Customs duty. So we pay enough to keep people quiet, but for the rest we need documents so we can deliver our goods without difficulties. A mason with a cartload of stone, a charcoal burner with logs, a farmer selling a load of hay – they all need documents, and if they are going to another town they need passports so that the cases of whisky and bales of wool underneath will not be discovered. Liberty, Fraternity, Bureaucracy – they were the watchwords of the Revolution. The pen is mightier than the sword,' he said sarcastically.

He picked up the quill pen and tapped his teeth with it. 'Now, how does my plan sound to you?'

'It sounds excellent,' Ramage said, 'but you're taking an enormous risk!'

'If anything goes wrong,' Louis said cheerfully, 'we'll all ride in the same tumbril, and can cheer each other up.'

Ramage thought for a moment. 'We'll be away several days. The *Marie* from Folkestone will be going to the rendezvous each night . . . I'd better send a report to England. I've found out how many vessels there are in Boulogne, and what each type can carry. It's little enough, but I'd better – '

'You'd better pass over every important scrap of information as you get it,' Louis interrupted grimly. 'It'll give Dyson and your two men something to do with the *Marie*. But be careful of giving too many details of our proposed journey, just in case . . .'

'I'll just mention that I have to leave Boulogne for a few days. Look, I'll write it now, and you tell Dyson that Jackson and Rossi will be down to join him in the morning, and they are to sail for the rendezvous tomorrow night.'

Louis nodded. 'Who actually delivers the report in England?'

'Jackson. He can transfer to the Folkestone *Marie*, deliver it, sail in her the following night and be back here in Dyson's boat the next morning.'

'Very well,' Louis said, 'it was fortunate I brought a pen! Now, let's get these passports and other documents completed, then I'll leave you to write your report.'

CHAPTER TEN

The two-wheeled postchaise normally carried only two people, with plenty of room for their luggage. There were grubby but comfortable cushions should they wish to sleep, and many pockets in the faded green leather upholstery in which could be stowed flasks, warm clothing, books for those hardy enough to read, and the cautious traveller's pistol, still the most reliable insurance against highwaymen and footpads. Louis had slipped all their travel documents into one such pocket, explaining later that French people were so accustomed to having a lot of papers that they became blasé.

Although the carriage, a cabriolet, was open in the front so that the passengers had a good view of the road and countryside, it smelled stuffy, a mixture of mildew and boiled cabbage. Louis sat on one side and Ramage on the other, with Stafford in the middle, so that no matter which side an inquiring gendarme opened the door, Stafford would not be expected to speak. Having told the coachman all about the two Italian passengers – with suitable winks and hints – Louis ensured that he would be able to describe various things of interest along the road without arousing suspicion.

The number of shops and houses that had been damaged or destroyed in the town of Boulogne had not been obvious in Ramage's walk round the port area. He assumed at first that it was the result of bombardment by British ships; then he saw that much of the damage could not have been caused by gunfire from seaward because other buildings or hills were in the way.

As the carriage rattled along the narrow cobbled streets and out through the town gates, Louis explained that it had happened in the early days of the Revolution: houses and shops owned by people accused of being anti-Revolutionary or pro-British were looted and then destroyed. Both Boulogne and Calais had suffered for their age-old association with the British, Louis said in a low voice, careful that the coachman could not hear. Even the shouted accusation of a jealous rival was enough to start the mob burning a shop or warehouse. And churches, convents, charitable institutions – all were wrecked in the first few weeks of Revolutionary enthusiasm.

The sun was just coming up over the horizon to reveal a cloudless sky as the 'chaise reached the open countryside and passed the hamlet of Samur. Ramage felt uncomfortable in his new clothes, although they were a passably good fit. The white kerseymere breeches would have benefited by an hour's attention from a good tailor, but the boots fitted and the worsted cotton stockings were comfortable enough. The coat was tight under the armpits and the skirt was (by London standards) unfashionably long, but the light grey was just the colour an Italian man of affairs would choose for a visit to France. It seemed strange to be wearing a round hat after so many years with a three-cornered one, but they were popular in France, according to Louis.

The damage to property was not confined to Boulogne: in even the smallest village there was usually at least one shop or cottage destroyed; in the larger villages and towns the churches had suffered too, and those left standing often had a sign in front, painted in Revolutionary colours, saying 'This is a Temple of Reason and Truth.' Louis pointed out the English convent at Montreuil which had been destroyed and was now just a heap of ruins, with bushes and shrubs growing where once nuns walked and worked and prayed. Most of the ruined houses nearby belonged to British families who had formed a flourishing little colony under the *ancien régime.*

Soon the journey established its own rhythm: at each *barrière* the coachman would call the amount of the toll and Louis would pass it out to the attendant; at each post Louis alighted to inspect the new horses, usually complaining (on principle, apparently) at the condition of at least one of them. Most of the people they passed along the road were poorly dressed. Few men were less than middle-aged and most much older, which was to be expected in a country where conscription was strictly enforced, but it had another effect for which Ramage was not prepared: in the few fields that were cultivated, women were doing most of the work.

He saw an old woman leading a pair of donkeys while another, her skirts hitched up to her knees, guided the plough; a mile down the road two young girls led a horse pulling a cart laden with cordwood. He had also seen several boys, fifteen or sixteen years old, begging quite openly, and Louis had explained that most such youths refused to learn a trade, knowing they would be conscripted the moment they reached eighteen, and were already dreaming of the martial glory that Bonaparte promised them.

The whole countryside showed one effect of the Royal Navy's strict blockade: almost every forest, wood and copse had been chopped down; even isolated trees in the hedgerows had been felled and one had fallen across a cottage, where it had been left. Ragged stumps, like rotten teeth, showed Bonaparte's hunger for timber to build his invasion barges and repair his ships, although it was significant that there was no sign of the arch-shaped two-wheeled timber carriers, no train of horses hauling trunks along the roads, no trees newly felled and lopped and waiting for transport. Whatever timber was now being cut into planks at the sawyers' pits at Boulogne and Calais must have been carried a long distance – by sea from the Biscay ports or Spain? It was unlikely that many ships would get through from the Baltic, Ramage thought; the blockade was too effective. But hauling trunks a couple of hundred miles along roads such as these would take weeks.

Shortage of wood was not just a lack of planking; far more critical would be the lack of compass timber, the wood that grew in natural crooks and curves and which was vital for constructing frames and rounded bows and tapered sterns. He realized that that alone would account for the box-shaped barges; that alone meant that no master shipwright could build a bow or stern that would allow a vessel to get to windward:

apart from the bow having to butt through the water, like a goat trying to get through a hedge, every wave would try to push it aside . . .

Even though the 'chaise's wheels were large and reasonably well sprung they could do little to disguise the big potholes which jarred each man's spine; soon Ramage was just staring numbly at the countryside until, at Montreuil, they rattled over a bridge across a river which Louis said was the Canche. The name was vaguely familiar and Louis tried to provide clues. It flowed through Hesdin to its source somewhere near St Pol, he said. Hesdin? And then Ramage remembered: Agincourt was ten miles or so to the north-east and Crécy the same distance to the south-west. Crécy-en-Ponthieu, to give it the full name. Had the great forest nearby – which they would soon pass – fallen to the axe to supply the boat-yards along the coast? Bonaparte would have no reason to be sentimental about Crécy, where the English longbow-men defeated the French cavalry in 1346 . . .

At Nampont the horses were changed again and later, as they skirted the old forest, Ramage noticed that only slender saplings and undergrowth stretched as far as he could see. From Nouvion – barely five miles from the actual battlefield of Crécy, Louis told him – the land was flat and uninteresting until the Frenchman pointed to the outskirts of a small town ahead: Abbeville, he said, his voice flat and expressionless.

There were three gendarmes at the guardhouse covering the roads from Montreuil and Hesdin and, with pistols tucked in their belts, unshaven and cocked hats askew, they slouched over to the 'chaise. Two stood back while the third held out his hand for the documents, which Louis handed him with a polite greeting, answered by a non-committal grunt.

After a cursory look at the papers he muttered something to the other two men and went back to the guardhouse. Louis glanced at Ramage and nodded his head slightly, then climbed out of the carriage, followed by Ramage, who signalled to Stafford to stay where he was.

Almost at once there was a peremptory shout from the guardhouse. 'He wants all three of us,' Louis growled, and beckoned to Stafford. Inside the guardhouse there was a small, high desk behind which the gendarme was perched on a stool, his cocked hat now on a hook behind him and the papers spread open across the top of the desk, each held down by a small stone.

'Which of you is Citizen Peyrachon?'

Louis reached across to fold his two papers, jerking his head as if Ramage should not see them. 'I am Citizen Peyrachon, and you know better than to leave Committee papers lying around like that,' he snapped.

The effect on the gendarme was startling, and Ramage saw that even he lived in terror of the Committee of Public Safety. The man slid off the stool as though it had been kicked from under him, and with what seemed to be one single movement he had his hat on his head and was offering Louis his papers, placating a member of the secret police.

'Of course, Citizen!' he said hastily. 'I have not checked the papers of the other two but . . .'

'I vouch for them, but check their papers; you have your duty to perform,' Louis said sternly.

The man snatched the first passport. 'Citizen di Stefano?'

'I am Signor di Stefano,' Ramage said pompously.

The gendarme slid a piece of paper across the desk towards him and dipped a quill in a bottle of ink. 'Would you please sign your name?'

With a flourish Ramage wrote 'Gianfranco di Stefano,' and passed the pen to Stafford, who wrote his assumed name beneath with all the assurance of a skilled actor.

The gendarme straightened his hat and compared the signatures with those on the two remaining passports. He ran a finger down the travel documents, folded them all and handed them back to Louis. '*Cela suffit, Citoyen,*' he said, 'have a good journey.' Louis took the documents and with a curt grunt turned on his heel and walked back to the carriage, as if he had bestowed a favour on the gendarme.

The coachman whipped up the horses and the 'chaise clattered through the cobbled streets of Abbeville. It was a wretched and gloomy town, depressing in its squalor. Many of the houses were wooden and bare of paint, with planks hanging down loose and obviously too rotten to hold any more nails. A number of houses had their windows and doors boarded up. The whole town looked as though half its inhabitants had fled several years ago at the rumour of an approaching invader and never returned. And that, Ramage realized, remembering Joseph Le Bon, was almost what happened; except that the enemy had been their own people, and Abbeville had been ravaged by fratricide, not war.

As they reached the square Louis pointed up at a long

balcony which ran the length of the first floor of a house, and then imitated a woman primping her hair and adjusting her hat, and Ramage knew that it was from there that the women of the town had watched the execution which had been delayed for their benefit by Joseph Le Bon. Louis stared ahead as the carriage passed the place where his wife had been beheaded.

Once through the square the 'chaise swung inland after running parallel with the coast for eighty kilometres and followed the valley of the River Somme. Nine miles beyond Abbeville they reached Ailly, and while the horses were being changed Louis pointed out the Red Cap of Liberty perched on top of the weathercock, which swung in the wind a point either side of south-west, reminding Ramage of a patient schoolmaster shaking his head in reproof.

A few miles farther on Ramage and Stafford saw their second symbol of the Revolution: Flixecourt, a village otherwise indistinguishable from most of the others on the Paris road, boasted its own Tree of Liberty. The damp air – probably helped by night mists from the River Somme – had rusted the metal trunk and branches, as though Liberty at Flixecourt had passed the autumn of its days and was now well into winter. Louis laughed bitterly at Ramage's comment and said: 'It began rusting the day the blacksmith finished making it!'

The coachman reined in at Picquigny for the last change of horses before Amiens and, to Ramage's surprise, began cursing the postmaster, swearing he would never reach Amiens before the curfew with such spavined and broken-winded beasts. Louis climbed out to add his voice to the protest. Two gendarmes strolled over to listen and were promptly involved by Louis, who invited them to note that the postmaster's villainy would be the cause of them reaching Amiens after the curfew, but they refused to become involved. With that Louis reached inside the 'chaise and took out his papers, beckoning to the gendarmes. There was a whispered conversation, with much nodding towards Ramage, who caught the phrase 'Committee of Public Safety,' and a few moments later both men walked over to the postmaster and told him peremptorily to provide good horses. The postmaster nodded sullenly and went back to the stable, signalling the coachman to follow him. 'Choose for yourself,' he mumbled, 'I cannot help it if the horses they provide are broken-winded. It happens to all of us at a certain age, and these horses are no exception.'

An hour later, with the sun setting behind them, they saw Amiens Cathedral high above the city, the sun's last rays turning the stone of the tall spires into pinnacles of pink marble. And then, with an almost startling suddenness as the sun dropped below the horizon, the city was in shadow; the Cathedral spires became menacing and stark grey fingers towering over narrow streets. Somewhere below them would be jail cells and police headquarters, guillotines and Trees of Liberty. Although France was at war, Ramage knew by now that the enemy the French people were still incited to fight in almost daily exhortations was not the English but almost every aspect of their lives before the Revolution: anything connected with the *ancien régime,* and a lot more besides.

The Church – although according to Louis there was talk of Bonaparte allowing the priests some freedom after recently signing the Concordat with the Pope – was obviously still a major enemy, and perhaps the hardest for the Revolution to fight (although by now the one from which it had least to fear), since both Church and priest had until a few years ago been so much part of people's lives. Charitable institutions were also the enemy; their almshouses and hospitals had been destroyed or taken over. Anyone faintly connected with the aristocracy had long since fled abroad or taken a tumbril to the guillotine and, Louis had told him, so had many people whose only connection with the aristocracy had been proud boasts of high-born relatives, boasts made before the Revolution and frequently imaginary, intended only to impress the neighbours.

The main enemy, the one said to lurk round every corner, was the anti-Revolutionary. To be so denounced to the local Committee of Public Safety or the police put any man's life in peril, since all too many tribunals set up by the Committees – there was one in every town – listened to the charges and, like Joseph Le Bon, either refused to listen to the evidence or disregarded it, along with any defence. The general view was that the guillotine settled any doubts: the thump of a head dropping into the basket was the sound that secured the Revolution from plotters. The guillotine was also a great boon to a man heavily in debt, Louis had said bitterly. It was surprising how many creditors were strapped down on the 'Widow' after being denounced by debtors, and equally surprising how many grocers and bakers and butchers expanded their businesses after their rivals were judged to be plotting against the Revolution.

All the facts that Louis had told him last night in that tiny room at the Chapeau Rouge in Boulogne, all the horrifying examples he had cited of the tribunals at work (not least the one that sent his own wife to her death), seemed to take on a new and more immediate meaning as the horses trotted towards Amiens. In Boulogne there had been risks. He never forgot for a moment that he was in an enemy country – the sudden unexpected arrival of the gendarme at the door yesterday morning had been a frightening enough reminder. But somehow Amiens seemed different; although for the moment he was not sure why, he was beginning to feel uneasy. Was it because Amiens was well inland, away from escape by sea? No, that was absurd; he was not a turtle that had to be near water. Nor was it due to the sheer size of the city.

It must be the atmosphere which, even from this distance and viewed from a jogging 'chaise, seemed sinister and full of foreboding. If he was taken prisoner and locked in the room of a house, with an armed sentry at the door, obviously he would feel trapped and more than aware of the danger he was in. But supposing he was taken prisoner in the same circumstances and locked in a cell in a fortress with an armed sentry at the door: he would be in no more and no less danger – but the heavy, cold atmosphere of a fortress cell would frighten him more, as if the sheer bulk of a fortress was menacing.

He wished he could talk about it to Louis; he was certain the Frenchman would understand his uneasiness. But whispered conversations as they approached the city would puzzle the coachman and might arouse his suspicions, even though he had been a jovial enough fellow so far. That was another reason for unease: everyone had been comparatively jovial while the 'chaise rattled along the road from Boulogne, but once it approached the shadows of Amiens itself the joviality had vanished – even the coachman had flared up at the postmaster at Picquigny – and for Ramage it had been replaced with a grey fear that came like evening mist in a valley, something that just formed without apparent effort or movement.

Louis pulled out his watch. 'We will be in just before the curfew, unless one of these horses goes lame.'

The Hotel de la Poste was in a street barely a hundred yards from the Cathedral, whose spires, more than 350 feet high, made the few clouds in the darkening sky seem torn pennons streaming from cavalrymen's lances. The owner, a surly man with sharp, shrewd eyes and who bore no resemblance to his Corporal brother in Boulogne, made no secret of the fact that his inn was almost empty, although he made it clear that that was no reason why anyone should expect the kind of service given in Paris. From the way he said it, he obviously had a hatred of Paris which extended to anyone who might be going to or coming from the city.

He rubbed the palms of his hands on his green baize apron as he inspected the three small bags the coachman handed down and then gave a contemptuous sniff, and Ramage guessed that despite his Revolutionary fervour, *m'sieur le patron* still judged the prosperity of his guests by the reliable *ancien régime* yardstick of the quantity and quality of their baggage.

Ramage left Louis to arrange the rooms and the Frenchman went into one of his now familiar winks-and-nods consulations with the owner, ending up by producing an almost cheerful look on the Norman's face when he heard they would be staying several days, accepting without question the explanation that the Italian wanted to visit some of the factories to look into the possibility of arranging a regular supply of the plush, woollen stuffs and goat-hair costumes for which Amiens was famous and all of which were hard to buy in Italy, though in great demand. Louis then spoiled the effect by adding a last flourish, saying that once his business was done here, Signor di Stefano would go on to Paris to conclude his business with the Ministry of Marine. The Norman gave a prodigious sniff which made it clear that nothing good ever happened in Paris, least of all to Italians. Picking up the lightest of the bags he led the way to the staircase.

There had been no sign of the innkeeper's daughter, although the Corporal's description of the shrewdness of his prosperous brother had proved accurate so far. Ramage wished he knew which room the *lieutenant-de-vaisseau* occupied during his twice-weekly visits: he had the impression that it would always be the same one, so that the linen need not be changed too frequently. The Corporal's brother

134

would be up to all those tricks, and probably more of his own devising – as became a successful hotelier, the Corporal would say with pride.

The room he was to share with Stafford was large and high-ceilinged, a domed bedstead standing in one corner with faded blue silk curtains and counterpane. Another bed, little more than a wooden frame made up with a mattress and a matching counterpane, stood in another corner, with a chest of drawers against the wall between them. A round table with four chairs in the centre of the room completed the furnishings, apart from long and faded green velvet curtains at the windows which had been washed so often that the remaining nap looked like patches of incipient mildew, and a threadbare carpet covering most of the floor. Ramage was relieved to notice that none of the floorboards creaked. Would the *lieutenant-de-vaisseau*'s room be furnished in the same way – with equally silent floorboards? He was thankful for Louis's shrewdness in demanding to be shown several rooms before deciding which they would take: the first two, on the floor above, were too small; two others on this same floor (the door of a third remained locked) were the same as the room he was in: a large and small bed, one chest of drawers, one table and four chairs. All the windows were tightly shut, so that each room smelled musty with the hint of trapped odours from the kitchen reminding Ramage that meals would be served in their rooms. It was a French habit for which he was thankful: dining-rooms were a danger because it was too easy for gendarmes to glance round at the diners as often as they wished, and conversation had to be guarded, with Stafford silent.

As Louis and the innkeeper left the room they were discussing the supper to be served for all three of them in Ramage's room in half an hour's time, and when Ramage shut the door behind them Stafford whispered: 'All right if I talk, sir?'

'Yes – just keep your voice down and listen for footsteps in the corridor.'

Ramage waited, and when the Cockney began unpacking his bag, emptying the contents on to the smaller bed but remaining silent, Ramage said: 'What were you going to say?'

Stafford looked round in surprise: ' Oh, there wasn't nothing I wanted to say right now, sir; it's just sitting in the coach not being able to say nothing that's so aggravatering.'

'Aggravating,' Ramage corrected automatically, long since accustomed to the Cockney's mispronunciations. 'Well, make the best of this evening because you'll have to be silent tomorrow.'

'Aye aye, sir,' Stafford said, walking over to the door and kneeling down, as though looking through the keyhole. He opened the door quietly and just enough to be able to look at the edge of the lock. Then he shut the door and walked back to his bed, picking up a small bag made of soft leather and pulling open the drawstring. He shook out several small strips of metal which had the ends bent into various shapes, picked one up and examined it, grunted and put them all back in the bag.

Ramage was unsure how to interpret the grunt and asked: 'Can you manage that kind of lock?'

Stafford looked hurt. 'Wiv a bent pin held in me toes, sir,' he said contemptuously.

That evening, after the innkeeper and his painfully thin wife had cleared away the supper and left the room, Ramage said, 'I haven't eaten a meal like that for a very long time. At least some good chefs survived the Revolution!'

'Wait until you see the bill,' Louis cautioned. 'Innkeepers are the new bankers . . .'

Ramage patted his stomach reflectively. 'Jowl of salmon, sole, roast pigeon, *bouillie* beef – I haven't had that for years – and roast fowl. Picardy beer – not much body to it, admittedly, but nice enough if you treat it as small beer – and Volnay wine. Better than salt pork and pease, eh, Stafford?'

The Cockney belched happily, his eyes slightly out of focus. 'Never tasted sole like that, and that there bully beef, or whatever you call it. Beer ain't up to much, like you say, sir, but the wine – ' he looked down at his empty glass, 'well, it'd ease the journey down a bumpy road, I reckon. Thought they was short of food!'

'Make no mistake,' Louis said, 'they are. There were food riots in many towns last year. This man Jobert knows where to get the delicacies – and he pays a high price. You can get anything – if you have the money. The ordinary people though: many of them have less than your people in England.'

'Nice to be rich,' Stafford commented contentedly, 'even if only for a few hours!'

Ramage pushed the carafe towards him. 'You and Louis

had better finish that up, but don't expect to eat like that every night we're here!'

Stafford shook his head. 'Once in a lifetime's enough, sir. Cor, wait until I tell the lads.' He topped up Louis's glass and then filled his own, and after putting the carafe down, carefully he raised his glass and looked Ramage straight in the eye.

''Ere's to you, sir, an' the Marcheezer, an' may you both live to a ripe hold hage – '

Louis reached for his glass, but Stafford had not finished. 'I'm a bit tipsy, sir, an' I ain't very good wiv words, but the other lads – not just Jacko and Rosey, but all the rest of them – well, they'd want me ter thank you for gettin' them out of trouble so often – ' He saw the puzzled expression on Ramage's face and hurriedly explained. 'Well, like when we rescued the Marcheezer, and then when that Don rammed us in the *Kathleen*, and the privateers at St Lucia with the *Triton*, an' the 'urricane, an' that skylarking in the Post Office brig . . .'

As if startled at the length of his speech he hurriedly gulped his wine, followed by Louis, and put his glass down nervously.

Ramage held out his own empty glass, and Louis poured some wine.

'Here's to you and the lads,' Ramage said soberly, not trusting himself to say more.

Louis finished his glass and said: 'Before we sleep, we should think of our plan for tomorrow.'

Ramage nodded. 'Since it's a Saturday, the *patron* won't expect us to try to do any business at the factories, so we'll establish ourselves as visitors. We can have a look at the Cathedral – after all, it's the biggest in France, and even though the Church is not popular here, we Italians are God-fearing people! After that we'll make sure we know all the roads leading away from this hotel, and you must find out where we can hire horses in an emergency – steal them, if necessary.'

He paused for a minute or two, deep in thought. 'Stafford has his picklocks; we have wax in case we have to break and repair a seal, candles, and the little lantern. You have that thin-bladed knife and each of us has a heavier one. Pen, paper and ink to copy any documents. Plaster and some box-wood in case we have to carve a copy of a seal, and the chisels and gouges. You have the sheets of notepaper with the

Ministry of Marine heading . . . Can you think of anything else?'

When Louis shook his head, Ramage asked Stafford: 'You have everything you might want?'

'Me picklocks, some thin wire, a spatula an' me fingers; that's all I need, sir.'

CHAPTER ELEVEN

Next morning Louis left them after explaining that he was going to make the necessary arrangements while Ramage and Stafford wandered through the city, establishing themselves as innocent visitors. The short walk to the great Cathedral was almost frightening. The whole city seemed to be silent and foreboding; silent although horses' hooves clattered over the cobbles and cartwheels rumbled; although people walked the streets talking to each other and shopkeepers stood at their doorways, calling out greetings and trying to beguile prospective customers.

There were a few of the noises one would expect in a city; but in an almost deserted city. These were not the noises of a normal city going about its daily business, and he and Stafford had almost reached the Cathedral before Ramage realized exactly what was missing: no one was laughing and no one was bustling: it was as though everyone had a secret guilt and feared that the pairs of gendarmes who seemed to stand at every corner were watching and waiting to make an arrest; that they knew only too well there was among the quiet streets of Amiens a building with barred windows where a man who laughed loudly or joked or behaved in a carefree manner might be dragged before a tribunal and accused of being an enemy of the Revolution.

But surely these people in the streets *were* the Revolution: surely it was for them, the *sans-culottes*, that the Revolution had been staged? With the aristocrats dead or exiled and their estates sold off to the people, with every man proclaimed as free and equal as his neighbour, and the armies of France standing astride Europe from the Mediterranean to the North Sea, surely now was the time for the people to be happy? Yet Ramage sensed that these people in Amiens were far from carefree; they were nervous and suspicious of each other, and looked at those gendarmes not as protectors against burglars, cutpurses and pickpockets but as honest men might be wary of large and unknown dogs.

Louis had told him all this; indeed, he had explained it with great care. Ramage admitted to himself that it had been easy enough to listen but too hard to visualize; one had to see it to believe it.

The majority of the French people had supported the idea of the Revolution: for generations under the monarchy taxation had been harsh and arbitrary, with the poorest always paying the most. But there had been such a struggle for power after the Revolution: such almost unbelievable cruelties and injustices committed with chilling cynicism in the name of the Revolution by those very leaders, as each struggled for personal power, that the people were bewildered and disillusioned. Debtors denouncing their creditors to avoid paying their bills, vicious men settling old scores by the same means – the people had seen too much of it. Louis must be right – the majority of them were sick of the metallic hiss and thud of the guillotine, sick of passing a tumbril laden with white-faced men and weeping women. This was an aspect of the Revolution they had never visualized and never wanted – seeing former neighbours (and often former friends and sometimes relatives) dragged off to the Widow . . . This bore no relation to getting rid of the tyrannical landowners and the iniquitous tax collectors of the *ancien régime*; it had nothing to do with driving out the grasping priests and seizing the vast lands owned by the Church.

But in several cases the grasping priests had cast off the soutane, snatched up the Red Cap of Liberty and returned – in the role of rabid Revolutionaries. Joseph Le Bon, the former *curé*, had probably killed more innocent Frenchmen in the time of the Revolution than Bonaparte's Army of Italy lost in the march to Rome; and Joseph Fouché, former *abbé* of Nantes and professor at its university, was now the Minister of Police and the most feared man in France. It was, Ramage reflected, as though the old fierceness of the Inquisition readily converted into Revolutionary zeal; merely a question of changing the Church's rack for the State's guillotine in the determination either to command men's souls or kill their bodies. As with the Inquisition so with the Revolution: mere acceptance was not enough; one had to be a zealot.

As he and Stafford side-stepped to avoid three pimply boys who were begging, watched without interest by the gendarmes, he realized that although no one seemed to be starving, few were wearing clothes which had not been carefully darned.

A cool and supercilious look at the outside of the Cathedral. Two more gendarmes standing fifteen yards from the main door watching lethargically, although a strange face was a reason for them slowly swivelling their heads to relieve the boredom. One removed his tricorn and inspected the inside before replacing it on his head.

The outside of the Cathedral had suffered the sort of damage you would expect from excited schoolboys drunk for the first time on Calvados: the heads of all the saints had been smashed off and sculptured groups had been crudely mutilated in an attempt to make them look ridiculous. Yet it was an attempt that was itself ridiculous, since the Cathedral had stood for nearly six hundred years, massive and graceful. Disfiguring the small, sculptured groups had as much effect on its majesty as a man relieving himself against a buttress.

Ramage walked through the main door, and despite the gloom saw at once that the great altarpiece spreading the whole breadth of the Cathedral was untouched. As he noted that the beautiful chapels on either side of the choir also appeared to be undamaged he saw five people kneeling. Four seemed to be old women, the fifth a crippled man, one of his legs stuck out sideways. A wooden leg. Their presence emphasized the vastness and the emptiness and the silence: there was none of the distant chanting or murmuring that you usually heard the moment you entered the main door of a great cathedral: simply the chilling silence of an abandoned building . . . As he walked towards the altar he saw that the famous marble statue of the weeping child had been damaged. The altar was bare – not surprisingly the Revolutionaries had taken the gold and silver candlesticks, and the rich red and purple hangings had vanished. Yet the stained-glass windows were mostly intact – a gap here and there in the delicate lacework of coloured glass showed where an eager fellow with a strong arm had lobbed a brick or fired a fowling-piece.

The crippled man hauled himself up with the clumsiness of pain and began hobbling towards the main door, but seeing Ramage and Stafford he waved his stick as if in greeting. He was tall, though his shoulders were now hunched; his hair was grey and his face lined, but Ramage guessed that pain and worry – or was it sadness? – had aged him more than the passing years.

'Good morning, Citizen,' he said carefully, as though wanting to pass the time of day but wary and unsure, like a man half afraid he was about to be accused of trespassing. Ramage thought of the two gendarmes near the main door. Perhaps they were more interested in visitors to the Cathedral than they seemed: a man attending church, albeit without there being a priest present, could be a man against the Revolution . . .

Ramage shook hands and, guessing that the man could satisfy his curiosity about the Cathedral's fate during the Revolution, waved towards the altar: 'Things have changed since I was last here.'

'You are not French. Italian, perhaps?'

Ramage nodded. 'From Genoa. I've been to Boulogne; now I go to Paris and then back home.'

'Italy . . . at the pass of Mont Cenis –' the man tapped his wooden leg with his stick '– that's where I left this leg.'

Was there fighting up among the Alps? Who would be crazy enough to have a battle among the mountains? The man saw his puzzled look and said: 'The snow – my regiment was part of the Army of Italy. We marched over the mountains in thick snow. Some of us were too weak to get over the pass . . .' He glanced at Stafford, uncertain whether to go on.

'And the weak ones were left behind?' Ramage asked quietly.

The man nodded. 'If an arm or a leg freezes it dies, and if it isn't amputated quickly gangrene sets in. It can set in even if it is amputated. I was lucky.'

'They carried you in a wagon?' Ramage asked innocently, hoping to draw the man out.

'They left me in the snow, just where I collapsed. There was a monastery nearby,' he added, almost absently. 'After the Army had gone the monks came along the pass to see what had been left behind. Not looking for loot, you understand; they were interested only in saving lives. They found me – and seventeen more like me. They carried us back to the monastery. They couldn't save my leg, but they saved my life. They had very little food, but they shared it with us – with eighteen atheists who up to a few hours earlier had belonged to the 24th *Infanterie de Ligne*. They nursed us and fed us and sheltered us. For the five of us that needed them, they made legs of wood, specially carved and fitted. It was five months before I was well again – and by then spring had come and the snow had melted and I could leave . . .'

'So you returned to your regiment?'

'With one leg?' He knew Ramage was encouraging him to talk and he smiled. 'There was war in Italy and war in Austria – there was war almost everywhere; but there was peace in the monastery near the top of Mont Cenis, so I stayed and tried to pay my debt. I helped hoe and sow and reap the year's harvest – it's a very brief season – and I left the following spring, when the snow had once again cleared, just a year and a half after I first arrived. I got back to my home here in Amiens as winter began; it was a long walk for a one-legged man.'

'But your family was glad to see you.'

'I found that my family was dead.' Again that flat, expressionless tone of voice. 'My brother and my wife had been denounced as anti-Revolutionaries and guillotined, and the shock had killed my old father . . .'

'Who denounced them?'

'The man who wanted our grocery shop,' he said simply. 'He is now the prefect of Amiens and the most powerful man in the city.'

'And you?' Ramage asked quietly. 'What do you do?'

The man glanced at the statue of the weeping child for a few moments, and then at the old women who were still kneeling. 'I come each morning and pray; I pray as I did before the Revolution and I pray as I learned to at the monastery. I pray for the souls of those I loved, and I have one other prayer which I can reveal to no man.' No flourish, no drama; just a plain statement by a man no longer afraid.

Louis had become an atheist at the Revolution; but now he prayed, too; he prayed that there was an after-life, so that Joseph Le Bon would be eternally punished. Had Le Bon worked here in Amiens?

'I have met men who have prayed for Citizen Le Bon,' Ramage said in a voice barely above a whisper.

The man's eyes held his. 'I'm sure you have; many true Normans say a prayer for him before they go to sleep at night.'

The man had spoken freely because he was beyond fear. At first he had been cautious – probably because he saw no reason to invite trouble – but Ramage thought he would probably talk as freely to a gendarme. Such a man had nothing more to lose to a régime which had abandoned him in the snow of an Alpine pass and slaughtered his wife and brother (and, to all intents and purposes, stolen the family business). Fortune held none of his family hostage because now he had none to submit. With one leg chopped off above the knee, he must find it hard to make a living – Louis had said something about the wounded being reduced to begging once the Navy or Army had finished with them, the same as it was in Britain – so threatening such a man with the guillotine was about the same as offering him a swift release from his misery.

Ramage glanced round at the great interior of the Cathedral. 'I expected to find more damage . . .'

The man smiled grimly. 'You haven't heard the story, then? It's one of which we Normans are proud. When the Revolutionary Army arrived from Paris after sacking and looting the churches and *châteaux* along the route, the people of Amiens decided they were going to save their Cathedral. The tocsin was sounded, the National Guard of Amiens assembled, and with drums beating they met the *sans-culottes*, who had already begun their work – you can see the damage they did to some of the statuary.

'Well, there was a pitched battle right here, where we are standing, and the people of Amiens drove them out and mounted guard over the Cathedral, to make sure no further damage was done. Eventually the Army left to carry out their evil business elsewhere, but the leaders in Paris learned their lesson: they could drive out the priests, chase off the bishop, steal the gold and silver ornaments – but they must leave us our Cathedral.'

He looked round at the four old women. 'Yes, you are right to be puzzled: how is it that in our city of 14,000 people – that is all that are left now – you find only four women and a cripple in the largest Cathedral in France and for which the people fought the Army? I'm not sure myself; I only know that the reason is complex. The Cathedral has stood here since 1220 – it *is* Amiens; the city has grown up in its shadow. But since the Revolution the Church as an organization has been regarded as anti-Revolutionary.

'Those that want to pray – well, they find it safer to pray in the privacy of their homes. A few, like those old widows –' he gestured at the women – 'are beyond caring what goes on in Paris, or in the rest of France: the Revolution has taken their sons and grandsons, and they have nothing more to lose. They refuse to surrender the only solace left to them. You could say they refuse to give up the habit of a life-time . . .'

He held out his hand and as Ramage shook it he said, 'They say Citizen Bonaparte has signed some agreement with the Pope, and we might be allowed to have a priest soon; per-haps even a bishop. But who knows – ' he shrugged his shoul-ders. 'At least they haven't locked the doors of the churches, even though they watch us.'

With that he left, and the only sound in the vast Cathedral was the click of his sticks and the muffled, dragging thump of his wooden leg. Somewhere out in the streets of Amiens, Louis, the man who had lost a wife at the hands of Le Bon, was talking secretly with men who, if they had not been be-reaved, at least had good reasons for working against the present régime. Ramage understood then that an ally was simply someone who shared the same aim, even if his motives were different.

Back in the Hotel de la Poste Ramage pulled off his boots and flopped back on the bed while Stafford poured water into a basin to wash his face.

'Whatcher make of it all, sir?' he asked, towelling his face vigorously. 'The town, I mean. Gives me the creeps. Like being in a graveyard.'

For all their long walk round the city after the visit to the Cathedral, they had been unable to talk for fear Stafford's voice would give them away, and Ramage had been curious to know how it all seemed to someone with the Cockney's straightforward and uncomplicated approach to life.

'It's about as I'd expect a city to be if an enemy was occupying it.'

'That's what puzzles me, sir,' Stafford said, hanging up the towel. 'After all, wasn't this 'ere Revolution supposed to make it better for 'em? In Boolong an' 'ere and all the places we went through, everyone 'ad a face as long as a yard o' pump water. Why, they've got as much food as we 'ave in Eng-land but not one in five score can squeeze a grin an' I don't reckon none of 'em knows how to laugh – '

He paused a moment, listening to footsteps outside in the corridor: the sharp thud of booted heels and the jingle of

144

spurs, the measured tread of a heavier man wearing lighter shoes, and what were obviously a woman's footsteps. The men's voices were little more than murmurs; the woman's voice was excited. There was silence for a few moments, then a door opened and shut.

The *lieutenant-de-vaisseau* had arrived. M'sieur Jobert was taking him to his room and Jobert's enamoured daughter was dancing attendance. What dispatches was the galloping lieutenant carrying to Paris?

Ramage had asked himself the question ironically, but as he thought about it he felt a chill of real fear creeping through him: up to now, thanks to Louis, the whole expedition had been successful enough, but up to now it had not really started. It was six o'clock and the lieutenant probably left for Paris by six o'clock tomorrow morning. Ramage had twelve hours in which he might be able to read the dispatches – and twelve hours during which he or Stafford might be caught as a spy . . . or find that the lieutenant carried not secret dispatches from Admiral Bruix to the First Consul, but dozens of the dreary reports required each week by the French Ministry of Marine's equivalent of the Navy Board. The frigate *Junon* reporting that a cask of salt beef marked '154' contained eleven fewer pieces; the sloop *Requin* reporting that seaman Charles Leblanc had deserted; the cutter *Mignon* asking for the third time for a bolt of canvas to patch her ancient mainsail. All navies floated in a sea of forms; it always amazed him that when a ship fired a broadside a thousand quill pens did not fly across the sea in place of round-shot.

He heard Jobert and his daughter walk past the door again, no doubt returning downstairs to start preparing supper. The lieutenant would be busy with soap and water, razor and comb, doing a self-refit after his long ride, making himself ready for supper.

Supper! Would he, too, eat in his room? He certainly would! In a moment Ramage saw his plans shredded: the lieutenant would have supper served in his room with the daughter (and the mother as chaperone). The *patron* might join him later, and after the ladies had retired to bed both men would probably settle down to an evening's drinking and conversation. The wretched courier might not quit his room until he left the hotel in the morning to climb on board his damned horse and steer for Paris. Which meant that the risks increased a thousandfold: Stafford would have to wait for him to go to sleep and then break into the room (admittedly that would be easy) and then, while the lieutenant slept, find the leather pouch and get it out. And surely the lieutenant would put it somewhere safe. Even tucking it under the mattress at the foot or head of his bed (anywhere else would make an uncomfortable bulge with these thin feather mattresses) would be bad enough: Stafford would need a light, and even a shielded lantern increased the risk enormously since the smell of a smoky candle might well rouse a sleeping man.

He sat up suddenly, as if physical movement would ease the tension, and Stafford glanced round. 'You all right, sir?' he asked anxiously, seeing Ramage's expression.

Keep the ship's company cheerful, Ramage told himself; don't alarm Stafford, who has the most dangerous job. A confident man succeeds where a nervous man is bound to fail. At that moment there was a double tap on the door and Louis came in, a ribald greeting on his lips for the benefit of anyone outside. He shut the door carefully and grinned.

'Was your tour of Amiens successful?'

'Interesting – we weren't doing anything in particular!'

'Visiting the Cathedral, talking to a man suspected of being an anti-Revolutionary, having lunch in a café frequented by agents of the Church . . .'

'We were being watched, then?' Ramage asked ruefully.

Louis shrugged his shoulders and continued speaking in French. 'No more than any other strangers walking round the city. The gendarmes are at every corner solely to keep an eye on everyone, and they report before they go off duty.'

'How do you know what they reported?' Ramage asked curiously.

'I have friends,' the Frenchman said with a wink. 'But don't worry, no one suspects you. As soon as you both left the Cathedral, the gendarmes checked that you were staying here and that your papers were in order. I'm only telling you so that you have an idea of how these people work. You are not used to a country where everyone is a potential spy, and where some men make a good living by acting as police informers.'

He sat down at the table and reached for the wine bottle. 'Well, our friend the lieutenant has arrived.'

'We heard him go to his room. He's still there,' Ramage

added gloomily. 'I've just realized he may have his supper there, too.'

'That would have made it difficult for Stafford, eh?'

'Of course it would – and may,' Ramage said sharply, irritated by the Frenchman's bantering tone.

'On the contrary,' Louis said cheerfully. 'Instead of the lieutenant eating in his room and we eating in ours, you and I will be eating downstairs at the same table. You'll be able to meet the lieutenant – and the landlord's pretty daughter. Who knows, you might make the lieutenant jealous!'

The Frenchman thought of everything. Ramage was both relieved and yet irritated: he hated being in another man's hands. He had commanded his own ship for too many years to like having the initiative taken out of his own hands. In the past he had received his orders and was accustomed to the brief nod of acknowledgment when he succeeded and had always been ready for the blame if he failed. But here in France, here on enemy soil, his world was turned upside down.

He had his orders, yes, and damnably difficult orders they were. Putting the success of his arrival in France in the hands of a smuggler – yes, that was unavoidable and had been anticipated by Lord Nelson. But being in the hands of another smuggler, a Frenchman into the bargain, for the rest of the operation: how could he ever explain *that* to His Lordship? Damnation, it was as much as he could do to accept it himself, even though he had absolutely no choice if he was to succeed. Well, success would be its own justification, and (he gave an involuntary shiver) if he failed the guillotine would make any explanations on his part not only unnecessary but impossible: the Admiralty would never know if it was the fault of Lieutenant Ramage, the First Consul or the fourth gendarme in the back row.

An orchestra! He grasped at the idea but knew it was a straw. Louis, Dyson, the two seamen, Stafford and himself – they were an orchestra, and unless he accepted the fact he would make his life a misery. Louis's part was making sure they did the right things in France; Stafford dealt with that part which – he could not suppress a grin – would land him in jail in London; Dyson and the two seamen looked after communications; and himself – well, he was the conductor. He waved his baton, having made sure everyone was playing the same music, and generally kept an eye on the whole thing, hoping no one would blow a wrong note or drop his instrument with a loud bang.

For a few moments he felt better; then he found himself thinking once again that it was not a nightmare; he really was sitting in a room at the Hotel de la Poste in Amiens with a French smuggler and a Cockney picklock: on their efforts, cunning and skill might depend whether or not the British Government would know in good time if Bonaparte's invasion plans were propaganda – a gigantic bluff intended to tie down Britain's Channel Fleet – or a vast operation which would go into action in a matter of weeks, if not days. And which, he told himself coldly in an attempt to drive out the fears, could result in the French Army of England becoming the Army of Occupation. If life in Boulogne and Amiens were examples of what the new France did to its own people, it required very little imagination to think what the new France would do to old England. Old Britain, he corrected himself.

'Supper is at seven o'clock,' Louis said. 'Unfortunately our friend Stafford has an upset stomach and looks too ill to come down, so he will be free to get on with his work while we and the lieutenant attack the soup – onion soup, the landlord tells me; his wife's speciality. And I think you will have to retire to your bed when you begin to feel ill after the sole – the same symptoms as Stafford and due to something the two of you ate for lunch in that wretched café, no doubt. That will leave you free to inspect Stafford's work while the lieutenant and I attend to the roast sucking pig that you requested me to order specially – and which,' he said with a broad grin, holding out a hand as if to fend off Ramage's protests, 'and which is the reason why we are all supping together downstairs tonight: you ordered roast sucking pig and invited the rest of the guests in the hotel to your table.

'The lieutenant is the only guest, apart from ourselves. The landlord was very impressed with the generosity of his Italian guest: no doubt it will show on your bill,' Louis added impishly. 'I am, incidentally, a connoisseur of sucking pig: I can tell in a moment if it has tasted anything but its mother's milk; any innkeeper who tries to serve me a wretched little under-sized beast which had been fed on grain for a few days – well he had better watch out! I shall report in due course if I received value for your money!'

Ramage had never felt so hungry, onion soup had never

been so delicious – or less satisfying. The sole melted in the mouth but did damned little to soften the hunger pains in his stomach. The lieutenant, young and fair-haired with long silky moustaches, was expansive and friendly; a casual on-looker would have assumed he was the host and Ramage and Louis his guests. The innkeeper wore a new blue apron and a frilled white shirt and walked round the room beaming, his dumpy daughter's cheeks were pink with barely controlled ex-citement and her eyes danced and were shiny with love for her lieutenant.

Louis spoke little and while not appearing to eat fast managed to consume twice as much as Ramage, who was obliged from time to time to answer the lieutenant's ques-tions. The lieutenant, he swore to himself, was an expert in asking short questions that needed long answers. And all the while the delicious aroma of the sucking pig roasting on its spit wafted through every time the door between the kitchen and the small dining-room was opened. Ramage glanced at Louis and thought that if he could have had a few slices of the sucking pig he would not care if a cunning farmer had fattened the runt of a litter with grain; in fact a few slices of the toughest old sow in the whole of Normandy would be welcome.

Upstairs an even hungrier Stafford was at work: Ramage had tried to avoid thinking about the Cockney, not because he feared that he would fail but, with the French lieutenant sitting on the opposite side of the table, he had the uncomfort-able feeling that if he thought about Stafford the Frenchman would suddenly remember something he wanted from his room. He had watched him all the time the soup was on the table: a splash of onion soup down the Frenchman's stock would be enough to send him upstairs to change. Then he had worried that a glass of wine would spill, or a piece of fish drop from a fork. And all the time Louis had eaten stolidly, eyes on his plate, shoulders hunched – but, Ramage sensed, his ears missing nothing, whether a horse's hooves in the street or the crackling of dripping fat as the sucking pig turned on its spit.

The innkeeper removed the plate which had been piled with sole and a moment later – for this was the signal – Louis was looking at him anxiously. 'Are you all right, M'sieur?'

In anticipation of the question, Ramage had been sur-reptitiously holding his breath until he felt dizzy. He put a hand to his head and groaned and with his head spinning found it required no acting skill. He stood up while he still felt dizzy and in a moment Louis was beside him, solicitous and reassuring the French lieutenant.

'He and his foreman – they lunched at a café. The foreman is already ill; now M'sieur is stricken.'

Ramage, suddenly afraid that the lieutenant would insist on helping him to his room and already worried about Stafford, found it easy to simulate a retch and a moment later retched again and tasted the onion soup. He muttered in Italian, brushed away Louis's hand, told them both to continue their meal and rushed for the door, as though about to be sick. As he closed the door behind him he heard Louis telling the innkeeper with artful hypocrisy that the Italians had to take the consequences if they chose to eat in cheap cafés . . .

He managed to stop himself running up the stairs two at a time; instead he walked up slowly and heavily, groaning every now and again. Would Stafford be back in their own room or still in the lieutenant's? For all his play-acting in the dining-room he now felt genuinely queasy, as though the sole had come to life in his stomach and was swimming round vigorously in the onion soup. He recognized it as an old friend (or enemy): the queasiness he always felt when fear and food met together. 'The condemned man ate a hearty breakfast.' Good luck to him; such a man had either no imagination or a stomach of iron.

He gave the pre-arranged triple tap on their door and heard a movement in the room. A moment later the door opened and as soon as he stepped inside was closed and quietly locked by Stafford. There was nothing on the table – and nothing on his bed or Stafford's. The seaman had failed. He must have entered the room but not found the satchel. Or the lieutenant was on his way to Paris to collect dispatches, not deliver them. The queasiness increased and he belched, a vile compôte of sole and soup.

He turned to ask Stafford what had gone wrong – and saw that the man was grinning.

The Cockney walked over to the chest of drawers, pulled out the second drawer and carried it to the table. Lifting out some clothes, he produced a shiny leather satchel the size of a family Bible and with a long shoulder strap. Ramage saw that the top flap was down and the clasp was locked.

With a flourish Stafford produced a thin sliver of metal, inserted it in the keyhole and turned. The flap sprang open from the natural stiffness of the leather, and Stafford took out a dozen letters and two slim packets.

Ramage sat down at the table, his heart pounding; one half of him wanted to snatch up the envelopes and see, from the superscriptions, if there was a dispatch from Bruix to the First Consul; the other half of him shied away like a horse balking at a fence, scared to take the plunge because the consequences of there being no such dispatch meant that he would have wasted several days by believing a fool of a corporal.

Stafford tapped one of the letters. 'My French is a bit rudeemental, sir –'

'Rudimentary,' Ramage corrected him absent-mindedly.

'– rudimentally, sir, but I think this is the one you want.'

Addressed to '*Le Citoyen Pierre-Alexandre-Laurent Forfait*,' at '*Le Ministère de la Marine et des Colonies*' in Paris, a line of writing above the seal on the back showed it was a dispatch from '*Eustache Bruix, Vice-amiral, Commandant, Force Navale de Boulogne.*'

Ramage put it to one side and looked through the rest. All were addressed to various departments in the Ministry; the sender's name on the back of each indicated its mundane contents – '*L'Ordonnateur de Marine à Boulogne*,' '*Bureau des Armements et Inscription Maritime au port de Boulogne*' and so on. None was addressed to the First Consul, but Ramage was not surprised: an admiral would report to his Minister. The First Consul was the Corporal's embellishment.

Stafford was setting out his equipment – a flat spatula with a wooden handle, several sticks of sealing-wax of varying shades of red, and a thin-bladed knife. He gestured to a candle already alight and standing on the chest of drawers – it would be an hour before it was dark and Ramage had not noticed it – and said: 'All right if I close the shutters, sir?'

Ramage looked out. Anyone at several windows in the house opposite could see into the room. The thought of the watchful gendarmes in their cocked hats decided him and he pulled the shutters close.

Stafford put the candle on the table and added paper, a bottle of ink and a quill to the collection of items. Ramage picked up Bruix's letter and examined it. The blob of red wax was perhaps half an inch in diameter, and soot from the clerk's candle flame had made black streaks in it. The oval crest – the impression of an anchor with '*Rep. Fran.*' at the top and '*Marine*' below – had been carelessly applied by the clerk who canted the seal as he pressed so that the wax was wafer-thin on the left side and a quarter of an inch thick on the right. Several small blobs of wax were spattered round it, as though the clerk's hands shook – or else he was a damned clumsy or careless fellow. Ramage could imagine what would happen if a British admiral ever saw his letter sent to the First Lord of the Admiralty in such a state: the clerk would suddenly find himself at sea as a cook's mate!

Stafford was holding the spatula blade in the candle flame, moving it so the metal heated evenly. 'That the one you want opening, sir?'

The Cockney was casual, almost offhand. Ramage had no idea how the devil the man was going to open a letter sealed with the stamp of the French Navy when he did not have the seal to make a fresh impression when he closed the letter again. Was he being too offhand? Did he realize that, apart from anything else, their lives might depend on his skill? 'Yes, but will you be able to seal it again so a clerk in Paris doesn't spot anything?'

'*You* won't be able to spot anything, sir.' He reached for the envelope. 'If you'll just hold this spatchler in the flame, movin' it like so, I'll get ready.'

Ramage took the blade, watching shadows dancing over the walls, and was reminded of a magician. Stafford picked up the letter and ran his fingers over it. 'One sheet of paper folded three times, ends turned into the middle, put inside a plain sheet which is folded three times and ends folded in the middle, an' a blob o' wax to seal it. People never learn!'

'Never learn what?'

Stafford grinned impishly. 'Never learn it ain't a safe way to send a secret letter wiv people like me around!' He picked up two sheets of plain paper from his pile and compared them with the letter. ''Bout the same thickness: that's lucky.'

'Why?'

'Means we can experimentate wiv the 'eat o' that blade.' He folded the first sheet into three, and then folded the two ends inwards so that they met edge to edge in the middle, running his fingers along the folds to crease them, and making a neat packet. He then took another sheet, put the packet in the middle and folded again in the same way, holding the ends down with his finger. He picked up a stick of sealing-wax.

'Have to use the candle for a moment, sir – can you hold it for me?'

He heated the stick of wax and ran it on to seal the paper, dripping enough until he had the same thickness as on Bruix's letter. 'That's it: now, if you'll carry on hotting up the spatchler, sir . . .'

He held his own packet in one hand and Bruix's letter in the other, as though comparing the weight; then he felt each of them with the forefinger and thumb of his right hand, as a tailor would examine cloth. 'Both about the same thickness,' he commented, putting Bruix's letter to one side and his own packet in front of him, next to it. 'That's what matters.' He took a piece of cloth from his pocket. 'Let me have the spatchler, sir!'

He wiped off the soot, slid it beneath his own packet directly under the wax, and pressed down, gently pulling up one end. In a few moments, as the spatula warmed the wax through several thicknesses of paper, the end lifted and he flicked away the spatula. 'Warm it up again, will yer, sir. Just right, that was.'

'Here, let me look at that,' Ramage demanded, and Stafford passed over his packet, taking the spatula and keeping it in the flame.

Ramage looked at the blob of wax. It was still the same shape except that it was neatly divided in two, half on one end of the paper, half on the other. Stafford's spatula had been warm enough to allow him to separate the ends, but not so hot that the heat distorted the impression of the seal.

'Can you guarantee to do that with the Admiral's letter – I mean, not damage the impression?'

'Bit 'ard to guarantee it, sir; just say I'm certain sure I can,' Stafford said, still waving the spatula through the flame. 'Look on the back – no scorching of the paper, eh?'

There was no sign that the warm blade had been used.

'That's it, see. Most people think o' wax as 'aving to be 'ot to work it, but warm is enough. 'Ot on top fer an impression with a seal, yus; but warm's enough to separate it underneath, like you saw. Now, see the clerk was careless; the wax is thin on one side and thick on the other. Very lucky we are.'

Ramage nodded. He guessed five minutes had passed – by now the landlord downstairs would be marching into the little dining-room with the roast sucking pig on a plate. In another five minutes it would be carved and the lieutenant and Louis busy eating. Fifteen minutes for them to eat and have more. Well, he and Stafford were not behind schedule – yet, anyway.

'I'd like you to 'old the letter down when we're ready, sir, so I get a clean lift up . . . Reckon this spatchler's about ready.' He watched as Ramage put Bruix's letter square in front of him, the wax seal uppermost. In almost one complete movement he removed the spatula from the flame, wiped off the soot and slid the blade under the letter. With a surprisingly gentle touch – surprising, Ramage thought, until you remembered his original trade – he lifted the corners at the exact moment the wax was warm enough to part, once again flicking the spatula clear. He blew on the wax to cool it and handed the packet to Ramage without bothering to look at the seal.

Ramage saw that the seal itself was both intact and perfect: the wax had parted at the thin side and softened enough on the thick side to allow Stafford to detach it from the paper before the heat came through to the impression. Carefully he removed the letter which was folded inside, and opened it.

Printed at the top was the same symbol that appeared on the seal: an oval shape with an anchor in the centre with '*Rep.*' on the left of the stock, '*Fran.*' on the right, and '*Marine*' beneath, following the curve of the crown and arms. '*Liberté*' was printed in large letters to the left of the oval and '*Egalité*' on the right.

The letter was written from Pont-de-Brique – that was where the Corporal had said Vice-Admiral Bruix had his head-quarters – and dated '*Le 13 Prairial.*' He could not remember the new system of dating the French used since the Revolution, with different names for the months and numbering the years from the Revolution instead of the birth of Christ, but yesterday was the first day of June.

Quickly he skimmed through the letter. Forfait's full name and title were repeated, and the letter itself began: '*Vous me demandez par votre dépêche du 1er de ce mois renseignement sur la . . .*'

And there it all was: apparently Minister Forfait was asking Bruix all the questions that the Admiralty wanted answering! Indeed, not just Forfait: the information was needed for the First Consul. Bruix was explaining that he had received the questions but that it would take him several days to obtain all the details for the three lists and his report. *Citoyen* Forfait would understand that while it was easy to prepare the first list – the various categories of vessels that were completed and could be commissioned by the *13 Messidor* – the shipyards would have to be inspected by naval officers to ensure the accuracy of the second list (showing the stage reached in each vessel under construction for the Invasion Flotilla at that date). The third list presented even more difficulties, because indicating how many of those under construction on *13 Messidor* could be completed and commissioned by *14 Thermidor* would depend on the number of workmen being employed, and that in turn depended on the money available for wages, on equipment and materials, all of which were in critically short supply.

Nevertheless, Bruix wrote, the complete report would be enclosed in his next weekly dispatch. He assured the Minister that he had always shared the First Consul's views on the need for urgency but 'you will understand, *Citoyen,* that I can only commission the vessels as they are launched from the shipyards if I have sufficient sails, cordage, blocks and armament, and it must be brought to the First Consul's attention that of the twenty-three barges already launched, only eleven could be rigged and commissioned ready for sea with the equipment at my disposal. Of the seventy-three gunboats so far completed, only nineteen are fit for sea and armed. We lack fifty-four guns and carriages for the remainder, and will need 359 guns and carriages to arm the gunboats required by the First Consul and ordered from the shipyards. I understand that General Soult is writing separately to Paris, in answer to the First Consul's questions about the Army's position, but I sincerely hope we shall not be expected to supply them with powder, shot or flints from our meagre stores.'

The rest of the letter was a subtle recapitulation of all the earlier requests that Bruix had made to Paris and seemed to be hinting to Forfait that he should prepare the First Consul for a disappointing report. Bruix said he would welcome by return an answer to his request for a total of 413 guns and carriages because, if only a portion was forthcoming, he would sooner transfer the workmen from the gunboats to the transports which required no guns. This was not to say, he added warily, that he considered the Invasion Flotilla could be protected by fewer gunboats than already decided on; simply that he was anxious to make the most economical use of the available workmen. He was also waiting for money to pay the carpenters and shipwrights whose wages were now eleven weeks in arrears. There were signs that many workers, particularly foreigners, were leaving the yards, which in turn were demanding payments which had been owing for several months.

Ramage reached for pen, ink and paper, and hurriedly noted down the main points of the letter, taking particular care not to make any mistake with the numbers of vessels or guns. He slid Bruix's letter back across the table to Stafford and, after folding his own copy, tucked it down the front of his shirt. In the meantime the Cockney was heating his spatula over the candle flame, having refolded the letter inside its cover.

'If you'll hold it ready, sir,' he said. 'Just make sure the edges are hard up against each other – that's it. I'll 'andle the spatchler an' 'otting up the wax as long as you keep the letter firm.' He touched the palm of his hand with the blade, winced and shook his head, putting the metal back in the flame. 'Take a bit more yet.'

He was utterly unconcerned; that was what impressed Ramage. No nervous twiddling, no silly jokes to reassure himself. Yet Stafford was smart enough to know that one mistake could result in them all being captured as spies, and he had seen enough guillotines in the past few days to have no illusions . . .

The Cockney picked up the cloth. 'Just about right, I reckon,' he said, wiping the soot from the blade and sliding it beneath the letter. 'No, sir, don't press down – just 'old it still.'

Watching the wax carefully, he moved the blade away for a moment and then slid it under again. He crouched over the seal like a cat about to pounce, hiding it from Ramage's sight. Suddenly the spatula was tossed aside again and Stafford was blowing hard at the seal.

He then stood upright and reached for the satchel. 'Any of these other letters interest you, sir?' When Ramage shook his head he put them back in the satchel and pointed at the dispatch. 'Pick it up and look if you want, sir; the wax has set now. All ready for the Minister, it is!'

He was not exaggerating: the red wax was adhering once again to both sides, and Ramage saw that Stafford had judged it perfectly, softening just enough of the wax to make it

156

stick together but not enough to affect the impression of the seal.

The Cockney was holding the satchel open, but before Ramage had time to put the letter in he tipped the other letters out again, closed the flap and locked it. Then he put the satchel flat on the table and punched it with a clubbing movement, both hands clasped together. The blow was heavy enough to flatten the satchel, and as he opened the lock again and replaced the letters he said: 'Worth knowing, that. If I'd 'ad trouble with the seal, we could've put all the letters together so the seals line up, and then jumped on the satchel. That would've cracked *all* the wax. Wiv every seal broken, the clerks in Paris would reckon the lieutenant's 'orse must 'ave sat on the satchel. Not very bright, clerks isn't.'

He lifted the candle to illuminate the inside of the drawer, took out his set of picklocks, and picked up the satchel. 'If you'd like to keep an ear open for anyone comin' hup the stairs, sir, I'll take the 'tenant's bag back. We all right for time?'

Ramage looked at his watch. 'Twenty-one minutes from the time I came in. Where did he hide the satchel?'

Stafford laughed dryly. 'Very horiginal, our 'tenant. Hid it under the bed!'

It was nearly midnight before Louis returned to the room. Ramage and Stafford, lying on their beds, heard the *lieutenant-de-vaisseau* and the smuggler stumbling up the stairs, joking and guffawing in the confidential and noisy manner of men who had spent the evening getting drunk together. Louis escorted the lieutenant to his room, said good night with a flourish, and stumbled back towards his own room. Ramage heard the lieutenant's door shut, and a moment later their own door opened.

'How is the sick man?' Louis asked loudly in French.

'A little better, if you mean me. My foreman is much better – and hungry!'

'I thought so,' Louis said drunkenly, 'wait a minute . . .'

They heard him stumble down the stairs again, to return with a jug in one hand, two bowls in the other and a loaf of bread tucked under his arm. Once he had pushed the door shut it was obvious he was as sober as when Ramage had left him at the table; the drunkenness was an act.

'Enough broth for both of you,' he said, putting it on the

157

table. 'With the landlord's compliments. Now, how did it go?' he asked Ramage quietly. 'I made sure the lieutenant was drunk when he went to bed, just in case!'

Ramage and Stafford sat down at the table as Louis served the soup and broke the loaf into pieces. 'The suckling pig was excellent,' he chuckled. 'The lieutenant was as appreciative as myself. He was critical of the sole – as became a naval officer, perhaps – and as a true Norman he approved the onion soup.'

Absent-mindedly he extracted two spoons from his pocket, handed them round, and sat down opposite Ramage. He was obviously anxious to hear their news but both Ramage and Stafford were too busy with the broth to pay much attention. Stafford finished the bowl and eyed the jug hopefully. 'Some left,' Louis said. 'More for you, sir?' Ramage shook his head and nodded towards Stafford.

Leaving Stafford to finish off the soup with noisy gusto, Ramage took his notes, smoothed them out on the table, and said in English: 'Stafford did an excellent job: we – er, borrowed – the satchel for fifteen minutes. There were sixteen letters in it, and a dispatch from Vice-Admiral Bruix to the Minister of Marine Citizen Forfait . . .' Ramage could not resist pausing to tantalize the Frenchman.

'Were you able . . .?'

'Stafford opened the seal and – '

'But was he able to close it again?' Louis interrupted anxiously.

' – and after I'd read the dispatch he seated it again so that the clerk who applied the original wax would never know. Stafford has – like you – skills not normally found in a sailor.'

'The dispatch,' Louis prompted.

'Ah yes – ' Ramage tapped the paper, 'most interesting. It seems that the Minister, on behalf of Bonaparte himself, has just asked Bruix nearly the same questions that the British Admiralty wants answering: how many of the various types of vessels forming the Invasion Flotilla have been completed and are ready for sea; how many will be completed in a month's time; and the situation regarding the rest.

'Oh yes, and Admiral Bruix is having a great deal of trouble getting enough money to pay the carpenters and shipwrights at the various yards – all of whom are eleven weeks behind with their wages. And he is reminding the Minister that he has asked for more than 350 guns and carriages for the gunboats. They must be 24-pounders – '

'One for each gunboat,' Louis said.

' – exactly,' Ramage said, glancing at his notes. 'Here we are – seventy-three gunboats completed so far, and only nineteen ready for sea. No guns for the remaining fifty-four. Then he needs another 359 guns for the rest of the gunboats ordered by the First Consul. Then he says twenty-three barges have been launched but he has masts, sails and cordage for only eleven of them. All that bears out what we saw in Boulogne.'

Louis sucked his teeth. 'More than four hundred gunboats ordered, and guns for only nineteen . . . Masts, spars and sails for less than half the barges launched, and probably four times more are ordered . . . That's how this man Bonaparte seeks to challenge the British Navy, which has kept nearly every one of its ships at sea, winter and summer, for the past eight or nine years. Fill the gunboats with farmers' boys and clerks from the counting-houses and send them across the Channel,' he said, mimicking the Bonaparte portrayed by English cartoonists.

Ramage felt a great sympathy for the man, and noticed that Stafford was watching him curiously. By Bonaparte's standards, Louis was a traitor to France; but by the standards of men like Louis and the man with only one leg who was abandoned in the Alpine snows, it was Bonaparte and the new régime who were the traitors. What a dreadful position for men to be in, when they find their country's official enemies are their only friends . . . As though all the jailbirds in Britain had suddenly seized control and, with their leader installed in St James's Palace, then set about making the country a safe place for thieves, murderers, panderers, blackmailers and sheepstealers to live in – and, the bitterest irony, did it all in the name of liberty, equality and the brotherhood of man.

Louis pointed at Ramage's notes, his finger emphasizing that they covered only one side of the page. 'Is that *all* Bruix reported? Surely it is not enough for your people!'

Ramage grinned. 'No, this is really only an acknowledgment of the Minister's request. I had the feeling that Admiral Bruix wanted to warn Citizen Forfait that the full report when it comes will not make cheerful reading for Bonaparte: he more than hints that the First Consul should be tactfully prepared in advance . . . And he's taking the opportunity to square his own yards, too, reminding Forfait that he has not received the guns, cordage, sailcloth and so forth that he has requested, quite apart from money to pay the workmen.'

'He'll need all the excuses he can think of, if the First Consul finds he has fallen behind schedule with the new Invasion Flotilla,' Louis commented sourly. 'And General Soult can abandon hope of ever getting a marshal's baton if the Army of England is not ready, right down to the last button and musket flint. But –' Louis hesitated, obviously still puzzled, 'what happens now?'

'The Admiral has asked the Minister to tell him by return – presumably he means by this same lieutenant – when he can expect the 413 guns and carriages, and the money to pay the workmen. He says the full report on the Invasion Flotilla will take a few days to prepare and will be included in his next weekly dispatch. So presumably it will be taken to Paris by our lieutenant this time next week.'

Ramage waited anxiously for Louis to absorb the significance of the timing. It was better to let the Frenchman think it out for himself. While lying on his bed waiting for Louis to return from the orgy with the sucking pig, he had considered all of the alternatives open to him. Thank goodness there were some: he was not forced into one course of action – except that in the last resort, if everything went wrong, then some time next Saturday the wretched *lieutenant-de-vaisseau* was going to be left for dead behind a hedge on the quietest stretch of road between Boulogne and Amiens.

Louis was slowly arranging the crumbs on the table in a neat little pile. He looked tired and there was a sheen of grease on his chin, a patch he'd missed when he wiped his mouth with the back of his hand after finishing the sucking pig. Damn the pig; he was still so hungry his thoughts kept going back to it. Now Ramage was having to wait, and regretting the way he'd tantalized Louis over the dispatch, though the Frenchman was not being deliberately slow. He was being thorough, if his past performance was anything to go by; like a good chess player he was calculating every move his opponent could make before deciding on his own.

He looked up and, with a gesture to Stafford, said, 'I talk in French; I can't think well in English.' He folded Ramage's notes along the original creases and then ran the edge of the paper along the line of his jaw, the paper rasping on the stubble.

'First, we need to look into the lieutenant's satchel again

when he returns from Paris on Monday, so we know when – or if – Admiral Bruix can expect his 413 guns and carriages?' When Ramage nodded he commented: 'Your people should regard that information as more vital than knowing when the vessels will be completed, since without a gun a gunboat is useless.'

Ramage nodded again: so far Louis's thoughts had run parallel with his own.

'Second, we need to look into the satchel again when the lieutenant returns to Paris from Boulogne next Saturday, so we can make a copy of Admiral Bruix's full report to the Minister. After that, your people will know as much about the Invasion Flotilla as the First Consul, eh?'

'Perhaps more,' Ramage said dryly. 'I think the Minister will edit it carefully to safeguard himself before presenting it to Bonaparte . . .'

'It's all politics,' Louis said gloomily. 'The Admiral will write an honest report because he has probably done an honest job: he has built as many vessels as he could with the money and materials provided, and commissioned as many as possible. The men in Paris are responsible for the deficit – they did not supply what was needed. Forfait knows that he has not supplied the materials – because he has been unable to get them. The Treasury has not supplied the money – because it is not available. But the First Consul is certainly not going to blame himself for ordering more ships than was possible to build with the money and materials available: oh no, he cannot be wrong. *Alors*, there will have to be scapegoats – something that Forfait and the Treasurer know only too well. If Forfait blames the Treasury, he knows he makes a mortal enemy; likewise the Treasurer probably knows that he cannot throw all the blame on Forfait. So –' Louis gave an expressive shrug, 'between them they carefully edit Admiral Bruix's report. After all, he is a hundred miles from Paris, and at times such as these I imagine a man is wise not to be more than a hundred metres from the First Consul's ear if he wishes to remain in favour.'

The rasping of the paper on Louis's jaw was getting on Ramage's nerves. He gave a passable imitation of a Gallic shrug. 'Politicians are the same the world over; it probably happens in London as well.'

'It even happens in every town hall,' Louis said bitterly, 'only there they're after money, not power. But we stray

161

from our problem. Can we safely stay here another week – that is what we have to decide.'

Ramage put his hands flat on the table. 'I accept your decision.'

'Without a good reason, it will be dangerous. Can you think of a reason?'

'Stafford's illness becomes worse?'

Louis shook his head. 'An illness means a doctor, and a doctor is likely to suspect Stafford does not speak Italian. Doctors know Latin, don't forget.' He looked up at Ramage and began laughing. 'You were the last one to be taken ill – and you speak Italian well enough to pass for one. I'm afraid you are the one who has to take to his bed. It is the most natural reason, apart from being the safest.'

The prospect of faking an illness for a whole week was far from pleasing, but Ramage knew there was no other way. Louis was quite right because the stage had already been set: both the landlord and the lieutenant had seen him taken ill at supper; they both knew the Italian's foreman had been taken ill a few hours earlier. Why, the damned *lieutenant-de-vaisseau* would no doubt be anxious to hear how *il signor* was progressing when he returned from Paris with his satchel.

'We have to get the word to Jackson that there's been a delay. He'll be returning from England and expecting us back in Boulogne by Monday. And I must send another report: the Admiralty will be interested in what we've discovered from the lieutenant's satchel.'

Louis nodded. 'Passing messages is the least of our problems.' He thought for a moment. 'If all went well, Jackson should be on his way back to Boulogne tonight. I can arrange for your report to reach him so that he and Dyson sail for the rendezvous again tomorrow night. He'd be in England on Monday and back in Boulogne by Tuesday.'

'Good: I'll write the report now, and orders for Jackson.'

'The sooner the better,' Louis said, 'it's a long ride from here to Boulogne, the way my man will have to go. And don't forget he might be caught: don't be too – well, too explicit. I don't mean in your report to the Admiralty,' he added hastily. 'Just make sure that if my man is caught and the papers read, no one can trace us here!'

Ramage jerked his hand up to his neck in a chopping motion. 'The sight of a guillotine blade guarantees caution . . .'

CHAPTER TWELVE

By Tuesday afternoon the tension in Ramage's room at the Hotel de la Poste was as taut as the strings of an overtuned cello: if Stafford walked across the room in his normal manner he was told not to stamp; if he walked silently he was ordered not to creep about. Only Louis, who was free to come and go and anyway had his own room, escaped Ramage's irritation.

The feeling of being trapped in the room was illogical; Ramage admitted that much to himself as he alternated between the hard, upright chairs and the hard but horizontal bed. He slept badly because the lack of exercise meant his body was not tired, his muscles ached from disuse, and all the while the worry of the *lieutenant-de-vaisseau*'s return kept his mind active. He knew all that well enough; he knew equally well that he had never had a cabin that was a quarter of the size of this room and, although he had occupied each one for months on end, he had never regarded any of them as small.

But immediately outside the cabins had been the ocean. Usually there were scores of miles to the nearest land in the Mediterranean, hundreds in the Caribbean, and thousands in the Atlantic. He had never really appreciated that freedom: just open the door, acknowledge the Marine sentry's salute, and a few steps up the companion ladder brought him on deck to look at a sea horizon. Not always a reassuring sight, admittedly, even in the Mediterranean and the Caribbean, since a summer storm in the Golfe du Lion stretched your seamanship to its limits and a Caribbean hurricane could take it beyond.

To pass the time, he had re-sailed every storm he had ever experienced while commanding his own ship. Not many, considering that it covered more than three years and the distance from Italy to Gibraltar and on to England, and from England across the Western Ocean to the West Indies, the length and breadth of the Caribbean, and back to England by a somewhat circuitous route. A couple of dozen gales, maybe double that number, since to a sailor they were as common and about as irritating as a shower of rain to a farmer gathering his harvest. One storm had been worrying, and that the one that caught the *Kathleen* cutter just after he had brought her westwards into the Atlantic through the Gut. The east wind had funnelled from the Mediterranean between the Atlas Mountains of Africa on one side and the mountains of Gibraltar and Spain on the other. For a few hours he had wondered whether the *Kathleen* would live through it. She had, since a ship can usually take more punishment than her men, and Ramage admitted to himself he had learned a lot (mainly that most of what he had learned as a midshipman and later as a lieutenant in big ships, had little to do with handling small ones), starting with the fact that following seas which looked like hills from the deck of a ship of the line seemed like mountains from the quarterdeck of the cutter.

And one hurricane. He had learned more about heavy weather in the forty-eight hours that its winds and seas had torn at the *Triton* brig that he would otherwise have learned in a lifetime at sea, and seen her masts go by the board. But the ship had stayed afloat – though that had been doubtful for what seemed like a lifetime. Yes, he had learned a good many lessons, though he would die a contented man if he never met another hurricane to put them into practice again. One lesson was as valid for a storm as for a hurricane, not to mention going into action or even taking a ship alongside a quay. It was simple enough – no reasonably trained and experienced captain with a well-found ship had much to fear providing his ship's company was well-trained and trusted him. The training part was obvious; the trusting less so. It had taken him several actions and a hurricane to find out what was probably the most important aspect of command.

Apparently its importance was not limited to being at sea; Stafford, who had served with him since his first command, was as cheerful shut up in this room as he would have been on the deck of the *Triton* brig running before the warm Trade winds and slicing her way towards the setting sun. He was exposed directly to his captain's bad temper – although only his captain would face the Admiralty's wrath if everything went wrong, all three of them would face the wrath of Bonaparte's men, and that in turn would mean being strapped down under the guillotine blade. Neither Stafford nor Louis had more nor less to lose than Lieutenant Ramage: the only thing at stake was whether they could keep their heads firmly on their shoulders and get back safely across the Channel . . .

Ramage vowed he would try to be less irritable in the future. The arrival of the *lieutenant-de-vaisseau* from Paris would ease some of the strain; his return from Boulogne on Saturday would see an end to it. On Saturday! The wait from Wednesday to Saturday would be twice as bad as this; what *really* mattered was Bruix's report. He found himself wondering for the hundredth time whether making the attempt on the satchel this time was worth the risk of wrecking everything for the attempt on Saturday.

Louis had reckoned it was; Stafford was indignant – or as indignant as he dared be – when Ramage had mentioned that a mistake with the wax seal of the Paris dispatch would endanger the whole operation. On Saturday, once they had read Bruix's dispatch, it would not matter if they jumped on the seal: by the time the satchel reached Paris and was opened at the Ministry of Marine on Monday, all three of them should be back on board the *Marie* and heading for Folkestone . . .

Once again Ramage went back to reading *Le Moniteur*: Louis regularly brought in old copies that he found in various places: it had taken only fifteen minutes to read the latest issue, which was about as interesting as the *London Gazette*, although the bombast of some of the official statements was amusing enough.

He had decided a hundred times to abandon tonight's attempt; he had changed his mind a hundred and one times. So – and he was ashamed to admit it even to himself – they would make the attempt, providing he did not change his mind yet again. Judging by the increasing rate, he had time for half a hundred more changes of mind before the *lieutenant-de-vaisseau* flopped into his bed tonight, secure in the knowledge that his satchel was safely hidden . . .

Supposing that Forfait did not bother to answer Bruix's questions about the 413 guns and the money for the workmen – or could not answer for a few days, until someone made a tally of the guns available and checked the money in the Treasury kitty . . .? The Admiralty in London would not give a tinker's cuss that there was a shortage of money – that was something faced every day by every ministry in every government in the whole world; but guns for the invasion flotilla's gunboats – that was different. Knowing that Bruix would get no more guns suitable for the gunboat was more important than knowing the rate at which new gunboats were being sent down slipways. Without guns, they were useless, since they were unsuitable for carrying troops, provisions or ammunition. On the other hand if Forfait said that no more guns would be available for, say, six months (until the foundries produced them, or the Army could be persuaded to hand some over and ship carriages could be made for them), then the Admiralty knew that for the next six months Bruix's only effective gunboats were those he had been able to commission.

You could go a stage further: Bruix would, left to his own devices (but of course the Minister or the First Consul might overrule him), probably finish the construction of those gunboats already on the stocks simply to get them out of the way, and then use all available extra carpenters and shipwrights (and sawyers and smiths, for that matter) to concentrate on building more barges – or if not more, then speeding up construction of those already started.

In fact you could very easily start getting quite sorry for Admiral Bruix's plight! The poor man was in the silly situation where he could build more transports for the Invasion Flotilla and carry an even larger Army of England across the Channel but, because he could not get the guns, he would have many fewer gunboats to escort them: the more transports he built, the less able he was to defend them.

It was some consolation that Lieutenant Ramage was not the only naval officer within fifty miles of the Channel who had problems, he reflected gloomily, but at least Bruix would not be strapped down on the guillotine if he failed.

Ramage was worried about Louis: from six o'clock he had been expected back to describe what plans he had made to ensure that the lieutenant once again had supper in the dining-room downstairs, but he had not arrived by seven o'clock. Ramage and Stafford had to return to their roles of invalids, undressed and in bed, waiting for supper. Both had to appear suitably ill, although the daily bulletin given to the landlord when he brought up their breakfast showed that Stafford was on the mend while Signor di Stefano made only slow progress. Fortunately the landlord himself had scorned the idea of calling a doctor: once Ramage had described the symptoms the landlord had clapped his hands and announced that the café where they had lunched was infamous for serving food that was bad, and that his wife had a family recipe for the medicine that would clear it all up *tout de suite*. He apologized that the Signor and his foreman should be taken ill in Amiens in this unfortunate way, but there was no need to worry. With every meal since then two small mugs of the medicine had appeared, a piping hot and evil brew of mint, rosemary and chicory for certain, and many other things that Ramage could not define but previously thought had their origins in drains. At every meal the two men had taken appreciative sips but, the moment the landlord was gone, poured the rest into old wine bottles which Louis had found for the purpose and took out of the hotel in his coat pocket to empty.

Louis arrived only a minute or two before the landlord and his wife came in with the supper trays. He had no time to report on his afternoon's work before the first course of his meal was served at the table, while the landlord's wife bustled back and forth between Ramage's and Stafford's beds, first with the mugs of medicine and then with bowls of broth.

Unfortunately for both men, part and parcel of the family remedy was a menu that went with the medicine: one which ensured that the patient received 'nourishing food'. This meant broth and bread, followed by boiled fish, for every meal, starting with breakfast.

Luckily Louis was treated as a trencherman, and the moment the landlord and his wife left the room after serving an enormous course he hurriedly shared it with Ramage and Stafford, making sure he was back at the table with a clean plate, and looking hungry, by the time they returned with the next offering. Only once, on the previous evening, had the plan gone adrift: they had forgotten to dispose of the medicine before the landlord's wife come back to clear the table. Amidst much clucking she stood by while Stafford and Ramage finished their mugs and, fighting to avoid vomiting, screwed up their face muscles into the nearest they could muster to appreciative smiles. Louis flattered her medical skill and incautiously – or so he claimed, though Ramage suspected an impish sense of humour – said they looked as though they could have drunk more.

As soon as supper was finished and the landlord and his wife had bidden them all good night, Louis looked quizzically up at Ramage. The tension throughout the meal had made it obvious that they were alarmed at his late appearance. Neither man had said anything during the brief periods when the landlord and his wife were out of the room between courses, Ramage from stubbornness and Louis for fear a man already under strain would lose his temper.

'It's all arranged,' Louis said. 'The lieutenant is here but hasn't gone up to his room yet. He – '

'How the devil is Stafford going to get the satchel?' Ramage snapped.

' – the lieutenant met an old friend and they are drinking together. He'll be going up to his room for a wash, and then go down to supper. After he has eaten, the friend and I join him for an hour or two playing cards . . .'

'All right,' Ramage said, giving a thin smile of relief, 'but you had me worrying because you were late back.'

'I was drinking with the lieutenant,' Louis explained hurriedly, before Ramage's bad temper had a chance of returning. 'He saw me as he came in and greeted me like a brother. A comfortable ride from Paris, he tells me; a little tired but pleased to see me and his old friend. He has given the landlord strict instructions to have some good Calvados ready and the card table set up.'

He rubbed his hand across his chin and the bristles rasped: Louis never had more than twenty-four hours' growth of beard but, as far as Ramage could see, never less. It was impossible to guess when he actually shaved, unless he always used a blunt razor. Yet the Frenchman looked worried and Ramage waited patiently. Finally Louis said: 'We need to cut down the risks even more: we don't want anything to stop us getting a sight of Admiral Bruix's dispatch on Saturday, and we don't want to lose any time getting a copy of the dispatch to England . . .'

Ramage thought for several moments, puzzled that the Frenchman should be so emphatic about something so obvious. 'Have you any suggestions?'

'Yes. To begin with, we should get your copy of the letter – or your notes – from the Minister out of this room as soon as possible. If you keep it here through the night until I can get it to Boulogne, you are holding on to evidence which can incriminate you. No one would search my room or suspect me; but you are different; a foreigner is always suspect . . .'

'But if the gendarmes became suspicious of me, it wouldn't take –'

'Even if they were, they are still only suspicious of an Italian shipbuilder,' Louis said impatiently. 'It would probably take two or three weeks to check on you. Your papers aren't forged – they are genuine, with an imaginary name written in. But if your room was searched and they found notes written in a foreign language, it wouldn't take long to get them translated. And then it would be so obvious what they were – and what *you* were! They would have no need to check. The only thing that could get you guillotined for certain within the week are those notes.'

The Frenchman was right. The first set of notes had been burned after he had written a report to Lord Nelson on Bruix's dispatch, and Jackson should now be on his way to Folkestone to deliver it. All he had to do tonight was make notes as soon as Stafford got hold of the Minister's reply, write out another report to Lord Nelson, and hide it somewhere until Louis could send it off to Boulogne to meet Jackson, who should be back by Thursday. The notes could be burned like the first set, and the same procedure followed on Saturday night. Providing Jackson could get over and back each time, the operation could not fail: the Admiralty would have all the information it required, even if Ramage and Stafford were arrested on Sunday morning.

Louis agreed when Ramage outlined his intentions. 'As soon as you've finished writing your letter to Lord Nelson tonight and burned your notes, take the letter to my room. You'll find a loaf of fresh bread in the top drawer of the chest – I've just put it there with cheese and a bottle of wine: anyone finding it would assume I keep it in case I get hungry. Now, if you press the bottom of the loaf you'll find a slit in it that is deep enough to take your dispatch. Push it in and put the loaf back. It's the loaf,' Louis explained with a grin, 'that will take the dispatch to Boulogne. It will sit in a basket with a bottle of wine and some cheese – the courier's lunch.'

'Supposing he eats the loaf?' Ramage asked.

'He'll have three loaves – one for himself, one in case another traveller wants some, and a third which he is taking to his widowed mother in Boulogne. That's the one with the dispatch. The courier leaves for Boulogne tomorrow morning and again Sunday morning,' Louis reminded Ramage.

'That's all arranged.'

'But we'll be leaving on Sunday,' Ramage said, and then he remembered. 'But we are supposed to be going on to Paris . . .'

Again Louis grinned and shook an admonitory finger. 'You see, you haven't got into the habit of life in France! You English – if you want to go from Dover to London, you just climb into a carriage or mount a horse. Or board a wagon. No travel documents, no passports – all you need is the money to pay the fare. Of course, Bonaparte would tell you that you haven't "*Liberté, Egalité, et Fraternité*" . . .'

'I've no doubt he would,' Ramage said impatiently, 'but how do we get back to Boulogne on Sunday morning?'

'You ask Louis if he has arranged for new travel documents and a carriage.'

'And what does Louis tell me,' Ramage asked sarcastically. 'That he has also forgotten all about them?'

'No, Louis would tell you that they'll all be here by Friday, along with a letter from the Port Captain at Boulogne asking the Signor to return urgently for more discussions – a request that makes you very angry, as the landlord will notice.'

'How did the Port Captain know I was still in Amiens and not in Paris?'

Louis thumped his hand against his forehead, then shook his head with exasperation. 'Remember, this is France! Any Frenchman could tell you. The police headquarters in Amiens know where you are staying. Any messenger trying to find you and knowing your route would simply inquire at the police headquarters in every big town.'

Ramage began to feel a chill creeping over him that had nothing to do with the fact that the sun had long since set: he pictured the police of France as a great octopus bestriding the country, a tentacle reaching into every town, with the suckers representing villages and police posts along the roads, and although unseen, touching the lives of every man and woman in the country.

Louis was watching him closely. 'I think at last you understand, *mon ami*,' he said quietly, and Ramage nodded.

Stafford's grin was infectious. As he held out the letter after opening the seal on the cover Ramage saw that the Cockney was completely unworried: there was not a trace of perspiration on his brow, his hand was steady, and he had worked quickly but without hurrying. Deftly, Ramage thought; that was the word. As he took the letter, Ramage made sure he did not have to hold out his own hand too far for too long: he knew it was trembling slightly. He knew he would laugh a little too loudly if Stafford made a joke – in fact a laugh might well sneak out as a giggle.

With great deliberation he put the letter to one side without glancing at it, drew the sheets of notepaper in front of him, placed the inkwell near his right hand and inspected the tip of the quill pen. Unhurriedly – although he knew the whole performance was for himself, because Stafford was completely absorbed with the watermarks in the paper used as an envelope – he unfolded the letter and began reading, almost skimming through it the first time. He found this was the best way of getting the 'atmosphere' of a letter written in a foreign language, relying on a second or third reading to yield the precise details.

One thing was immediately so clear as to be startling: *Citoyen* Pierre-Alexandre-Laurent Forfait, Minister of the Marine and Colonies, was writing an extremely chilly reply to Admiral Bruix; far colder and more formal than Ramage would have expected, having read the Admiral's dispatch to the Minister. It *might* be Forfait's manner – in which case would the Admiral (who obviously knew him well) have written what was by comparison a friendly dispatch?

He read the Minister's letter again more slowly, lingering over some of the phrases and examining them. Hmm . . . there was no doubt about it; the letter was *intended* to be cold. Ramage had the feeling that someone (presumably Bonaparte himself) was very angry with Bruix's request – repeated request – for money, while the Minister was alarmed at Bruix's warning that the full report on the Invasion Flotilla would prove disappointing to the First Consul when it arrived in Paris.

Citoyen Forfait was more than alarmed; he was obviously a very frightened man. Ramage saw him as a nervous individual who understood the danger of standing between the First Consul and one of his admirals. When things were going well, it was a splendid position for an ambitious politician, since he received the praise and could hold on to as much as he wished before passing on the remainder to the admiral concerned. When things were going badly, Bonaparte's wrath – and from what Louis said, the Corsican had more than his share of his island's hot temper – landed fairly and squarely on the minister's unprotected head. From the tone of Bruix's dispatch Ramage guessed that the First Consul's original orders for the construction and commissioning of the Invasion Flotilla had been impossible from the outset. He pictured an anxious Minister nodding his head, bowing his way out of the First Consul's presence, and rushing off to give the orders to Bruix . . .

Ramage glanced at his watch and realized that he was wasting time.

Hurriedly he began making notes. Admiral Bruix's request for fifty-four guns at once for the gunboats already completed, and 359 more for the remaining gunboats that were ordered, 'had been noted.' However, Citoyen Bruix would have observed, the Minister wrote icily, that there was a general shortage of all sizes of naval guns, particularly 24-pounders, and the foundries were, at the First Consul's express order, working overtime. However, there were seventeen 24-pounder guns and carriages at Antwerp, and orders had been sent for them to be taken by sea to Boulogne. Since most of the coast between Antwerp and Boulogne fell within Citoyen Bruix's command, the Minister hoped that the British would not be allowed to intercept the vessels carrying them.

The request for money was ill-timed, Forfait wrote, and the First Consul, when told of it by the Controller-General (since the request had to be made to the Treasury, 'there being no funds available at the Ministry'), had given instructions that Citoyen Bruix would be responsible for ensuring that the shipyards continued to give of their best 'even though accounts were outstanding,' and that the workmen did not leave their jobs. Any man that did – or threatened to – would be conscripted immediately. Citoyen Bruix was to issue a warning to that effect. In the meantime the First Consul waited 'with unconcealed impatience' for the complete report he had requested.

Ramage handed the letter back to Stafford as he scribbled the last of his notes. He had been careful to copy whole sentences where necessary – he knew that although Lord Nelson might accept his word that as a precaution Citizen Forfait was putting out an anchor to windward, their Lordships at the Admiralty most certainly would not. Nor could he blame them, he thought, as he watched Stafford carefully folding the paper and beginning to heat the spatula again;

172

Their Lordships would also find it impossible to picture Lieutenant Ramage and Ordinary Seaman Stafford juggling with candle, spatula and sealing-wax and reading the correspondence between Vice-Admiral Bruix and Bonaparte's Minister of Marine – in fact even Lieutenant Ramage was finding it hard to believe, though Will Stafford, Ordinary Seaman, seemed to take it in his stride.

As soon as the letter to Bruix was sealed, Stafford put it back in the satchel and vanished from the room to return it to its resting place under the *lieutenant-de-vaisseau*'s bed. Ramage took another sheet of paper and began his report to Lord Nelson. He had already decided that he must write it on the assumption that he might not get back to England to make a personal report: a euphemistic way of avoiding having to admit that the French might catch him and put his neck under the guillotine blade. He must also write it in such a way that if it was intercepted it would not reveal how the Minister's mail had been read.

'An opportunity presented itself to read the reply made to the sender of the dispatch referred to in my first letter,' he wrote carefully. From that, Lord Nelson would know it was Forfait's reply to Bruix, since he had given both names in his previous report, which had already reached Jackson safely. He glanced up as Stafford slid back into the room, and then continued writing.

Stafford sat down on his bed, wondering if he would ever stop feeling hungry. He stifled a belch, but tasted the medicine yet again. The damned Frogs: he had not trusted them the moment the *Marie* arrived in Boulogne, and nothing had happened since to make him change his mind.

Marvellous how the Captain gabbled away in the lingo: he sounded as French as Louis, except when he was talking Italian, of course. To hear him and the Marchesa rattling on was an education – they talked so fast they certainly got their money's worth for every breath they took! It was funny how being shut up in this room was getting the Captain rattled. Unlike him – he was usually ... Stafford cudgelled his memory for a phrase he had heard one of the Captain's friends use: 'My deah Remmedge, y're disgustin'ly cheerful!' He usually was, too. In fact, when they went into action the more dangerous it got the more cheerful he became. Jacko once said that if the Captain ever died in battle, he would probably be laughing his head off.

173

Stafford glanced across to see him writing, his face in profile against the flickering candle. He looked very strained these days. Dark patches under his eyes – squinting, too, so the two vertical creases between the inboard ends of his eyebrows look like the fairleads for heavy rope. And blinking, as he did when he was thinking hard and rubbing the upper of those two scars over his brow. If only he knew how well his ship's company knew all his little habits!

The two vertical creases between the eyebrows, and the mouth shut in a straight line like a mousetrap meant someone had done something wrong, and stand by for a chilly blast, m'lads. Creases, mouth normal, blinking and rubbing the upper scar on the brow meant difficult situation and I'm thinking hard. Creases, mousetrap mouth and rubbing the scar meant get your heads well down everyone 'cos the Captain is about to explode. The exception was when they were going into action and the odds were not favourable (and that was the way the Captain usually went into action!). The creases, mousetrap and rubbing the scar vanished with the sound of the first gun; then the Captain's eyes fairly glowed, like polished chestnuts, and he would sling the same sort of grin across his face as he used when the Marchesa teased him.

Stafford had never seen the Captain worried like this, though. Like a bear in a cage, those bears they have at Vauxhall Gardens, nasty-tempered brutes, and you could see that all they wanted was to be set free, so they could roam where they wanted, eating people from time to time or just growling like the Captain. Trouble was he had been talking French to Louis most of the time, so it was hard to know exactly what was going on. Sitting here and getting the satchel and opening the letters might seem difficult to the Captain, but as far as William Stafford was concerned it was a lot better than reefing a topsail in a high wind, or polishing brass and scrubbing decks on board a ship of the line at anchor at Spithead.

There were not many other captains he would care to be with on a jaunt like this one; in fact Mr Ramage was the only one he could think of. All the rest would be stiff and sort of gritty, like dried sand on the deck after holystoning; the idea of having to share a room with a common seaman – well, demmit, sir! That was what made Mr Ramage the Captain he was: it all came natural to him – joking with the men, sharing a room with one of them when necessary, and all

174

the rest that went with it. Dignity – that was it. Any of those other captains would lose their dignity if they did that; they would find the men getting familiar. It did not work that way with Mr Ramage, though; if anything, it worked the other way – he gained in dignity because he had the men's respect. Assured of himself, he was, as if he wore his assurance like a skin and never realized he had it, and because of that was not for ever scared of losing it. It was only whores who kept harping on their virginity.

Funny how Mr Ramage watched that game with the wax seals: he seemed to think it magic. And opening a lock! Well, every man to his own trade – it always seems like magic the way he takes the ship into action. And every time he out-smarts the French – even old Mr Southwick, who had been in more battles than most men have eaten mince pies, reckons there's no one like him.

Handsome, too. Face a bit on the lean side, and not a bit of spare meat on the carcase. Father owns a big estate so there must be a lot of money there. Good looks, money, a nice chap, and the Marchesa too. But the way he goes about things you would think he had nothing to lose if a French cannonball lopped his head off. Those two scars on his forehead – each was a memento of boarding a French ship with a sword in one hand and a pistol in the other. Each time he had ended up unconscious and covered in blood, the lads thinking he was dead. You would think that he would go more carefully with so much to lose, since he had so much to stay alive for. But no, show him a French ship and off he goes, breathing fire and smoke and taking a swipe with his sword.

Stafford smiled to himself. Watching him sitting at the table, tapping his teeth with the feather of his pen, reminded him of a schoolboy trying to do his lessons! A good caning for you in the morning, my boy, unless you learn ten more verses of that Euclid. Though maybe Euclid was not a language – never heard of anyone speaking it. Come to think of it, it might be a sort of sums? He shrugged his shoulders, thankful that neither sums nor Euclid were needed to pick a lock or open a sealed letter.

Although Louis was good the way he shared his meal the minute the old trout and her husband left the room, he was hungry. That damned medicine tasted so awful it stopped the rest of the food going down properly, like something nasty

blocking a drain. Looks as though Mr Ramage has finished
Wipe the pen, screw the cap on the inkpot, fold the letter and
reach for the sealing-wax . . . Stafford walked over to the
table.

'Top drawer in Louis's chest,' Ramage said, giving him the
letter. 'A loaf of bread. It has a slit in the bottom of it large
enough for this. Take the candle . . .'

Late that night Louis woke Ramage apologetically. 'I forgot
to settle one thing, and I want to send word by the courier
when he leaves for Boulogne in the morning . . .'

Ramage nodded to indicate he was fully awake and listening.

'The *Marie* – we should be back in Boulogne by Sunday
evening. If you want to sail at once for Folkestone, I'd better
pass the word for Dyson to have everything ready.'

'Can we get to Boulogne all right on Sunday? We can
get a carriage?'

'It's the best day of the week: few people travelling, so
there's no trouble getting fresh horses. The gendarmes at
the *barrières* have usually eaten a big enough meal and drunk
enough wine to be sleepy in the afternoon.'

'Would the *Marie* normally go fishing on Sunday night?'

'Any night,' Louis said emphatically. 'We've always avoided
regular sailings, so that if we miss a voyage or make an
extra one, nobody notices.'

In five days' time they might be on their way back to England. Was it too much to hope? 'Very well, we'll sail on
Sunday night. And –' he hesitated, as if talking about it
might make it happen. 'I'll write orders for Jackson.'

Louis rubbed his chin. 'It would be a pity if we didn't get
the third letter. Two out of three is better than nothing, but
the one that'll cover you with glory – ' he grinned amiably –
'is the third one.'

'It'll be a very quiet glory – if only for the sake of you and
your smuggler friends,' Ramage said, getting out of bed and
rubbing his eyes. 'Put that candle of yours down on the table
while I write Jackson's orders. Hope that loaf isn't stale by
the time it gets to Boulogne.'

'By the way,' Louis said, 'I won a lot of money from the
lieutenant tonight: I've promised him a chance of revenge
next Saturday night – providing you still haven't recovered
enough for us to carry on to Paris.'

CHAPTER THIRTEEN

In anticipation of the arrival of the fake letter from the Port Captain at Boulogne asking him to return for more talks, Ramage's slow recovery began on Thursday morning. When the landlord arrived with breakfast he was delighted to find Ramage sitting up at the table, pretending a shakiness he did not feel and claiming to be on the mend. By Thursday evening the landlord's wife, as she laid the table for the evening meal, was claiming a victory for her family recipe, encouraged by Louis.

On Friday afternoon the landlord was knocking on their door and announcing as though he was the town crier that a special messenger had brought a letter from Boulogne for the Signor, and was waiting.

Ramage went to the door, took the letter with a flourish, told the landlord to come in and wait, walked back to the table and sat down importantly. After breaking the seal he began reading, and sniffed with annoyance. '*Mama mia . . . accidente!*'

Louis jumped up from Stafford's bed as if in alarm. 'Is something wrong, Signor?'

'Wrong?' Ramage banged the letter down on the table. 'That twice-damned Port Captain at Boulogne – who would think I spent two whole weeks with him, discussing everything from the price of workmen to providing saws and adzes? Now he wants me to go back for *more* talks. "Urgent," he says; "very urgent," and that is why he is sending a special messenger after me. Well,' Ramage said wrathfully, noticing the landlord was obviously very impressed by what he was hearing, 'the Port Captain is lucky that I got no farther than Amiens; if I'd reached Paris I'd be damned if I'd travel back all that way. Even now, I'm not so sure that –'

'Oh, please,' Louis wheedled. 'For the good of the Republic, Signor . . . we need the help of men such as yourself : why, by using the methods you employ in your shipyard in Genoa – well, I heard the Port Captain's adjutant saying he reckoned it would halve the time they're taking at Boulogne and Calais to build the barges.'

'It would indeed,' Ramage said, obviously undecided. 'But they expect me to bring my men up here and put them to work for a pittance. Charity – that's what the Port Captain expects. Hardly becomes the First Consul and the new Republic, I must say.' He gave a contemptuous sniff. 'If you want to build an invasion *flotilla*, then you need money, materials and men. Talk and promises never planked a ship –'

'Well, they've sent a special messenger after you, Signor,' Louis said. 'That shows the importance they attach to you, doesn't it, Jobert?'

'Oh yes, indeed,' the landlord said hurriedly. 'I knew it at once – that is why I rushed up here the moment the messenger arrived.'

'Very well, I'll be guided by you,' Ramage said in a voice that showed he was mollified. 'I shall be well enough to travel by – well, no earlier than Sunday.'

'Shall I tell the messenger, Signor?' When Jobert scurried down the passage Ramage said anxiously to Louis: 'What about the travel documents – there was only this.' He held up the single sheet of paper.

'I expect the messenger has special instructions not to hand over the travel documents until he is sure you are going to Boulogne,' the Frenchman said lightly. 'Such documents would be worth a hundred gold *livres* to spies and other enemies of the Republic!'

'Quite so, quite so,' Ramage murmured. 'One can't be too careful.'

A few minutes later Jobert returned, holding a small packet. 'I signed a receipt for this, Signor,' he said in the sort of awed voice he might have used to confess that he had sold his soul to the Devil. 'The messenger is returning to Boulogne with the good news.'

'Thank you, landlord, thank you: it is a great inconvenience to everyone.'

'Oh no, Signor, an inconvenience to you, without doubt; but for us it is a pleasure that you will be staying until Sunday.' He intercepted a glance from Louis and excused himself.

Once the door had shut and they heard the man going down the stairs, Ramage handed the packet to Louis. 'You'd better check this over.'

The Frenchman opened it and took out several sheets of paper. He read them through and nodded. 'All correct – and I can vouch for them being absolutely genuine. The documents, anyway; I don't know about the three men named in them!'

Ramage slept badly that Friday night. Stafford and Louis has drunk a lot of wine at supper, and while the Frenchman had not turned a hair the Cockney went to bed tipsy and snored with a violence that reminded Ramage of a small boy running a stick along iron railings. The snoring and an imagination running riot left Ramage tossing and turning in his bed, going over in his mind every possible danger and difficulty they would face before they boarded the *Marie* and sailed for Folkestone. Nor was sleep helped by the fact that in his imagination the room was now turning into a prison cell; he had been trapped in it for a week and the walls and ceiling seemed to be closing in. Even in the darkness he felt that they were squeezing him like a clothes press.

Next morning at breakfast he told the landlord that he felt so much better that he was going for a walk; both he and his foreman needed some fresh air. The landlord hastened to suggest that the Cathedral square with its trees was a good place for a promenade. But the café, he said tactfully: he hoped the Signor would not visit it again . . .

The day was sunny and under a cloudless sky the city of Amiens looked shabby but a little more cheerful. It would take many coats of paint on shops and houses, and the people would have to be wearing less darned clothes and at least one in a dozen needed to be smiling before Ramage would rate it more cheerful than the day he had arrived. The two of them walked until noon, when Ramage led the way back to their room feeling considerably better: within eight or nine hours he should be reading Admiral Bruix's dispatch; in twenty or so they should all be rattling along the road to Boulogne. Beyond that he dared not think.

He was getting increasingly superstitious. Was it the effect of this damned room, was he losing his nerve? The knowledge that there was a guillotine in the north-western corner of the Cathedral square in the shade of a row of plane trees was depressing. The heavy blade was missing (presumably the executioner kept it at home, well greased against rusting) but it was still easy to see how it worked. Stafford had an unhealthy curiosity about the way the victim was 'turned off', and because Ramage would not let him betray his interest as they walked past, he checked after lunch with Louis.

The Frenchman was neither squeamish nor superstitious about 'The Widow', pointing out that it was the régime that had killed his family, not a piece of machinery. He was proud of its sheer efficiency, pointing out that it was quicker and surer than the hangman's noose used in England, far less crude and brutal than the garotte used in Spain, and more certain than the headsman's axe previously used in France. It was not uncommon for a man to be alive ten minutes after being 'turned off' on the gallows, he told Stafford, while the garotte suffocated a man very slowly. With 'The Widow' it was over in a flash.

When Stafford began to argue the point, saying that at Newgate prison they now had a special hinged platform on which the condemned man stood, Louis silenced him with a wave of the hand. 'The noose or the axe depends on the skill of the individual executioner. If the drop is too short from the gallows, the victim strangles slowly; if it is too long, the noose just about wrenches his head off. If the axeman makes the slightest mistake, the axe can land across a man's shoulders or slice off the top of his skull, as you might cut the top off a boiled egg.'

'What you really mean is, the axeman might be drunk and miss his aim,' Stafford said contemptuously.

'Yes, drunk, nervous – or just tired.'

'Tired?' Stafford exclaimed, 'Well, he oughter get a good night's sleep first!'

Louis said patiently, *'Mon ami*, you don't understand. This morning you walked past the guillotine near the Cathedral, and I expect you thought of a man – or a woman – being executed there, with perhaps a crowd gathered round the platform.' Stafford nodded and the Frenchman continued: 'Well, try and picture the whole of that square filled with an excited, screaming mob of Revolutionaries – thousands of them, all yelling for blood. Imagine tumbrils – like hay carts – coming into the square one after another and packed full of terrified men and women, young and old, with their hands tied behind their backs and all condemned to death. Imagine the mob yelling insults and threats, throwing stones and rotten fruit at the condemned, many of whom are praying loudly, or weeping, or shrieking with fear.

'Imagine the gendarmes climbing up into the tumbrils as they come to a stop near the guillotine and pushing these people out. Because their hands are bound they lose their balance and fall, and from up on the guillotine platform, the *bourreau* – the executioner – is shouting at his assistants to

180

hurry up as they lash the next victim's ankles together . . .

'Two hundred people have been executed by that guillotine in one day, Stafford, all the work of one *bourreau*. If he still used an axe, I think he'd have been tired after the first fifty. He'd be excited, and with all that crowd, no doubt he'd be drunk. With the guillotine, it hardly matters if he is drunk . . .'

'Two hundred?' Stafford repeated unbelievingly.

'Only two hundred, because Amiens is a small city. In Paris it was nothing for a single guillotine to execute five hundred in a day. What slows down the rate is getting the decapitated bodies out of the way . . .'

'Why is it called a guillotine?' Ramage found himself asking, fascinated by Louis's narrative. 'Did a M. Guillotine invent it?'

'Not exactly. A few years before the Revolution a member of the Assembly called Dr Guillotin (there was no final "e") proposed a resolution that a way of executing people should be found which was swift and avoided the risk of mistakes by an executioner. His motives were of the highest. The College of Surgeons were consulted about the swiftest and most painless method, and the decapitating machine with a falling blade was designed. When it was adopted for executions it was named after Dr Guillotin, who still lives in Paris. I heard he had a quarrel with Citizen Robespierre and was imprisoned during the Revolution, though I believe he has been set free by now.'

''Ow does it work?' Stafford asked, and Ramage knew he shared the Cockney's fascination, although it was unlikely Stafford shared his fears.

'Well, you saw how it looks: a vertical frame in which the blade falls is built at the end of a bench on which the victim lies, his head protruding over the end so that the neck is exactly below the blade.

'The neck rests in a shaped piece like the lower half of a pair of stocks, and there's an upper piece that is clamped down when the victim is in position. Some guillotines have a fixed bench so that the condemned person – who of course is bound – has to be lifted on to it. The newest ones have a *bascule* which pivots on an axle like a seesaw between vertical and horizontal.

'The guillotine blade (which is very heavy) has a diagonal cutting edge and is hoisted up by the *bourreau* – the executioner – who hauls on a rope. The rope is attached to the upper side of the blade, goes up through a pulley at the top of the frame, and comes down to a cleat at the side. There's a basket to catch the head, and a long basket to one side of the *bascule* for the body.

'Now, this is what happens at an execution: the *bourreau*'s assistants – they are called *valets* – seize the man. His wrists are tied behind his back, and his ankles are secured. The *bascule* is swung up vertically and the man is pushed against it. It is just the right length, so that he is looking over the top edge at the frame and blade.

'The *valets* push his shoulders so that he swings over with the *bascule* like someone lying on a seesaw, and is now horizontal, his neck resting in the shaped piece. The upper piece is clamped in position as though he has his head in the stocks, and the *valets* jump back out of the way in case they get their fingers nipped by the blade.

'The *bourreau,* who has already hoisted up the blade, flips the rope off the cleat and the blade falls so quickly the eye can hardly follow it. There is a thud, the head falls in the basket, and it is all over. The body is pushed sideways into the other basket and the *bourreau* hoists the blade again. It is kept well honed, although towards the end of a busy day it gets blunt and – '

'That's enough, Louis,' Ramage interrupted. 'My neck feels sore already, and if Stafford can't picture it by now he never will.'

'You must admit it's interesting, sir,' Stafford said. 'You ever seen anyone get turned orf at Newgate?'

'No. I know it is regarded as great entertainment, but somehow I . . .'

'Oh, it's not too bad,' Stafford said enthusiastically. 'It's worse when you know the condemned man. Saw a cousin o' mine turned orf, once. Stood there a couple o' hours I did, waiting. Then as they fetched him out, St Sepulchre's church bell began tolling, the parson began saying the funeral service, an' that was that. Born to be cropped, my cousin was.'

'Cropped?' Louis asked, puzzled at the word.

'Yus, "Knocked down fer a crop." That's when the judge says the cramp words.'

The Frenchman shook his head, mystified, and Ramage looked puzzled. 'It's slang, yes, but what does it mean?'

'Mean yer don't know, sir?' Stafford said disbelievingly. 'Well, the cramp words is what the judge says when he knocks

– when he sentences yer ter death. An' sentencing a man to death is – well, it's putting the noose round the neck and cropping 'im on collar day.'

'Collar day?' Louis exclaimed. '*Mon Dieu*, what English is this?'

'The noose fits like a collar,' Stafford explained crossly. 'Honest, Louis, yer don't speak English very good, really.'

'I do my best,' the Frenchman said wryly.

When Jobert and his wife brought up their supper promptly at seven o'clock there was still no sign of the *lieutenant-de-vaisseau*. Louis came in while the food was being served and as he sat down he said casually to the landlord: 'I hope the lieutenant won't be too late tonight; we have a card tournament arranged.'

'Ah, we do not know what has delayed him. His other friend – the one you were playing cards with on Monday night – called in a few minutes ago. He said he did not want to miss another exciting evening.'

His wife made a disapproving noise and Louis raised his eyebrows questioningly. 'Gambling,' she sniffed. 'Such a waste of good time!'

'The citizens must choose how they divert themselves,' the landlord said reprovingly. 'They work hard for the Republic, and they deserve some relaxation.'

The woman muttered something Ramage and Louis could not catch, but her husband turned to them apologetically. 'My daughter – she is upset. She has not seen much of the lieutenant on his last two visits. I keep telling them that it is not often we have citizens in the hotel with whom the lieutenant can relax, but . . .'

Louis was quick to make profuse apologies to the woman. 'This is our last night here,' he concluded sadly.

She sniffed. 'You have not settled your account yet, Citizen,' she said acidly.

'*Mon Dieu!*' Louis muttered, and helped himself to more soup.

As soon as they had finished eating and Jobert had cleared the table, Louis followed him downstairs to settle the bill. He returned fifteen minutes later, cursing the landlord for a thief.

'There is a special charge for the "medicine",' he said angrily. 'And they've charged for a full meal every time you and Stafford had a plate of broth. The "medicine" is . . .'

'But you paid?' Ramage interrupted anxiously. 'We don't want – '

'Don't worry, I made just the amount of fuss a French landlord would expect another Frenchman to make, and I made him reduce the bill by twenty per cent. He would have been suspicious if I'd paid the full amount!'

'No sign of the lieutenant?'

'No, the landlord is quite worried and his daughter in tears. He has never been as late as this. The girl is sure he has been thrown from his horse and is lying dead in a ditch.'

Ramage took out his watch. 'Just before nine o'clock. I hope she's not right!'

'Tonight of all nights,' Louis said grimly. 'I thought everything had been going too well.' He rubbed his bristly chin in a characteristic gesture. 'Of course it could be the fault of Admiral Bruix . . .'

Ramage said nothing. From the time they had told the landlord that they would be returning to Boulogne on Sunday morning, he had known that the one thing that could wreck all their plans was the Admiral being late with the report. He might not finish it until late Saturday evening, and the lieutenant would get orders to ride direct to Paris without stopping – a hard ride but not impossible. The Admiral might not finish it until Sunday, and even then the lieutenant could still arrive in Paris in time to deliver it to the Minister on Monday.

Come to think of it – and he cursed himself for not paying more attention to the point – there was really nothing in Bruix's earlier letter that promised the Minister that the report would be sent off from Boulogne on Saturday. It was all his own assumption – that because the weekly dispatch to the Minister was always sent off on a Saturday, the special report would be treated in the same way. Yet the fact that it was a special report could mean that it would be dealt with specially: sent off to Paris as soon as it was ready, rather than have it dispatched in the regular way.

All this damned waiting, being cooped up in this room for a week, that damnable medicine, too, most likely for nothing. The more he thought about it, the more certain he became. He glanced up at Louis and knew the same thoughts were crossing the Frenchman's mind.

'If we can think of a reason to tell the landlord for staying longer, are those travel papers all right?'

'Yes, only the date that they were issued is written down, and they are for a single journey from Amiens to Boulogne. There is no final date, but they are valid for one month.'

'I'll have to have a relapse. Hmm, no,' he finally decided, this was an occasion when he would take advantage of being an officer. 'I think Stafford will have a relapse. With a couple more blankets on his bed, he'll pass for feverish.'

The Cockney looked up at hearing his name, a puzzled grin on his face.

'I was telling Louis that if the lieutenant doesn't come tonight, we'll have to stay here until he does. We'll need a reason – and you look a bit feverish.'

'Aye aye, sir,' Stafford said cheerfully, and then his face fell. 'It don't mean more of that medicine, do it?'

'I won't hear a word against it – Louis says they've charged us three times the price of brandy for it.'

'Ah, 'tis too expensive for the likes of me,' Stafford said quickly. 'I'll make do with broth.' He looked keenly at Ramage and recognized the worried look. 'Is it dangerous, staying on 'ere, sir? I mean, would you rarver go somewhere else an' 'ide? Louis is bound to know a safe 'ouse. I can 'eave this case an' bring you the satchel.'

'Heave this case?'

Had Stafford been a girl, Ramage would have said he suddenly looked coy as he said: 'I always tell a clerk ter put down "locksmith", sir, but – well, a'fore the press gang took me up I sort o' worked in Bridewell Lane on me own account, like.'

'At night, you mean,' Ramage said helpfully.

'That's right, sir.' He grinned when he realized that Ramage was pulling his leg. 'We can keep a watch on the 'tenant's window each night. When we see a light we know 'e's 'ere. When the light goes out we know 'e's gorn fer 'is grub, an' our Will is up the drainpipe and darn again with the satchel a'fore you can say Jack Ketch.'

Ramage envied the Cockney's nonchalance. 'Heave the case,' he reminded him.

Stafford's jaw dropped for a moment, and then he grinned again. 'Our slang, sir. "Heave" is – well, you'd call it burgle. A "case" is – ' he thought hard for a moment, 'well, it's the place wot gets burgled. Like the Italian word.'

'*Casa*? But that means "house".'

'Exackly,' Stafford said triumphantly. 'Yer see . . .'

His voice tailed off as all three men's eyes went to the door. There were heavy footsteps coming up the stairs. Two men . . . the landlord was speaking, although it was impossible to distinguish his words. They reached the corridor, and still the landlord was talking. He sounded anxious. Another guest who was doubtful about the quality of the rooms? Then the coarse laugh of the lieutenant.

Louis sighed with relief and sat down at the table.

After Louis had gone downstairs to join the lieutenant, Ramage decided to write the first part of his report to Lord Nelson, so wording it that he could then copy the facts and figures from Admiral Bruix's letter without delay. Louis's concern the previous Monday night about having incriminating papers in the room had been justified, though Ramage was more than worried that he was himself becoming obsessed about it.

As previously arranged, Louis came back into the room after an hour, ostensibly because he had forgotten his purse but actually to tell Ramage that supper was over and they were just settling down to play cards, and Ramage had to fight with his own impatience and nervousness to let five minutes pass before nodding to Stafford.

As the Cockney left the room Ramage's heart began to thud. The game begins . . . like going into action and waiting for the first enemy gun to fire and drive away the fear. The long wait was nearly over: in the next few minutes he would know if he had the answers to every question the Admiralty could think of, not just those covered by his orders. If he succeeded, the First Lord got a bonus. If he failed – even thinking about it was making his breathing shallow and chilly perspiration was trickling down his spine. His stomach seemed full of a cold liquid churning round. It was not often he could sit quietly in a chair observing his own fear. It was far worse than being on his own quarterdeck while he was taking the ship into action. At sea there were tactics to decide (and sometimes hastily changed at the last moment), sails to be trimmed, orders to be given: with so much to do there was no time to think of fear as such; it crept in, like a misty rain which soaks clothes and chills bodies, unless he was busy. Fear did not get a chance to take a grip on him on a quarterdeck, and the busier he was the more likely it was that someone who did not understand fear would say he was brave.

The real test – and one Ramage wouldn't pass – was sitting in a chair and waiting for things to happen over which he had no control. Stafford had gone to get the satchel; he had orders to open it, and then open the seal of a dispatch. The only trouble was that Ramage had no control over whether or not the dispatch was in the satchel ...

Ramage was watching the door so intently that when it swung open suddenly he gave such a start that he bit his tongue. Cursing to himself, he licked a finger to see if he had drawn blood and, after Stafford walked in and tossed the satchel on the table in a gesture which nearly blew out the candle, Ramage decided that he was too tense to watch him open the seal – providing the Admiral's letter was there.

I'll watch him sort the letters, then I'll take my jacket off slowly and hang it up, he told himself; anything to avoid watching the hot spatula sliding under the paper and knowing we've lost everything if Stafford heats the metal a fraction too much. Not everything, of course; with this last dispatch it did not really matter so much. The melted seal would not be discovered until the satchel was opened in Paris on Monday morning: but it was still better if the French never discovered that the satchel had been opened ...

Stafford selected the right picklock, gave a few wiggles and the flap of the satchel sprang open. Same satchel but someone had been polishing it: the deep scratch below the lock was still there but stained by the polish.

One thickish packet and – one, two ... seven ... nine ... fourteen ... fifteen other letters. Only the packet is addressed to the Minister; the rest are for various departments in the Ministry. Stafford is already heating the spatula with a cheery grin as he pulls the packet in front of him, seal uppermost, and runs a hand through his hair. In Stafford it was confidence; in others it might have been mistaken for bravado. The spatula blade was discolouring with the heat and collecting soot ... Stafford testing it on the back of his hand and put it back in the flame, leaving a smear of soot on the skin of his hand. A full minute passed before he tried it again then, after a quick movement to wipe the soot on his trousers, he slid the spatula under the packet.

Ramage looked away but he knew he could not stand up and take off his jacket with the nonchalance he had intended. He must stay sitting there; Stafford might want him to hold something. He kept his eyes off the seal and looked at the

187

candle but that was no good – when he 'looked away there were candle flames all over the place. Back to the seal with the wax turning shiny as the heat gets to it. Is this how a rabbit feels when a ferret is staring at it? Now Stafford is flicking the spatula away and the packet is open, and the look on his face means that everything has gone well.

'There y'are, sir.'

Ramage unfolded it carefully and found five pages. Paragraphs of neat writing and many figures. He reached for the paper, unscrewed the top of the inkwell, but did not bother to check the tip of the quill because it had been all right half an hour ago.

Bruix's report began with all the polite preliminaries: the French might have fought a Revolution but they still clung to the sort of archaic phrases beloved by the Admiralty. And here, Citizen Minister, is the situation of the Invasion Flotilla at the time of writing . . . Ah, how nice of Bruix! 'I have given first the type of vessel and, for convenience of reference, its capacity. Then I have listed the total number ordered by the First Consul, followed by the number actually launched, commissioned, awaiting commissioning or under construction, and finally the deficit at the time of writing.

'The vessels noted as "awaiting commissioning",' Bruix continued, 'are those which have been launched but which cannot be completed because we lack masts, sails, rigging and guns. You can see how many vessels are under construction, and although there has not been time to distinguish the precise stage each has reached, I have indicated how many are more than half completed.'

Ramage skimmed through and finally read the last few paragraphs of the dispatch in which Bruix acknowledged the Minister's last letter. The shipyards had been told that they would be paid as soon as funds arrived from Paris, but he regretted having to report that it had proved impossible to prevent a number of workmen ('especially skilled shipwrights and carpenters, who can command high wages by working in the cities making and repairing furniture') from running away. Guards were on duty at the shipyards, but the men were billeted in private homes and it was impossible to keep a watch on them day and night. A proclamation had been read to all the men warning them that they risked conscription.

Bruix took this opportunity of listing once against the deficiency in guns so that the Minister should have, in one dispatch, all the facts at his disposal. In view of the Minister's reference to providing funds for the shipyards and wages, Bruix said, he forebore from repeating the actual requirements to settle all accounts and wages to date.

Ramage sighed. Now to copy the facts and figures. He turned back to the first page and began writing:

'*Flotille de grande espèce*

'Barges carrying 4,320 men and intended to sail in two divisions. Each barge to carry 50 cavalry, 25 infantry, 3 officers and 2 non-combatants, and a cargo of 27 muskets, 20 bayonets, 200 tools, 1200 cartridges, 1500 rations of biscuit, 500 of oats and 500 of bran, 50 horses, 60 saddles and 6 sheep.

'Ordered – 54. Launched – 23. Of these there were sufficient masts, spars, cordage and sails to complete and commission only 11. Under construction – 5 (all less than half completed). Deficit – 26.

'Sloops, forming the Second Flotilla, each with a pinnace in company, and carrying a total for the Second Flotilla of 35,964. Each sloop to carry 3 officers of a company, 91 officers and men, 2 officers of a battalion staff, 1 officer of the general staff, 3 gunners, 3 wagoners, 8 surgeons. The cargo to comprise 27 muskets, 20 bayonets, 27 pioneers' tools, 1,200 flints, 12,000 cartridges, 1,200 rations of biscuit, 150 pints of brandy and 4 sheep.

'Ordered – 324. Launched – 109. Of these, only 69 could be commissioned. Under construction – 15 (of which four are more than half completed). Deficit – 200.

'Gunboats, to form the Third Flotilla, each with a pinnace in company and carrying 130 men for a total of 56,160 (including 3,456 surgeons). Each gunboat to be armed with one 24-pounder gun and also to carry 1 piece of field artillery and the same cargo as sloops, plus 2 horses, 10 bushels of oats and bran, and 200 rounds of shot.

'Ordered – 432. Launched – 73. Of these, only 19 have been commissioned. Still under construction – 14 (of which 12 are more than half completed). Deficit – 345.

'Caiques, forming the Fourth Flotilla. To carry a total of 2,160 men with 216,000 cartridges, 21,600 rations of biscuit, 1,080 rations of brandy and 108 sheep.

'Required – 540. Requisitioned, commandeered or captured – 127. (Note: only 63 of these have arrived at Boulogne, Calais, Étaples, St Valery or Wimereux. Another 11 have reached Le Havre and Cherbourg. The remaining 53 are in various ports between Antwerp and St Jean de Luz awaiting safe convoy.) Deficit – 413.

'Corvettes, forming the Fifth Flotilla, each carrying 40 men for a total of 3,240. These to carry the same cargo as gunboats but no artillery or ammunition.

'Ordered – 81. Launched – 10. (Note: 27 old corvettes have been refitted but none is less than 25 years old.) Deficit – 44.

'Fishing boats, forming the Sixth Flotilla, and to carry 2,160 horses and riders, with a double supply of horses and riders.

'Required – 108. Requisitioned, commandeered or captured – 108.

'Fishing boats of six different types to form the Transport Flotilla, and intended to carry 3 million cartridges, 1,208 horses, 3,560 officers and men, 1,760 canteen women, and a considerable quantity of other military stores too numerous to list here.

'Required – 464. Requisitioned, commandeered or captured: 276. Deficit – 188.

'Another Flotilla comprising 100 to 150 large, armed fishing boats have yet to be found,' Bruix wrote. 'These are intended to carry 200 horses, 1,000 men, 10,000 rations of biscuit, 10,000 rations each of brandy, oats and bran, and 200 sheep.'

From the preceding figures, Bruix noted, it will be seen the number of men that the vessels ordered or required can carry, 110,324, is less than the required strength of the Army of Invasion (working on a total of 113,474, comprising 76,798 infantrymen, 11,640 cavalry, 3,780 artillerymen, 3,780 wagoners and 17,476 non-combatants), but it is anticipated that each vessel will be able to carry an extra dozen or so men.

'The search still goes on in all ports from Antwerp to St Jean de Luz,' the Admiral added, 'for 300 merchant ships of less than seven feet draught and each of which can carry 100 men. Although there had been some success in finding a number, several of these have since been captured by British cruisers and privateers while making for Boulogne.'

Bruix concluded with what Ramage read as a plea to Forfait to make it clear to the First Consul that he had done the best he could with the money, men and materials available, and he continued to doubt the wisdom of trying to make seaworthy those craft built for similar projects in the 1760s: they required a disproportionate amount of men and materials – particularly men, since only skilled shipwrights could be used for that type of work.

Ramage drew a line and then signed his name. Then he put down the pen and screwed the top on the inkwell. He gave a sigh of relief and looked at his watch. It had taken twenty-five minutes. 'Here, you'd better seal this and take it to Louis's room. I hope he remembered to get a fresh loaf!'

'He did, sir, an' he told me he'd slit it ready for up to six sheets of paper. You've only used –' Stafford flicked through the pages, 'three. I'll seal them first.' He folded them and ran his thumb nail along the creases to flatten them. Picking up a stick of red wax he glanced at Ramage's signet ring. 'Want ter use the seal, sir?'

Ramage shook his head. 'Too risky – if that was intercepted and I was caught . . .'

As soon as the blobs of wax sealed Ramage's letter, Stafford left the room in his usual silent manner, returning to say that it was secure in the loaf.

'Want ter glance at any of these, sir?' He gestured towards the remaining letters.

'No – we've done enough for tonight. Just seal up the Admiral's dispatch and get that satchel back under the lieutenant's bed, so we can get to sleep!'

The job was nearly done. Almost unbelievably, they had succeeded. It remained only for Stafford to reheat the spatula and fix the seal, put all the correspondence back in the satchel, and return it. Ramage decided to lie on his bed to savour the feeling of relief: Stafford needed no help, and Ramage was beginning to feel weak from relaxation of tension and almost unbelievably tired.

The bed creaked, and as he stretched out he realized just how weary he was. Stafford was humming quietly to himself and Ramage watched the shadow of the Cockney's head dancing across the ceiling.

'That's it, me beauty,' Stafford muttered and blew vigorously. 'Ah – just as good as the horiginal. In yer go.' Ramage was reminded of a poacher talking to his ferret. There was a click as he turned the lock on the satchel. 'Right, that's that, sir; I'll be off darn the corridor.'

Ramage murmured contentedly. Drowsily he wondered if Louis was winning at cards. Tomorrow morning, in a few hours' time, all three of them would be in a carriage rattling along the road to Boulogne, with the report preceding them, safe from interception should they be captured. Jackson and

Rossi would be waiting at Boulogne with the *Marie* and Dyson. Curious that a scoundrel like Dyson should eventually do something that made up for all his past crimes. Dare he tell Lord Nelson all about him, so that Dyson would not go through the rest of his life a wanted man? Plenty of time to think about that later; now it was good to sleep knowing that the work was done, and it only remained to escape . . .

A woman's shrill scream went through him like a dagger. She screamed again and again in desperate fear; then he heard her running along the corridor and down the stairs, still screaming as she went. The landlord's daughter?

He leapt out of bed and grabbed Stafford's spatula, the stick of wax and the remaining bundle of picklocks. Where could he hide them? The screaming had stopped but he could hear thumping below, as though men were coming up the stairs. Stafford had not come back and it was difficult to know what had happened.

Hurriedly he tossed the picklocks, wax and spatula up on top of the canopy over the bed, then dragged off his clothes and pulled on his nightshirt, blew out the candle and hurried to the door, waiting a few seconds before opening it as the first of the men ran past.

It was the lieutenant with a lantern, followed by Louis and then the landlord.

'What's happening?' Ramage asked sleepily and with suitable nervousness.

'Burglars!' the landlord said, using Ramage's appearance to leave the other two men to run into the lieutenant's room. 'My daughter found them and raised the alarm!'

'What was she doing up here?'

'She had written a *billet doux* for the lieutenant and crept up to put it under his pillow, I think. Then she saw all these men. Half a dozen or more, she says . . .'

Ramage murmured sympathetic noises as he listened. A few moments later the lieutenant strode out, chest puffed with importance. 'There is no one there – and the dispatches are safe –' he waved the satchel he was holding. 'The window is wide open – the villains escaped. Landlord! Fetch the gendarmes – we must start a search for them. Six men!'

The landlord scurried down the stairs.

'Did you see anything, M'sieur?' he lieutenant asked Ramage.

'Nothing – I heard screaming. It woke me up.'

Louis said, 'M'sieur still looks half asleep, for all that!'

Ramage took the hint. He rubbed his eyes. 'I am, too. Did they get away with anything valuable?'

'Nothing that I can see,' the lieutenant said complacently. He held up the satchel. 'This is all that matters. That is still firmly locked, as you can see –' he tugged at the flap. 'The only keys that will open it are in Boulogne and in Paris. The Admiral's dispatches to the Minister of Marine.'

'Do you think the burglars were after that?' Louis asked innocently.

The lieutenant shook his head vigorously. 'Not a chance. Who could know that I carry dispatches? And anyway, the satchel is always concealed. I rely on your discretion, gentlemen,' he said confidentially.

'Just common thieves,' Louis said. 'They probably looked through the window and saw we were playing cards. Why,' he exclaimed, 'they'd have seen me, too! Here, lend me your lantern, I must see if I've been robbed!'

Louis fiddled with the key for a few moments – Ramage remembered he had left the door unlocked and obviously wanted to conceal the fact from the lieutenant – swung the door open and went inside.

'Everything is all right,' he said when he emerged. 'They must have decided to search your room first. They recognized you as a man of substance,' he added slyly.

'You are winning at cards,' the lieutenant grumbled. 'Second time running. A month's pay you've taken off me so far –'

He broke off. Strange voices were coming up the stairs and Ramage saw two gendarmes, each with a lantern. They clumped along the corridor and stopped.

'Which of you is the Italian, di Stefano?'

Ramage stepped forward, puzzled.

'Get dressed,' one of the gendarmes snapped, 'you are under arrest.'

CHAPTER FOURTEEN

The police headquarters were on the south side of the square, looking out across the pavé to the guillotine under the plane trees on the far side. The two gendarmes pushed Ramage through the open door with a series of oaths and one of them kept him covered with a pistol while the other went along a corridor and knocked on a door. A minute or two later he called and the man with the pistol gestured to Ramage to follow.

Sitting at the desk in the middle of the room was a man in an officer's uniform whose thin face was heavily lined. Every few moments his right eye suddenly closed momentarily, as though he was winking, followed by a spasmodic jerk of his right shoulder. For a moment Ramage was reminded of a puppet, some of whose strings were broken.

The man pulled his lips back, as though about to bite something juicy, and exposing a mouthful of yellowed teeth. 'Passport,' he hissed.

Ramage dug into his coat pocket and then handed it over.

'Gianfranco di Stefano, eh? You speak French? You are Italian?'

Ramage nodded.

'What are you doing in Amiens?'

'Travelling to Paris. I was taken ill.'

One of the gendarmes whispered to the officer.

'Paris? You were travelling to Boulogne. You have a carriage ordered for tomorrow. You and two other men.'

'I have been to Boulogne and was going back to Paris when I was taken ill,' Ramage explained with a nervousness far from feigned. 'Before I recovered, word came from Boulogne that there was still some unfinished business there and asking me to return.'

'What business? Who asked you?'

Ramage guessed that he was trapped if this man was thorough. He could bluff it out for a few days, but the moment the police checked with the Port Captain in Boulogne, they would find out that there was no such person as Signor di Stefano; that his documents were genuine but the blank spaces had been filled in with a false name. And then the fun would start: they would set to work on him to find out what it was all about. 'Set to work' – he was avoiding using the word 'torture,' but that was what he meant.

'I have nothing to say,' Ramage said crossly. 'Why am I under arrest?'

He had to keep his mouth shut for long enough for Louis to get the dispatch to Boulogne, and be sure the *Marie* had sailed for the rendezvous. Once he could be sure that the dispatches were in Lord Nelson's hands, his job was done. Then he could talk as freely as he wanted – making sure not to incriminate Louis and his comrades – or remain silent. The final result was likely to be the same: he would swing over on the *bascule* and the executioner would let the blade drop. *Le Moniteur* would probably print some florid announcement that an English spy had been executed at Amiens (or an Italian one, if he stayed silent), and eventually someone in the Admiralty in London might connect the execution with the fact that Lieutenant Ramage had disappeared after sending a final report from Amiens ...

'You have nothing to say, eh? Well, I have,' the officer said. 'You are under arrest because your man – your foreman, I believe? – was seen by the daughter of the landlord in the room of another guest. An officer of the Republic,' he added ominously.

'I thought she said she saw *several* men.' It was a glimmer of hope but no more.

'She may have done; what concerns you is that your foreman is the one she definitely recognized.'

Ramage shrugged his shoulders. 'That's what she says. I was asleep and have no idea what was going on. Was she in the room with my foreman? Did they have an assignation?'

It was a weak enough answer, but for the moment he was trying to gain time to think. Where the devil was Stafford now – obviously he had escaped out of the window, but how long could he avoid recapture? He did not speak a word of French, had no money and no map to help him get back to Boulogne. The only thing on his side was a natural Cockney shrewdness.

'What was your foreman doing?'

'Seducing her, perhaps? How should I know – I told you, I was asleep.'

Where was Louis now? Had he escaped before anyone checked up on his story that he was acting as the spy-cum-guard to the Italian travellers? Ramage could not remember seeing him from the moment the gendarmes said, 'Get dressed ...' On the other hand he might still be at the hotel, pretending to be as puzzled over Stafford's behaviour as the gendarmes. That would make sense! At the moment the only thing the gendarmes knew was that Stafford had been seen in the lieutenant's room. Nothing had been stolen so there was nothing to incriminate either Signor di Stefano or Louis. If

Louis suddenly vanished it would be taken as proof of complicity.

In fact he and Louis would be cleared completely if the gendarmes accepted that whatever Stafford was doing had nothing to do with his employer or Louis. Let's see what happens, Ramage thought. For the moment I remain the Italian shipbuilder outraged that he should be lodged in jail for the night . . . All that gaunt-faced policeman knows is that my foreman was in someone else's room: no one has challenged my story that I was asleep at the time. With a bit of luck they'll release me tomorrow with suitable apologies!

Ramage thought of asking to be allowed to write to his own country's ambassador in Paris protesting at his arrest, but he remembered, just in time, that the Republic of Genoa, whence he allegedly came, was now Bonaparte's Ligurian Republic. Then the officer, who had been staring at the top of his desk for several moments, looked up.

'If he was trying to seduce her with her consent,' he said coldly, his voice sounding to Ramage like that of every outraged father or cuckolded husband, 'why did she scream?'

Ramage shrugged his shoulders expressively. 'How should I know? Perhaps she changed her mind.'

'She is in love with the lieutenant,' the officer said doggedly. 'It is impossible that she went to the room to meet your foreman.'

'Very well,' Ramage said in a bored voice, 'she had an assignation with the lieutenant in his room. Clearly not a very virtuous young lady, eh?'

'She did *not* have an assignation with the lieutenant in his room,' the officer said angrily, his right eye winking and his shoulder jerking.

'What was she doing in the room, then? Meeting my foreman instead?'

'She had written a note for the lieutenant and was leaving it in his room. Where is your foreman now?' Again the wink and shoulder twitch.

'I don't know,' Ramage said impatiently. 'Perhaps he has an assignation with the young lady's mother – have you inquired?'

It must be midnight by now. Had Louis managed to get that damned loaf to the courier? If Ramage could be sure that the report – he found himself trying to avoid even thinking of the name Bruix, as if the police officer might read his thoughts

– reached Jackson on board the *Marie*, it would make it worthwhile. *What* worthwhile, he found himself asking. Stop thinking in euphemisms. If I know that my copy of Vice-Admiral Bruix's report on the state of the *Flotille de Grande Espèce* has reached Vice-Admiral Lord Nelson safely, then tipping over on the *bascule*, and staring down into the basket which will catch my head a fraction of a second after the guillotine blade lops it off, will be a little easier to bear.

It must be easier to die when you know you have achieved something. On the average, Ramage had gone into action four times a year, for the past three years, never expecting to come out of it alive. There had been a good chance that a French or Spanish roundshot would knock his head off or – involuntarily he reached up and rubbed the scars on the right side of his brow – he would be cut down by a cutlass or skewered on a boarding-pike.

For Lieutenant Ramage, there was no difference between having his head knocked off by roundshot or lopped off by guillotine. Yet, in a bizarre sort of way, there was. If the copy of Bruix's dispatch reached Lord Nelson safely, there could be nothing more in his career (even if he lived to become an admiral) that could match it in importance. The sort of things that involved the risk of having your head knocked off by a roundshot were relatively trivial: it is only when you play for the very highest stakes that you risk 'marrying the Widow.'

The officer was staring at him and when he caught Ramage's eye he asked curiously: 'What were you thinking about?'

'That if my foreman *did* have an assignation with the landlord's daughter, I envied him. Pretty girl – have you seen her?'

The officer flushed, a redness that stained his lined and wrinkled face like wine soaking through *lasagna*, and Ramage realized that the man must have been speculating about her.

'The other man you were with – the Frenchman: who is he?'

'You mean to say you don't know?' Ramage was scornful. 'Why should I?' the officer asked defensively.

'One of your ministries sent him along to spy on me wherever I go, that's all I know!' As soon as he saw the officer nodding, as though the information was credible, Ramage decided to embellish it. 'I can tell you, I've had enough of his company. "Won't you have another bottle of wine, M'sieur?" he says ... And I have half a glass and he finishes the whole bottle. Who pays, eh? *I* do. Liqueurs – you tell me why all the liqueurs go on my bill? And the brandy – *Mama mia*, how much that man can drink! I pay for it, every drop. Not –' Ramage added hastily, as though suddenly nervous, 'that I'm saying anything against him, you understand.'

The police officer nodded sympathetically. 'He was sent from Paris, no doubt.'

'Yes, he joined me in Paris after my visit to Boulogne was arranged.'

Nothing said about Louis up to now could incriminate either of them. This local police officer might accept that Louis was working for some ministry or committee – he would be used in secrecy – without checking up. He might well think that arresting a foreigner who was being supervised by the employee of a ministry or committee would leave him open to an accusation of interfering . . . it was a faint hope.

'Where is he, anyway?' Ramage asked crossly. 'Let him speak for himself – he's always very secretive, although he keeps a sharp enough watch on me.'

'Probably writing a report on this affair for his superiors,' the officer said. 'I expect he'll be in to see me later.'

'Well,' Ramage said calmly, 'he can tell you all about everything, so there's no need for me to stay. You'll find me at the hotel.'

He had not walked two paces before the officer was shouting. Ramage turned to find himself covered by the pistols of the two gendarmes.

'You are going to a cell!' the officer said angrily. He pulled a large book towards him, a book that reminded Ramage of a ledger in a counting-house. 'Now, I want your full name and address, and all the details of why you are in France . . .'

The cell was square, five paces along one side and five paces along the other. It had a chill of its own, something which had nothing to do with the outside temperature, for it was a warm night. Ramage only saw the inside for a brief moment, in the light of the guard's lantern, before being pushed in and having the door slammed behind him. As his eyes became accustomed to the darkness he saw that there was a single small window high in one wall, and although it was barely large enough for a man to put his head through, there were iron bars.

He had seen a low wooden cot but in the darkness misjudged the distance, finding it by banging his shin painfully on a corner. A moment later he kicked over a bucket, and from the smell guessed its purpose. There was a thin palliasse of sacking and straw on the cot, and he thought momentarily of all the bedbugs lurking in there, waiting for the majesty of French law to provide them with their next meal.

He sat down on the cot and realized how tired he was. The strain of the last hour had drained his energy, and he hoped he was tired enough to drop off to sleep quickly, instead of finding his mind invaded by a dozen worries which tightened his muscles and chased sleep away. Having already been caught once in his nightshirt he decided that undressing would be confined to his boots.

The interview had not gone too badly. The officer was suspicious but not more so than was to be expected. His main interest obviously centred on Stafford, and Ramage was sure he had accepted the story of Louis being the representative from some ministry or committee in Paris.

As he stretched out on the cot he reflected that whatever happened – and for the moment there was no need to be too pessimistic – Louis had almost certainly had time to get the report out of his room and into the courier's hands. Sleep, that was what he needed; worrying could achieve nothing, since once again everything was in Louis's hands.

Dawn was a pale grey square at the window when he was woken by the rasp of bolts being pulled back. A moment later the door creaked open and a wedge of yellow lantern light on the floor showed a small bowl being put down on the floor just inside the cell. The door slammed shut, cutting off the light, and the bolts rasped again, all without anyone saying a word.

Ramage rubbed his eyes and heard the faint rasp of other bolts: presumably the inmate of another cell was also receiving his breakfast. He walked carefully over to the door and picked up the bowl. It was a watery gruel which had a vague smell of dried peas, and he saw something he had not noticed at first, a large crust of bread, the end of a long loaf.

There was no spoon – presumably they were afraid of a prisoner using it to beat in the guard's head, although heaving the bread like a half brick would do more damage. He tilted the bowl and began drinking, and was reminded immediately of the landlady's medicine. The taste was not the same; the prison gruel had far less body but hinted at the same strange origins. Certainly the gruel owed most of its substance to cabbage water, although the peas floating around in it might well have been rabbit droppings for all the taste or sustenance they offered.

Birds began to chatter outside the window as it grew lighter. There were a few high clouds and the wind seemed to be from the south-west. With luck it would hold there long enough to give Jackson a fast reach over to Folkestone tonight. Was Louis's courier already heading towards the coast from Amiens? Already through Picquigny, Abbeville and Montreuil? In his imagination Ramage travelled the road back to Boulogne, crossed the Channel, hired a horse at Folkestone and rode to Aldington, where his clothes and perhaps Gianna, were waiting . . .

He put the bowl down angrily: of all the thoughts that had tried to fight their way into his mind in the past week, the one he had resisted most successfully until this moment was of Gianna, and he knew he had to continue to shut her out. Men were supposed to be spurred on to great feats of daring and bravery by the thought of beautiful women, but he was damned if it worked for him. He had often thought of Gianna just before going into action, but all that happened was that the prospect of getting his head knocked off became even less attractive. Now there was a possibility of getting it lopped off by the guillotine he found even this brief glimpse of her painful. Next week, he whispered to himself, she must go away now and come back next week . . .

There was no sign of life inside the police station although outside the window the occasional clatter of hooves showed that the people of Amiens were beginning to stir. He felt grubby and greasy; his chin and cheeks were ready for a shave, though presumably prisoners were not trusted with a razor.

It was Sunday morning, and in London it would be another couple of hours before the family came down to breakfast. Then – he stood up abruptly to shake off the thought and began pacing up and down the cell. Five paces to the window, turn, five paces back. The floor was made of stone blocks: the same stone as the walls. He passed by the door and noted that it was made of four thick baulks of timber, braced and strengthened by iron crossbars, with the whole surface closely studded with iron bolts which would presumably deflect the blade of an axe, whether wielded from inside or outside the cell.

For the moment the question of escaping did not arise, he decided, but to give himself something to do he began going over every inch of the cell. The window was so small he would have difficulty getting his head through it, let alone his shoulders, so there was no point in testing the bars. The outside wall – stone blocks, each four feet wide by a foot thick, with the bars of the window set in the middle. The inner walls – again solid granite blocks, probably a foot or more thick. The ceiling was a good nine feet high, and rust marks in the plaster showed him that it was made up of iron rods spaced about six inches apart. A woodsman's axe would make no impression on the door itself and the hinges were outside in the corridor. Whoever designed and built this cell knew his job. Despite all the stories of daring escapes from barred cells, the fact was that the only way out of this, without the key to the door, would be by igniting a barrel of powder . . .

Supposing things did go wrong, and it came to escaping? He shrugged his shoulders and sat down on the cot. The only way out was through the door, and the only way of opening the door was by sliding back the bolts and turning the key in the lock from outside. If Stafford had been there he might have been able to pick the lock from inside, but even he could not slide back those big bolts.

Which left no alternative but to overpower the jailer. Get the man inside the cell under some pretext or other, knock him out, walk blithely out of the building and hope to vanish down the side streets. It would be wise to watch the habits of the jailers. The one on duty at the moment was a cautious beggar who opened the door just enough to push the bowl in and then slammed it shut. Habit or orders? Was one jailer on duty at a time, or was there another one sitting or standing out there as well? He needed to know that before he made any move.

Then he pushed the thoughts away: it was still early on Sunday, and the courier would not yet have reached Boulogne. All being well, Dyson, Jackson and Rossi would sail tonight for the rendezvous and Jackson would transfer to the Folkestone *Marie* to arrive in England tomorrow morning. He would deliver the report and be back in the Folkestone boat ready to sail for the rendezvous on Monday night, meet the

French *Marie,* and be back in Boulogne on Tuesday.

There could be a delay of course – the courier for Amiens might be a day late getting to Boulogne; the *Marie* might lose twenty-four hours if she could not leave Boulogne early enough to reach the rendezvous that night. Hellfire and damnation, it was hard to guess . . . All right, say the courier reaches Boulogne too late for the *Marie* to sail tonight to get to the rendezvous, Dyson would sail on Monday night instead, and Jackson deliver the dispatch on Tuesday and get back to Boulogne soon after dawn on Wednesday.

Say Louis and Stafford managed to escape from Amiens and made their way to Boulogne, they would miss the *Marie* sailing with the dispatch, so they would have to wait for her to return on Tuesday or possibly not until Wednesday. They would be safe enough hidden on board her all day Wednesday, until they could sail on Wednesday night.

This meant that to give them all a chance of getting away – which was the least he owed the men – he needed to keep his secret until dawn on Wednesday. After that he could confess, tell blatant lies, bait the gendarmes or do whatever he wanted, knowing that he would not endanger the men or the dispatch. It was a long time to wait; today, Monday and Tuesday: seventy-two hours.

He stood up suddenly, as if to drive away the hours. It might not arise; Louis might convince the officer that all the trouble had been caused by a foreman with a roving eye. I'll be back at the hotel by this afternoon, he told himself, and began pacing up and down the cell.

He was used to walking in a confined space – the quarter-deck of his last two ships had not allowed more than a dozen uninterrupted paces – but this cell was even smaller and the constant turning made him feel dizzy. Queasy, perhaps; the turning was swilling the gruel around in his protesting stomach, and the few pieces of stale bread he managed to swallow did nothing to ballast it down.

He flopped down on the cot and shut his eyes. He had felt trapped in the hotel room, but it had not really given him the slightest idea of what it was like to be locked in a cell. Once when he was a boy he had nearly drowned, and he remembered the terrible feeling of being utterly trapped, and the desperate way he had kicked his legs and flailed his arms to escape from the water which enclosed him like glue . . . A few days in this cell could drive a man mad. How did anyone endure being jailed for years? That's something I'll never know, he thought grimly; I'll have been freed, escaped, or they'll be leading me across the square to the guillotine long before a week has passed.

An hour later he heard the bolts being pulled back and the key turning in the lock. The door swung open and a gendarme with a pistol walked into the room, motioning him to remain sitting on the bed. He was followed by the gaunt officer, who nodded briefly.

'I trust you slept well,' Ramage said sarcastically. 'I'm sorry to be the cause of you getting to bed rather late.'

'I have my duty,' the man said, his right shoulder twitching. 'We guardians of the Republic's safety must always be alert.'

Ramage avoided saying 'Amen' and looked at the floor, waiting for the officer to start questioning him. Instead, the man said nothing. He stood and stared down at Ramage who, able to see what the man was doing out of the corner of his eye, was thankful he had begun looking at the floor before the officer began his curious vigil.

Ramage started counting the seconds, and had reached three and a half minutes before the man said: 'Are you ready to confess?'

Ramage was so startled that, without thinking, he said: 'Why, is there a priest here?'

The gendarme shook his head impatiently. 'Don't be ridiculous,' he said sternly, 'I mean, are you ready to confess what you and your foreman have been doing?'

'Doing!' Ramage said angrily. 'Well, all the time we have been in Amiens we have been sick – thanks to the bad food we were served. We shall be glad to say goodbye to Amiens, I can tell you.'

'The *lieutenant-de-vaisseau* – do you know what his orders are?'

'Of course I don't. Hardly to sail a ship, though; he seems to be a horseman rather than a seaman.'

'He is Admiral Bruix's personal courier,' the officer said, emphasizing each word.

'Indeed?' Ramage raised his eyebrows. 'What does he do, ride to Paris once a week and bring back the Admiral's truffles?'

The officer ignored the gibe. 'He carries the Admiral's dispatches to Paris, and brings back the orders from the Minister.'

'And . . .?' Ramage prompted.

'And nothing!' he snapped. 'It is a very important task; surely you realize that, don't you? Admiral Bruix commands the Channel coast.'

'He must be kept busy; all I heard in Boulogne were complaints about the British frigates capturing ships, so that supplies never arrived.'

'Your words sound very much like treason,' the officer said coldly.

Ramage stood up with a suddenness that made the gendarme with the pistol swing the muzzle up towards him. 'Treason!' Ramage yelled angrily, deciding that the moment had come for outraged indignation. 'You dare accuse *me* of talking treason! *Mama mia!* I, an Italian, come all the way from Genoa to Boulogne – right across the Alps and the Juras, no less, and all at my own expense, because your own shipbuilders can't launch vessels for the Invasion Flotilla fast enough! You are so behind with construction that unless something is done quickly, you will not be able to invade England for another two years.

'Your Admiral Bruix knows that – though,' he dropped his voice confidentially, 'he may not tell the First Consul, that is something only those two know, but I do know the Admiral found it necessary to send a thousand kilometres for a particular man. And who was that man?' He let his voice rise indignantly. 'Come on, name him! Who was this Italian shipbuilder that Admiral Bruix decided could help speed up the building of his Invasion Flotilla? You don't know perhaps, but I'll tell you – it was *me*. Gianfranco di Stefano, shipbuilder and master shipwright – master shipwright at my age, that surprises you, doesn't it – and loyal subject of the Ligurian Republic. *That* is the man you accuse of treason!'

The officer was now looking worried. Ramage saw that his outburst had impressed him, but he feared that the fellow was plodding and tenacious, a man who would carry out an investigation like a keen chess player analysing all the possible moves.

'I did not accuse you of treason, M'sieur; I merely said your words sounded very much like treason, which – '

'That is just as insulting as a direct accusation,' Ramage said huffily.

'I assure you that it isn't, M'sieur. If I accused you directly,

204

you would be charged with treason. Now tell me, where is your foreman?'

Ramage sighed and sat down. 'You might just as well accuse me of witchcraft to ask me where that thrice-damned foreman is! How can I possibly know? You have kept me locked up all night, so how can I look for him? In some *bordello,* if I know him, and better a *bordello* than a cell, I assure you, since I now have experience of both.'

'The Frenchman,' the officer persisted, 'this Louis Peyrachon: where is he?'

'In his room at the Hotel de la Poste, I imagine,' Ramage said, playing for time as he absorbed the good news that the police officer had just revealed. 'Or with my foreman in the *bordello.* How else to spend a Saturday night in a town like Amiens? You French do not know how to live! Everyone seems to go to bed as soon as the sun goes down!'

'What did you arrange with him?'

'Arrange? What do you mean by that? After we had supper he went downstairs to play cards with your precious lieutenant, and I did not see him again until he came upstairs with the lieutenant after that silly girl started screaming.'

The police officer nodded, as though what Ramage had just said fitted in with information received from other sources. 'Where did you meet this man?'

'I told you that last night. I didn't "meet" him; he was ordered to travel with me. Which ministry he works for I do not know – he did not tell me, and I did not ask. I resented – and still resent – having someone escorting me everywhere, as though I was a dog on a leash.'

'Is it not strange, M'sieur, that the moment a young woman screams because she finds a man in the room of à naval courier, two men in your suite suddenly vanish?'

'*Two* men vanish?' Ramage exclaimed, his surprise unfeigned. 'Are you referring to the Frenchman? How can you say he vanished when I saw him – the lieutenant and the landlord can confirm that – in the corridor afterwards? I did not see my foreman from the time I went to bed, but the Frenchman, Louis, I did see. And don't refer to him as being in my "suite"; he was a thoroughly unwelcome addition, I assure you; as unwelcome as the *grippe* my foreman and I caught here in Amiens.'

'The Frenchman was not in his room this morning . . .'
'So?'

'The room was completely empty,' the officers said.

'You mean he left with all the furniture?' Ramage asked sarcastically, still trying to gauge whether the policeman was setting some sort of trap.

'Of course not!' He was getting impatient at last, Ramage noted, with eye winking and shoulder twitching. 'I mean he packed his bag and vanished.'

'I hope he has gone to Paris to report to his masters that you have locked Signor Gianfranco di Stefano in your stinking prison.'

'We shall know in good time,' the officer said, obviously unperturbed at the prospect. 'In the meantime one of my men is riding to Boulogne. He has instructions to see if you are known at Admiral Bruix's headquarters, and to inquire into your passport and travel documents. What answers will he get, M'sieur?'

'You make a habit of asking questions that no one could possibly answer!'

'I'll ask you one that you can answer, then. In Paris, at the Ministry of Marine, what was the name of the official who arranged your visit to Boulogne?'

'Official? I saw at least a dozen. I asked to see the Minister, but I was passed from one man to another. I told one of them that the way they were treating me, anyone would think I was going to try to steal the Invasion Flotilla, instead of help to build it!'

'Surely you can remember at least one name?'

'Well, I can't; why should I remember the names of petty officials?' he said arrogantly. 'Imbeciles, most of them –' he suddenly had an inspiration, 'and so obsessed with secrecy they must regard their names as State secrets, judging from the way they behave. They all talk out of the sides of their mouths, like this.' Ramage pulled a face. 'Who do they suspect – their colleagues in the ministries? Who do they suspect of being spies – those same colleagues?'

'I neither know nor care what goes on in Paris,' the officer said obstinately. 'I am only concerned with what goes on here in Amiens.'

'But why are you keeping me in prison?'

'Because I have inquiries to make in Boulogne.'

'Why cannot I stay at the Hotel? No one can travel in France without documents.'

'The two men travelling with you have just vanished,' the

policeman said coldly. 'If I release you, what is to stop you vanishing as well?'

'I don't know what has been going on,' Ramage said angrily, 'but if I had anything to do with it, surely I would have vanished too, instead of going to bed!'

'Perhaps – who knows?' the policeman said, shrugging his shoulders. 'The whole thing is a puzzle.'

'What was stolen from the lieutenant's room?'

'Nothing as far as we know, but – '

'There you are!' Ramage interrupted crossly. '*Nothing* has been stolen; all that seems to have happened is my foreman and the landlord's daughter had an assignation in the lieutenant's room. For that *I* am locked up!'

'I was going to say that the lieutenant was carrying a satchel full of letters and dispatches from Admiral Bruix's headquarters to the Ministry of Marine. Until the lieutenant arrives in Paris we do not know if any of those letters and dispatches were stolen.'

'Why on earth should anyone want to steal a few letters?'

'They are State secrets!'

'In that case,' Ramage pointed out sourly, 'why would anyone steal just one or two? Why not the whole satchel?'

'Be patient,' the policeman said. 'As soon as the inquiries are complete . . .' He left the sentence unfinished and went to the door. 'If you want anything better than prison fare, you can send out to the hotel. You pay for it, of course.'

Ramage found the rest of Sunday the longest day he had ever experienced, but Monday was far worse. The walls of the cell were so thick that apart from a few street noises coming through the tiny window and an occasional sound from inside the building which managed to penetrate the thick wooden door, he might have been sitting on a raft in the middle of the Western Ocean: his sense of isolation was almost overwhelming.

He could do nothing about trying to escape until Wednesday . . . He found himself looking forward to the arrival of the turnkey who brought his meals from the hotel, even though the man was a sullen brute who took an obvious delight in slamming the tray down on the floor so hard that soup slopped over the edge of the bowl and meat slid off the plate on to the dusty flagstones.

The turnkey was his only visitor on Monday, and he spent

most of the day wondering what has happened to Louis and Stafford and speculating whether, if he could not escape, he would eventually be given a trial or simply marched out and executed. The inquiries in Boulogne ruled out any chance of his being released. In an otherwise uncertain world, that much was sure enough.

Even as he sat on the wooden cot he imagined a gendarme visiting various offices in Boulogne – no doubt he had been given a list – and systematically asking if they had had any discussions with an Italian named Gianfranco di Stefano, shipbuilder. One after another the officials would say no . . . and, with the last office visited, and the last official questioned, the man would return to Amiens and report.

By then the lieutenant would be back after delivering his satchel to the Ministry in Paris. All the seals would have been examined closely. Had Stafford been a little careless this time, a little too confident? Ramage cursed himself for not examining the seal after the dispatch had been done up again. Would it stand comparison with a new seal? Had the wax sagged slightly? Not obvious if you compared it with another one that had not been opened and re-sealed?

They had thought of a clerk – or even the Minister – picking up the dispatch and breaking the seal: unless there was something radically wrong about the impression, it would not arouse suspicion. He had not thought – though perhaps he was being unfair to Stafford, who was a shrewd enough fellow – in terms of the seal being closely compared with others.

The net was gradually tightening; there was no escaping that fact. Evidence would soon be on its way to Amiens from Boulogne that would show that Signor di Stefano was not the man he claimed to be. That evidence would be damning enough, and anyway the police officer would soon hear from Paris. If the report from the Ministry of Marine said that the seal of the dispatch from Admiral Bruix had been tampered with, then Signor di Stefano had an appointment with the Widow across the *place* without delay. If they found nothing wrong with the seal there might be a respite.

He shivered as he thought that his life might depend on a piece of wax; on whether or not suspicious men in Paris could detect that a wax seal had been opened and stuck down again. His life was balanced, not on a knife edge but on a piece of sealing-wax.

The landlord of the Hotel de la Poste had obviously made up his mind that Signor di Stefano would not be a guest at his establishment again: he was charging exactly double the normal price for each meal, and insisting on a large deposit against the bowl, plate, mug, and tray. Some of the meat was so tough that Ramage had difficulty in tearing it apart with his fingers and, even worse, the tray was too flimsy to use as a weapon.

By two o'clock in the afternoon of Tuesday, Ramage was counting the hours to Wednesday morning, when he could begin to watch for an opportunity to escape. Then the door of the cell swung open unexpectedly. A gendarme walked in with a pistol, motioning Ramage to stand in a corner. A moment later two more gendarmes came in and one of them tossed a pair of irons on the floor by Ramage's feet. 'Put them on your wrists,' he ordered.

As soon as Ramage had fitted them, the man slid a padlock through the slot and locked it. He gave Ramage a push towards the door. 'Come this way.'

Ramage, expecting another interrogation by the police officer, was startled to find himself escorted into a large room in the centre of which was a long table. Three men sat at the table, one in the middle of the far side and one at each end. Halfway between the door and the table was a chair, and the escorts marched him up to it.

The man sitting at the end of the table on Ramage's right was the gaunt police officer, now freshly shaven, with his uniform newly pressed and his cocked hat resting on the table in front of him, as though it was a symbol of authority.

Sitting at the middle of the table was a plump, sharp-eyed man who was not in uniform. His hair was iron-grey and he was watching every move that Ramage made. The third man wore a uniform Ramage did not recognize, but he had similar gaunt features to the police officer at the other end of the table: their eyes were sunken and they reminded Ramage of the paintings he had seen of the Inquisition at work: ruthless men, burning with zeal but cold and detached, who put no value on human life as they sought out heretics with the tenacity of sharks round a piece of bloody meat.

The police officer turned towards Ramage and said: 'This is a tribunal set up under the relevant section of the military code. Sit down and –'

'What am I –'

'— sit down and remain silent while the preliminaries are completed.'

Ramage sat down and tried to compose himself: he was an Italian shipbuilder, unwashed and unshaven but on his dignity. He would keep up the pretence for as long as possible, and after that remain silent. Well, perhaps not silent; he would be able to give them a few jabs with his tongue. It was the only satisfaction he was likely to get since they had the guillotine to ensure the last laugh.

'Gianfranco di Stefano?'

Ramage glanced up: it was the man in the centre of the table who had spoken. Now was as good a time as any to start prodding. 'Yes, but you have the advantage of me.' It did not translate well into French and he suddenly remembered that it was an English phrase. Anyone who spoke English well enough would be suspicious at hearing it said in French by an alleged Italian. The Frenchman smiled; an amiable smile, but also the smile of a man who knew he had all the advantages.

'Signor di Stefano, this tribunal has assembled by the order of the Military Governor of the district of Amiens, and I am appointed its judge. *Citoyen* Houdan –' he gestured to the police officer, 'is the prosecutor and *Citoyen* Garlin will present your defence.' Both men nodded at Ramage; cold and distant nods, the kind of nods a farmer gives when selecting particular animals to go to the slaughterhouse.

'I will read the charges,' the judge said, picking up the top sheet from a small pile of papers in front of him. ' "That the said Gianfranco di Stefano did illegally enter the Republic of France for the purpose of spying; that the said Gianfranco di Stefano, using stolen and forged passports and travel documents, did travel to Boulogne for the purpose of spying on the Invasion Flotilla and on the encampments of the Army of England; that the said Gianfranco di Stefano did stay in Amiens for the purpose of spying on the courier carrying State documents between the headquarters of Vice-Admiral Bruix at Boulogne and the Ministry of Marine and Colonies in Paris; that the said Gianfranco di Stefano and two accomplices did attempt to intercept the said documents; and that the crimes listed above, each and every one, are punishable by death under the military and civil codes of the Republic." '

The judge looked up at Ramage. 'You understand the charges?'

'I am an Italian subject; I request a translator.'

'Request refused,' the judge said brusquely. 'How do you plead?'

'Does it make any difference?' Ramage asked sarcastically.

'Yes, it makes a considerable difference,' the judge said, missing the sarcasm. 'If you confess, it will save the tribunal's time.'

'Confess to what?'

'To the crimes with which you are charged, of course,' the judge said impatiently.

'The charges are very flattering seen through the eyes of a simple Italian shipbuilder; but I would be boasting if I confessed to such things.'

'Oh, we have no objection to you boasting,' the judge said quickly. 'If you wish to confess . . .'

'No, no,' Ramage said modestly, 'apart from boasting, I should also be telling lies if I confessed.'

'Very well, *Citoyen* Prosecutor, let us hear the evidence against this traitor!'

Ramage jumped up, the irons on his wrists clanking. 'Don't call me a traitor! Why, you haven't heard a word of evidence yet!'

'You are unduly sensitive, M'sieur,' the judge said calmly. 'You are a traitor – we know it and you know it, but there are certain formalities we have to go through. Continue, *Citoyen* Houdan, and ignore this traitor's interruptions.'

'When arrested at the Hotel de la Poste by members of the Committee of Public Safety,' Houdan said, 'the accused di Stefano was unable to account for the whereabouts of his accomplice, who had a few moments earlier been detected in the room of a naval officer carrying dispatches to the Ministry of Marine. The said accomplice was denounced by the daughter of the landlord of the Hotel de la Poste, who saw him.

'The accused di Stefano claimed to be an Italian citizen and a shipbuilder concerned with the Invasion Flotilla at Boulogne. He produced a passport and travel documents to prove this assertion and claimed that he had been recalled to Boulogne for further talks with the naval authorities there.

'I produce exhibits A, B and C which disprove these claims.

'Exhibit A is a letter from the Port Captain of Boulogne, duly notarized, which says that the accused has never had any discussions with the naval administration whatsoever. Exhibit B is an affidavit from Admiral Bruix saying that the naval lieutenant in whose room di Stefano's accomplice was found is the regular courier carrying highly secret documents between the Ministry of Marine in Paris and the naval headquarters in Boulogne.

'Exhibit C –,' he waved a sheet of paper which was liberally covered with red seals, 'is an affidavit from the Ministry of Marine which says that among the dispatches carried by the courier on this particular day was one from Admiral Bruix giving information upon which the whole future of the war depends. Information,' Houdan said, raising his voice aggressively, 'whose value to the English would be beyond price.'

With that, Houdan passed the papers to the judge, who turned to the man on the right. '*Citoyen* Garlin, you will put forward the defence.'

For a few moments Ramage was dumbfounded: he had heard enough from Louis to know that the administration of justice in France was crude, but he had not expected this. He stood up. 'Surely the court will not hear my defence until it has heard the prosecution's attempt to prove the charges against me?'

Again the judge smiled. 'You were not paying attention. The charges have been read and the prosecution has proved their truth. You –'

'Witnesses,' Ramage said angrily, 'why, not even the landlord's daughter –'

'The witnesses have been heard,' the judge said, picking up the papers which Houdan had passed over to him. 'Who can doubt the word of the Port Captain of Boulogne, Admiral Bruix, and a senior official of the Ministry of Marine? And do you deny that the landlord's daughter saw your man in the lieutenant's room?'

'But no one's proved I had anything to do with it! The prosecution has to prove I was trying to read the dispatches!'

'Weren't you?' the judge asked quizzically.

'Of course I was not. I would have needed supernatural powers to know that the lieutenant was carrying papers of any sort, and considerably more than supernatural powers to have known that on Saturday night he was carrying a dispatch which you say is "beyond price". Apart from all that I have absolutely no interest in such things.'

The judge rapped the table impatiently with a gavel. 'You must not interrupt the court's proceedings with all these irrelevancies: *Citoyen* Garlin will make your defence.'

'But I haven't spoken a word to this man!' Ramage exclaimed. 'He knows nothing about me – why, he has never seen me before!'

Garlin smiled slyly. 'The accused has little understanding of the judicial process,' he said to the judge, who nodded and turned to Ramage.

'Your defence counsel is correct, and for your information *Citoyen* Garlin has defended hundreds of criminals who –'

'Has he ever defended an innocent man?'

The judge looked embarrassed and then angry. 'Of course,' he said peremptorily. 'Now be silent and listen to your defence.'

'Ah yes,' Garlin said. 'The defence acknowledges the impossibility of providing a translator into the Italian language at such short notice. Regarding the charges, the accused accepts that he is unable to explain the whereabouts of his accomplice, and he further admits he was in possession of a forged passport and travel documents ...'

Ramage knew he was trapped so completely that any protest would be a waste of breath. Providing there had been no hitch, Jackson would have arrived in Folkestone by now, found Lord Nelson and delivered the report. After dawn tomorrow there would be no need to play for more time. On the other hand, there was no need to rush things today: although he was understandably anxious to hurry through all this nonsense, saving ten minutes here only brought him ten minutes nearer the guillotine ...

Garlin coughed, as if he realized that Ramage's attention was wandering. 'The accused admits that in the absence of his foreman it is impossible to prove his innocence as far as entering the room of the lieutenant is concerned –' he waited, as if expecting an interruption from Ramage, but none came. 'The prosecution has proved the charges concerning the passport and travel documents, so the accused can only ask for the court's clemency. As to the third charge, the accused can only state that, since the seal on the Admiral's dispatch was intact when it arrived in Paris, obviously he did not open it.'

Ramage looked up and stared at the judge, who looked back at him with unblinking eyes and said: 'The court will adjourn until tomorrow morning to consider the verdict.'

Ramage stood up and bowed. 'I assume it is customary to consider an accused man's guilt without hearing his defence.'

'The court has just heard your defence,' the judge said. 'It was very ably stated by *Citoyen* Garlin.'

'*Citoyen* Garlin made an interesting statement,' Ramage said contemptuously. 'He was obviously speaking for himself, since what he said had nothing to do with my case and was certainly made without consultation with me.'

'The court is satisfied,' the judge said, unperturbed, and signalled to the guards, each of whom took an arm and swung Ramage round and marched him out. Before the door shut behind him, Ramage heard the three men laughing among themselves.

Ramage woke next morning with a curious sense of relief: Wednesday had arrived at long last, the day by which Louis and the rest of them should be safely out of the way. Now he could seize the first opportunity to escape that offered itself. That opportunity could only arise outside the cell, or at least at a time when the door was open. He had already missed his first chance – he had been sound asleep when the jailer slid the breakfast tray on to the floor.

He rubbed his chin: four days' growth and it was beginning to feel like a scrubbing brush: all appeals for water to wash in had been brushed aside and he felt filthy. He ate the food and left the tray beside the cot: that meant the jailer had to open the door wide enough to shout at him to bring the tray to the doorway. That might lead to something . . .

He was still daydreaming, imagining Lord Nelson in his cabin reading the copy of Admiral Bruix's report, when suddenly the bolts slammed back and the door was flung open. One guard came in and covered him with the pistol while two more once again locked irons on to his wrists. They were the same guards as the day before but, Ramage noted sourly, they were now clean-shaven and their uniforms were much smarter, as though it was Sunday. They waited a minute or two and then called down the corridor. A fourth man appeared, holding a musket. 'We're ready,' one of them said and, preceded by the musket, Ramage was marched out of the cell.

After going along the corridors and past the room where his so-called trial had been held, Ramage was surprised to see that they had reached the front door of the police station. As a sentry swung the doors open to allow them through, Ramage looked right across the square to the guillotine. Suddenly he was frightened. Would they continue marching to the guillotine platform? Was that why the court had laughed?

The idea was so strong in Ramage's mind that he was startled when one of the guards bumped into him and then swung him round, so that they marched to the left, along the side of the square. He just had time to see the word MAIRIE carved in the keystone of the doorway of the next building before he was bundled inside and along a corridor.

The building smelled musty, and he was just cursing that any attempt to bolt from his guards while in the street outside would have resulted in a pistol ball between the shoulder blades when he realized that he could hear the distant murmur of many voices. Suddenly the leading guard with the musket stopped and flung open a door.

The murmur became louder, and then he was being marched into a large hall in which a hundred or more people sat on forms. Like the audience at a theatre, they were all facing a raised platform where three men – the trio who had formed yesterday's tribunal – sat at a table covered by a large but faded Tricolour. In front of the table was a box on which a raggedly dressed, unshaven man was balanced, his hands manacled, a gendarme at either side.

Ramage's escort jerked him to a stop and, as he realized that he had been brought to some sort of ceremony, the man on the box, with a suddenness which took the gendarmes by surprise, knelt with his manacled hands held upwards in a gesture of supplication, and almost immediately began a terrible wail.

As the audience began to jeer, the judge in the centre of the trio at the table made a contemptuous gesture of dismissal, and the guard on either side of the prisoner tugged at his arms.

'Mercy!' the man shrieked. 'In the name of God, mercy – my wife –'

'You appeal to God, do you!' the judge bellowed angrily. 'Very well, let's see if He shows you mercy, because no traitor deserves any from the Republic!'

The man, knees sagging and barely able to support himself, was dragged out through a door on the far side of the hall. Ramage was just bracing himself to be marched to the box when he saw another prisoner, who had been kept against the wall farther down the hall, being pushed towards the table.

The man was so frightened that, unbalanced by having his hands manacled, the gendarmes had to hoist him up and then hold him in position.

'Jean-Baptiste le Brun!' the judge thundered, and Ramage watched the audience. Most of them were grinning, teeth bared and sitting forward on their forms. All of them were enjoying it – with the exception of a white-faced woman sitting near the back: she was now standing, tears streaming down her face, gripping her hands and moving her head from side to side.

'The court has heard the charges against you, and your defence, and the sentence of this court is – death.'

The audience waited a moment – to Ramage it seemed they wanted the man to scream, or collapse – and when they saw him turn to get down from the box they lost interest and began gossiping. The wretched man had disappointed them; Ramage sensed that if there were many more performances like that they would leave and go to the nearest café.

Once down from the box the man braced himself, shaking off the hands of the gendarmes. Then he stopped and turned to the crowd and waved to the weeping woman. It was a poignant gesture; all a condemned man could say to the woman he loved. Ramage knew it was all he would want to signal to Gianna if she was there. And perhaps he would wave to her when his time came; it would puzzle all the ghouls – there would be scores of people round the platform of the guillotine – and they would glance over their shoulders to see who he was waving at, never guessing that she was on the other side of the Channel.

The gendarmes were pushing him now, and he braced himself and strode down towards the box, at the last moment walking a little faster than the guards so that he could jump on to the box without their help.

He held the judge's eyes and the man's lips curled into a sneer.

'Gianfranco di Stefano,' he said softly, as though savouring the words, 'the court has heard the charges against you, and your defence – ' he lingered over the words, as if to provoke an outburst from Ramage, 'and the sentence of this court is – death.'

Still Ramage held the man's eyes, thinking to himself: so this is what it is like . . . far less frightening than staring into the muzzles of the enemy's guns.

A moment before the guards tugged at his arms, he jumped sideways and down, turned to the door and walked out, shoulders back, head erect, not too quickly, but just fast enough for his guards, all of whom were short men, to have to scurry to keep up with him.

As the door was shut behind him he realized that there had been no jeering. He almost laughed when he reflected that every one of them in that hall, judge, prosecutor, defence counsel and audience, had been cheated: they thought they had sentenced to death an Italian shipbuilder (indeed, the audience did not know even that much: to them a man with an Italian name had been sentenced to death), whereas in fact they had caught a British naval officer, who, despite the affidavit from their own Ministry of Marine that the seal on Admiral Bruix's dispatch was untouched, had read the dispatch and passed the information it contained to Lord Nelson.

There seemed to be a certain cachet about being condemned to death. For a start, two guards now brought each meal, one covering him with a pistol while the other carried the tray. It was as though they too knew that the only way of getting out of the cell was by overpowering a guard. Yet they put the tray down carefully, instead of giving it the bang that spilled the soup.

The improvement did not spread to the Hotel de la Poste: on the contrary, the landlord obviously took the view that selling good food to a condemned man was a wicked waste, and Ramage found himself eating little more than kitchen scraps.

There was a subtle change in the cell, too: previously it was just the cell in which he was locked; now it was a condemned cell. He told himself the cell had not changed; only his attitude to it had altered. Maybe that was so – being sentenced to death certainly required some adjustment on the part of the condemned man. Apart from anything else, he thought grimly, unless he found a way of escaping within a few hours, he was measuring time with a clock rather than a calendar.

The more he thought about it, the more he realized that certain quaint phrases took on a fresh significance. 'Composing himself for death,' for instance: in England priests and parsons were nearly always on hand to help a dying man to do that. Previously he had never quite understood what it entailed, but now that he had nothing else to think about, it made more sense.

An old man would naturally be more composed. His active life was past, and the physical restrictions of age plus the knowledge that no matter what he did, life held no more challenges (at least, no more challenges to which he could respond), probably meant that he could resign himself to the inevitability of death. If it was preceded by a long or painful illness, or perhaps poverty or loneliness, it might even come as a relief.

But a young man faced death with so much of life to lose – he had to fight not just the fear of the unknown (everyone faced that, no matter what their age!) but the feeling of being cheated out of so many years, so many experiences, so many sights. Looking back on the various times he had previously faced death, there was a consistent pattern: on each occasion there had been very little time to think about being killed. The longest period when he had been convinced he would die had been the dozen or so hours in the middle of the hurricane with the *Triton* brig, but the raw power of the hurricane, the shrieking wind which numbed the brain, the sheer weariness, had meant that he gave little thought to what death really was; he thought of it as the next huge wave, or the next increase in the strength of the wind.

Death had a different face when you were going into action: it was a sudden threat – usually the guns were firing within less than an hour of the first hint of battle, and you were so damned busy that it was only during those awful moments as the enemy came in range and you found yourself staring at the muzzles of his guns that fear suddenly reminded you of death. Then the muzzles would give that dull red wink and spout smoke, and there was no more time to think; all your efforts went into handling the ship well. When the battle was over, relief at still being alive brushed aside the thought of death.

Sitting in a condemned cell made a man realize that most people's attitude towards bravery was entirely wrong: to them heroes were men who climbed on board an enemy ship, cutlass in hand, and slashed and sliced their way to victory, or led a cavalry charge, or at least did something active to defeat an enemy. But really (in Ramage's experience, anyway) apart from a few moments' doubts and fear right at the beginning, once it all started you were carried along by an almost hysterical exhilaration and the knowledge that if you stopped to think you would probably be killed.

No matter how many times you gave the order to fire, or raced across an enemy's deck like a run-amok butcher in a slaughterhouse, you learned nothing about facing death that was of the slightest help in a condemned cell. Death might come at the end of a year's painful sickness or it might come as the red-eyed wink of a gun muzzle, but the sick man would no more recognize the death dealt out by the gun than the fighting man would recognize the drawn-out death from sickness. The label on the bottle might be the same but the contents were different.

Now Ramage had two alternatives: either he managed to escape, or one morning soon they would march him across the *place* to the guillotine. It was only a hundred yards, but would it seem a long walk or a short one? He found he was far from sure. How did a man who had only a few more minutes to live measure distance? The question had a horrible fascination, and the more he considered it the less sure he was. Knowing that the walk from the police station door to the guillotine was the last he would make, the condemned man (Ramage carefully avoided identifying himself with the victim; he would have escaped by then) might find it all too short: walking a mile might give him time to compose himself. On the other hand, walking a hundred yards to meet the executioner might seem an enormous distance; the condemned man might well prefer to walk out through the cell door and meet him three paces down the corridor, and get it over quickly.

He suddenly stood up to shake off the thoughts: in an hour or so – if he was not very careful – he would be screaming and hammering at that damned door.

Instead he thought of Louis and Stafford and hoped that they were safe. At least they had not been caught – he was sure of that, since the prosecutor would have been quick to confront him with either of them. For Louis, death at the guillotine might well be something of a release: it had claimed his family, and looking back on the brief time he had known the man, Ramage thought that he was lost, a ship without sails or compass, a man deprived of any purpose in life except revenge. The Cockney Stafford would meet death with the same jauntiness that he had faced life. If they caught Stafford,

Ramage only wanted to say one thing to him – it was bad luck that led to their discovery. Even when warned that Admiral Bruix's dispatch might have been opened, the Ministry officials in Paris had found nothing wrong with the seal. Stafford would want to know that.

What about Jackson, Rossi and Slushy Dyson? If Jackson had received the dispatch for Lord Nelson, only death would prevent the three men from delivering it. Curious that he was sure that even if Dyson was the only survivor he would still do his best, as though it would give him some sort of absolution for having planned a mutiny and then deserted.

He finally thought of Gianna, though he had been trying to keep her out of his mind. As there seemed little future for the two of them, why not think of the past? Be thankful for what had been, rather than bitter at the thought of what might have been. For her sake, it would have been better if she had never met him – she might be left to live her life long after his head dropped into that damned basket, and it was always worse for those left behind.

She loved him – there was no doubt about that. Yet even if he lived, their future might not lie together. Everyone avoided facing up to it – his own fault, since he dodged it as a topic of conversation – but there were many obstacles in the way of them getting married. For a start, as ruler of the state of Volterra she had to be prepared for her return after Bonaparte's troops had been driven out. She would probably find chaos there, with bitter quarrels between those who had collaborated with Bonaparte and those who had not. It would require real statesmanship to resolve those quarrels between leading families. Was Gianna capable of managing it? He was doubtful: she was too headstrong, too impatient, and perhaps even too demanding. She saw things in black and white rather than in shades of grey, and she would find it hard to understand why people had collaborated with Bonaparte, assuming that it was to gain some advantage, whereas Ramage knew that in at least some instances it would have been from an instinct for survival.

Anyway, whatever happened and whatever the problems, it would be of no help for her to arrive back in Volterra with a foreigner for a husband. Not that the word 'foreigner' existed in the Italian language, but for a citizen of the state of Vol-

terra a straniero, a stranger, was someone who came from somewhere else, be it Venice, England or the land of the Laps.

It was all very sad and all very interesting, and it helped to pass away the time, but it had no relevance for Lieutenant Ramage. By the time the watch in his pocket had run down, he would either have escaped or he would be dead. Curious that they had forgotten to search him. He decided that if he could not escape, the last thing he would do before they marched out of the cell to the *place* (call it the guillotine, he told himself; using euphemisms does not help) would be to stamp on his watch, just to avoid a gendarme stealing it from his corpse.

He was just going to sit down on the cot again when he heard the key turn and the bolts being slid back, and a moment later the door swung open and the prosecutor came in, preceded by a guard holding a pistol.

'Prisoner di Stefano . . .' Houdan paused, obviously to give the maximum effect to whatever he was going to say.

'Prisoner Houdan,' Ramage said sarcastically.

The effect on the Frenchman was remarkable. Instead of his face flushing with anger, it went pale, and the muscles pulled down the corners of his mouth. 'Why do you call me that?' he demanded tightly.

Ramage shrugged his shoulders. 'You are as much a prisoner as I . . .'

'Don't be absurd! Why, within four or five hours you will be marched to the guillotine!'

Ramage was surprised at the way he was able to nod so casually, as though Houdan was relaying old news. 'Yes, I go in a few hours, and you? You'll follow – in a few weeks, or a few months; even in a year or two. But you'll follow, Prisoner Houdan . . .' He was delighted at the way he had pitched his voice: no lamenting priest could have spoken more dolefully.

Certainly it was having an effect on Houdan who, instead of hitting him, whispered: 'Why do you say that?'

'The swing of the pendulum, my friend; at the moment it is swung all the way over to your side, and you and your friends just snap your fingers and send your enemies to the guillotine. But one day the pendulum will swing back the other way. All the relatives and friends of those you have murdered have been waiting patiently, and they'll snap *their*

221

fingers, and then you and your friends will know what it is like to swing over on the *bascule* and lie there staring into the basket.'

Houdan was shaking his head, unbelievingly, and Ramage could not resist giving the knife yet another twist.

'The crowd watching and jeering yesterday – I suppose they'll clap and cheer round the guillotine as the blade drops, too. But a crowd is fickle, Prisoner Houdan; it doesn't mind who dies, man or woman, young or old, Royalist or Republican, Breton or Burgundian. It would find it amusing to watch the prosecutor being decapitated.' The phrase in French did not have the same ring as in English, but Houdan's mouth was now hanging slack and he was obviously staring into some private hell about which he had never before dared even to think.

A full minute passed, during which time the sentry started moving uncomfortably, as though he too was considering the pendulum and his own position. Then Houdan pulled his eyes back into focus, braced his back and repeated, as though they were his first words since he came into the cell: 'Prisoner di Stefano, your appeal for clemency has been rejected!'

'You are mistaking me for someone else,' Ramage said coldly. 'I made no appeal, nor shall I.'

'An appeal is routine after the sentence of death,' Houdan said.

'And its rejection is equally routine?' Ramage inquired.

'Not necessarily. Now, I have one last question. You are not Gianfranco di Stefano. Who are you?'

'Ah – so you have found me out,' Ramage said sadly, and noted the triumphant look on Houdan's face: the Frenchman was obviously enjoying the thought of getting his revenge for all the baiting he had received.

'Who are you, then?'

'Ah,' Ramage lowered his head sorrowfully, 'the last in an ancient line; when the blade drops, a noble family vanishes, as though it never existed. A few tombstones, a mausoleum here and a palace there . . . a sad thought.'

'Your name,' Houdan persisted.

'The *Duca di Noia*.'

The Frenchman's eyes widened and then his face became animated: a Royalist! He plunged a hand into his pocket and fished out a piece of paper and pencil. 'Spell it!' he demanded.

222

As soon as he had it written down he asked: 'Where is that?'

'Where is what?' Ramage asked innocently.

'Noia – the place of which you are the Duke. *Were* the Duke,' he corrected himself.

'Oh, Noia isn't a place, it is a – how should I say, the translation is a little difficult. Now, in French, it would " *Le Duc d'Ennui*".'

Houdan stared at him suspiciously. '*Ennui?* Are you sure you have not make a mistake? Are you saying there is no such place as Noia?'

' "Noia" is an Italian word,' Ramage said patronizingly. 'It means – well, boredom, tedium . . . I assure you that after a few hours locked up in a cell, anyone becomes the *Duca di Noia*. After a week or two in a French cell I dare say he becomes *Le Grand Duc d'Ennui*.'

Houdan looked at him with narrowed eyes, his face revealing hatred. 'Your execution is arranged for ten o'clock tomorrow morning.'

'Thank you,' Ramage said. 'It's a civilized hour: I was afraid you would make it dawn.'

Houdan left the cell and the door slammed shut. Ramage sat down on the cot and felt violently sick. You needed the continued presence of someone like Houdan to play the role of the blasé cynic: the moment you were left alone it all seemed so empty and useless. But, he thought sourly, hurrah for the *Duca di Noia*; he made sure that long after Gianfranco di Stefano or Lieutenant Ramage had escaped or shuffled off this mortal coil, Houdan will wake up in the early hours of the morning and think of the pendulum.

It would be the devil of a gesture (one that would leave not just Houdan but the tribunal looking stupid) if just before they shoved him against the *bascule*, he said casually, 'By the way, I am not an Italian shipbuilder, I'm a British naval officer, and I did read that dispatch . . .' But it would be a pointless gesture; far better to let the French remain unaware that the British knew the details of their Invasion Flotilla.

Ten o'clock tomorrow morning. He pulled out his watch and saw that it was a few minutes past eleven o'clock. Twenty-three hours was not a long time – yet before the guards came to fetch him it might seem endless. He was disappointed that there had been no word from Louis; that neither he nor his friends had smuggled in a weapon of some sort – even a long hatpin in a loaf of bread might have done some good. He needed something more than a bowl or a mug to attack two jailers, one of whom always had a pistol. Nor had the French authorities been much help: the trial one day and sentencing the next hardly gave a man time to plan an escape! But time was running out: he had better start thinking hard . . .

CHAPTER FIFTEEN

At seven o'clock next morning Ramage was just finishing a cup of cold acorn coffee when he heard boots marching in the corridor outside the cell. It was the regular thud made by men who had been drilled. Halt, one, two! They had stopped at his door. A firing-squad? No, here in France they use guillotines . . . The key turned, the top bolt slid back, then the bottom, and the door swung open.

Houdan was standing there, a smirk on his face, with a gendarme on either side and several soldiers drawn up in single file behind him, along the wall of the corridor.

'Prisoner di Stefano,' he said in a voice which matched his expression, 'your fame has spread to Boulogne: the naval authorities want to question you. Apparently there is a suspicion that you saw more than was realized in Paris. You are being taken to Boulogne for interrogation and I should warn you that the naval authorities will not treat you as gently as we have here in Amiens.'

'Travel broadens the mind,' Ramage said casually. 'Don't you find that?'

'In your case it also lengthens your life by two or three days. The sergeant of the guard has the warrant for your execution and after handing you over to the naval authorities he will deliver it to the police station in Boulogne. They have a guillotine there . . .'

'I am sure they have, but you have put yours in *such* an attractive position: the plane trees make a colourful contrast with the shiny blade against the green of the leaves and the bark of the trees. I hope you will appreciate it –' he paused for a moment, 'yes, I am sure you'll appreciate it . . .

when your time comes.'

Houdan stepped back as though he had been slapped in the face, and turned to the sergeant. 'Here is your prisoner; guard him well. You have the warrant, and you have your instructions. You've signed my receipt – ah yes, I have it here; a receipt for the body of Gianfranco di Stefano.'

The sergeant, a burly and red-faced man who looked as though he enjoyed his Calvados, grunted and jerked a thumb at Ramage. 'Come out here – that's right – stand there. Four men in front – hurry, there! And you four behind. Right now, attention! Quick march!'

The sergeant marched them down the corridor, boots booming like drum rolls, and halted them in front of the large double doors leading to the square. He then marched to the head of the file, made a flourish towards the gendarme to open both doors, and led the file of men out into the early morning sunshine, down the steps and into the *place*.

'Shoulders back!' he shouted when he saw a group of women on the corner of the square, and he increased his stride. It is many miles to Boulogne, Ramage thought to himself gleefully: many miles and at least a couple of night stops. There should be several opportunities to escape. A chance to make a bolt for it in open country was what he needed; open country just before darkness. He would march like a particularly docile prisoner all the first day. A day and a night would be enough to make these soldiers regard their prisoner as a well-behaved fellow.

By tomorrow they would be near the coast, with the guards bored and weary. Tomorrow evening he would make a bolt for it, no matter what the risk. He braced his shoulders back and swung his arms: he was beginning to feel more cheerful; at last he had a sporting chance!

It was a pleasant summer's morning: the sun, still weak, presented the city of Amiens in a friendly light. Only a few people were about, although from the smell of bread and the smoke from the chimney the baker had nearly finished his work. Past the shops and the last of the houses was the barricade. The sergeant produced a handful of papers, waved airily towards his prisoner and said something that provoked a snigger among the gendarmes, and the march began in earnest . . . Soon there were open fields stretching into the distance all round, except for a small wood half a mile ahead. The soldiers dropped into an easier step and two or three of

225

them started talking among themselves. The sergeant still strode ahead but at a comfortable pace, knowing that there were many miles to cover before sunset. Insects buzzed, and occasionally a startled bird flew overhead. The sound of marching feet had been replaced by a sort of prolonged scuffling noise, with the occasional curse as a man had to lengthen or shorten a step to avoid twisting his ankle in a pothole.

Ramage suddenly saw two more soldiers standing beside a tree forty or fifty yards ahead: obviously stragglers who had fallen out of the column on its way into the city, and now meant to catch up after their rest. At that moment one of the waiting soldiers began walking into the middle of the road, and his gait seemed curiously familiar. Then the second one joined him. A minute or two later his escort had stopped and he was staring at Stafford's grinning face. Beside him was Louis – they both looked incongruous in the uniform of soldiers of France.

'Mornin', sir,' Stafford said, 'wotcher fink of this rig?'

The shock of hearing not just English, but Stafford's unique version of it, spoken again left Ramage feeling faint from the mixture of relief and shock, and unsure whether it was easier to laugh or cry.

'Good morning, Stafford,' he managed to say in an even voice, and then broke off suddenly, realizing that whatever else he said would be repeated with glee to the rest of Stafford's shipmates, men who had sailed with Ramage for upwards of a couple of years. 'You are late, Stafford,' he said with mock harshness. 'What were you doing, paying another call on the landlord's daughter?'

But Stafford had served with him too long to be fooled. 'Me and Louis *did* think of waiting until you was being led up to the Widder, sir, but we reckoned the crowd might fink they was being cheated, once they got a sight of yer.'

Louis's ugly face was as cheerful as Ramage had ever seen it. 'Good morning, Lieutenant, I'm sorry we could not let you know in time for you to have shaved, but I have breakfast almost ready – in the wood just ahead.'

Ramage giggled. It was a brief giggle and he managed to stifle it before it ran away with him, but he knew that, after the events of the past few days, his self-control was very weak. 'Fresh eggs, eh?'

'As many as you want; I'll make you a fine omelette,' Louis

said, and went on as though still discussing a menu. 'I'm sorry we could not get you out yesterday evening, but I decided that it was better to leave you to a miserable night rather than risk a slip-up in our plans by rushing things.'

'Where did you recruit your army?'

'Nine men are not too difficult, really, although rather expensive: we will have to hold a pay parade before we dismiss them. They are – although you'd hardly think so to look at them – some of the cream of the Channel smugglers. They are all,' he added quietly, 'men who have as little affection for the Republic as I have. It took me a little time to find ones who were not known by sight in Amiens.'

'But the uniforms . . .'

'I'll tell you all about it as we eat breakfast,' Louis said.

They reached the wood and turned off the road, following a track among the trees. After a hundred yards they reached a glade where a man in fisherman's clothes was prodding a small bonfire over which hung a kettle. The soldiers split up and sat down around the fire, joking with the fisherman who began breaking eggs into a large pan.

Ramage beckoned to Stafford and sat down with Louis on a fallen tree trunk. 'Tell me what happened,' Ramage said, 'from the beginning.'

'That screaming,' Louis said in English, 'the moment I heard it I guessed that the daughter or the mother had gone to the lieutenant's room, and as we all ran up the stairs I had time to think. I was hoping you were still in your room, and you were. So I listened to what was going on for a moment or two, slipped into my room to get the loaf with your papers in it – and found Stafford already there.' He gestured to the Cockney to carry on.

'Yus, well, that there screaming at the door froze me fer a moment or two. Then when she ran, I 'opped out of the window an' managed to work meself along a ledge to Louis's room ter try an' get 'old o' the bread. I just reached the drawer when the door opens an' Louis an' me finds ourselves starin' at each uvver. We just had time to arrange a rendy voo an' then out the winder I goes and Louis marches out wiv the loaf stuffed darn 'is trouser leg.'

Louis laughed at the memory. 'After I pretended to inspect my room and you were arrested, I delivered the loaf to the courier and told him what had happened. I knew our main job was done, so I then had to sit down quietly and work out a plan to rescue you – it wasn't too difficult since I knew what the gendarmes would do – and before the courier left for Boulogne at dawn I was able to give him some instructions.

'I guessed we had until Wednesday to arrange things, because the regular sentencings are always on Wednesdays, and the gendarmes like to keep to a schedule – trials on Tuesdays, sentencing on Wednesdays and executions on Thursdays. Well, certain isolated Army camps in the Boulogne-Calais area lost various pieces of uniform on Monday, while other camps lost a few muskets. The losses were so scattered that no one would connect them, and the booty arrived in Amiens late on Tuesday. On Tuesday and Wednesday various men arrived at Amiens, though few of them passed through the police barricades: fortunately the police have the quaint idea that all visitors to a city come in by road.

'I had a friend at the police station who was able to keep me informed about your trial – what did you say that so infuriated the court? – and I was sitting in the back of the hall at the *Mairie* when you were sentenced, although you would not have recognized me. I was proud of you, by the way! You created quite an impression.

'The rest you can guess: all these men met me here during the night, we put on our uniforms, and the sergeant marched them into the city. Stafford and I stayed here because we might have been recognized.'

'What about the documents that the sergeant showed to the prosecutor, and those for the police at the barricade?' Ramage asked.

'They came up from Boulogne. There's a standard wording for most of these official documents, you know. The important thing is to have a supply of the correct stationery with the appropriate heading printed at the top, and some wax and a seal. Most ministries and committees use the same seal . . . I think that omelette is done. By the way, your last dispatch was delivered safely.'

As Ramage listened to Louis describing the arrangements for getting him back to England, he was thankful for the Frenchman's clear, practical mind. Louis had done his best to eliminate chance: tomorrow night the *Marie* would be fishing along the three-fathom line off Le Tréport, which was not only the nearest fishing port to Amiens but easily spotted from the sea. The great white and grey chalk cliffs of the coast of Normandy flattened out as they stretched north-eastward to curve inland and vanish altogether three or four miles beyond Le Tréport. The little fishing port itself was built at the foot of Mount Huon, at the entrance to a valley through which flowed the River Bresle.

If the weather was bad, Louis said, Slushy Dyson would bring the *Marie* into the actual harbour, small as it was, and let her dry out in the mud at low water, along with the other boats belonging to the port. Le Tréport was about the southern limit for boats fishing from Boulogne, but since bad weather would be the only reason why Dyson would come in, it also provided its own good excuse. A jib stowed below in the cuddy, Louis explained, was held together only by the boltropes, two seams having ripped once in a squall so that a complete panel was missing. 'Our alibi,' Louis said with a wink. 'It gives us a reason for going into anywhere. "Stress of weather," you know. Then we sail direct to England: there will be no time to get to the rendezvous with the Folkestone *Marie*.'

Ramage, thinking of the thin soles of his boots, asked: 'How many kilometres to Abbeville?'

'About forty-five – that's about twenty-eight miles.'

'And on to Le Tréport?'

'About eighteen miles by road, but we shall be riding cross-country from Abbeville.' Louis saw that Ramage was looking worried and said reassuringly, 'We march on to Abbeville at a reasonable pace. We go through the town and continue on the road to Boulogne, explaining to the guards at the barricades that we have orders to get you to Boulogne as quickly as possible.

'Once we are clear of Abbeville we leave the road, wait until it is dark, say goodbye to our friends, and climb on board some horses which will be waiting for us. A pleasant night ride to Le Tréport, keeping a mile or two north of the road. We reach a particular house at a village called Mers, on the coast just north of Le Tréport, where we are assured of a welcome and a chance to sleep. We'll then find out if the *Marie* is in the harbour or out fishing.'

'And if she's out fishing?'

'Then – after resting all day Thursday – we have to haul a small boat down the beach, launch it, and row out to the three-fathom line.

'But if we're seen?'

'We shall be seen: we'll have a lantern, and anyone sufficiently interested in our activities will see that we are busy
fishing. If a fishing-boat called *Marie* from Boulogne happens
to see a boat out fishing on the three-fathom line and sails
over towards it, well, we shall be half a mile or so offshore
and it won't take long for three men to get on board.'

'Three? So you are coming back with us?'

Louis nodded. 'I would like to stay behind, but my friends
in Boulogne think it would be a good idea if I went on a
holiday until they are absolutely sure that I was not identified
at Amiens or at the inn you used at Boulogne. They can
deal with the Corporal at the *Chapeau Rouge* – no, not kill
him!' Louis said hastily when he saw Ramage's expression.
'They'll just explain what he has to gain by having a bad
memory for names and faces – but he may have gossiped
already . . .'

'You'll have nothing to fear from the British authorities,'
Ramage said. 'I will make sure you are given – well, whatever
you need.'

Louis held up a hand and grinned. 'You don't have to
reassure me! But I have friends over there, you know . . .'

Ramage thought a moment, and then said: 'Louis, I want
to help you with papers because – no, wait a moment, let me
explain – if you rely on your friends, you are relying on
men who are outside the law. Oh yes, I know some of the
smugglers' leaders are important men, but there is no need for
you to enter the country as a smuggler on the run. With
me, you enter the country as someone who has helped a
British naval officer. I shall write a report for Lord St
Vincent, and you'll be given any papers you need to live in
England legally, so that –'

'No, please no,' Louis interrupted. 'I am grateful, and I
know there would be no problems. I'll go further – you have
already thought what you would do if the Admiralty will not
pay a reward, haven't you . . .?'

Once again Ramage was startled how easily the Frenchman
read his thoughts, for he had been thinking that his father
would be only too anxious to reward any man who saved his
son's life: a lump sum, an allowance, a house on the estate,
work if he wished for it . . . 'Yes,' he said, 'I've learned not
to place too much reliance on the official mind!'

'Well, it does not matter. You see, I want to stay only until

I hear from Boulogne that it is all right for me to come back. Although I am a man without an allegiance, I am not a man without a country. I am a true Norman – although I seem to spend a lot of my time in Picardy!'

'Very well,' Ramage said, 'but if you ever need a hand, get in touch with Dyson: I'll leave my father's address with him. My father would know what to do.'

'Thank you,' Louis said, 'and I will if necessary. Now,' he looked round at the rest of the men and said in French, 'if everyone has had enough to eat, it is time we marched on again.'

The man who had been tending the bonfire when they arrived kicked the charred embers until he was sure all were extinguished. The rest of them picked up their muskets, and the march began again.

They left their escort beyond Abbeville and the night ride to Mers was alternately alarming and hilarious: Stafford, who had never ridden before but did not bother to mention the fact, mounted the horse in the wood where they had been hidden and immediately jerked the reins and shouted, 'Giddy-yup!' No one was quite sure whether the horse objected to Stafford's accent or the jerk on the bit, but it promptly cantered off the track and among the trees, passing under a branch sticking out at the height of Stafford's chest. The startled seaman, as he related it afterwards, suddenly found himself shoved aft along the horse's back 'and dropped over 'is transom on to me 'ead!' In the half an hour it took to retrieve the horse, Stafford had recovered from his fall and been shown the rudiments of riding. Ramage and Louis decided the horse originally given to Stafford was too skittish, so Ramage took it and a chastened Stafford agreed to let Louis lead on his horse, holding the reins of Stafford's.

It seemed almost impossible to ride cross-country at night without causing a lot of noise: startled birds flew out of hedges and trees, squawking in alarm, while the thud of the horses' hooves seemed to echo across the fields and were punctuated by the jingle of harness. Occasionally an owl glided past, while bats darted overhead. A heavy dew gradually made their clothes damp.

They had left Abbeville behind and were just skirting the village of Cambron, with a moon in its first quarter giving enough light for them to distinguish hedges and ditches, when suddenly the yell of a frightened man right in front of them, followed by the excited barking of a dog, made Ramage's horse rear in alarm and Louis's horse back a few steps so that Stafford ran into it, pitching the Cockney over its head. Stafford managed to roll clear of the hooves and Ramage, seeing Louis slipping from the saddle and running towards the noise, grabbed both sets of reins.

Expecting any moment to hear the sound of shots, Ramage had calmed his own horse and seen Stafford remounted by the time Louis returned. 'A poacher,' he said contemptuously. 'He thought we were gendarmes deliberately riding him down.'

'Is he likely to raise –'

'No, he still thinks we are gendarmes. I told him to go home to his wife and stop poaching . . .'

A few miles farther on Louis slowed down and then stopped. 'This is the road between Beauchamps and St Valery – we're near a village called Woincourt. How are you getting on, Stafford?'

The Cockney groaned. 'Must 'ave worn the seat out o' these trousers and it's chafing 'ard on wot was in 'em. Much farver ter go, Louis?'

'Five or six miles. Can you manage it?'

'Not much choice, eh mate?'

Ramage smiled to himself in the darkness: the expression was typically Stafford; cheerfully grumbling yet remarkably stoical.

They reached the village of Mers at three o'clock in the morning, lucky not to have had a horse break a fetlock, but they seemed to see better in the darkness than their riders. Ramage could hear the dull swish of the waves as they rode slowly towards half a dozen houses scattered along a mile of road only fifty yards back from the beach. The last house – which was also the nearest to Le Tréport – had a dim light at a window, and Louis rode towards it, making no attempt to hide his appearance from anyone who might be watching from the other houses.

They reached the door and Louis dismounted, walked up to it and knocked loudly. For several moments nothing happened, and then a voice to the right – was there a man standing at the entrance to the outhouse? – said 'Picardy,' to which Louis promptly replied 'Normandy,' Ramage recognized it as a challenge and reply, and at once the man went to the door of the house, opened it and invited them in.

The atmosphere in the large room was typical of a fisherman's home: the clean, sharp smell of tarred nets and ropes hanging from the rafters fought with the stench of fish; the sooty smell of a badly-trimmed oil-lamp standing on the table mingled with that of boiled vegetables. A kettle was humming on the stove, and while the man tied up the horses, his wife bustled round making room for them to sit down.

'Were you responsible for the challenge?' Ramage asked Louis, and the Frenchman gave a dry laugh.

'I was responsible for it, but I didn't think of it. These people know I am a Norman, and the River Bresle – which is only a few hundred yards down the road from here – marks the boundary. This side is Picardy, the other side Normandy.'

As they talked, the woman was placing mugs on the table, and when the man came in to report that the horses were tethered, she handed him a bottle. He poured and gave mugs to Ramage and Stafford.

'Calvados – the blood of the true Norman,' he said with a wink, and pushed a third mug across to Louis while Ramage translated for Stafford.

'What we call applejack, ain't it, sir?'

'It is, and very potent,' Ramage said pointedly.

'Aye aye, sir,' the Cockney said. 'I'll go carefully. When do we start lookin' fer Slushy an' the *Marie*?'

'You have a whole day's rest ahead of you. We go out after dark tonight.' Ramage looked across at Louis and said in French, 'Does our friend here have any news of the *Marie*?'

The two men spoke for a few minutes and the fisherman's report was noncommittal: he had received instructions from Boulogne to expect Louis and two friends by road, been told the password, and warned that he would have to dispose of three horses: all that he had arranged. But no one had mentioned the *Marie* by name and he had not been to Le Tréport for several days, so he did not know if she was in the harbour. The *Marie* had not been fishing within sight of Mers the previous day, he said, because he could recognize her – he grinned as he said that, and Ramage guessed that Mers was one of the places used for landing contraband.

'She won't be here before tonight, anyway,' Louis said. 'Dyson won't waste a day hanging about out there – that would be taking an unnecessary risk. It wouldn't surprise me if you see a Royal Navy cutter come close in and have a look; even a frigate. They keep a sharp watch along this coast!'

'We ought to stand by and row out,' Ramage joked.

'Wait until one comes in sight!' Louis said. 'You'll see a patrol of cavalry galloping along the road, keeping abreast of her. The soldiers seem worried that one day a cutter is going to land an army to march on Paris!'

The fisherman had been whispering with his wife, and as soon as Louis stopped talking he said: 'Supper is ready, and mattresses and blankets are prepared. After you've eaten I suggest you have a good sleep. I'll deal with the horses and then go into Le Tréport to see if the *Marie* is there. Is there a message for Dyson?'

Louis shook his head. 'Don't take any risks. If you can tell him that all is well, do so; but he has his instructions, and everything so far is going according to plan – for once!'

As the setting sun balanced like a red-hot coin standing on the western horizon, Ramage rested his arms on the window ledge and looked seaward through the fisherman's battered telescope. The horizon was clear except for a distant frigate whose hull was hidden below the curvature of the earth: only her sails were still in sight, tiny squares darkened by shadow. A routine patrol – one of Lord Nelson's squadron 'on a Particular Service,' running up and down this end of the Channel, making sure the French Army of England had not put to sea. She had probably just looked into Havre de Grace, fifty miles away along the coast to the south. The *Marie* would have slipped past such frigates in the darkness, on her way with Ramage's dispatches which told Lord Nelson that no Army of England could sail for many months.

'No sign of her?' Louis asked.

'No, just that frigate we saw earlier. Still, with this west wind she'll make a fast passage. But I must admit I'm getting nervous. Ah –' he looked round as the fisherman's wife came in and began setting plates and cutlery on the table, 'well, it makes me hungry too.'

They ate a leisurely supper, the fisherman and Louis telling stories of smuggling and shipwreck along the Normandy coast. When they had finished Ramage looked at his watch. He was not particularly tired but several years at sea had taught him to take advantage of any opportunity for a nap.

After a word to the fisherman, Ramage stretched out on a mattress.

It seemed only a moment later that the fisherman was waking him, and as he rubbed his eyes he saw that Stafford and Louis were crouched over a bucket, washing their faces.

'Midnight,' the man said, 'and time for fishing . . .'

The boat was heavily built, beamy with what seemed a low freeboard to anyone used to a ship of war's boats. The fisherman put a small lantern and a bucket abaft the centre thwart. 'There's the bait,' he told Louis. 'Look – lines here, and watch out for the hooks. And here is the grapnel with plenty of line, more than enough to anchor inside the three-fathom line. Don't forget – '

'Yes, yes,' Louis interrupted impatiently, 'we've been over all that before and you're coming with us anyway; let's get her launched!'

The boat was hauled up well above the high-water mark, and heavy wooden beams had been sunk into the beach down as far as the line of seaweed. Below that, planks had just been laid so that the boat could be slid down to the water's edge.

Ramage checked the oars: there were six in the boat, but they were large and heavy with balanced looms. Stafford was fitting the thole pins – the waves breaking on the beach were just large enough so that once the boat began to float it would need some vigorous rowing for a few minutes to prevent her broaching and tipping them all out.

Both Stafford and Ramage were looking at the bulk of the boat and wondering how four of them were going to get her started – once she began sliding it would be easy – when the fisherman stuck a finger and thumb in his mouth and gave a piercing whistle. A minute or two later Ramage saw men coming from the nearby houses, shadowy figures in the moonlight.

Without a word they positioned themselves round the boat and, joined by Ramage, Louis, Stafford and the fisherman, ran her down into the water, wading to hold her while the four men climbed in, dropped the oars into position and began rowing.

The boat rowed well, and Ramage looked along the shore, watching the sea breaking on the rocky ledges which ran out for a couple of hundred yards from the beach to the north. Although the broken water sparkled and danced in the faint moonlight, the rocks themselves were grey and evil-looking, as though waiting patiently yet hungrily for a ship to be caught in a storm and driven on to them.

Soon they were far enough out to see the saddle-like gap in the cliffs in which both Le Tréport and Mers nestled, and the fisherman grunted, shipping his oar. They had rowed perhaps a thousand yards, and already Ramage felt the muscles across his shoulders tightening uncomfortably and others in the lower part of his back giving a hint that they would soon start aching.

The fisherman shifted the lantern and began coiling up a line along which pieces of cloth and twists of leather marked distances. Finally he had it coiled, and lifted up the small lead weight attached to the end and shaped like the weight in a grandfather clock. He leaned over the side and let the weight go, the line rushing out from the coil in his right hand. Suddenly it slowed down and stopped, and he seized it, dropping the coil and pulling in the weight end until he felt it just lifting off the bottom with the line taut. He felt the nearest marker on the line and muttered the depth. Three and a half fathoms.

'We'll start here,' he said, hauling in the leadline. 'Louis, begin baiting the hooks.'

Three hours later there was still no sign of the *Marie* although, the fisherman commented enthusiastically, the fishing was very good despite the moon. Ramage fervently wished the fish would stop biting but, knowing how the families at Mers depended on fish for their food, he thought it would be churlish to suggest they just sat there quietly without the lines over the side, either lying to the grapnel or rowing up to the west for half an hour and letting the wind and current carry them back parallel with the coast.

As more fish were hauled into the boat, twisting and thumping, covering everything with scales and slime, Ramage looked wistfully at the grapnel and line. He remembered all the boats he had seen in various parts of the world, comfortably anchored, with the men in them fishing by dangling lines over bow and stern, occasionally hauling in a line to find the bait had been taken. Three hours of rowing and drifting seemed to have knotted most of his muscles. It was unlikely – though pride prevented him from inspecting them in the light of the lantern – that his palms had any skin left on them; the sharpness of the pain when a dollop of spray soaked them again indicated that blisters had burst.

They were just rowing the boat round to get back to the westward again when Stafford said, almost as though it was of no consequence, 'There she is.'

Ramage glanced round and saw a darker shape: the *Marie* reaching down towards them, perhaps five hundred yards away and down moon. The fisherman hurriedly shipped his oar, tipped the bait out of the bucket and shook it to make sure no water was left inside, and put it over the lantern. The light had not been bright, but suddenly dousing it made Ramage realize just how much it had affected their night vision and allowed the *Marie* to get so close.

'We hide the light now in case someone watches from the shore with night-glasses,' he explained to Ramage. 'It is best, eh?' he asked, and Ramage suddenly realized how determined the man was to make a good impression on the two Britons.

Ramage rested on his oar and leaned over to the fisherman. 'While there is time – ' he held out his hand, and winced as the fisherman shook it enthusiastically, 'thank you.' There was nothing more than could be put into words and the fisherman seemed to understand.

'You will be all right with Dyson,' the fisherman said reassuringly, 'he is a good man.'

Ramage sat and watched the approaching fishing-boat. Dyson was bringing her along thirty yards or so to leeward of the rowing-boat, obviously intending to luff up and then heave-to, leaving them a few yards to row to get alongside.

Ramage glanced towards the beach: the odd patches of cloud crossing the moon, combined with the fact the moon was now low in the sky, made it impossible to distinguish the cluster of houses at Mers, nor could he see the large tower of the church in Le Tréport, St Jacques tower, according to Louis. Even using a good night-glass it would be impossible to spot the rendezvous between the rowing-boat and the *Marie*.

There was a sudden hiss of water and flapping of canvas and Ramage turned to see the *Marie* coming up into the wind, her jib flapping and the blocks squeaking as the mainsheet was hurriedly hauled in. The fishing-boat lost way as she turned north-west, the jib stopped flapping as the wind caught it aback, and a man was leaning on the tiller, keeping the helm over, so the rudder tried to push the bow round to larboard against the thrust of the backed jib trying to force it over to starboard.

The fisherman snapped an order, they bent to the oars, and a couple of minutes later Louis was standing in the bow throwing a line to a man on the stern of the *Marie*. The nearness of the two boats emphasized the height of the waves: it was far safer to board the *Marie* over her stern rather than risk the two vessels crashing together if the rowing boat went alongside.

With the line secured, Ramage and Stafford stowed the oars neatly, despite the protests of the fisherman that he would do that later. Ramage told the Cockney to board first and Louis waited for a smooth patch, then hauled on the line to bring the bow close. Stafford leapt up, and a moment later Ramage followed him. The *Marie*'s stern began to lift as she seesawed over a crest and Louis waited a minute or two. By the time he had jumped on board Ramage had recognized the dark figures on the *Marie*'s deck as Jackson and Rossi. A hurried question thrown at Jackson as they shouted good-bye to the fisherman and began to sheet in the backed jib brought the reply that all the dispatches had been delivered to Lord Nelson, who was on board a frigate at anchor in the Downs.

Five minutes later the *Marie* was reaching up to the nor'-nor'-west on the larboard tack with Dyson explaining that he wanted to get into the deep bay between Dungeness and Hythe and then bear away for the Downs, so that as far as any nosey Revenue cutter was concerned they had been fishing off the 'Ness.

Then, sitting in the little cockpit with Dyson crouched over the compass and Louis, Stafford and Rossi down in the cuddy, Ramage was able to extract from a Jackson obviously impatient to hear of his captain's adventures a full report on the delivery of the dispatches to Lord Nelson. The last courier had arrived in Boulogne on Sunday evening, Jackson said, with the news that 'the Italian gentleman' had been arrested by the gendarmes, although at the time he left Amiens both Louis and Stafford were still free. He had emphasized to Jackson that the dispatch he was delivering was of enormous importance.

Jackson said that as soon as he told Dyson they prepared to sail. By nightfall they were a mile off Boulogne and heading for the rendezvous. Fortunately the other *Marie* was fishing near the rendezvous, and leaving Dyson and Rossi to return to Boulogne, he went direct to Lord Nelson's frigate in the

Downs. Fifteen minutes after handing over the dispatch he had been hurried below to the Admiral's cabin and ordered to tell him everything he knew.

'I tried to avoid saying *anything* about the smugglers, sir, apart from the name of the smack,' Jackson said defensively, as if anticipating Ramage's wrath, 'but His Lordship said he wasn't interested in people breaking a few laws, he was concerned about what had happened to you.

'So I just told him the bare bones of it, about how you'd been arrested in Amiens, but he saw through me: he might only have one eye, sir, but he can see through a six-inch plank. He got angry and told me you'd probably be guillotined, and the only chance of saving you depended on him knowing all the details.

'Well, I may have done the wrong thing, sir, but I then told him all I know – about the Corporal's brother, and how you and Staff had gone off to Amiens with Louis, and how you'd passed the dispatches back to Boulogne. At the end of it all he seemed very upset; he turned to the captain of the frigate and said, "We've got what we wanted, but it's cost us young Ramage: those damned French will chop his head off – probably have already. Damme, we can't afford to lose young men like him!"

'Well, sir, I hadn't much hope for you when we left Boulogne, and hearing His Lordship say that put the seal on it. When I got back on board the Boulogne *Marie* that night and told Slushy, he wouldn't believe it though – credit where credit's due. He reckoned that Louis was a match for them French policemen. Seems he was right!'

The hiss of a bow wave, the rattle of blocks and the flap of a sail high overhead made Ramage realize with a sudden shock which turned his stomach to water that the dark patch on the *Marie*'s larboard bow was a large ship steering north. A blinding flash and thud warned him that she had opened fire.

'Wear round and run inshore!' Ramage shouted at Dyson. 'That was only a warning shot!'

Dyson thrust the tiller over and Jackson leapt to overhaul the mainsheet. Rossi, Louis and Stafford scrambled up out of the cuddy as the *Marie*'s bow began to swing.

The jib flapped and a moment later the big boom slammed over and the *Marie* heeled in response. Hurriedly the jib was sheeted in and Ramage looked astern. She was a frigate–

that much was clear in the darkness – and the *Marie*'s sudden right-angled jink had taken her by surprise: already she had ploughed on to the north and the fishing-boat was safe from her broadside guns, though alert men at the stern-chasers might get in a shot.

As the frigate disappeared in the darkness, occasional shafts of moonlight through the clouds lit up her sails. No, she wasn't wearing round after the *Marie*. Ramage looked round warily to the south: no, she wasn't leaving the *Marie* to a consort following along astern.

'Sleepy lot over there,' Jackson commented to Stafford. 'They left it too late to fire that warning shot.'

'I ain't complaining,' the Cockney said. 'So 'elp me, 'ow the 'ell are we going to tell 'em we're reelly friends?'

Ramage strained his eyes in the darkness as a cloud across the moon hid the frigate's sails. There was something damned strange about the whole episode. Her captain was not sleepy – he was wide awake and probably standing on the quarter-deck with his night-glass: no one patrolling close inshore, watching for French ships trying to run the blockade, was anything but alert, and all his officers and lookouts too. There would be six lookouts – two on each bow, beam and quarter, and with a moon like this probably a man aloft as well.

Yet that warning shot had been fired astern of the *Marie* and much too late. It was fired when the frigate was in no position to cut her off and almost too far past to loose off a broadside. Given that she could not stop the *Marie* escaping, why fire a warning shot? Why fire when there was no time to wait for a response and, if none was forthcoming, follow it up with a broadside?

Ramage shrugged his shoulders: perhaps he was making too much of it: the frigate may have just fired a random shot to frighten a French fishing smack back into port, having spotted her at the last moment against the land and decided not to bother with a broadside. For the moment he was thankful that they were all still alive. But it was a long way to the English coast and that frigate might well turn south again, and she was certainly not the only one out patrolling that night.

They must assume that the *Marie* would meet her again. They could try to sneak out and hope for the best, risking the frigate thundering down and firing a broadside that would lift the *Marie* out of the water and scatter the pieces like drift-wood. Or they could try getting close enough – waving a lantern, perhaps – and hailing her, explaining that the *Marie* was English. British, rather. He put himself in a frigate captain's position and knew it would not work until they were within a few miles of the English coast. No frigate captain would believe a British fishing-boat could be sailing close along the French coast: he would immediately assume it was some sort of trick and open fire – and who could blame him: why risk a frigate for the sake of some wild shouts from a fishing smack?

One thing was certain: the *Marie* couldn't spend the rest of the night sailing up and down the coast off Le Tréport. Of the alternatives, trying to sneak across the Channel was the most likely to succeed. Once again Ramage was puzzled by the frigate's last-minute warning shot. It was as if she had been expecting to find a ship to seaward of her, and had only spotted the *Marie* inshore at the last moment . . .

'We're getting close to the beach, sir,' Dyson murmured. 'Water gets a bit shallow!'

'Very well, bear up and run south, parallel with the shore. Jackson, Stafford – stand by the mainsheet; Rossi and Louis – jib sheet!'

Dyson leaned on the tiller and the seamen heaved in the sheets until both jib and mainsail were trimmed to the wind now on their starboard beam. The clouds, still broken up, let patches of moonlight skim across the surface of the sea, but there was no sign now of the frigate's sails over on the starboard quarter: she must have carried on northwards, probably intending to go up as far as Boulogne before turning south again. It was idle to speculate; all that mattered for the moment was that she had not turned back to investigate the *Marie*. No doubt her captain assumed that she was a French fishing-boat and had scurried back into port.

Scurry back into port! Yes, the last thing the frigate captain would expect was that she would go boldly offshore, heading for the middle of the Channel. Do the unexpected: surprise won battles. Ramage knew that most of his successful actions in the past owed more to achieving surprise than to clever planning.

'Stand by at the sheets! Dyson, we're going to bear up again: I want to get well out into the Channel. Forget that damned compass; just get her bowling along hard on the wind.

South-west on the starboard tack should keep us clear of the frigate.'

'Aye aye, sir,' Dyson said crisply as the other four men made sure the sheets were clear.

For the first time in many days (weeks, in fact) Ramage felt exhilarated: he was back at sea, making his own decisions and with a good crew. Admittedly the vessel he commanded was very small, but it was only a matter of scale: a fishing-boat escaping from a frigate; a frigate escaping from a ship of the line . . . The problem was the same.

The men were ready and he gave Dyson the order. The *Marie* slowly edged round to starboard and the men grunted and swore as they hardened in the sheets, while Dyson edged her closer and closer to the wind. With the sheets turned up on the cleats, Ramage looked questioningly at Dyson: the *Marie* seemed a little sluggish.

'She likes a bit more jib, sir,' he said almost apologetically. 'Bit 'ard-mouthed she is, at the moment.'

'Rossi, give him a couple of feet on that jib sheet,' Ramage said. 'Easy now, mind it doesn't run away with you. Here, Stafford, tail on the end!'

Almost at once the *Marie* came to life; the sluggishness vanished and she was as skittish as a fresh horse, her bow rising and falling gracefully as she drove to windward across the crests and troughs, her stem bursting random wavetops into sheets of spray.

Ramage tapped Dyson on the shoulder as he hunched to one side of the tiller. 'I didn't know she had it in her; she's a real thoroughbred!' And Dyson knew how to get the best out of her, that was clear enough. Not only get the best out of her, Ramage suddenly realized, but how to sneak her past the frigates! He had probably been doing it once a week for several years! Ramage felt a bit sheepish at his earlier fears and was thankful he had kept them to himself. Not that this was the time to relax – the frigates would be patrolling very close in to Boulogne, since that was nearly every blockade-runner's destination. Down here, where the coast was a series of bays and headlands, they would be patrolling a much wider band, since blockade-runners might try to stand several miles out or creep along a mile off the beach.

Ramage gestured to the seamen. 'Stafford and Rossi – you keep a sharp lookout to larboard; Jackson and Louis – take the starboard side. We're small enough to stand a chance of

242

spotting someone else before they see us, so we'll be able to dodge.'

The jail cell at Amiens seemed a lifetime away now; the time he and Stafford had spent hunched over the candle in the hotel room opening those seals was so remote that it might have happened to someone else. Soon, all being well, they would be working their way into Folkestone. No, not Folkestone! It would be too complicated trying to explain to the Revenue men why there were two identical smacks called *Marie* in the same port! If they made for the Downs, it would give him time to explain things to Lord Nelson. Then, perhaps, the Admiralty would write a discreet letter to the Board of Customs, and after a few expressions of outraged indignation, the Customs might agree . . .

'Fine on the larboard bow, sir!' Stafford hissed. 'A schooner or summat: hundred yards away an' convergin'.'

'Bear away!' Ramage snapped. 'Let the sheets run, lads!'

Rakish hull, two masts, fore-and-aft rig – that much Ramage could see as the *Marie* began to turn away and then he was momentarily blinded by a ripple of flashes along the stranger's bulwarks. Above the squealing of the sheets running through the blocks, the flogging of the heavy sails and the creak of the gaff jaws on the *Marie*'s mast, he could hear the dull popping of muskets.

Thank goodness the *Marie* turned on her heel like a dancer. A French *chasse-marée*! Damnation, that was what the frigate had been hunting! He dodged across the *Marie*'s deck to keep her in sight as the fishing-boat headed inshore again, and saw that both hull and sails were shortening: she was turning after them: any moment she would wear and, with the wind right aft, she would be down on them long before they could get into shallow water.

Where the devil was that frigate now, he thought bitterly as he watched first the big mainsail and then the foresail swing over on the *chasse-marée*. They were in no hurry because they had their quarry in sight and knew they had the legs of her. The *Marie* had only one advantage, and that slight enough: she could tack and wear more swiftly, jinking like a snipe in front of a sportsman's gun.

If the *Marie* waited until she was nearly on her, until the *chasse-marée*'s damnably long bowsprit was almost poking down their collars, then wore right across her bow at the last moment, risking a collision? It might catch the French ruffians unawares because they would expect the *Marie* to turn the other way. Not much of a surprise really, except that the men with the muskets would be waiting on the starboard side, and would have to dash over to the larboard as the *Marie* suddenly ducked under her bow.

The *chasse-marée* captain must be out of his mind, risking revealing his position to a British frigate by firing a lot of muskets at a fishing smack, for the flashes could be seen a long way off. Unless the Frenchman did not know the frigate was around . . . But surely he must have seen the flash of her warning shot at the *Marie*?

'There's a battery on the coast just north of Mers,' Dyson said, as though reading Ramage's thoughts. 'That *chasse-marée* probably thought they fired the shot, not the frigate, and came up to have a look. Not our night, it ain't . . .'

Ramage guessed that that explained why a *chasse-marée* had opened fire on what was apparently a French smack: a shot from a shore battery would tell her that an enemy vessel was around. But there was no more time for idle thoughts: the *chasse-marée* was now racing up astern, her bow wave showing clearly in the patches of moonlight. She was slightly to larboard of the *Marie*'s wake and fifty yards away: any minute now those muskets would start popping, trying the range.

'Dyson,' Ramage snapped, 'we're going to wear right across this fellow's bow at the very last moment. Just shave his stem. I'll give the word, but be ready. The rest of you, stand by at the sheets. One kinked rope jamming in a block and she'll cut us in half, so have a care!'

He looked back over the *Marie*'s larboard quarter but, as he turned his head, he caught sight of a large, dark shape: a dark shape topped by a series of rectangles that glowed in the moonlight like distant phosphorescence – the frigate was back, reaching south along the coast and steering to intercept the *chasse-marée*, which seemed to have not yet sighted her.

'Belay all that,' he told Dyson hastily, 'here comes the frigate!'

At that moment the *chasse-marée* sighted her and immediately wore round to larboard, her booms and gaffs crashing across with a noise that could be heard from the *Marie*, hardening in sheets at the run and obviously hoping to claw up to windward of the frigate. But it was going to be close. It was the Frenchmen's only chance, and a desperate one, with the *chasse-marée*'s captain gambling that he could pass the frigate so fast on an almost opposite course that their combined speeds would spoil the British gunners' aim.

The frigate's starboard side suddenly dissolved in a blinding flash. The roar and rumble of her whole broadside came across the water and moments later echoed back from the cliffs.

'Cor, that blinded me!' Stafford exclaimed.

'Likely to have done more than that to the Frenchies,' Dyson said. 'An 'ole broadside!'

'Dismasted her,' Jackson said quietly. 'I can just see her. She's lying –'

'I see her,' Ramage said, 'but that damned frigate's seen us: she's going to leave the Frenchman for a few minutes and deal with us.'

The frigate ploughed on towards the *Marie* and Ramage knew there was now no chance: she would be on them before they were close enough inshore to get her captain worried about the depth of water under her keel, and with her gunners alert the *Marie*'s chances of tacking and wearing her way out of trouble were nil.

Surrender! The frigate would soon heave-to and hoist out boats to deal with the dismasted *chasse-marée*, so there was a chance they would accept the *Marie*'s surrender, and that would give him time to identify himself.

'Jackson and Stafford – let go the main halyards! Watch your head, Dyson! Rossi, let the jib halyard run!'

At the same time Ramage jumped over and let the jib sheet fly: the sail started flogging immediately, and he jumped back to the weather side with Dyson as the heavy boom, mainsail and the gaff crashed down like a collapsed tent.

Slowly the *Marie* lost way and paid off with the wind and sea on her beam. A minute or two later the frigate was to windward and Ramage heard shouts and blocks squealing as she tacked, and a voice shouted in bad French: 'You surrender?'

'We're British,' Ramage bellowed. 'Yes, we'll wait here!'

'You surrender,' ordered the voice, magnified by a speaking-trumpet, in a disbelieving and uncompromising tone. 'We'll send a boat in a few minutes.'

With that the frigate bore away and headed back to the *chasse-marée*, now a wallowing hulk, and hove-to just to windward. Ramage could imagine the bustle as boats were hoisted out. One would be enough for the Frenchmen – they would have no fight left in them, and the frigate was perfectly placed to give them another broadside if necessary. And one boat would be enough for the little *Marie*!

'Dyson, see if you can get into the cuddy: we need a lantern. It might save a lot of misunderstanding when the boat gets here.'

With that they began hauling the heavy folds of sail away from the hatch. It was hard work, with both boom and gaff sliding a few inches one way and another as the *Marie* rolled. Several minutes later they had cleared enough space for Dyson to slide down into the cuddy while the five of them leaned hard against the boom in case it slipped and crushed him.

Suddenly Dyson vanished and a moment later began swearing violently. 'Me ankle!' he shouted. 'I slipped and wrenched it! I can't even stand up again!'

Ramage was nearest to the hatch. 'Hold tight,' he told the men, 'I'll go down and fetch him out.'

He lowered himself, carefully feeling with his feet so that he landed astride Dyson, who was lying on the cabin sole, groaning and cursing.

'Left leg, sir,' he muttered. 'That's it – ow! Cor, I think it's busted. Oow,' he screeched, as Ramage ran his hand over it.

It was broken, and how the devil were they to hoist Dyson out of this mess?

'Where's the brandy?'

'Locker by the step,' Dyson grunted.

A few moments later Ramage pulled the cork out and gave Dyson the bottle.

Jackson was peering down into the cuddy. 'Is it broken, sir?'

'Afraid so,' Ramage said. 'Find some light line and take this locker lid: smash it up and give me a piece of wood for a splint.' The American disappeared and a few moments later Ramage heard thudding as he broke up the lid.

'You've had enough of that brandy, Dyson.'

'Just another sip, sir, it 'urts cruel 'ard.'

'I know it does, but I don't want you being sick over everything; it's difficult enough down here as it is.'

Dyson gave him the bottle and he corked it. 'Another tot when we get you up on deck.'

246

Jackson handed down a strip of wood and several lines. 'Shall I come down and give you a hand, sir?'

'There's no room; Dyson's lying here like a couple of sacks of potatoes.' Ramage braced himself, tucking all but one of the lines under a knee. 'Now, this is going to hurt, Dyson, but we can't move you until I've got a splint on it.'

Dyson grunted from time to time but he did not say a word. Ramage was not sure if the brandy was taking effect or whether the man realized that cursing and complaining would only cause delay. And time, he thought to himself as he gently knotted the first line, is getting short: the frigate's boarding party will soon be here.

The *Marie* was now rolling more violently: probably the water was getting shallower and the uneven bottom was kicking up an awkward swell with the wind against an ebb tide.

'How are you up there with that boom?' he shouted to Jackson.

'Trying to secure it with the mainsheet, sir. The topping lift's carried away. We've got to move it back across the hatch for a minute; we can't get at the bitter end: the boom's jamming the cleat.'

'Carry on but hurry; it's hot down here!'

The little cabin exaggerated every noise on deck; the boom being dragged a few feet sounded as if the hull was collapsing.

Ramage reached for another line and carefully slid it under Dyson's leg, trying to wedge his own body so that the rolling did not dislodge him. He tied a reef knot and took the third line. That passed round easily and he reached for the fourth, wishing Jackson would hurry and get the sail off the hatch.

Suddenly there was a heavy thud against the hull, a babble of voices, and a startled exclamation in French by Louis. Almost at once Jackson was shouting in English and Stafford joined in. The frigate's boat had got alongside without the men, busy securing the main boom, seeing them.

Many feet were pattering over the deck overhead; some-one – he sounded like an excited midshipman – was giving shrill orders.

'Hold on a minute,' Ramage told Dyson and stood up, clawing at the canvas and finally thrusting his head and shoulders clear. There was at least a dozen men on board, all with cutlasses or boarding pikes pointing at Jackson and his men.

'Ahoy there!' Ramage bellowed, 'we are –' he broke off as he sensed a movement above him, a swift movement which showed against the stars: it looked like the butt of a pistol coming –.

CHAPTER SIXTEEN

His head was thudding as if someone was beating it with heavy drumsticks; his body was lying horizontally and swaying, as though suspended between sky and sea. Slowly he forced his eyes open and found himself looking up at the deckhead of a ship. His wrists seemed to be curiously angular and jammed in the pit of his stomach, and then he realized that they were locked in irons. Cautiously he tried to move his ankles, but he was held in leg irons, too. In irons and in a hammock . . .

The effort was too much and he lost consciousness again, and what seemed hours later woke up to the sound of distant shouting: shouting in English; orders for clewing up sails. Another shout echoed through a speaking trumpet and an anchor splashed into the sea and a minute later there was a smell of burning from the friction of the cable running out through the hawsehole.

He tried to sit up but a hand pushed him back in the hammock. He tried to look round, but his head seemed to be stuck in a cloth helmet. 'Who is that?'

'Never you mind,' said a surly voice. 'Just you lie there nice and still.'

'Fetch an officer! I am Lieutenant Ramage!' His voice was little more than a croak.

'And I'm Father Christmas, and I don't want no trouble!'

The man had moved round so that by turning his head slightly Ramage could distinguish a Marine uniform.

'Where are the other prisoners?'

'All secure in irons, except the one with the bad leg: the surgeon's still working on 'im.'

'What's tied round my head?'

The Marine came closer and stared at him curiously. 'It's a bandage. You was hit on the 'ead.'

'So I was,' Ramage muttered. 'What ship is this?'

'The *Calliope* frigate.'

It took a befuddled Ramage a moment to recognize the name because the Marine pronounced it Cally-oh-pee.

'And where have we just anchored?'

"Ere, matey, you want to know a lot for a traitor, don't you! The Downs, that's where we are—' he paused as a boat was hoisted out, 'and that'll be the capting going over to tell Admiral Nelson we 'ad a good night's hunting. They'll have you and your mates 'anging from the yardarm by Monday,' he added without apparent malice. 'Very 'ard on traitors they are.'

'Quick,' Ramage said, trying to sit up and again being pushed flat, 'fetch an officer! Dammit, man, I am a King's officer: tell him Lieutenant Ramage wants to see him urgently!'

'A King's officer, eh?' the Marine said sarcastically. 'Well, all I can see is a face that ain't been shaved fer a week, topped off by a bloodstained rag. Yer clothes is in tatters and yer stink like a farmyard. When did yer last wash?'

Ramage dared not try to sit up again: the sudden thrust back made his head spin. As he tried to think of a way to persuade the Marine to fetch an officer, the man said phlegmatically: 'The sergeant said I was to guard you an' fetch you a clout if there was any monkey business.'

'Didn't he say you were to report when I recovered consciousness?'

'Yes,' the man said patiently, 'he did, but there ain't anyone else 'ere, and I ain't leaving you alone; it's no good you trying that trick on me.'

Pleading, cajoling, bullying: what the devil would work with a man like this?

'Listen, this is extremely urgent. You hail until someone comes. Then send him to tell the officer of the watch that one of the prisoners is Lieutenant Ramage.'

'Ramage, eh,' the Marine said conversationally. 'There was an officer of that name in a cutter called the *Kathleen*—'

'Did you serve in her?' Ramage exclaimed.

'No, my mate did. Quite a lad, *that* Ramage was.'

'But I'm the same one!'

'Ah,' the Marine said, 'then why did you ask me if I served in her? If I did, you'd know, wouldn't you?'

'Damnation, yes I would, but it's almost dark down here and I haven't had a chance of looking at you: every time I try to sit up, you push me down again!'

'You certainly *sound* like an officer,' the Marine admitted. 'But you was in that French fishing smack, so you can't be.'

Ramage felt like weeping with frustration. 'Look, just hail someone – you'll look a fool if they find you are guarding a British officer!'

'Aye, but I'll look a bigger fool if I start shouting that a man my sergeant says is a traitor is a British officer: I can just guess what my sergeant will say!'

Then Ramage remembered: 'Perkins – that's the name of your captain; stocky man, red face, comes from Devon –'

'Dorset,' the Marine said. 'See, you're wrong again.'

'Don't be stupid! Do you think a French fisherman would speak English like me and know about your captain?'

'Belike he would; you can't trust Frenchies. Anyway, no one says you're French. That Lieutenant Ramage's father was in the Navy – an admiral,' the man said conversationally. 'Served with him once, years ago.'

Ramage tried to control himself. 'I'll tell you about him: then you'll see. My father is Admiral the Earl of Blazey; he's tall with brown eyes and his nickname is "Old Blazeaway." If you tell me where you served with him, I'll tell you the name of the ship.'

'He was a Rear-Admiral then, on the Leeward Islands station.'

'The *Phoenix*,' Ramage said promptly.

'You're right, too. Now what do I do?' the Marine muttered, clearly overcome by his discovery.

'Hail until someone comes, then pass the word for the officer of the watch.'

'Just my luck to get a duty like this,' the Marine grumbled as he moved out of Ramage's sight and a moment later began bellowing towards the hatch. A seaman must have appeared and was sent off to fetch the sergeant of Marines.

Ramage groaned: the chain of command . . .

Finally he found a Marine sergeant looking down at him while the sentry whispered. The sergeant turned on his heel without a word.

'You'll be all right now, sir,' the sentry murmured confidentially. 'One of the best, our sergeant. He was the one what clouted you across the head.'

'I'm glad to meet him,' Ramage said, and closed his eyes.

'Will you say something, please – sir,' a shrill voice said

nervously, and Ramage looked over the edge of the hammock at a young midshipman, who had obviously been sent by the officer of the watch.

'Young man,' Ramage said heavily, 'I am going to say this once, and then you report it immediately to the officer of the watch. I am Lieutenant Ramage, I have been working under the direct orders of Vice-Admiral Lord Nelson, and I was escaping from France in the French fishing vessel which you captured during the night. Now, look lively!'

The boy vanished and the Marine sentry moved close again. 'Don't you fret, sir,' he said soothingly, 'everything'll be all right: we'll have you out of those irons in a minute, but watch that 'ead of yours; if I know the sergeant, he give you a fair old clout!'

Suddenly he sprang to attention and Ramage saw a lieutenant eyeing him.

'Good morning,' Ramage said wearily, 'I'm now saying this for the third or fourth time. I'd be glad if you would report it at once to Captain Perkins.' Once again he described who he was and under whose orders he had been working.

The lieutenant listened, and when Ramage finished he said: 'I'm inclined to believe you; but the captain is with His Lordship at this moment. I'd be grateful if you'd wait a few minutes until he gets back . . .'

Ramage could not blame him; even as he told his story he knew it sounded improbable.

'Tell me what happened to the rest of the men in the smack.'

'Oh, they're all in irons. All except the one whose leg or ankle was broken: the surgeon's been attending to him.'

'How many of them?'

'Let me see – there was twenty-seven from the *chasse-marée* and six from the smack.'

'What happened to the *chasse-marée*?'

'She sank: when her foremast went by the board it stove in the bulwarks and opened up some planking.'

'And the *Marie* – the smack?'

'We towed her in; in fact we're just getting her anchored now.'

A midshipman came up and whispered to the lieutenant who, before he left, said: 'The Captain is coming back on board.'

Five minutes later Captain Perkins, a couple of lieutenants

and the Marine sergeant were helping Ramage out of the hammock, with the Captain shouting angrily for the master-at-arms to bring the key to the irons.

Ramage was too dizzy to stand and they sat him on the deck. Captain Perkins knelt beside him.

'I'm sorry, Ramage; you realize we had no idea – ?'

Ramage nodded and regretted it a moment later as his head began spinning again.

'I was just reporting to his Lordship,' Captain Perkins continued, 'and happened to mention the name of the smack. His Lordship – well, he became rather excited and told me I was to send you on board at once!'

Ramage pointed to his torn clothes and unshaven face, but Perkins said: 'His Lordship was most emphatic that I sent you over immediately if in fact you had been on board the smack. I told him you would want to clean yourself up, but His Lordship has already got his lieutenants finding you clothes – ah, here's the master-at-arms. Hurry, man! Don't fumble with those keys!'

Fifteen minutes later a shaky, unshaven and smelly Ramage was waiting in the Admiral's cabin on board the *Minerva* frigate. Outside the door the sentry suddenly stamped to attention; a moment later the Admiral walked into the cabin, a small, slim man who had no need to bend his head to avoid bumping the deckhead. His empty right sleeve was pinned to his coat; his good eye was bright. He smiled the moment he saw Ramage hurriedly getting up from the chair.

'Ah, Mr Ramage rises from the dead!'

'Good morning, sir; I must apologize for my appearance –'

'Don't apologize; I wanted to see you at once. Hmmm!' He eyed Ramage from head to feet. 'You don't have that furtive look of a jailbird yet – but obviously you haven't been staying in the best hotels! I'm told the knock on the head is not too serious. Ah,' he turned as a tall, heavily built man with a round, cheerful face knocked and walked into the cabin, 'here's Captain Ross. Meet the *Calliope*'s prisoner, Ross; a desperate-looking rogue, you'll have to admit.'

Captain Ross, who commanded the *Minerva*, gave a friendly grin. 'The last we heard of you, young man, was your coxswain – what's his name? Jackson, was it? – telling us you were in a French jail and about to be hauled off to the guillotine any moment,'

'Aye,' the Admiral said, 'I'm afraid I anticipated your death, Ramage: I didn't expect the French would let you slip through their fingers!'

'You anticipated . . .' a puzzled Ramage broke off lamely.

'Yes, I wrote a private letter to your father giving him all the news we had. I didn't say you'd been executed, but the inference was obvious. You'd better send word to him at once – give me the letter and I'll see it goes up to London in the Admiralty bag tonight.'

'Thank you, sir,' Ramage said, 'it was kind of you – '

'Telling a father his son is probably dead is not a kindness, young man; and I expect the Marchesa has shed a tear or two,' he said, adding in a brisker tone: 'Now, sit down and tell me what happened – begin from the time you left me at Dover Castle.'

At that moment Ramage cursed himself for not having considered how he would describe the roles of people like Simpson, Dyson and Louis. Well, Dyson desrved some kind of recognition for his work, even though he was a deserter, and Simpson deserved to have his anonymity preserved: his smuggling activities were a matter between him and the Revenue men.

'Well, sir,' Ramage began hesitantly, 'to get to France I had to enlist the help of some men who – well, who – '

'I know all about that,' Nelson said crisply. 'I anticipated you would, and your coxswain told me. Don't back and fill, man, I don't care if you emptied Newgate and used the prisoners: I'm not a Revenue officer, and the Admiralty is sufficiently satisfied with the result of your work to take a generous view in the matter of rewards – within reason, of course.'

The hint was broad enough, and Ramage described all his activities, without naming Simpson. The Admiral was intrigued by the story of Dyson and commented to Captain Ross: 'Probably best to leave him to carry on smuggling – he won't thank us for clearing him: that would mean a court martial and then a pardon. The Admiralty might make a note of his name, in case he is ever picked up – still,' he said to Ramage, 'have a talk with the man and see what he wants. He's done more work for the country as a deserter and smuggler than he'd ever do as a pressed seaman!'

When Ramage finished his story by explaining why one *Marie* was now anchored near the *Calliope* while another was in Folkestone, the Admiral nodded several times. 'The *Calliope* won't claim her as a prize. Well, you're a lucky fellow. You realize you lived up to your reputation for disobeying orders, I suppose?'

Ramage, startled by the sudden change in Lord Nelson's voice, glanced up quickly, the alarm showing on his face. 'I – well, sir, there – '

'Your orders,' the Admiral said relentlessly, 'were to go to Boulogne and make the best estimate you could of the number and type of invasion craft ready for sea and some estimate of their capacity and when they could sail. Is that not so?'

'Yes, sir,' Ramage admitted nervously.

'Very well; if you were given those orders, then you could assume that that was what the Admiralty intended you to do. Am I right?'

'Of course, sir.'

'And what did you do? You had a look round Boulogne and then went off to Amiens, no doubt a nice enough town in peacetime but no place for a British officer in wartime.'

'But sir, Admiral Bruix's dispatch – '

Suddenly the Admiral was laughing. 'Have you ever seen such a long face, Ross? He has a guilty conscience! I'll bet he looked more cheerful when they sentenced him to the guillotine, eh?'

'Not surprising, sir, if I may say so,' Captain Ross said mildly. 'I suspect you frighten him more than Bonaparte did!'

'I don't mind telling you, Ramage, that I had to word my report to the First Lord very carefully, otherwise His Lordship *would* have jumped on you for disobeying orders. So, remember that as far as Lord St Vincent is concerned, my orders were wide enough to allow your – ah, your visit to Amiens.'

'Thank you, sir,' Ramage said soberly. 'May I – '

'Get yourself cleaned up and report to the First Lord at the Admiralty,' Lord Nelson said. 'I am writing to him this evening and he'll receive the letter before you arrive. It might be a good time to see about further employment. You've done me out of a job – you realize that, don't you?'

Ramage looked flabbergasted. 'But – you're commanding the Squadron, aren't you, sir?'

'I am at the moment, with orders to watch Bonaparte's Invasion Flotilla and make sure it never crosses the Channel. Your sight of Admiral Bruix's dispatches means we have nothing to fear this year – so probably the Squadron for "a Particular Service" will be dispersed.'

'I'm very sorry, sir,' Ramage said apologetically, 'but –'

'I have no regrets; indeed, at the risk of being indiscreet I don't mind admitting, young man, that you've done me a good turn: commanding this Squadron is not my idea of fighting the war. I just sit here, cold, damp and ill, my cough much worse and my eye inflamed . . .'

Ramage tried to look sympathetic and Captain Ross glanced away: Lord Nelson's obsession with his health was always in violent contrast with his obsession for fighting the French wherever there was water enough to float a ship. However ill he was, though, the chance of battle always cured him.

The Admiral stood up and smiled at Ramage. Holding out his left hand he said as Ramage shook it: 'Tell Lord St Vincent the story in the same way you told it to me, Amiens and all; and my best wishes to the Marchesa: you are a lucky young man.'

Fontana Paperbacks: Fiction

Fontana is a leading paperback publisher of both non-fiction, popular and academic, and fiction. Below are some recent fiction titles.

- ☐ SO MANY PARTINGS Cathy Cash Spellman £2.50
- ☐ TRAITOR'S BLOOD Reginald Hill £1.95
- ☐ THE KREMLIN CONTROL Owen Sela £1.95
- ☐ PATHS OF FORTUNE Susan Moore £1.95
- ☐ DAYS OF GRACE Brenda Jagger £1.95
- ☐ RAVEN William Kinsolving £1.95
- ☐ FLOODGATE Alistair MacLean £1.95
- ☐ FAMILY TIES Syrell Leahy £1.95
- ☐ DEATH IN SPRINGTIME Magdalen Nabb £1.50
- ☐ LEGION William Blatty £1.75
- ☐ A CROWNING MERCY Susannah Kells £1.95
- ☐ BLIND PROPHET Bart Davis £1.95
- ☐ ALL THINGS IN THEIR SEASON Helen Chappell £2.50
- ☐ A CRY IN THE NIGHT Mary Higgins Clark £1.75
- ☐ SUNRISE Rosie Thomas £1.95

You can buy Fontana paperbacks at your local bookshop or newsagent. Or you can order them from Fontana Paperbacks, Cash Sales Department, Box 29, Douglas, Isle of Man. Please send a cheque, postal or money order (not currency) worth the purchase price plus 15p per book for postage (maximum postage is £3.00 for orders within the UK).

NAME (Block letters) _____

ADDRESS _____

_____